Praise for *H*

"This is one of the most moving works of exile literature I have ever read, the poignant account of a deracinated soul… the writer she most resembles is Virginia Woolf. But Phipps differs from Wolf insofar as the memory is both personal and deeply historical."

— Kenneth Asher, author of *Literature, Ethics, and the Emotions*

"This novel is transformative… I am transfixed by it… Sheer poetry… Phipps is a major voice in the rich literature of exile, and she opens painful doors for the reader, and for this, I am grateful."

— Patrick Bellegarde-Smith, author of *Haiti: The Breached Citadel*

"*House of Fossils* poetically gathers together a polarity of alluring attractions, of exile and return, of the mysterious sea ebbing and returning."

— LeGrace Benson, author of *Art and Culture of Haiti*

"Yes, Marilene Phipps' *House of Fossils* is a novel both personal and political refracted through the lens of history and memory and multiple migrations. It is at once haunting and luminous. This is all done with a poet's fascination with and attention to language and a painter's exactness with and consideration for color and detail. A truly riveting and compelling read."

— Jacqueline Bishop, author of *The Gymnast and Other Positions*

"This is an important book—one that will move you and stir serious discussion with others and, most importantly, with yourself."

— MJ Fievre, author of *A Sky the Color of Chaos*

"In this stunning book, Marilène Phipps expands her mastery of the poetic, short-story and memoir forms into a compelling novel. *House of Fossils* draws a delicate portrait of a woman torn between traditions, geographic locations, and languages while also sketching the disasters, man-made and natural, which mar Haiti's history. This is a fascinating addition to the literature of immigration."

— Henry Louis Gates, Jr., Harvard professor, prolific author and presenter of the PBS series *Finding Your Roots*

"*House of Fossils* is a profound and moving wonder of a novel. Here is Io, a daughter of Haiti, descendent of that troubled, chaotic nation, held in its orbit, living her satellite existence in Cambridge, Massachusetts. Her imagination is in constant uproar, beholden to the fact that no one gets to choose what she remembers or dreams. Io is a kind of mystic, foreign even to herself, she tells us, a troubled subject of this homeland where it is "as if no one lives a natural life or dies a natural death," and where she witnesses the tragic elaborations of revenge exacted over and over again, generation after generation. Marilene Phipps has composed a holy and irreducible vision of Haiti and its innumerable tangled histories and peoples."

– Paul Harding, Pulitzer Prize Winner for his novel *Tinkers*

"*House of Fossils* reckons with what it means to be from Haiti, with grace and authority. It is an exhumation – the exhumation of an understanding of self from the dirt of history and experience. It is achieved without bitterness or agenda, unflinchingly, with the tenderness of a confession."

– Eli MacLaren, author of *Dominion and Agency: Copyright and the Structuring of the Canadian Book Trade, 1867–1918*

"Marilène Phipps guides us back to the Mysteries, to forces strong and incomprehensible, the experiences that defy language and evade easy meaning. By turns earthy and ethereal, she presents the world we know— its seaweed, its cities, its laws, its longings—and takes us also to the vaster realms, of ghosts and souls, unknowable and infinite. Set in Canada, New England, the author's native Haiti, *House of Fossils* explores the place where memory, imagination, and history mingle. Most of all, in luminous, numinous, lyrical prose, she takes us deep into the depths of our ever-shifting internal seas."

– Nina MacLaughlin, Boston Globe critic; author of *Wake, Siren*

"*House of Fossils* expands our understanding, not only of linguistic tensions in the Caribbean but also the historical implications of colonialism in the Americas."

– Geoffrey Philp, author of *Garvey's Ghost*

"Marilene Phipps is our generation's Joseph Conrad. The voyage through *House of Fossils* is grounded in dazzling detail, but informed by psychological awareness and spiritual connection. The book is a poetic and masterful portrayal of personal exodus."

– Susan E. Reed, author and journalist writing for The Times Literary Supplement, The Washington Post, The Boston Globe and The New York Times

"Dreams, ghosts, fossils, memories, race, family, loss, and migration animate this fascinating novel that combines sharp intellectual dialogue with bone-and-blood emotion. Io, the central character, is "fully Caribbean and fully Haitian." Her struggle becomes ours, and it's no spoiler to reveal her glorious realization: she can rescue herself."

– Renee Shea, author of The Language of Composition

"*House of Fossils* by Marilène Phipps surpasses the usual limits of superb prose. Every sentence evokes the art of storytelling at its absolute best. This is required reading for anyone seeking to commune with humankind on a level that transcends language, country of birth, or even the physical world. *House of Fossils* pulsates with her inimitable brilliance. It is at once a masterpiece by an award-winning poet, fiction writer, memoirist, and celebrated painter."

– Katia D. Ulysse, author of Mouths Don't Speak

"In *House of Fossils*, Marilène Phipps weaves a soul-stirring narrative around her main character, Io, a daughter of Haiti, going from haunting stories of shipwrecks to revealing encounters and discussions about race and class in Haiti and its diaspora. She leaves no stone unturned in this provocative book about how we connect to others, close and distant."

– Joëlle Vitiello, Macalester College; writer and scholar on francophone and Haitian literature

House of Fossils

Marilène Phipps

**CALUMET
EDITIONS**

Minneapolis

**CALUMET
EDITIONS**
Minneapolis

Printed in the United States of America.
10 9 8 7 6 5 4 3 2 1

Cover oil painting by Marilène Phipps, *The House on Laurel Street*
Cover and interior design by Gary Lindberg

ISBN: 978-1-950743-21-6

For my mother

"We had the experience but missed the meaning. The past experience revived in the meaning is not the experience of one life only but of many generations…"

T.S. Eliot, *The Dry Salvages*

Table of Contents

I.   The Ghost of the Mary Celeste   1
II.   The Law of the Land   40
III. Family Totems   64
IV.   Cacao   128
V.   The Love of Mothers   158
VI. Haïti Homecoming   204

Also by Marilène Phipps

Unseen Worlds

The Company of Heaven: Stories from Haiti

Crossroads and Unholy Water

House of Fossils

Marilène Phipps

I. The Ghost of the Mary Celeste

Io in the Year 2004...

HOPING FOR THE FOG TO LIFT, I entered the house in Spencer's Island and set my heavy leather bags down. Saul agreed to rent it to me for the night when we first spoke and showed me the way. We started by veering off from the main road of that small Nova Scotia town and walked along a barren, pebbly path that followed the seashore. I declined Saul's offer to carry my things, saying that I was used to managing alone. The sea was at low tide, and the beach was a dark stretch of rocks and seaweed. The horizon stretched hazy and far behind a small island surfacing across from us. Presumably, the town owed its name to it. Gulls flew soundlessly above like aviators in a reachable infinite. I walked behind Saul as quietly as he did. He was a tall, vigorous, skinny man in his mid-forties, wearing jeans and a gray T-shirt. Beneath a worn baseball cap, his eyes shone a piercing blue behind round glasses, yet were strikingly soft in contrast to his sharp-edged nose, thin lips and jawbones as angular as his body. His skin appeared etched by excessive exposure to scorching sun and wintry wind. The pathway was short, so we had soon reached the house. Saul unlocked the front door and stepped aside to let me in, revealing a couple of potted geraniums flowering beneath brambles in a corner. The flowers' sudden, vivid red jolted me as if I heard a shriek. Yet I bent down and softly rubbed one of their velvety leaves between two fingers to release their distinct aroma on my skin and breathe it in.

Entering the house felt like crossing a threshold into a calm, gentle space existing outside the world I carried with me. The entrance room was more than a hallway. A simple, rectangular oak dining table, looking worn, abraded, and even showing some deep gouges in a few places, was set over a bare-wood floor along with a pair of equally rustic-looking chairs that did not match. A white refrigerator, whose bottom edges were rusting, stood in line with the wall opposite the door. The room's sparse furnishings created a detached, monastic mood. The wooden walls had been hung with an eclectic number of small shelves and exuded the salty smell coming from the nearby sea. A strange kind of mist hovered just below the ceiling. Subdued hues of a late afternoon light filtered through dusty windowpanes on my left and shimmered like silk floating over silence.

The silence came from fossils. It is as if a veil had lifted, and I was now permitted to see them looming out of an internal, timeless fog invisibly floating all around me. Their sudden materialization was unsettling in the manner that ghosts are. But startling as they were, no sense of menace hung in the room's atmosphere. Perhaps I felt from them only a kind of gentle curiosity towards the stranger who had infiltrated herself in their space. Furnishings in the house must have, in fact, been purposely minimized to accommodate them. This was their house to inhabit, and not decorate. Fossils appeared to be waiting, ordered in great number like an army maintained by a sharp-edged sense of time, the color of slate. They were of all sizes and in many shades of grey, stiffly laid on every shelf and flat surface or propped up in rigid alignment against the walls.

Saul stayed discreetly by the door while I ventured further into the house, turned to the right and stood still to look into another room from the open archway. More fossils. A petrified branch, a remnant of some immemorial tree, ran across the whole length of the left side of the living room, bypassing a black wood stove and the big black armchair stationed next to it. It looked as if a spirit had once taken form in this sizeable branch and remained confined in matter for a boundless expanse of time. A wide, cut section of a fossilized tree trunk was anchored in front of the stove and next to a solid-oak coffee table that looked flimsy by contrast, despite its heavy legs. Two windows allowed a view to the outside. A delicate row of fossils was lined up on each of their sills. I could see the island seemingly floating in the hazy distance through the window directly across from me. I then walked to the other window to my right and looked through it, only to catch another sight of the pathway, geraniums and front door. On an aged writing desk with its matching chair placed in the corner to my left between the two windows, a high pile of yellowed books loomed over a delicate display of smaller fossil fragments. The spine of the hardbound book at the bottom of the pile read *Design and Construction in Tree Drawings*.

I sat down.

I felt myself in the presence of a long-lost friend whose features I was gradually being brought to recognize, not as much by sight as is commonly experienced, but with other senses. My feet rested on the edge of a round braided rug laid at the center of the room. It seemed as a mysteriously spiraling doorway to other dimensions that children in fairy tales unwittingly cross. I withdrew my feet.

* * *

HAVING SPENT THE PREVIOUS night in the town of Parrsboro because of the sudden burning smell coming out of my car engine during the afternoon, a Sunday when everything was closed, I began to wonder, while taking in my new surroundings that were remarkably filled with an abundance of fossils, why a series of unremarkable but fortuitous events that Monday had forced me, each time, to retrace my steps back to this Parrsboro-Spencer's Island area.

For example, I was hardly out of the garage, where my car had been worked on until late in the morning, when I had to drive right back to retrieve the credit card I forgot on the counter.

"Io?" The mechanic questioned with a curious smile when I identified myself to claim the card. "What kind of a name is 'Io'?"

"As good as any," I replied, shrugging my shoulders.

Then, after a late lunch at the Cape d'Or Lighthouse, I was forced back to the pottery shop in Spencer's Island where I had left my summer hat. And so, the day had gone until it was too late to drive anywhere, and I found myself needing a place to spend a second night while the few local places with available rooms were either closed or already rented out. Perhaps Monday was a bad day to arrive anywhere unprepared.

In search of a room, I had come to Spencer's Island down one of its two roads. They trace a big letter "Y". Fishermen's houses bunch up and huddle in the "V" section of the roads and along its flanks. They were painted in white or pastels like freshly-powdered old ladies emerging from stuffy parlors to air themselves. A charming B&B whose windowsills and porch overflowed with petunias planted in clay pots towered reassuringly over the lot. But this B&B was also closed. However, I noticed a man working on the façade of the house next door. I crossed over to ask him for help.

This was Saul. The day I met him, he was busy with a house-painting job. I explained that I was on a summer vacation, and it had been nearly a month since I started a trip around Nova Scotia. I still had a long way to go. I had been driving through towns I sometimes stopped in to visit or sat on beaches where I collected pebbles. But as things stood at that moment, I needed a room for the night.

"I have a little house," he said. "An old fisherman's house. It's empty. You can have it for the price of a song." Saul smiled at his own comment, and without further ceremony, put his paintbrush down and shut the lid over the paint can. "It's close by. We can walk. Take your things. No need to lock your car, but you can if you want to."

We started down the single road at the tail-end below the "V" section within this Y-shaped road that turned out to be a steep down-hill slope pointing directly at the beach where it ends. On the brief landing where this road ends and meets the sea at high tide, stands a rock monument erected in memory of a lost ship, the *Mary Celeste*. Out at sea, a breast-shaped island emerges from a distance, a floating green formation lost in an edgeless horizon where, most days, blue sea lines up against blue sky.

* * *

SAUL AND I eventually stood in the living room of the small house filled with fossils. After we agreed on the rent, we found ourselves involved in an easy conversation that had recurring inner movements like the roll of the waves outside. We spoke softly, revealing thoughts that we might never share with friends. It seems there are realms of the heart that people open more easily to a passing stranger in whose eyes we recognize the kindness and timeless patience we imagine exist in the infinite. We thus find words to express inner substance that had pressured us imprecisely until then. It's as if ghost stories heard in childhood occupy rooms in the mind where secret creatures remain trapped in an inaudible existence, needing to be exhibited to light that would both disclose and disintegrate them. And so, for someone we will never see again and who will quickly discard us from memory, we extirpate the hitherto inarticulate refinement of our unique soul.

"You'll find here what exists nowhere else," Saul finally said. "You'll regret it if you drive further and don't spend your time here instead."

Saul was a fisherman of Scottish descent who had recently sold his boat. "I won't fish anymore," he explained, "not to make a living anyway. Fishing to make a living turns men into predators. Fishermen fight each other for the same spoils." He walked to the window to the left of the desk and looked out towards the sea straight ahead, his back turned to me. "A fisherman's got no time to both love the sea and what it gives. We use the sea to transport the things of our greed, but greed will destroy us. The sea is angry about that. Now that I don't go after fish, I have time to notice things. Look."

I approached Saul by the window to see what he was pointing to. It was a shriveled golden leaf hung on a long, silvery spider's thread. It was gently swaying behind the window on whose frame the thread was attached, remnant of a once delicate, complex, lustrous web. In the same frame of vision, and in strong contrast to the leaf, I noticed a little farther and standing at the edge of the beach on the other side of the street, the pyramidal rock monument built in memory of the brigantine *Mary Celeste*, the lost ship.

Looking out the window, no traces of a once vibrant history were to be seen on the beach. The view was of a peaceful coastal town. While I was imagining and visualizing the buoyant economic life the waters once exhibited, it was nevertheless for Saul's sensitivity that I expressed wonder. "You see the small things in which poetry lies," I said.

Saul shrugged his shoulders. "I don't know why I tell you this."

"Perhaps it's because they haunt you like a poet is haunted by the way the world hits her sensibility?"

Saul fell silent. He picked up a small piece of fossil from the windowsill in front of him and toyed with it. "No," he finally said abruptly. "It's just that I grow older, and I value other things. But I usually keep these thoughts to myself, so I don't get laughed at. A real man in Spencer's Island is one that cusses, spits and guts fish."

"Saul, I have to tell you that I am a writer. I also write poetry, and I paint."

"You paint? I wish I did."

"I do love to paint. But from what I've observed so far, artists and poets we imagine as uniquely sensitive people, well, they're no less competitive or at each other's throats than the greed-filled fishermen you describe, or lawyers we make fun of in hundreds of shark jokes."

Saul smiled, turned around and walked slowly to the woodstove. He stood there absentmindedly caressing the big pipe where it curved up into the ceiling, and spoke again, "My wife, each day I love her more. A man isn't supposed to show emotions. But me, each time I leave the house, I have to kiss her before I walk out. If I don't, something is missing the whole day."

I sat on the wooden chair by the desk. The head of a nail was pushing up my left thigh, but I ignored it. "Nothing reassures me more than a man who loves his wife."

Saul nodded approvingly. "It's the right thing," he murmured.

A reverie was starting to come over me, so I spoke again quickly in order not to be overcome by it. "Your wife's lucky," I said. I felt no envy and only the admiration from one who stands before a thing of beauty. "It must be glorious to be so loved. I have never felt that kind of love from a man. It seems that their love has been more what they wanted from me than what they had to give."

Saul raised his head and looked into my eyes intently. "Who knows? Maybe you just misunderstood them."

I wanted to give him a playful repartee to hide signs on my face that his words had moved me. I then thought that I should say something profound. But I said nothing of either sort and asked instead, "So, Saul, do you still eat fish?"

Saul smirked, "I do. But I say a prayer before each meal. Got to give thanks. I see each fish we pull out of the ocean like it's an embryo I ripped from its amniotic fluid. In the way it struggles, the fish shows you its pain and the pain of its mother, the sea."

"How can you still eat it then?"

"It shows you, so you know, not so you don't take it," Saul replied slowly. "And it shows you, so you know that it too knows."

"Knows what?"

"About the other side of things. The reverse of life. Death. You're closer to God then. God uses the fish to teach you. You watch the fish quietly while it shows you, and you don't forget." Saul stopped speaking and looked at his hands. He then glanced at me briefly but intensely as if he wanted to read my face and guess my reactions. "With you seeing it," he continued, "the fish's already in you before you eat it. You carry it and its pain inside. Yet, it keeps you alive. You need that to live. I'll be damned if…"

I interrupted Saul, "Do you believe in God?"

Saul paced quietly in a circle. He then slumped into the big, worn armchair next to the woodstove. "Sometimes, I feel I understand nothing. Nothing is simple. Everything's more than it seems. I don't know what *real* is. I don't know who's real."

"Saul? How about you? Are you real or a ghost washed up on the shore?"

"Wonder about that myself!" Saul exclaimed, and laughed. "Stay long enough, maybe you'll find out!"

"I told you, I'm only staying a night." I suddenly got up from the chair, no longer able to ignore the nail head pushing into my thigh.

I went back to the window and stood in front of it but with my back turned to the sea.

"Only you know what you got to do…" Saul said in a sudden somber tone. "Just like the wind that shifts without warnings but knows why. The sea knows itself too. Even if the sea is mysterious to us, it knows its own tempest, its own rage, its own tears. Its appetite shows you the feelings in its heart. It swallows our ships. It swallows men. Sometimes I like to think it has already swallowed me but gave me back."

"Ha! We've come back to my question. Are you a ghost, Saul?" I said, hoping to reverse our solemn tone.

Saul smiled and explained, "It's like those men on the Pictou. A huge wave washed two men off the deck, and the next wave washed them right back on board. The sea sometimes wants to show you it knows each one it takes and each one it lets go. It has its reasons for what it does, and it has memory. Its graves are in its mind and its belly. But sometimes it spits them out."

"What an unusual way to look at these things. Tell me more."

"Yeah… It's like it sends you a notice. Things you find washed up on the shore, like marbles, pipe stems, things like that. I used to collect these things. I don't anymore."

"Why not?"

Saul stretched his legs with a slight groan and put his head back to rest on the armchair. "A doll," he said, looking at the ceiling. "Early evening, I found what's left of an old doll. Looks like porcelain. It's not quite whole. It's missing some parts."

"What did you do with it?"

"It's in my house. I put it on a windowsill in the bedroom so it can look out to sea. Thought it would like being able to see where it came from or was rescued from, whichever way you look at it." Saul leaned forward, put his elbows on his knees and rested his face in his cupped hands. His blue eyes were smiling with the glint of a challenge. "Ain't it true sometimes that where you come from is where you wanna be rescued from?" He looked at me and asked gently, "Why are you so far from home?" Before I could answer, he turned his gaze away, saying, "Anyways, the doll made me sad the way pipe stems don't."

"How come?"

"Dunno. It's like the doll's looking out the window but not at the sea. It's more like she's looking for something else. It's crazy, but I got to wonder how the doll feels, and only sad thoughts came up." Saul shifted position again in his armchair, twisting right and then left.

I walked to the other window, gazed briefly at the geranium, and with my back to Saul, I said, "Some people argue that mediums can pick up visual images from objects. It's like things have memory. You hold them and somehow see where the object has been, who owned it, where. Some mediums even describe the house where the object was placed. Maybe your doll does remember. Maybe you unconsciously pick images up from the doll and feel its own nostalgia and sadness. It has to be a story full of loss that comes from an old doll washed ashore."

"Yeah. I took the doll to an antique store in Parrsboro. The woman there said it's more than one hundred years old. Makes you wonder about the girl who lost that doll and the girl's parents. It's been over a month now since I found it. I feel like it's changed me. Ah, maybe I'm losing my mind some! You think that's what's happening, maybe?"

I laughed. "Absolutely!"

Saul suddenly bolted out of the armchair and walked to the space adjoining the dining room where I had noticed a stove, a sink and a small painted cupboard. He looked all around like he was checking things, and then said, "Think I should plug in the fridge and the oven for you?"

"Don't bother. I have nothing to put in the fridge, and I don't intend to cook."

"No? My wife's the best cook in the world. If I wasn't so hard-working, I'd be round as a tub."

"I'm only staying one night, remember?"

* * *

DURING MY FIRST EVENING in the house, I sat ensconced in
the old black armchair next to the black-iron woodstove. The black
wrought-iron lamp standing on the pine chest to my left had a black
shade whose outline cut a sharp triangle against the white walls. Hung
above me, framed in black, a yellowed black and white print showed
Owl's Head Mountain emerging out of Lake Memphremagog, and
topped by horizontal streams of clouds looking as ominous as the
waves that crashed on its flanks. The small, carved wood loon that I
had bought early in my trip and which had become my mascot, itself
exhibiting white dots over black, was at that moment settled on the
writing table, having somehow found its proper home.

The braided rug under my feet swirled like the eye of a hurricane, sucking the room into a whirling, timeless vortex: I was traveling through limbs of trees that had lasted and come to me from an
unfathomable slice of our universe. They brought intimations of life
far beyond my own and yet to which my life somehow belonged.

When we had stood in the house a few hours earlier and he
noticed my astonishment at the fossils, Saul explained how the Bay
of Fundy is the area where the three continents were joined before
the earth's plate tectonic system pulled them apart. He explained
that one might find fossils in the region, such as crocodile footprints,
which are the same as fossils found on the African continent. He
smiled at the expression on my face when he mentioned that we
were standing amid things that had been formed four hundred million years ago.

Such numbers are beyond the human comprehension of time or
space, so I tried to understand them in terms of weight. Yet, the exhil-
aration I felt in this house denied all feelings of weight. The only
mental abstraction that allowed me to relate to these fossils that could
encompass notions of time, space and weight, was the word *presence*.

There was no doubt in my mind then that the *presence* had
intelligence, patience, wisdom, compassion, and a sense of humor. I
sensed that part of me existed in the way these petrified limbs did and

would somehow endure similarly. I was never less alone in my life than the night I sat in the company of fossils.

Familiar people, cherished places, cruel events through which I lived, all became remote like something I had dreamt. There was endearment in the memory but no sense of loss or melancholy about the past. I had shed my "crew" the way the *Mary Celeste* had, the empty ship that mysteriously endured through tempest or scorching sun until it finally sank off the coast of Haiti, the Caribbean island that once sheltered pirates and privateers, and was the place of my birth.

My meandering coast drive had unwittingly led me to this seashore town and house. From one roadside antique store to the next, I collected a number of bird and duck carvings. I set a Drake Bluehill duck on the pine chest under the black lampshade and a Canadian goose in the bedroom where its softly curving black neck had a nice consonance with the smooth iron bedposts.

After I placed these wooden birds, sold to me as "antiques," side by side with fossils, I started to think differently about antiquity. Also, by the time I arrived in Spencer's Island, these worn antiques had acquired a joyous familiarity that made them seem young, lighthearted, thus affording me a sense of comfort and security during the evening when I became drawn in by the staggering notion of deep time, nestled as I was in the soft darkness of an old armchair.

Yet, while I held the fossils in the palms of my hands, I felt from them a different sense of the familiar than what I feel from ordinary objects in my home, one impossible to articulate. Assuredly, it was a feeling created by an intellect infused with some knowledge of paleontology and geology. Yet it was a wholly spiritual feeling, somehow explainable only to me at the time by the notion of a universal soul from which both the fossils and my deep being were born.

My first night in the house was all but comfortable.

Perhaps the night had really been stormy like skies in my dream across which the winds moaned, indistinguishable from voices calling to each other? Perhaps my body, in its tossing and disquiet, had only been expressing feelings and phenomena occurring in the larger world outside?

Perhaps the dream's incessant knocking on a window that I kept trying to unlock until it shattered when I finally succeeded in opening it, was in reality inspired by the actual tapping of a single branch from an outside tree shaken by night winds on the loose, winds out on a hunt for a kill? Perhaps the dream also came from the lingering in my unconscious of the old print of Cape Splits that hung over the bed and which I had admired at some length before going to sleep?

The print showed three sailboats thrashing amid enormous waves. They flailed like blackbirds, uselessly fighting against the inevitable crash against the cliffs of Cape Splits, cliffs looking like the murderous teeth of a giant. Yet, seagulls the color of spume flew above while a great stream of light arched in the horizon.

* * *

AFTER I WOKE from that dream on my first morning in Spencer's Island, I went to the window that faces out to sea near the writing table. I was startled to notice that the shriveled leaf, suspended on a spider's thread, was still there, unchanged.

Were there not any winds blowing outside during the night? I asked myself. I even began to doubt that I had indeed seen Saul and a little girl walking together on the beach at dusk after I had returned from an early dinner in a nearby restaurant.

While I felt perplexed by my perception of what was reality or dream at that moment, the morning fog had not yet lifted. It was nevertheless not opaque or blocking the view in any way but appeared to be only moisture meant to dampen and clean the sky's waking eyes.

I dressed quickly and went out to look for Saul. I hoped that he might be where I first met him the previous afternoon.

He saw me before I saw him. I had not yet reached the house up the road where he had been painting the day before. Instead, I found him working on the foundation walls of an old house, walls that serve as a supporting, square belt around it. He had taken a number of rocks out of the side of the basement wall that faced the street and had propped himself on the high pile they made. Settled on this heaped mass of rocks and debris, Saul was taking a short rest. He was watching the street from the hole in the wall when he saw me passing.

The house had been leaning dangerously to one side, and Saul was hired to fix it. He had propped four, tall metal beams up against the one side of the house where he started the work. He had positioned and secured the beams so they pushed up that side of the house and maintained it with enough support, keeping it from caving in, while he dug out the foundation belt-wall.

Working on one side at a time, he would be positioning the beams first, afterward removing the rocks, and then rebuilding the strip of wall with fresh cement, using the same rocks. When he was done with all four sides, the house would be as strong and straight as new.

Someone calling my name with cheerfulness startled me out of my reverie. "Io! How did you sleep?"

Saul was waving to me from the shade of the basement.

"How long can I stay?" I asked.

He did not reply. Through the hole in the basement wall, I saw him hop off the pile of rocks, disappear up the basement stairway, and reappear at the front door. He lifted his cap, slapped it on one thigh to get the dust off, and adjusted it right back on. This was the first time I had caught a glimpse of Saul's head. He was bald. Suddenly seeing the complete nakedness of a skull usually covered with a cap or normally covered with hair was startling, especially in contrast to a still youthful face. I felt a kind of embarrassment as if I had unwittingly caught sight of an intimate part of Saul. No wonder men and women throughout the world created ways to cover or adorn their heads in public places or during their devotions to God. It seemed that I should have averted my eyes, but the surprise and quickness of his gesture had given me no time.

Saul lifted his cap again and slapped it vigorously. More of the dirt flew off, but there was heavy red soil still sticking. He shrugged his shoulders with a grin. "Guess my wife will have to wash it."

"Yes, she'll have to," I said, smiling as well. "And how's your little girl?"

"What little girl?"

"The one with you last night on the beach."

"That's not my little girl."

"Who is she then?"

"Dunno. She showed up three or four weeks ago. She came to me like she knew me. But that girl's not a talker. Just told me her name. She keeps me company while I collect dulse. She tries to help, but I can see she really doesn't like to touch seaweed. But she loves sand dollars!"

"Does she live nearby?"

"Dunno. I asked her, but she doesn't answer. She's different, all right! Very quiet. The sky's like her watch. She looks up and checks it now and then to know when she needs to leave. When it's time, she points to it. But no matter what day, when I get to the beach, she's there. Early evening. Most days, it's just her and me on that beach. Still, she always sees me before I see her. I know it because when I spot her, she's already walking towards me."

"She seems very sweet," I said. "She made me think of my own little girl."

"You have a child?"

"Yes and no."

"What do you mean, *yes and no?*"

"She was adopted. An orphan. Got her out of Haitian slums."

"From Haiti, huh? Lucky girl!"

"But I lost her some time ago after a nasty divorce."

"Oh, I'm very sorry. Those damn lawyers!"

"No. It wasn't the lawyers. We had joint custody, although that was after a two-year legal battle. In the end, it was the weekly back and forth that proved difficult for a child. Plus, her father remarried. That didn't help. It was good for her with him but not good for her with me. I think she felt pressure to choose. He comes from an educated family with lots of money, social connections, and lots of siblings, all of them married with children, so she had lots of cousins. I have none of that. It's just me, an immigrant in America. Remember how yesterday you asked me why I am so far from home? The reasons are complex. It would take a whole book to explain. I think she made the sensible choice. And that too would be a long story."

"What's her name?"

"Eveline."

"Nice name! Did you choose it?"

"Yes. I liked the sounds in it. I liked the *Eve* part. It was the first mother, therefore, the first daughter, at least in my Christian tradition. And I liked the syllable *line,* like in bloodline. She was the only child I'll ever have."

"It's really too bad it went wrong. Must've been hard."

"I'm okay now. It's been a while."

Saul's face suddenly looked somber. I felt sorry to have caused it. I thought about my mother at that moment and how she would surely say about him that he has the long face of a day without bread. He kept his eyes downcast for a little while. Without their lovely pale blue color shining through, his face seemed to have lost its light. His glasses were still speckled white like they were the previous afternoon when I first met him. "Are you house painting again today?" I asked.

"Nope. Not today. I should take a spin over there though, I'm not done."

"Is your house painted white too?"

"No way! Not my house. Everyone can tell my house by the color. It's different from all the other houses here."

"What color is it?"

"Blood red."

* * *

AT THE END OF THAT FIRST AFTERNOON in Spencer's Island when I initially met Saul and we had a long, relaxed conversation after agreeing on the rent, I had gone for an early dinner at a nearby restaurant. I had noticed a sign advertising lobster and hoped they would also have lemon meringue pie.

When I came back to the house of the fossils, it was still light outside, and I decided to walk on the beach. I believed that I'd be going on my way the next day, and I wanted to take advantage of the natural beauty available at my doorstep. The tide was out very far, and the fog had left the shore to go hang low over the sea at a good distance away. Large, dark formations of sharp rocks covered with a thick mass of seaweed could be seen strewn all over the beach after having been concealed under high tide when I arrived. "The tide here is the highest in the world," Saul had told me.

I started walking, glad that I was wearing sneakers because the beach turned out to be mostly pebbles. Even areas of sand were prickly with rejects from the sea. The light was fading, and I had to be careful where I stepped. In the distance, I could make out the silhouettes of two people bent over the dark waters in which they stood covered up to their knees. I wondered about what they could be looking for at such an hour and with so little light.

Feeling curious, I started towards them instead of returning to the house, while they, in turn, seemed to be heading my way at the same moment. By then, it was almost night, and even while I was getting closer, I could not make out the features of the two people until I heard, "How was dinner?"

Saul was smiling, face relaxed under his cap. There was a girl with him, and it seemed to me that she could only be his daughter. He was carrying armloads of seaweed. "It's dulse," he said, noticing the direction of my gaze. "It's good to eat, plus it has all sorts of healing properties."

"Is that what you were looking for in the water then?"

"Yeah."

"But why not simply pick it off the rocks?"

"That's not dulse. You can't eat that one, although it makes the best fertilizer and insecticide."

I tried to speak to the girl, asking her some questions, but she only stared. I figured that she was shy. Noticing my embarrassment at the girl's lack of response, Saul said, "Here, why don't you touch the dulse?"

Expecting it to feel like snakes, I reached for the dulse with hesitation while remarking, "How wonderful to have this beach where you can relax at the end of each day! You're a lucky man."

"I know. This is my playground."

"Did you grow up around here?"

"Yes, in Advocate."

"You never left the area?"

"I did. I lived in Halifax for a while. I met my wife there. But I missed this place."

"This must have been heaven to grow up in."

Saul bent down and laid the dulse across a big piece of driftwood. Then he stood back up straight, setting his legs wider apart. He crossed his arms and looked me in the eyes. "I had the best childhood one can ever have. I grew up very poor. But we had a roof, and we had food. And we had love. So, I didn't feel poor. I come from a long line of fishermen. My father still gets up every day to go fishing. He'll probably die fishing. There was no question back then that I'd be a fisherman like him. That was all one could be, it seemed. But when I was a boy, I made money mowing the lawn of the Advocate Cemetery. Lots of money. It's on a hill. I could look at the sea in the distance and think, 'my father is there'. Yeah. Best childhood!"

"You mowed the lawn of the *cemetery*?"

"I did. In the summer."

"What's it like to be a child and to be mowing the lawn of a cemetery?"

"Sunny. It was sunny. I ate my sandwich and read names on the tombstones. I knew all the families. One tomb had a life-size sculpture of a deer right next to it."

"Was it not spooky to be sitting surrounded with bones of dead people?"

"There aren't that many bones. Most of the tombstones read, 'Lost at Sea.'" Saul squatted near the driftwood and started idling with the dulse with his index finger. The girl had traced an invisible hopscotch in her mind over which she was hopping, switching from one foot to the other. It was completely dark by then, but neither of them seemed ready to say good night.

"Empty tombs?" I asked. "Is the ghost supposed to come and find his tomb?"

"In a way, yes. But it's more a question of memory. And respect. Plus, a soul must rest."

I was puzzled. "If there's such a thing as a soul, do you think it needs a grave in order to rest?"

Saul said, "A grave's like an anchor with a long rope." He got up again and turned to face the dark ocean ahead. "The shipwrecked and the drowned, they haven't said their proper goodbye. The grave gives them that place where they can do that."

"Do what? Get a proper goodbye?"

"Yeah. And this way too, they know they're dead and should be off." He laughed. "We don't want ghosts sticking around, do we?"

"Saul? Do you believe in ghosts? And what do you think about reincarnation?"

"Dunno. Maybe for some of us. Not everyone." Saul sat down on the driftwood next to the dulse. He pushed his cap to the back of his head, baring his forehead. The girl stopped playing hopscotch and came back near us. I thought that she would be asking to go home, but she did not. She just looked at me. She did not seem annoyed. I caught myself remembering my own little girl again, my Eveline.

"Which ones of us don't reincarnate?" I asked.

"Those that are ghosts," Saul answered with a chuckle.

"So, you do believe in ghosts, Saul."

"Dunno. But dead or not dead, people need a proper goodbye. When we separate, we need a proper goodbye. If not, we suffer haunt."

"Haunt?" I asked. It was my turn to squat, needing to get closer to Saul for this conversation. I had not gotten a proper goodbye from Eveline. I still hoped that I would. Talking about ghosts demanded that we be near, with ears close enough for whispering. The girl remained standing, however.

"Yeah. Feelings or ghosts, they work the same way," Saul said. I secretly agreed with him in my heart. He pulled his cap down his forehead again. "They stick around 'til they get a proper goodbye. And so, there are some people you see in front of you, you think they're real and yet they're not. I suppose that's what a ghost is, somehow looks real, but isn't."

"And where do they go after they have had their 'proper goodbye'?"

"Dunno."

A breeze started to lift, and the girl looked at the sky. She closed her arms around her chest as if she were cold. Still, she said nothing.

"Who do they need the proper goodbye from?" I asked.

"People they knew, obviously," Saul answered. "People they loved. People who loved them."

Hearing this, I wondered, *Could it be that it's not just the dead who want a proper goodbye and that my Eveline still hopes for a proper goodbye from me too?* "But Saul," I said, "at some point, people they knew would sooner or later die too. What you're saying suggests that you believe in an afterlife where the dead continue on. And if they're in an afterlife where there appears to be remembering and feeling since there's wanting a proper goodbye, that means there's life after death, and that we too will end up there and reunite. And what you're saying could also mean you believe in reincarnation and that people would need to get a proper goodbye before they leave the afterlife realm and return to this world and be reborn somewhere else?"

Saul picked up a pebble at his feet and threw it far ahead of us. "Dunno. It's a lot of complication you're bringing up. But see that monument to the *Mary Celeste* over there? It's the grave left for these ten people. Sure as I am alive today, they came here at some point for their proper goodbye."

"Did they get it?"

"Dunno. But they came for it."

"Do you think that writing a book about someone you miss can serve as a monument for giving a proper goodbye?"

"Dunno. Why not?"

"Ever seen a ghost, Saul?"

Saul got up and arched himself back, filling his lungs with air. The girl looked again at the sky. I wondered what she saw. She took Saul's hand.

"If you wanna talk to people who see ghosts, you're in the wrong place," Saul said. "No ghosts in Spencer's Island! Go to Barra or South Uist. That's where you find ghosts."

"Well, for now, I'm here, and I better be off so you people can go home. We all need a good night's sleep." I wished them a good night and turned to walk towards the little house full of fossils. It already felt like a friend waiting for me to come home.

"Ever heard the line?" Saul asked from a distance.

I turned around. "What line?"

"He ain't dead, just buried."

We were both laughing when the girl suddenly came running to me, gently took my left hand and put something in it. It was a sand dollar.

"Thank you!" I said, "How lovely! How perfect! Will you tell me your name?"

"Mattie." She was shy.

* * *

THE LAUNCHING OF THE *MARY CELESTE* in 1861, a wooden sailing vessel initially named *The Amazon*, had marked the beginnings of the shipbuilding industry in Spencer's Island. The beach area there was an ideal site for a shipyard, needing minimal facilities to house carpenters' benches, a forge and a wood-fired steam-box. It also provided an abundance of raw materials within easy reach.

That a vessel I had heard about all my life, the legendary *Mary Celeste*, was built in this obscure place, which I had unwittingly stumbled upon, amazed me. There remains a mystery about its disappearance. People keep telling the story made of facts and conjectures alike.

There were ten people aboard, Captain Benjamin Briggs and seven crew, as well as his wife Sarah and young daughter Sophia-Mathilde, who had joined him for this voyage. They sailed out of New York on November 7, 1872, loaded with 1,701 barrels of spirits—poisonous denatured alcohol—destined for Genoa, Italy. It is thus that the brigantine started eastward across the Atlantic Ocean, known to be tempestuous during late fall.

According to the records, November of that particular year was unusually stormy. Vessel after vessel arriving in ports along the eastern seaboard of Canada and the United States reported continuous gale-force winds and violent seas.

Sailors from a similar ship called *Dei Gratia* had sighted the *Mary Celeste* in December 1872. They described it as a ship haunting the sea, out of control, sailing empty.

Yet, after boarding the ghost ship, men of the *Dei Gratia* observed that the *Mary Celeste* was undamaged, except for the sails. No trace of struggle was left on the deck or anywhere in either the cabins or the hold. Its cargo was intact. Coats were hanging on racks. Loose coins and pipes ready to be smoked were lying on the dining table. But not a soul was on board. The entire crew had vanished.

The most sensible theory about what happened to the *Mary Celeste* is that somehow fearing an explosion of the brigantine from leakage of its alcohol cargo, Captain Briggs ordered everyone off it and into the lifeboat. The rope from the skylied was pulled off in a matter of minutes. It would give the lifeboat a good three hundred yards for it to tow behind the ship. Ten people dangerously overloading the small boat would be watching their ship anxiously waiting for developments.

* * *

PEOPLE IN MY DREAMS can be said to rise up from my brain's dangerously overloaded lifeboat as well. I think of them as having followed me all day from the indeterminable distance of the unconscious until they can climb aboard my psyche at night.

My sleep is the time when they take the opportunity to infiltrate and take over. They noisily clamber on deck, search all rooms until they can lower themselves into the hold and close off access. They act on me as the tempestuous sea did on the *Mary Celeste*, tossing and flooding her over while sails ripped. They banter in my brain all night and settle back down in the lifeboat at dawn.

On waking some mornings, I felt the need to drop anchor, to stabilize myself after a night of hurricane dreams. I would search for solid form, reach for any fossil, select one black-slate fossil from the bedside table and follow with my fingertip vein-like traces that tiny ferns left on it four hundred million years ago.

It was on one such morning, while sitting on a large piece of driftwood in the sunlight outside my front door, that I noticed Saul walking towards me. "Did you say you're a writer?" he asked as he got closer, not bothering with phatic greetings.

"This morning, I don't know who or what I am," I said.

"Well then, it might help you remember if I introduced you to a man here. He's written many books, but one is about the *Mary Celeste*. Seems to me you're curious about that story, right?"

"The ghost-ship?"

"Yeah. But according to him, no ghost at all. What happened is clear as day. Wanna come?"

I got up right away, asking, "Tell me first, do people here hunt at night?" and started following him down the pathway leading to the main street.

"Nobody hunts at night that I know of," he said. "The only thing we hunt here is dulse and fish. Why do you ask?"

"I heard calls, tapping, knocking and cracking sounds. I am not sure if I was awake or not. It's as if all of nature joined forces to get my attention. Even the wind's howling sounded alive. I am not even sure what it is I heard. Ah, it's silly. But it unsettled me. You're going to think I'm crazy."

"New place. New sounds," he said, shrugging his shoulders. "It's nothing to worry about. There's a part of us that lives in the jungle. It likes the hunt. Misses it. But it fears it too."

"Possibly. But still, it's crazy."

"Listen, that jungle animal inside us, people around here take it out to sea or to the hockey field. Take my wife, for example. She's a wild wolf! You should see her on the ice. She's a hockey champion! Nothing stops her. She attacks like a beast. She goes out there for a kill. I tell you, she's scary. Then she goes home and bakes blueberry muffins. Go figure."

"You sound so proud of her," I said distractedly, suddenly remembering a friend who lost his fiancée. They had been ice-skating, young, in love, the date set for a spring wedding. But the ice broke, and she went straight down deep. "But, how's Mattie?" I asked.

"The usual. Come at dusk to look for dulse, and you'll see her. She'll be there. She'll see you before you see her."

Saul had led me just past the front of the B&B and was now crossing the street to a pretty white house. He went around to the back door and rang the bell. A man in his seventies opened the door. Saul introduced us and then excused himself. I should not have been surprised, but I was disappointed that he left. "By the way," he said, walking away, "that doll I was telling you about? I'm giving it back to the sea."

"But why, Saul?"

* * *

"SO, WHAT BRINGS YOU to the Bay of Fundy?" my host courteously asked as he was ushering me into his house.

"Gale winds," I said with laughter. I entered the soft light of a space filled with marvelous paintings and old prints of all manner of ships. My mouth opened slightly from a sense of wonder.

"You say *winds* brought you here," my host argued. "All considering, you should say *seas*."

"What do you mean?"

"I mean that the Bay of Fundy bears some 170 miles into the very heart of New Brunswick and Nova Scotia," he answered with a smile that never left his lips although the downward curve of the corners of his mouth seemed to indicate a more somber temperament. His eyes analyzed me behind dark-framed glasses. "Twice a day," he continued, "some 115 billion tons of water move in and out of the bay and generate what is estimated to be 200 million horsepower. It takes a little over twelve hours for each tide to complete its cycle of flooding and ebbing."

"The highest tide in the world?"

"Yes."

"But how's it that you remember these exact numbers?" I asked.

"I should have them in mind. I have written enough about it."

"Saul mentioned your book, *The Saga of the Mary Celeste*."

"Yes. A fine vessel."

"A fine mystery and a fine book, too, from what I hear."

"I hope. And it was a *fine mystery* indeed. But I am afraid that the days when the waters of the bay were alive with commercial vessels and fishermen passing up and down are long gone."

"What happened?"

"Hard to say. Progress maybe? I should also mention that the waters were frequently used by privately owned vessels of war fitted-out for the capture of the enemy's merchandise. They were known to attack coastal communities regularly. Actually, they were little more than pirates."

"I'm a descendent of pirates!" I said, smiling.

"Really? But where do you actually come from?"

"Haiti."

"How about that! Do you know that the *Mary Celeste* ended its days in the bay of Port-au-Prince?"

"I grew up in a house overlooking that bay. Do you think the *Mary Celeste* somehow brought me here?"

"I see that you like ghost stories."

"But what really happened to the Mary Celeste?"

"One hears many theories," he said with eyes full of play. "What if I told you that a giant octopus gripped the entire ship from underneath, sucked all the crew one by one, and then spat their bones out?"

"No... really...?"

"Or if I told you that a pirate ship that lost most of its men to disease had attacked the *Mary Celeste* in order to kidnap and put its crew into forced labor so they could replace their own dead crewmen?"

"That doesn't make sense either!"

We both laughed. "And what if I told you instead that Captain Briggs, on the *Mary Celeste*, actually feared an explosion from the alcohol cargo he carried because the brigantine had passed the Eastern point of Santa Maria where the warmer temperatures of the Azores would have created increased pressure on the leaking alcohol? There's always some leakage with such cargo. Then, tell me which theory would seem more plausible to you?"

"The octopus! Without a doubt!"

"And right you are!"

We laughed again with the insouciance of children.

"But, tell me about these," I asked, pointing to the paintings all around us. "I so love old ships!"

"I come from a long line of seamen that unfortunately ends with me," my host said. "These you see in the paintings in this room are all ships that my grandfather manned. My father passed the paintings on to my brother and to me."

"But this one?" I asked, "Isn't that the Cape d'Or lighthouse?"

"Yes. A friend painted that. Have you been there?"

"I have and keep returning. I met someone who is staying there for a couple of nights. That horn would drive me crazy. I would not be able to sleep."

"There's always a lot of fog there. It's all automated now, but it's not so long ago that men lived in lighthouses and took care of them. Only a special kind of person is able to stay alone all winter long."

"You asked me if I liked ghost stories. It isn't ghosts I like. The ocean is what fascinates me. Yet, I grow increasingly afraid of it. Cape d'Or is terrifying. I think it wants me to jump."

"Goodness."

"Don't worry, I won't. But you know, the sea on a Caribbean beach is not the same that one contemplates when one stands over the cliff at Cape d'Or or on any cliff in Nova Scotia."

"It's a special ocean, all right."

"The jagged, black rocks help create a different mood," I explained. "But it isn't just that—it's like there's a depth in front of your eyes that gives significance to the words *the great beyond*."

The man was attentive, but I then grew silent, searching for words. I wanted to tell him how the Caribbean Sea has the warmth of beginnings, benevolent temperatures and color that befit play; how its sandy shores slope towards the water very gradually and how one may view that ocean as an immense, joyful bathtub suited to yellow rafts and red flippers. But here, at Cape d'Or, one senses a profound, intriguing life deep below that makes one shiver, somberness and cold being paired. The dark green waves feel immensely familiar to the rhythms in one's own body.

My host then interrupted my thoughts. "You're mute now. Have I lost you?" he asked gently.

"No. But there're so many thoughts coming at once. The easiest way to express them is to say that the deep movement of the waves makes me feel there is a kind of infinity that lives, breathes in me and all around."

My host took his glasses off and rubbed his eyes. "I understand," he said.

"Do you?" I asked softly.

"Yes. Have you heard of Captain Joshua Slocum?"

"No."

"Very few people have. He was the first man to travel alone in a boat around the world. His boat was called the *Spray*. It took him three years. He wrote about it in *Sailing Alone Around the World*. After crossing the Atlantic from Yarmouth, he put in at the Azores for several days."

"The Azores again!"

"Well, yes. Anyway, Slocum described how he was given food-stuff that included plums and some white cheese. He ate all that eagerly. After he set sail again, he was beset with horrible stomach cramps while a terrible gale had lifted. He double-reefed the mainsail and set the *Spray* on its course right before he threw himself on the cabin floor, suffering great pain. He rose many hours later and looked out. There was a tall man at the wheel dressed in garbs that resembled what a pirate might wear. This man introduced himself as the pilot of the *Pinta*, one of Christopher Columbus's vessels. Then he told Slo-cum he should rest some more."

"The *Pinta*!" I remarked joyously. "*La Nina, La Pinta*, and *La Santa Maria*! I learnt about these in my schoolbooks. I sang these names in my childhood play songs. They are the three ships with which Columbus is said to have discovered Haiti. That pilot who saved Slo-cum must've been among those who set foot on my island too."

"Yes, that pilot must've been in your Haiti. At any rate, after Slocum awoke the next morning, he realized that the *Spray* had sailed 90 miles on rough seas, and yet was still exactly on course."

* * *

MOST DAYS, THE HEART knows how to pace itself. I am not counting moments when it suddenly takes to jumping in quickened beats as if an owl had just hooted in the night.

Waking up from a strong, painful dream however, the heart does not know itself yet. It weighs with self-doubt, imprisoned in an unformulated clutch. Alive but alone is what the heart feels when waking from such dreams. It is as if you had just crossed through many lives, being the half-drowned survivor of a shipwreck washed ashore onto a deserted island, bruised with the imprints from people's features lingering over the mind, people you thought were familiar, cherished, yet whom you have just rediscovered, found them to be unknown, concealed, mysterious, while you still suffer in all layers of your flesh the poisonous lair that each one has dug.

You sit on the edge of the bed as odd to yourself and vulnerable as if you were standing on that very beach of your wrecked survival and escape. And so you make some steps towards the bathroom, or towards the kitchen, as you might towards natives you hope are hidden in nearby bushes so you could tell them that you also are human, and belong to the real world.

From such a dream I woke on my last night spent in the small town called Spencer's Island. I got up and walked through the house awkwardly. I looked apologetically at the fossils as if I had been an intruder in their house, and they had only tolerated my presence, although they might have somehow desired it. They had been patient with me until now as good parents are with a child learning to stand and who, at long last, takes a step. They seemed like parents filled with humble dignity and delight, yet also sobered by the distance and infallibility that belong to those imbued with ancient knowledge. I tenderly touched the fossils, feeling jagged edges, marks of brutal breaks and unnatural separation.

The fossils no longer had that inner quiet of beings that exist in receding time. They had the pathos of a broken jawbone found in sand—a testimony to sacrilege. A piece had been ripped from the whole to which it belongs and for which it forever yearns.

I had once thought of my good fortune at finding myself in a house full of fossils. I relished their discovery as a similarly thrilling opportunity as when we get a sighting of whales, dark, sleek, awe-inspiring, emerging boldly in full sight like an idea suddenly might before plunging back into the deep, leaving us with the persistent longing for what they had helped us briefly glimpse.

My intellectual distance had ebbed. I no longer saw tectonic plates simply as matter forced away by movement and heat that once shaped the earth and continue to do so. Tectonic plates were now living entities while human beings themselves seemed to be tectonic plates, each confronted with, and manipulated in their core by forces incomprehensible, uncontrollable, and viciously whimsical. I saw the tragedy of these tectonic plates and how, in their sloping movement and shifting away, they irretrievably left parts of themselves behind.

Human life itself seemed a voyage on a tectonic plate: we are slowly and imperceptibly drifting away, losing sight of our original shores. Childhood is a hazy landscape where our roots encroach and weigh like petrified eggs that never hatch as we dreamed they would.

While I stood in the house, surrounded by inanimate fossils, I felt myself instead in the company of animate forms resulting from the continuous fragmentation of their being through millennia. I saw fellow human beings in them—dark, frayed, misshapen, brittle, divided, randomly shelved to accent the small house our universe makes.

Feeling overwhelmed and at a loss, I picked up my hat from the dining table and walked out.

The fog brought inland with the evening tide hovered all around. A different light could be glimpsed out of a distant rent in the low sky. I sat on the big tree trunk that was now no more than a large piece of driftwood washed up in front of the house. This grey-white skeleton had a kind of softened hip bone where I nested my buttocks, sitting with my back straight up, eyes focused far out to sea.

Stripped of all its former majesty as a tree, the big driftwood was now a random bench where the idle sit, a shelf where shells are lined up, counted carefully and then abandoned.

* * *

FROM DRIFTWOOD TO SHIPWRECK, the mind can trace a direct trail. I thought of the book about Cape Breton shipwreck stories that I had bought in a woodcarver's store. Reading these stories, a little each day, I developed an ever-increasing respect for seamen. Thoughts and emotions originally awakened from hearing about the *Mary Celeste* progressively magnified and expanded.

I felt inwardly changed by these tales of brazen courage, defiance towards the wrath of the sea, the denial of danger; tales of men self-less and loyal, risking their lives to save those of others shipwrecked at sea, mocking death when it comes, mocking it more when it failed to take them away, going back to sea at the first opportunity, daring to act in ways thought mad by most. These stories created a shift in the way I saw the world. I wondered if the real madmen are, in fact, those of us landlocked in cities.

My dream during the last night I was to spend in the house of fossils had showed me how I mourned things of the sea and dreaded my return to the city, to the kind of death I lived there, having lost my previous life where the sea, one made in the measure of a person's heart and in the image of a person's soul, gives one repeated opportunities to reveal one's greater humanity and revel in it.

I reflected on the time when sea travel was at the center of North American life and its economic power. In the age of sail, when the brigantine *Mary Celeste* was launched out of Spencer's Island, the sea was the last frontier, like cyberspace, or the mysteries of what lies beyond our solar system. The ocean was unmarked territory. The very first explorers believed that the earth was flat and that you could fall off its edges if you sailed far enough. Whaling crews were composed of men as bold as the first astronauts. Seafaring men remained undaunted by the constant tragedies that befell their neighbors or their own kin. Out of the twenty-five people that perished in the wreck of the steamer *Dorcas* and the barge in its tow, the *Etta Stewart*, sixteen were from Louisburg alone, a village of only about 900 people; from this one shipwreck, seven women were widowed, and thirty children left without fathers. One woman lost both husband and brother. The chief engineer of the *Dorcas* lost his entire family on board with him: his pregnant wife, three children and one girl in his care.

Sitting on the lone driftwood in front of the house of fossils, I was still somehow in my dream of the previous night, seeing in my mind images of silent bodies sinking slowly in a bottomless ocean, feeling the ancient despair of one woman drowned, huddled onto herself, detached like a single musical note etched on a dark green, empty sheet, her disheveled long hair entangled with seaweed that wrapped around her naked white form in long strips resembling the final dress of a mummified being.

I shivered, crossed my arms over my breast, and shut my eyes. But the intimate darkness in which I then sat brought me no calm; it became instead a screen on which my thoughts projected the black face of my grandmother's manservant in Haiti. Louis's face seemed to represent all the shipwrecked from the slave trade, revealing how his life as a servant was no less shipwrecked than those who drowned in the *Mary Celeste*. My mind still sees how he stood in a ghostly uniform behind the chair of a kindly old lady preparing to feast at a table where she used a small silver bell to call for dinner to be served. I asked myself if a ripe old age reached at the cost of such suffering really holds joy for mortal man. Louis kept his white uniform spotless and his black face stern. His gold front tooth appeared to be the point where all possible joy had gathered and fossilized.

* * *

AT LAST, I GOT UP from the driftwood, but it was as an orphaned daughter aching to bury my face in my father's neck and recognize his scent the way one does precious wood. At that moment, I noticed a sand dollar on the driftwood, left somehow at the spot where I habitually sat during my days in Spencer's Island. I had been so caught up in my reverie that I had not noticed it.

I picked up the sand dollar with care and followed the star on its back with my fingertip. *You,* I said inwardly, *I shall always keep.*

I walked back into the house. The bedroom had a sullen look. I pulled its window curtains open and looked out. The fog was trying to lift, a blue sky readying to take its place. I let the curtain drop and sat on the lonely bed, thinking, *where have they all gone?*

It was a rather defiant thought I had when I held the sand dollar, thinking that I might always keep something or someone because I will it so. We cannot possess those we hold dear. My experience with Eveline taught me that much. Life is made of motion. Remembering becomes sorrowful; forgetting is a relief. I have wondered why my family life felt like a collage of disparate pieces temporarily brought together, a tapestry woven from threads soon torn apart. I have wondered if there is an ancestral debt that we pay for the slave trade that benefited several generations of us descendants of colons and continues to. I question whether a blood debt can ever be erased and if a curse ever ends.

Haiti has not recovered from cries of people in slave ships, people stolen from their land, ripped away from their families, even if they have somehow endured.

Slave traders and colonial masters have endured as well. Children they fathered with slave women turned into the revolutionaries who joined forces with slaves in 1804 and massacred the white masters, setting ablaze the plantation world they knew. Thereafter, however, these children were only able to reproduce the social systems they abhorred but which had given them birth.

A great rift eventually occurred between these revolutionary brothers. They developed two different modes of occupying the island.

Slaves in Haiti had come from twenty-four different African ethnic groups. After the revolution, these purely African groups remained in what was called the *pays-en-dehors*—the outside country. They were identified as the *Bossales,* or unrefined ones, and created a society that followed both an African model and a European feudal one. They remained uninvolved in politics. They spoke only Creole, and their religion was the Vodou that developed from African ancestral worship traditions.

The other group was called the *Creoles*, or mixed bloods. They were the minority population that kept occidental values and culture; they spoke French; they remained Catholics, creating a state that excluded the *Bossales* majority population while using them as servants, keeping all political power, huddling near port cities due to their dependency on foreign goods and culture. They highly rated a whiter skin color and did their best to retain the little they had, while they were identified by it and resented for it. Later arrivals from Europe in the nineteenth century in the form of fortune seekers, adventurous men dreaming of commerce, or whole families fleeing the revolutionary turmoil in their own countries, came to add their number and aspirations to the Haitians' ongoing battle of race and class. They quickly came to embody the former colonial elite and took positions in society that were previously occupied by them.

The children of Haiti thus continue to clash with each other as they sink in bitter waters. The fight of men drowning is all the children of Haiti know about living. Haiti has become the *Mary Celeste* but sails the Caribbean Sea in greater scale and horror. Haiti tells a story where no ill is ever undone, where souls of the drowned and the battered accumulate in the wind and where blood poured at sea never dissipates. Like the *Mary Celeste's*, Haiti's cargo is in constant danger of exploding.

The crew began to leave long ago and continues to pour out of Haiti. The best of every generation has panicked and fled. Every generation of elite Haitians has known exile. They are a race of captains that abandoned the ship they filled and manned carelessly, thinking only of profit. They watch from a roped distance to know when political unrest has abated, and they can return. The *Bossale* population, neglected, held in contempt, resented but abused by the *Creoles*, yet also often by each other, soon became aware and felt the attraction of the outer world. They began a desperate mass exodus on flimsy boats that never made it to their Miami destination, feeding their bodies to the sea as their ancestors had, dying on slave ships whose cruelties they did not survive.

Remembering my family's past life as I sat on the bed in Spencer's island, I knew that I had reached a point of no return. I could never go back and stay. The pull on the towrope would, however, never cease, as it again rekindled my emotions at that moment, my thoughts filling with longings and their ensuing disquiet—my grandmother's silver bell ringing furiously... cries of a little girl... lips scrubbed with bitter soap... the little girl spits over and over but the poison will last... Was it Louis who did it?... It is just as well if the womb was spoiled for breeding—no cries will be born from that womb... mildew coats scar tissue and unmerited shame so that seeds can only rot... You must never have a child. Your sister must never either... The nakedness of an abused black man has infected us with desolation and abandonment.

I know that eyes don't cry with tears in that place of remembrance. All during my stay in Spencer's Island, my mind remained inhabited, as it always does, with the memory of the small orphan girl I had once adopted and taken out of Haiti to raise as my child, be my family, my delicate sand dollar, my Eveline.

I had shared with her the family name I received from my father, and he from *his* father, going back through all generations of time. Eveline bore my family name with glee, but only a short while before our story also became one of separation instead of redemption. It has been a long time since I last heard her ask, "Mommy? Are you as tall as our house?"

Like Mattie's, Eveline's life is forever connected to the sea and Caribbean shores. From her, I learnt that poison also bears flowers. I wait for her return while my mind continuously sorts through disparate yet strangely connected memories that seem points of juncture between past and present seasons of life—I see my father kissing me goodbye at the gate, and me, watching him walk away on an infinite street... "I believe in you," he had said. "But how about my debilitated sister?" I had asked, "my frail, ash powder, bitter sister? What part did God play in this injustice and damage?" And all the while, my mother would moan… "Don't kiss me, don't touch me, don't…"

A fragment of a modern shipwreck has washed ashore Spencer's Island and grips the barren sand… I am that fragment, a panicked leaper from a dangerous vessel.

The memory of how the child I was played in the garden persists… But she crossed over—she ran… she ran. She runs… *Will she ever rest?*

Saul had thrown the doll back far into the sea, and I somehow knew that Mattie would consequently never be seen again on the beach at Spencer's Island. Saul will gather dulse alone for a long time.

Mattie had missed her doll, the very one that Saul had picked up on the shore and propped on the windowsill, facing the sea. The doll had called Mattie out of invisibility, called her to cross the veil between life and death and come get her. They briefly played in the light of day together again. In the ocean's memory, Mattie and the doll were one. In placing the doll on the windowsill, Saul unwittingly created a kind of altar and small monument through which Mattie could return to say her own proper goodbye, one distinct from those goodbyes possibly made at the monument on the landing by others aboard the *Mary Celeste*. The voice of a child holding her doll is a pure, distinct note, far lonelier, and it needs its own conduit.

* * *

IT IS AS IF INSTANCES OF MY PREVIOUS night's dream had waited for that image of Saul alone on the beach in order to engulf me all over again but now in the form of a vivid reverie. It came over me the way people who have neared death claim that their entire life unfurled in their mind's eye. Except that this dream was not my life but a staged play. Like a grand lady who owns many stunning dresses, Death had wished to impress me with her collection and had me try one on.

The previous night's dream had fed and added to a bold reverie I indulged before leaving Spencer's Island, its people, its lore, its mysteries. I felt I saw all that had happened to Mattie and the people on the *Mary Celeste*. I understood their story. Perhaps the fossils told it to my unconscious that, in turn, fed it to my consciousness, adding to the information I gathered from my conversation with the old historian and learning from records kept of what was found in the *Mary Celeste* by the sailors of the *Dorca*.

In the reverie, I found myself in a ship's cabin. I saw myself playing a melodeon and singing a hymn. The cabin windows are covered over with canvas and boards. On a berth, and playing with toys, sits a little girl for whom I'm singing. I can't make out her face or how old she is. I feel that she's my daughter. I sense great happiness in that cabin.

Under the berth, there is an old sword. Next to a table piled with books stands a sewing machine and a pretty sewing box. The temperature is warm—it must be sunny outside.

A tall man suddenly barges into the cabin, dressed as a ship's captain. I instantly know that he is my husband and the girl's father. He grabs me by the shoulders. "We are in grave danger!" he cries. "We must leave the ship right away!"

He hastily picks the little girl up from the berth. She tries to wriggle out of his arms and starts to cry. I grab a doll and hand it to her—it is the lovely porcelain doll she loves most. Clutching the doll, she is quieted for the moment. The three of us run up to the deck.

We are then outside and on deck. I see panic in the eyes of the crew, but they are nevertheless focused on the captain and follow his orders.

Men are folding some of the sails while others are pulling the main peak halyard out of its various blocks. One big sail is still lying loose and unfolded when the captain shouts new orders, "Get that rope down! We need it!" Men start pulling at the main peak halyard. When it is all released, they tie it to the ship at one end and to the ship's lifeboat at the other.

I don't understand what the fear is about, but the sense of threat and danger is strong. No one has a face I can yet make out, even the captain's face. I distinguish him from the men by his clothes. No matter where he stands, he feels central.

While the men are busy with the halyard, the captain hands the little girl over to me. I grip her hand.

He runs down to the cabin and quickly returns with what looks like a chronometer, a book, and some third object I can't distinguish. He then yells new orders. "Everyone aboard the boat! We have to get away from the ship!"

The little girl starts screaming, pulls her hand free of mine and runs towards the opposite direction to where we are supposed to go.

"Sophia-Mathilde! Get back to your mother!" the captain yells, running to catch her. I see the intense fear in his eyes, and Oh! I can see his face now! Oh God! It is the face of Captain Briggs! The man in the photo portrait I had seen in the book about the *Mary Celeste*, the same beautiful man. How I love that man! Like an ocean swell pushing inside my breast, pressure from love restrained now hurts.

The little girl suddenly stops short, tightens her clutch on the doll, hesitating about her next move. In that instant, her father grabs her and rushes back towards me.

He helps us all get in the lifeboat. He gets in last, and the crewmen lower it into the waves.

Now the lifeboat is tethered behind the ship, linked to it by a very long cord. I suppose it is the halyard I had seen the men pull at earlier. We are all packed in. The small boat is dangerously overloaded.

But it is morning, sunny, and the breeze calm. No one has taken a coat. The sea is a brilliant blue, and if it were not for the hasty way in which we got into the lifeboat, it could be thought that we are having a small outing.

Captain Briggs is sitting at the stern. I am next to him. In spite of the gentle sea, everyone's attention is fixed onto the ship. She is towing us. Some of the sails had been folded down according to orders from the captain, and so she has much less speed than she otherwise would have.

We wait, I do not know for what. I am apprehensive but silent. Since we got into the boat, Sophia-Mathilde has been sitting in my lap. She keeps her head low, but I can hear her sobs. She holds her porcelain doll tight to her little chest. "Hush, my sweet," I say to her. Hearing my words, she raises her face towards mine and looks in my eyes. Although she smiles, I see her fear. And yet suddenly, I can see her face! Oh! What shock—I know this face—it is Mattie's face! Mattie—Saul's friend in Spencer's Island. "Hush, my sweet," I say again. "Hush Mattie…" But it is a much smaller Mattie who now sits in my lap. I hold her closer still. She is quieted by the hug, and her fingers lightly enclose the sand dollar pendant around my neck. I understand her want—I untie the ribbon and secure the pendant around her neck. I make her notice the star design on the back of the white disk. I trace it with my fingertip. "Mattie, listen to me. I'll tell you what your father said when he gave me this sand dollar: 'You are my North Star,' he said. 'You give direction to my life. I shall never lose you. You shall never be lost.'"

Just then, the weather starts to change.

The change is above in the color of the sky and underneath us, where we feel the boat has a new, startling movement. The sky takes on the colorlessness of the dead. Swells begin to form all around us from a disturbance elsewhere and of which the breeze, turning into sudden, strong wind, brings us terrifying news.

A fluttering of gray mackerel goes right over us.

The ship ahead also has felt the change, and she pulls the cord so tight it seems we are like a baby being pulled out of the womb by hands that know the umbilical cord is wrapped around its neck.

Big rounded swells come one after another. The lifeboat goes up one side of each mountainous swell and then slides unsteadily down the other side. We sink deeper into the boat each time, but this is not a situation of each man for himself. Death will come from being dragged under together or being tipped into the furious sea. If we untie ourselves from the *Mary Celeste*, we are doomed; if we remain tied to the ship speeding ahead, we are doomed.

We all understand that if any one of these swells breaks over us, we are dead. Each man knows his only chance of survival is to stay screwed to that bottle-cork of a boat, and yet only if the God of Miracles also decides to show that He is the Almighty who can do anything He pleases—a God who will demonstrate how it is as much fun to unnerve a poor-devil-of-a-man by saving him from horrifying hell as it is to petrify this man enough that he spills his guts out from between his legs while begging Death to hurry up and take him.

Although her sails were trimmed purposefully so the lifeboat would not be dragged too fast, the wind has made the ship gallop like a panicked horse. The sails flap and billow like the wings of a trapped albatross or the flailing robes of a dying angel.

The men gasp. Terror allows them sounds and new features. These men, who had until now crouched in silence and facelessness, suddenly acquire definition, and I can distinguish one face from the other. It is as if men who lead obscure lives, find themselves when death comes—becoming clear, true, and his very own only when he faces his last minutes.

Mattie is now clasped in her father's arms—his strength is greater than mine. Her crying has stopped. She knows her fate. It is as if the distinction between the child and the adult is erased when confronted with death. Something ageless comes over us and needs larger, staring eyes to encompass the breadth of the situation: we want to remember and carry to the realm of soul the small amount of eternal dust we reaped from this earth and for which some of us will be praised by a forgiving God.

But in my heart, I cry for Mattie in case God forgets to cry for her. My last thoughts are taken up with sorrow for her life—so little of life she has had! And yet, perhaps it is good not to have had time to find, and carve, the singular wood out of which one's cross is made. Has she yet known suffering? What makes the tears of a child so fluid? Is there sorrow with which we are born and carry from the onset?

It is strange how we sometimes suffer more keenly in our dreams than when we are awake, moving as we do in the living world. What is this formless space into which we hurl ourselves? In this vivid, living reverie, on the verge of death, I discover the immense pain of a mother unable to save her child, and even though her baby's few months in the womb gave her an illusory sense of having power and miraculous shelter within her.

The big storm comes after the swells and keeps building up. The wind hisses and keens over the turbulent waves. It tears off their crests with a blast meant for our blinded, water-pitted faces. Spume and sea spray are like venom expelled from a wrathful mouth. It is one hell of a sound this roar from a breaking wave. You know your own horse, even coming from a galloping herd in the distance. You recognize him and are awed that you can tell him apart from the others. Not that he is more beautiful, but that he is yours.

When my husband takes my hand, I know that he has seen it too.

He has seen the wave, dark and fuming like a horse under the whip of the wind, getting ready to lift its huge body on its hind legs to full height before dropping its monstrous weight and crashing its front hoofs into our skulls.

He pulls me up as he stands in the shaking boat, holding Mattie fast against his chest with one arm. Struggling to maintain balance, we gaze together at the wave roaring toward us. We appraise the grey slate of it, menacing like the pelt of a great animal that will envelop us and keep us submerged for an endless, iced journey.

II. The Law of the Land

Io in the Year 2006...

ONE BOSTON PLACE. Where's that? It's not a street, not a number, and I am subpoenaed to be there at ten or my goose is cooked.

Google Maps on the iPhone signals that it's between Washington and State Streets. I can't see any street signs. Everybody around me is speed walking in a dark suit. They all seem to be carrying a black leather briefcase with a metal locking device, the ones you have to dynamite if you forget the secret code that opens it.

A black man in a brown suit stops (or was it a brown man in a black suit?), "Ma'am, are you lost?"

"Yes. Does it show?"

But he doesn't know where One Boston Place is either. He looks at my iPhone and agrees—it's close. It's a good thing I'm early.

iPhone, iMac, iPad, I, I, I—everything here is about ego—I own, therefore I am. I am, therefore I think. I think, therefore I am anxious. So here I am, anxious as hell, little me in a cold city looking for a lawyer's office when all I want is to be left alone on an island to dream of tadpoles and dragonflies. If what I see going on around me qualifies as "Life", I don't want to be part of it.

So far, I hadn't been. I'd done a good job staying out of life for a few years, flirting with the light at the margin of days.

But now, this ex-husband of mine, after nine years of playing me for dead—nine years of not having much life at all—he decides that he wants the child support I owe him for the girl we adopted together. And to think that she's now nineteen years old, and probably about to leave home, if she hasn't already. He now no longer would need to cook up stories that present me as an unfit mother as he did so he wouldn't have to share her with me. Fortunately, the divorce agreement eventually ordered he should.

So, Ex sends his lawyer after me, pulls me out of my peaceful non-existence like a snail yanked out of its shell to be eaten in one gulp. Yes, that's what I feel like right now, looking for One Boston Place while I really should be searching for a bathroom.

I'm looking for an invisible address, while all that my mind can visualize at the moment is a toilet. But instead of the deep release I need, what I've been getting these past few weeks is chest constriction, an internal instruction to die (or a "suggestion?"), while panic attacks burn my skin and electrocute to high hell my eggplant of a brain. My old fears walk on strong legs and haunt vacant hallways in my brain, all of them wearing yellow and red Tibetan masks with snarling mouths and popping eyes.

So, this feeling of being on the electric chair since I heard from my Ex and his subpoena got me running back for treatment to my Chinese herbalists.

Between Chinatown and Allston's Harvard Street, you get all of Massachusetts' Chinese health care concentrated in one area. All the herbalists I know are either called Wong or Wang. I'd be dead already if it weren't for these Wangs. I owe my life to an assortment of Wongs.

* * *

THIS TIME, I tried a new one in Allston. He is a third-generation herbalist. People come from all over the United States to see him. It's "Mind over Medicine," he claims. First come, first served. No appointments. Suits me fine. You enter the place, and you're in China. Magic carpet. Zoom straight out of America.

First, it's the smell of the herbs. They're stored there, they're boiled there, they're sold there, along with all manner of fortifying, calming, energizing, libido enhancing, or wart killing medicine, and presented in lime green, fuchsia pink, or turquoise blue packaging that display black Chinese calligraphy.

High ceilings and dull wood floors—the room is vast. It looks more like a small hangar used for too few shelves of medicine and too many gray metal folding chairs, some of them left open, waiting-for-Godot style, while the majority are folded, stacked in a corner as if in preparation, or hope, for a crowd of variously crippled, cantankerous, contaminated patients.

Behind a cherry vinyl counter directly opposite the glass entrance door where three man-sized Jade trees stand guard, two short women with cropped hair and drab clothes welcome you with stern faces. You ask them for the herbalist, and they both point with their chins and a vague wave of the hand in the direction of a corner opposite their counter, to the left, street side.

I go and sit, mentally evaluating the waiting-time by the number of waiting-bodies, all of them glum-faced, one of them particularly anxious—me.

I love it when my time comes. My middle-aged herbalist has the calm of a contented spiritual man. Right then and there, I know I'll be cured. I'll no longer walk around town focusing on the least painful or messy way I could end my life. People call it "depression." I call it "death-lust." And if you really believe in the existence of God, as I do, why not hurry to join Him? And my herbalist agrees with me, in a way. When I tell him my thoughts about death, he says, "Is good to prepare for death." But then he adds, "For now, we want make you more happy."

He takes a fresh Kleenex out of a box to his left and adds it to an existing pile accumulating on top of a thick foam pad on which he rests my wrist, starting with the right one. He has rounded, flexible fingers that he presses softly over a couple of different spots on the inside of my wrist. He talks to himself, "Liver, not good…" and then to me, "Are you angry? How sleep?" and then to himself again, "Kidney… sad…" And so, it goes for a slow, gentle moment while I run my eyes over his face thoroughly, then over his surroundings vaguely, and he quietly continues to probe my wrists and inner being.

The harmony in his face is strangely contradicted by the eclectic clutter of Chinese bric-a-brac to the left of the large wooden desk behind which he sits—porcelain cats each waving a front paw, wooden rabbits, bronze Buddhas, grandiloquent, golden goddesses, nude acupuncture dolls, finely-veined red and dotted black over beige plastic, and lying next to silk flower bouquets, all of them absent-mindedly displayed atop the very long shelf that hangs right at the level of the glass window overlooking Harvard Street in a way that somehow shields him from the bustle outside and from the inquisitive eyes of people passing by.

* * *

MY PROBLEM started with the first subpoena delivered to my door by a tall, balding man in a suit. Wham! You're remembered after all, and now a wanted "criminal." You owe eighty-thousand dollars of child support, compounded interest all included. You're given one week to pay it all, have your lawyer respond, or Lady, your ass is grass.

Lady? I usually am one and also a university graduate who lives in New England, where I try to fit in. That's the problem. I'm proper. I hold it all inside—the anger, the outrage, the injustice, the hurt.

Well, no more! Foul language's the only language that can articulate my feelings about foul play. Take my truth! "Fucking asshole, shithead," that's what I need to say, especially when, in my case, the law seems to be a set of rules at the service of a farce.

So, I'm telling you my story like it was, like it is, like it's happening right now, living in the present. It's the way memory works anyhow, the past being always in the present while the future's in the present as well because of the anxiety we waste over planning for it, to make it safe, predictable and tidy.

I'm, therefore, not putting any proper present, past or future tense in my story. It's all jumbled the way it feels in my mind where every moment stands in a continuous line to worry me, and I spend my present time trying to shove the past back into the past where it doesn't want to stay. Time makes a mockery of bridges and passages I build between slices of time of my life. Just like I imagine it might for this ex-husband, this ex-adopted daughter of mine, and their ex-lawyer, who they hired again to be their present-day lawyer.

Some thirteen years ago, she went after me like a formidable stage director who would redefine the life of my family in self-justifying defense of a poor-poor, abandoned man, left with a poor-poor, abandoned child. During the two-year divorce procedures, she proved to be a masterful shapeshifter who dissolved form, summoned shades, turning every good I'd ever done into believable evil. Starting divorce procedures was shown to be an illegal and criminal act for which I'd be damned, and not a legal chance for someone to get out of an untenable situation.

The divorce wouldn't've lasted this long if my Ex hadn't tried to deprive me of real time and overnight visits with my child, trumpeting to whoever would hear that I was an unfit mother.

Never mind that I'd paid all adoption expenses for the rescue of this little girl recently orphaned in the slums of Haiti. Never mind that I'd supported my Ex with the fruits of my work for all of the ten years our lopsided marriage lasted while he kept at a writing career with very poor prospects. A back injury that happened before our marriage had left him mildly handicapped, his torso locked and vulnerable. While I progressively turned servant to him during our marriage, rather than a wife, he turned more frightened, manipulative, and greedy.

The long divorce wasn't about money then, even if he did try to dispossess me of some, and even if he fought to receive child support for a child in whose caretaking he fought not to let me share. And despite appearances, it still isn't about money now. It's personal. It's revenge. The money he now has far surpasses mine.

I call his lawyer Robin Hood, for the way she comes after the evil mother again and for her sanctimonious righteousness in her fight for Life's disinherited wretches.

My own lawyer says, "A lawyer's just a hired gun." And, looking at the old divorce agreement, she also asks, "Why did you cave in so easily?"

Try and fill the skin of a poet! Of a naïve, youngish woman without family or personal ties in America who could support and comfort her, an immigrant unfamiliar with American law, disserved by a lawyer who, at the time, neglected her case because he saw no real money in it, leaving her open to further chiseled scrutiny of her every action by the other party's lawyer, letting the proceedings drag over time until that very time was used as additional argument against her.

Try to experience life as this head-in-the-clouds woman (as my father called me when he lived), when she was being legally attacked by a shrewd, angry man who claimed he'd suffered abuse, and this, while he was being actively served by an army of lawyers—his own father and mother supported and aided by their law school friends and colleagues; his lawyer sister, lawyer brother, and their lawyer spouses. Imagine this army of outraged, loving, well-trained people banded together, riding behind a Robin-Hood-Hired-Puppet to destroy this Haitian Chiquita-Banana whom Fate had found fit to land in Massachusetts where, it turns out, a child's not a legal adult until she's twenty-three.

When this Chiquita was only nineteen, she was already an anonymous immigrant working in an El Paso, Texas, dry-cleaning facility. You'd think I'd swum over the Rio Grande illegally the way Texans treated me in department stores, seeing my yellow skin. My Ex complained of abuse. Well, I'm familiar with suffering abuse, but not inflicting it.

I'm now an anonymous, gray woman in Massachusetts where I'm told that no judge sitting in a court will send this ex-husband of mine packing, telling him, "your child's grown. You alienated the child from her mother. You prevented her from visiting her mother. You never contacted her mother about the child support you only now claim you needed. You never gave the mother any news of her child while you were both in the same town. Too much time has passed. Case closed."

My lawyer says, "This isn't gonna happen."

"Why not?"

"Concerning child support, Massachusetts laws won't budge. The law's made for deadbeat dads. It doesn't leave room for special cases like yours. Judges are tired and impatient. A divorce agreement's only seen as a contract. You agreed to pay this money. You owe it."

* * *

AH... THE GLEE OF A RAT! Running free, high up on a power line, tasting the sun, feeling alive under its dark hide, russet eyes glowing from the thought of ripe mangoes into which it'll soon sink its teeth. The rat's gloating inside, thinking himself clever for having gone up the electric post, circumventing the wide, slippery shield of corrugated iron that has been nailed at the bottom of the mango tree and around all the fruit trees of the land. That tree near the house is the creature's favorite. From the power line over which he speeds, the rat finally hops onto the branch of the tree most laden with fruit. This is picking season! Without hesitation, the rodent grabs for the first reachable fruit, the riper the better, ah... what joys to be had!

Inside the house, rat traps and pink rat poison were waiting.

Branches of the mango tree already rose as high as the second-floor balcony near my parents' bedroom. Rats that had avoided all traps or pink poison were eventually found drowned in chamber pots that were placed by the bedside at a comfortable stretch for the drugged sleeper who lived in a big old house with many bedrooms, and whose bathroom was at the end of a long, dark hallway.

It's hard to decide which was the better death for the rat.

First choice was a spine broken through its middle by a metal bar that snapped down shut on the creature. It separated him into two singular mounds of gray bristles; his stubby, ineffective, little legs helplessly grabbed at the air and empty space above, pain frying the brain in short electric waves that culminated into a soundlessly gaping, useless, open jaw.

Second choice would've been to succumb to the temptation of pink rat poison sprinkled with care in selected areas instead of picking at the cheese cubes of the above-mentioned first-choice traps. Such a soft color, this pink... do rats see color? But that death was also a slow death from untranslatable colic; a thousand small, bewildering daggers piercing guts everywhere; body cells slowly being reduced to puree, entire lines of blood vessels included, all channels, all resulting in an internal hemorrhage, an inner drowning from which I imagined, as a child, the soul of the rat raising a disabled, white flag.

As a third option, drowning in high levels of patriarchal piss could hardly have been a better death. It's hard to imagine what got the rat to jump or crawl in to begin with. It's nevertheless not hard to imagine the rodent, almost submerged, drenched in that smelly, yellow pool of piss, back legs pushing in repeated, jerky, slipping attempts to get some spring upward, front claws reaching up as well, but time and again screeching down the vertical, white-enameled inner slopes of the piss-pot, until fatigue or perhaps a backward fall into the pool got the better of the animal who stopped struggling, finally accepting this end of a tropical rat's life.

I come from generations of colonial rat killers.

Cockroaches and frogs did not fare well in my ancestors' hands either. Cockroaches are invisible, but you know they are there. You just know. It's life in the tropics.

Turn on the light in the middle of the night, and you will see them—these dark, glimmering, flattened, two-inch-long, oval shields that ferret around trash cans, scutter along kitchen counters to escape down the gray, mildew-collecting pipes of the sink, or into wall cracks behind which they live like illegal aliens.

The cockroach invader you commonly find in Haiti is identified on the Internet as the American Cockroach. This invader's to be distinguished from the German, Australian or Oriental Cockroach, among others. One way used by Haitians to kill these American pests, and for them to be shown openly in the light of day, is to spray the kitchen with Baygon bug killer at night before going to bed.

In the morning, floors, counters and kitchen sink are strewn with cockroaches dead on their backs. Their six spike-covered, little legs, and their geometrically-compartmented, lighter-colored bellies, then reveal the surprising vulnerability existing in complex designs; life forms easily turned into pellets, droppings, or excreta, then brushed off and dumped into the trash can that, in life, they reveled in.

Along with the interest in learning about the agonized death of a cockroach, there can also be a certain strength to be derived from observing how living creatures can still thrive while having to hide in dark, hot, humid areas of the earth's otherwise astonishing landscapes—these sentient beings who exhibit a strong desire for life, living in anonymity and trash.

Rats, cockroaches and frogs all live in the shadows. The only one you can hear is the frog. The night resounds with their calls. They seem to come from all directions. The calls are charming until you find a frog in your pool or worse—hundreds of its wriggling, black-tailed children. There's no swimming in a pool with a frog in it even if it has flattened itself along a vertical slope of the pool, tucked all the way down near the bottom where human eyes usually refuse to look.

The net used to clean leaves off the surface of the pool is also good for pulling frogs off the bottom. The poor frog is dragged all the way to the top edge until a decisive hand grabs it firmly and smashes it against the poolside.

One hit is all it takes. But invariably, the hand seems to feel a compulsion to repeat the gesture. The hand stops only when the once delicately articulated, gentle, brown-skinned frog is reduced to a heap of purplish organs exposed within meandering rivulets of its own blood.

Rat, cockroach, and frog are all sentient beings that are to be respected no less than a white cow that won't budge from the middle of a Calcutta street.

Rat, cockroach and frog are also God's creatures. They're entitled to life no less that we humans are.

If the Old Testament is right, and our sins will be brought down to our children, one generation to the next, I'd like to know how many generations of dead rats I'm paying for, down the generations of my colonial ancestors, down generations of patriarchal piss, for me to find myself looking for One Boston Place.

* * *

REMEMBERING old parental advice, I arrived early. Not only was I close to One Boston Place, I was actually standing right in front of it. It's an end-street building whose façade cuts the corner at an angle.

The letters that spell One Boston Place are formed out of gray cement applied onto the gray facade, just above eye level.

Vast entrance lobby. Cold gray marble walls and floor. Enormous, plush, black leather couch and armchairs shrink and lose themselves. No rug. At the front desk, a young black man and a young Asian woman stand, wearing navy blue jackets over white shirts.

The man's name tag says, "Mohammed." The woman's says, "Emiko." Emiko is on the phone, so I address Mohammed. "Is there a bathroom in the lobby?"

"Bathrooms are located only on office floors. Are you meeting someone here?"

"Yes. My lawyer."

"Which office?"

"She doesn't work here. We're meeting another lawyer."

"What's the name?"

"Robin Hood... Listen, I really must find a bathroom before I meet with anyone, and..."

"I've to get the okay from the office..." Mohammed interrupts me. "You need a name tag first. Show me an ID. Once I've got the okay, I can type in your name and address. Then, the machine prints your name tag..."

While he's talking, I'm thinking, *Listen, Mohammed, I'm not carrying a bomb. What you can't see under my vest is only shit I'm trying to rid myself of...* But still, all I say is, "I'm going back outside to look for a place that simply offers a bathroom and doesn't see the use of a toilet as a security issue."

* * *

"YES, YOUR HONOR, my Eveline was wonderful. Yes, I'm sad to hear that my child's been in therapy all these nine years. I hadn't thought this possible. She was so strong and healthy.

"Yes, your Honor, I regret it all. But should I also be sad to learn that she's in her second year of college, that her father's financial statement to the court reveals his one hundred thousand dollar a year income and his half-million-dollar worth of assets and insurance?

Yes, should I be dismayed that he could afford to put her in a private college, has enough money to hire a lawyer and sue me for money he doesn't need, never needed before, and won't need in the future?

"Sorry, your Honor. Allow me to rephrase. What I should've said is that it's real sad to remember, with love for her still in my heart, this scrawny black orphan from the Port-au-Prince slums at the time when she found herself spending her first American summer in Maine within the secure walls of a seven-bedroom, two-bathroom, three-living room, two-kitchen, hill-top family mansion overlooking blueberry barrens, ponds and endless woods. A four-year-old child, who on her first night in America, was lovingly placed at the head of a dining table where fifteen family members sat under the distant eye of a gray-bearded rabbi surveying us from an antique portrait hung high.

"Your Honor? Can you ever imagine the euphoria of the disinherited who finds a chest of riches? A girl who didn't have a dress to her name when I first met her, not even the undersized, faded rag she wore?

"Imagine her now, that summer in Maine, wearing a pink bathing suit, her first, an item of clothing she didn't know existed, while running free on a Camden beach, or dipping a finger in the water to taste its salt, delighted by the wonder of it, refusing to go in, but refusing to leave just the same.

"Or imagine her at the playground at Harborside, a goblin's town whose low, narrow, quaint, worn, brightly colored cottages nearly touching each other may've seemed less foreign to the Caribbean child than the large, sober-colored New England houses that were now surrounding her.

"She sat on the swing, asking me to push her harder and higher, higher, higher, while her embroidered gingham skirt with matching pink lace at the hem swelled open like a rose umbrella above the blue ocean which she seemed to be gulping whole with wide-open mouth, bows in her hair flapping wildly all the while.

"In the morning, she woke up early in a room she shared with no one else, this child who before then had only slept on the beaten-earth floor of a single room shack, a flimsy, thatch-wood and mud construction she occupied with five others. This Creole speaker had me as her new mother, a yellow Banana from the same country of origin as hers, the only person she could communicate with in her native Creole tongue, and her only friend all week long.

"Can you really imagine, your Honor, how BIG all of this must have seemed, and how it will forever loom in her mind? An unimaginable preciousness that must never, never, never be lost, no matter the cost, no matter even if that cost is the betrayal of her mother?

"I admit, your Honor, it was hard being a mother and a nanny, suddenly, late in life, having to lower the topic of my conversations and limit my vocabulary for so many hours of the day. My own thoughts no longer had room to spread. My work had been my life, and now my life was claimed by another.

"But yes, I'm very sad. I never thought that she'd still be in therapy once I gave up on her visits. By removing myself, I thought I was removing the problem.

"I never imagined that all the last nine years of her childhood... O my... going every week to cry on a therapist's shoulder, a woman paid to listen to her. I'd have listened for nothing. I paid to liberate her from the pain of the slums. I didn't get paid to do it. I thought that letting her go was the best thing for her, for us all, and for me as well, I admit. I needed help too. And it didn't look like she needed mine any longer. Neither of them seemed to want me or my money.

"It is only now that I understand the burden of betrayal put on this child's soul. Even her father wouldn't have seen it, even him, otherwise he wouldn't have done his devil's work just to suit himself, he wouldn't have, if he'd foreseen the consequences on her, his jewel.

"But I now grasp it all better. It makes sense, this psychiatrist. It sadly does, really. Eveline would indeed need help to carry the guilt of causing the shame, the demise, the elimination, the spiritual death even, of her mother. And not just any mother either, but a woman who owed her nothing and still had offered herself to give all she could at the time, a woman who saved her from her own death in the slums, like her parents had suffered. I was the mother of her second life, her only life now, her real life.

"Betrayal. I saw it.

"I saw it then, that first summer in Maine. Her father, my ex-husband, had started the first job he'd had since I knew him just so the adoption agency would see him as suitable, a man able to support his family (and lo and behold, he really did!). He worked during the week and spent the weekends with us in Maine. He came by bus on Friday nights. I saw the betrayal, but I couldn't explain it yet.

"The first Friday night that he came to join us, the minute he stepped through the door, 'Hi Sweetie!' and the four-year-old's head immediately drooped and bent to the right. Her large eyelids lowered slowly and heavily like petals gone to wilt over her full cheeks. The remaining slice of her eyes that I could still glimpse looked to the floor in a disoriented way and, in an almost inaudible agony, she said, 'Hiii…Daaaddy…'

"Her father immediately stared at me angrily and questioningly, but spoke only to the despondent child: 'What's the matter, Sweetie? Talk to your daddy.' And this man, who could no longer bend down painlessly to tie his own shoes, found a way to get on his knees in front of the tiny girl and hug her, hug her tenderly, and then quietly tie her shoelaces that had become undone an hour earlier while she and I were running free, chasing each other in the blueberry field, she with boundless delight, yet carefully holding an Indian basket full of blueberries so as not to lose a single one because if she did, she'd stop and pick up the round, purple gem very delicately.

"This complex behavior of hers became a Friday night performance that I chose to ignore.

"So, your Honor, I should've been prepared for what happened on that Easter vacation some six years later, before her tenth birthday. I was already divorced and sharing her time with her father. This Easter was my chance to have my child for a whole week. I worried that she might not see it as a chance like I did. The first vacation in Maine when she was happy to have me as her only friend was a bygone time. She was a different girl now, fluent in English, popular at school, her Creole language rejected, and all but forgotten. Her father and I were kept busy with her social calendar. But, that Easter, all her friends had gone out of town, and I was to be her only playmate.

"I went to Pearl's Arts and Crafts on Massachusetts Avenue with her early that first afternoon. Right after, we went home where I helped her build a small, prefabricated pine box and paint it all up with made-up animals. When we were done with the box, she sat on my lap, rubbing one cheek tenderly on mine and murmuring, 'You're the best Mommy ever.' She then went to her room and closed the door. I went to my room to make a call. I picked up the phone. She was already using it. I heard her voice, 'Daddy, I'm dying here. When are you coming to get me?'

"With a trembling hand, I carefully replaced the receiver and went to the kitchen. A while after, she joined me there and wrapped her arms around me tightly, pressed her face against my belly, declaring joyfully, 'I love you so much, Mommy! You and I are the best mommy and daughter ever!'

"I continued to prepare dinner with silent determination. After dinner, I told her what I'd overheard her say. She stared at me, her face tight and colorless. No words came out of her. I didn't question her about it or reproached her. I was too embarrassed and hurt to say any more besides letting her know that I was on to her.

"But it didn't stop there, your Honor. The Wednesday before Mother's Day weekend, I went to pick her up at soccer. In those days, that small-frame, wiry little girl was a fireball on the soccer field. Anything she chased, she was determined to get. And once she got it, she'd never let go. The coach loved her.

"I was fifteen minutes early. I'd never been early before. I'm always scrambling to be on time, then, now, forever. There's never enough time. I imagine that on my deathbed, I'll feel that I'd not had enough time either and that my life was just a scrambling to get there, onto that deathbed, feeling rushed. Anyway, I watched the end of her game absentmindedly until I saw something flashing in her ears. I thought, *She's got those earrings she wanted! I bet she won't have them on when she comes to the car.*

"Once she was in the car, I asked, 'Where're the earrings?'"

"'What earrings?'"

"'The ones you were playing soccer with.'"

"'I don't have earrings.'"

"'Give them to me right now.'"

"She sullenly pulled very large loop earrings out of her backpack.

"'Did your father buy them?'"

"'Yes.'"

"'Did I not say that I didn't want you to wear loop earrings, especially the large ones because they are dangerous on a child and you could get your ears torn, especially playing soccer? And they're inappropriate for your age.'"

"She said nothing. She looked at me fixedly, her eyes blacker than usual. Almost in a whisper, I managed to ask her, 'Do you understand that mother and daughter have to be able to trust each other?'"

"And so, your Honor, this is what happened next, the Friday before Mother's Day weekend, my ex-husband called me and said, 'You'll not be picking her up tonight.'"

"'And why's that?'"

"'She's afraid of you. She never knows what mood you'll be in and how you'll treat her. She doesn't want to see you.'"

"'Is this about the earrings I confiscated? Is she too ashamed to face me? Is this a joke?'"

"Your Honor, I made the mistake of shrugging my shoulders, thinking that *This too shall pass.* I'd had enough violence in my childhood and adult life. I witnessed great cruelty in Haiti. I didn't want to use force on a child. I decided to wait.

"But it didn't pass. I received the same phone call from my ex-husband the next Wednesday, and the next weekend. 'She doesn't want to see you.'

"Your Honor, I didn't know what to do. I was intimidated by this blockade and hearing that my daughter didn't want to see me. I was insecure about not being her blood mother. I didn't feel entitled to her.

"Later, I was informed that my child was taken to a therapist without my counsel or consent and that I too had to make an appointment to see her. The doctor declared that I was to wait until she gave me permission to see my daughter again. Three months went by. Finally, the doctor called. 'Just take her to a movie. Don't engage her in any long conversation. Be light-handed and easy.'

"So, imagine this. Here I am, trembling to be allowed to speak to my child again. I call, and still, she doesn't want to talk to me. When she finally picks up the phone after what I overheard to be a long discussion with her father, I quickly say, 'I have a birthday gift for you.'

"'I don't want it,' she tells me.

"'I can mail it,' I say.

"'No.'

"My ex-husband then takes the phone from her. 'I'm getting married. We're taking family pictures. My daughter will now have two stepsisters. They're all the same age. We're busy. Now isn't a good time.' He hung up.

"That was the last time I ever spoke with my daughter.

"Your Honor, I soon went back to Haiti to be among my own kind and abide by familiar rules. I went to my mother.

"I was gone a long time. During my first year of absence, I wrote several times to my daughter. I sent pre-stamped envelopes and postcards for her to write back. None ever came. I decided it best to let her have a stable life undisturbed by the needs of a negligible mother figure, not be torn between parents at war, two homes, two families, two countries.

"When I returned to the US, I settled in the Cambridge neighborhood where I'd lived before. Old acquaintances noticed and recognized me. They'd be sure to alert my Ex, I thought. Years went by, unnoticed. There were years when at first, I felt like I haunted the place, not lived in it. But I made new friends and formed other attachments of significance. It seems now that my Ex was just biding his time, waiting to get at me when there'd be nothing for him to lose, and he wouldn't again have to share our child with me. And that's the story, your Honor, of how I became a dead-beat Mom."

* * *

THE ABOVE CONVERSATION never happened. No court in Massachusetts would've given me a chance to tell my story, so I tell it to myself, repeatedly. However, scientific studies on the workings of memory reveal that each time you recount a story, it's slightly different.

Memory works towards peace and closure within oneself, but not towards a cover-up. It'll hound the person's mind until an acceptable version of the recollection is discovered, and feels true. The peace then attained becomes fixed. This is what it means to be free.

To free my daughter with a proper goodbye is why I asked my lawyer to request one last visit with her, finally claiming a right I hadn't realized I always had. The concept of a monument, erected for those lost at sea, to have a place where they could have a proper goodbye from their family, had haunted me since I learnt about it from my friend Saul in Spencer's Island.

And at last, it's all arranged; the setting is my lawyer's office.

So, I now find myself in a New England office overwhelmed by a conference table. Disparate antique chairs are set around the table, taking up the rest of the floor space. Yellowed prints of English foxhunts hang on the walls. But I can't really look or think of anything other than the face of my child.

I don't recognize her when she enters the room—she's tall, beautiful, elegantly dressed, tears are running down her cheeks. Her eyes look hesitantly for mine while she sits in a chair opposite me, one hand fumbling for the armrest. I'd stood up when she came in, but perhaps it hadn't been obvious to her that I'd have gladly embraced her.

"Do you recognize me?" I ask.

"Yes, I'd recognize you anywhere."

Because I don't want to cry, I start talking right away. "I want you to know that I haven't asked you here to reproach or demand anything. I only wanted a proper goodbye and tell you that you mustn't carry any burden in your heart regarding what happened between us. It hurt for a long time, I admit. It doesn't anymore. You were a child trying to survive in the midst of too much adult complexity. I'm free, and I want you to be free. If you never want to see me again, that's all right. And if you only want to see me again in order to learn who your birth parents were, what I know of them, if you only want to know your story of origins, and then close the part where I entered, that's fine too. And here, I brought photos of you and me when we knew each other. I brought them so you could remember that what we had together was beautiful, not something to cry over. You can do what you want with them. I have carried them long enough so I could give them to you, hand over your past, and you can decide for yourself what to make of it. You must become your own storyteller, my child. You don't need a therapist to tell you who you are or explain what you're feeling. You know what you feel as you're feeling it. You must accept your feelings for what they are, even if you think they're ugly. Every story has many facets. So, choose the best angle and write a beautiful story, because a beautiful story is what you deserve, what all of us deserve really, and what God intended for us before the devil got on the stage wanting to have a voice, wanting to be heard, wanting to have some say in the way events unfold in the world."

I stopped talking because my child slowly pulled a handkerchief out of the pocket of her jacket and softly blew her nose. She explained that she didn't want the photos to be tear-stained.

The top photograph was of her in the first blue dress I bought her. She stood in my bedroom in Haiti beneath a large painting of Mother Nature personified as a brown-skinned woman holding herself with great composure, surrounded by children, wearing a long, red, wide skirt adorned with green and golden leaves. The second photograph showed me with her at Christmas after the divorce. She wore a red velvet dress with a white lace collar, black patent shoes and white lace tights. She sat on my lap, her hair braided in as many braids as possible, all of them like arrows shooting straight out of her head, as piercing, as uncontainable as the huge glee and laughter stretching her lips, uncovering an amount of teeth that still didn't seem enough to express the bursting joy alive in her. And then there was the photograph of us wearing embroidered Mexican peasant dresses—hers pink, mine yellow. And then the photograph of her first winter in Massachusetts, a time during which a storm piled snow so high that all the parked cars were buried and the roads blocked. The image shows my child lying in the snow after I threw her up in the air, and she landed in a thick cushioning layer that was yet too magical for her to feel cold, and that made her chortle. For some reason, she asked, "Mommy, are you as tall as our house?"

But no, the meeting with my girl didn't happen like that. The truth's different.

Yes, there was the huge table that seemed to represent the overwhelming discomfort between us, while the foxhunt pictures predicted a killing. Yes, there were the photographs I'd brought, but she didn't want to look at them. There were no tears either, no embrace, and she wasn't pretty. She wore gray, casual sports clothes. Evidently, the occasion hadn't been worth dressing up for.

While her face could've gone in the way of her birthmother's prettiness, it went in the way of her father's plainness. I recognized him in her. She had his dark, honey color but also his large droopy eyes, his sizable square head and jaw, too big on top of her small frame and height; all of these features appearing bigger on her than they did on her father because his was the body of a man—albeit a short one—accustomed to carrying heavy loads until it killed him.

Her hair had finally given in to too much processing. It was thin, short, uneven, sticking out in rigid spikes, resistant to pomade. I remembered how I argued with her father so he wouldn't take her to a hair-processing salon, in spite of her pleading, and have her kinky hair straightened. She was tired of the stiff, architectural braiding I learnt to do for her. Each morning I persisted in combing her hair—the likes of which I was totally unfamiliar—so she'd look pretty at school, feel proud, adorned with a crown of multicolored beads that made her look exotic. But all she wanted, I understand now, was to look normal, invisible even, not feel self-conscious and weary of being a black child in a white family. She also now lived in a white country that must've seemed like the entire world, the only world there was, a world in which she wanted to fit, yet one in which she was destined to feel singular.

I had dressed up to honor the moment and, even sitting, I was the taller of us. And yes, there was my conciliatory monologue, one contrasting with her hostility, to which she listened with unfeigned coolness.

There was no freeing her. She was more than free. I didn't exist and hadn't for years. There was no one in the room meaningful enough for her to have need of a proper goodbye.

Despite her mood, and perhaps due to the imposing austerity of the lawyer's office, she remained in her chair, listening. But the beautiful sentiments I tried to express and to which she might have been sensitive, even grateful, proved to be an added offense.

She looked at me with what I read to be dispassionate hatred, and I imagined her thinking, *You Bitch, what do you think I ought to be grateful for? Grateful because you made yourself feel good by adopting the poor little black orphan who should, therefore, be enslaved emotionally to you for the rest of her life? Grateful that you went against your social class and your own father (if he hadn't died already), and went ahead to take this availably-cheap-feel-good-little-black-toy of a girl whose parents, ancestors, generations of her ancestors, had been servants to your parents and to generations of them before? You want to free me of some guilt while you were freeing yourself then, as you are now, of your own? Some ancestral guilt that you really should be feeling for all eternity, down the generations of children you never had, never will have, and should never have because your kind is just evil, and when they aren't quite evil, they're weak and stupid, like you.*

Lady, you owe me. And for the shame you made me feel over some words on the phone at Easter or over earrings my good Daddy bought me, my sweet Daddy, well, these nine years have been payback time for you. It was time you learn how it is to be frightened, to be small, without means, and afraid for your life.

But that did not happen either.

In fact, meeting my girl might never happen. Robin Hood tells my lawyer that the girl isn't her client and that we should ask the doctor's permission—the girl is the doctor's client. And the doctor says that the father is her client, he is the one who hired her, and that we should get permission from him for me to talk to my daughter. Then the father argued that the girl is the doctor's patient, and it's the doctor who should give permission. So, in the end, I can't get to the daughter without the father's permission, I can't get to the father without going through the lawyer, and the lawyer keeps sending me back to the doctor, who sends me back to the father, who sends me back to the doctor.

My lawyer is frustrated. So, I tell her, "With the power of the legal system behind you, you can't get me a visit with my daughter. Can you imagine better what I went through nine years ago?" She groans but says nothing. "Who's the law for?" I ask. "My ex-husband's rights, as written on the divorce agreement, are being protected, while mine aren't."

* * *

THESE SCENARIOS WERE filling my head, and later on as well, while I anxiously looked for a bathroom the morning that I had a meeting with lawyers at One Boston Place. But even Starbucks and Dunkin Donuts didn't have one in that area. I went back to One Boston Place and headed straight for Mohammed, standing at the desk in the lobby. But in the corner of my eye, I saw my lawyer. She was waving furiously at me, her slim body ensconced in the black leather couch set in the middle of the vast lobby and its gray marble floor.

It turned out that our meeting with Robin Hood had been canceled at the last minute with no real excuse and too late for her secretary to warn her, or me, in time to have saved us this trip to Boston.

"I know why they canceled," she said with irritation and satisfaction, "they're pissed, real pissed. I found an irrefutable law, by accident mind you, stating that they can't force you to pay compounded interest on Child Support, or any interest whatsoever. Your debt's cut in half. They're furious."

I was stunned. "Miracles do happen!"

"Yep!"

"And what's to come next?"

"Since the attempt to settle out of court failed today, I suppose what's next is that we'll go to the court hearing scheduled at the end of this month."

"Am I going to have to see that man again?"

"Yep. He'll be in court too."

"I've really got to find a bathroom now," I said, grabbing my shoulders as if I were suddenly very cold.

She smiled.

At last, Mohammed had a name tag ready for me. Following his instructions, I went to the 15th floor. Out of the elevator, I found myself walking on the same cold gray marble floor that was in the lobby. A large hallway running on either side of the elevator led to immense, glass double-doors where, behind a large marble-top counter, stood a receptionist wearing a navy blue suit and a white shirt. She gave me the secret code to the bathroom—*256. I punched the number on the lock at the door and entered a sparkling, cream marble bathroom that exhibited mirrors all around and boasted six large empty stalls. I was the only person there. I went to the largest, most comfortable stall, the one for the handicapped.

* * *

FINALLY, I did see my daughter—on Facebook. It was my lawyer's idea.

There she was, strings of photographs of her, claiming 372 Facebook friends, a lovely, vivacious, young woman with big, bright eyes, a wide, exotic smile, and breasts, new breasts that remind me that I never saw my child become a woman.

Breasts in a green, long evening gown, then a white gown, then a red gown...blowing a kiss to the camera... blowing candles over a pink cake... amber breasts in a pink bikini, afloat bubbling water of an indoor hot tub set in front of a glass wall behind which a snowed-in garden confesses the cold of New England... bright breasts beneath a radiant black face adorned with an outpouring of ringlets gathered at

the top of her head, lovely ringlets I knew to be synthetic hair exten-
sions, gathered atop her graceful head and falling overboard like an
explosion of fireworks.

My daughter was the uncontestable star of her Facebook page
and the only black person there.

She smiled in a dizzying display of photos with not a single
man around save for an unidentified elbow in a suit through which
her white-gloved hand is slipped. There are no family pictures, either.

The only other people showing on my daughter's Facebook page
are an array of blond girlfriends propped on either side of her like
window mannequins. The blond girls seem to adulate her while she
stares only at the camera.

I thought of Van Gogh's painting of irises in a garden. *Why did
Van Gogh paint only one white iris among purple ones?*

I thought again of my friend Saul in Spencer's Island, and how he
wanted to know why I was so far from home and said, "Isn't it funny
how where we come from is where we wanna be rescued from?"

Is it lonely for you, Eveline, to be an adopted, black orphan in a
family full of white cousins who resemble their parents? Is it lonely
to be an orphan, long-ago born from love between illiterate servants
living in slums where they died young from diseases that are consequences of malnutrition while you now sit in the plush living rooms of
educated white folks who'll claim you as theirs until death? Is it lonely
to watch television among them while news of hurricanes, drought,
famine and other forms of disaster having struck Haiti (as they once
did your parents' hut when they lived) are now and then broadcasted?
Is it lonely to listen to it all with an impassive photo-trained face as
if this news has nothing to do with who you are or where you come
from—you never belonged there at all—nothing to do with your fate,
what circles of world society you'll move in, what access to the beautiful you'll maintain, no matter what, so help me God?

Is it lonely, my daughter, to have turned your back on the one
person who knew the color of the Haiti mud shack she pulled you out
of, the one remaining mother who knows your story of origins—this
witness that you were a hungry black orphan from a no-name slum in

a country that no longer counts the people it has abandoned or whose loyalty it has discouraged—me, the one person who now understands that she need not take it personally that you were willing to play the incriminating role in a crucifying play?

I also wonder, considering our present estrangement and how it came about, how I might have somehow disappointed or hurt you further than you already were, and if you feel it would have been better for me not to have interfered with your life's prospects as they looked to me at the time I met you, deciding to make space for you in mine, troubled or limited as it was?

Ah, but I'll never know your feelings. We're all incomprehensibly blinded by the need for survival in a world where we all feel we're strangers passing by. We're learning rules as we go. We're tightrope dancers. Blood can be called black, white, yellow or whatever. But it's simply red—a strong, resistant color. Come what may, it'll keep running!

III. Family Totems

Io in the Year 2008...

IT BEGAN ON A FALL Sunday afternoon in Massachusetts. Clouds in a light gray sky looked like old men in a slow procession towards the infinite. Thomas and I chatted on the white couch of our apartment on Garden Street. Leo sat on the window-ledge behind us, cleaning himself. The movement of leafless branches agitated by the wind outside attracted him suddenly, and he stared watching something invisible that lay beyond the row of trees and the shadows they cast at the Radcliffe Library across the street. His focus was on things that only he saw, but now and then, he turned a puzzled gaze toward us.

Similarly mysterious, a golden statue of Avalokiteshvara—the Indian Buddha of Compassion—stood on the console opposite the couch. Its many arms spread like open wings. A painted eye observes humanity in the palms of its many hands.

Thomas and I sat close to each other. "The divine world fascinates me," I said, tucking my hand under his arm. "I was seven years old when my mother surprised me with a children's book about Saint Bernadette. I fell in love with saints."

"Why saints?" Thomas asked, turning to me with a gentle smile.

"Why saints? Well, I discovered people who had God as their daily companion. I wished to be among them in a world of miracles. I'd rummage through the house to find candle stubs. There were always some forgotten pieces around the living room or the bedrooms since we had blackouts every evening."

"What did *you* need candle stubs for?"

"I lit them so God would be able to locate my room in the dark. I felt so small, and the night sky seemed so vast. I actually hoped he'd reach for my hand under the mosquito net."

"Ah, Io... my wife... so odd, and so dear," Thomas said, reaching for my hand. "And you still light candles, even though I'm here, and my hand's forever yours."

"Maybe I light them for a different reason now?"

"What reason?"

"Ah... that's for another conversation. For now, I'm telling you about my childhood. And you need to know."

"I'm all ears."

I laughed. "Here it goes. About candles, the reality then was that rich and poor used candles or gas lamps every night. The neighborhood was quiet except for dogs barking in the slums and in the hills. And our dog would respond. His name was Boulie. He was actually our neighbor's dog, but he adopted us. Father would yell at him to shut up. Boulie would stop only for a brief while. He couldn't resist. Father would yell again."

"What happened to Boulie?"

"He died."

"How?"

"Dunno. I was sent to boarding school in France, and when I came back, Boulie was gone... but anyway... I was saying... in those days, Father, Mother, Europa and I sat on a green bench every evening. Father loved sitting under the stars. We could hear the brisk sound of bats when they grazed the water of the swimming pool. There wasn't much entertainment for us in those days, with blackouts and all... and curfew..."

"Curfew too?"

"Yes. We lived under the Duvalier dictatorship. And Father wouldn't let us play cards either."

"Why's that?"

"Silence. He wanted silence and calm."

"Hum… tough for a child."

"Yes. But it must've been hard enough for him during the day, making a living for his family under these political circumstances, and going about his business with the sense of constant danger… the threat of random killing of people on the sidewalk, people targeted unfairly… and the fear you might suddenly become one of them… your whole family gets killed in the process too… and usually at night… bodies put out for public display and discovered in the morning. You can imagine how one might really long for a calm retreat at home at the close of such a day. Every day."

"Why did they kill innocent people?"

"Why? Perhaps they thought they were guilty, or perhaps they weren't so innocent either. There also were constant false accusations coming from neighbors or deceitful friends. People wanting to appropriate what others had, and they manipulated Duvalier's fear of rivalry and being overthrown? Haitian history is full of that. Presidents never lasted long before the Duvalier dictatorships that passed from father to son. I also imagine that revenge over old personal issues was being solved in this way too. I don't know. Why Herod in the bible? No one really knew why or how things happened until sometimes years later. All sorts of theories went around town until the next murder caught everyone's attention… so you can understand why the green bench under the stars and the sound of crickets at night felt like a haven."

Thomas let out a sigh.

"And besides," I said with a smile, "Europa and I did argue loudly over cards."

"How so?"

"She complained I cheated."

"Did you?"

I laughed. "Would I, now? Well… I might've cheated a teeny bit when the game was slow… this made things move or ended the damn game. I didn't like playing cards. It bored me. I didn't really mind not being allowed to play."

"I'm not crazy about them either... But did you feel sad, sitting on the green bench?"

"Yes, but for Mother. Europa and I were relieved. Our father was content instead of angry. Normally he was angry a lot. I suppose it was stress. So, the whole family also ended up stressed by his moods. Up and down all the time. I also loved the quiet because I could hear insects. They made a joyful chorus... it was like all of nature held hands. I felt they held mine too, and the world wasn't so empty... But nowadays, what you hear in our old neighborhood are air-condition-ers and home generators. Wealthy families watch television, not stars. People in the slums have each other for entertainment and the sea breeze to cool their shacks. They chat until late at night. They share a common bed under a mosquito net... I use to fantasize about their closeness to each other."

"How do you know about what goes on in the slums at night?"

"I spied... Slums were right across the river at the bottom of our garden. We were in a valley. I roamed in the slums during the day and spied on them at night... Haitians love children. They didn't mind me there during the day. My parents didn't know I walked around in the slums."

"How come?"

"Father was at the office, and Mother always out and about... Sometimes when I'd hear her car starting, I'd run to the garage to catch her before she drove out, or I'd run after her car so she'd stop and let me go with her ... she rarely did."

"Poor little Io... And are these the slums where Eveline was born, and where her parents died?

"Yes. Who would've ever guessed that one day I'd adopt a child from the slums where I myself roamed as a child?"

Thomas put his arm around my shoulders. "But, darling... you're shivering... Come here. I'm so sorry... is it because I asked about Eveline? I don't know why she suddenly came to mind... The thing is, I worry about your hurt over this whole Eveline affair. The way she turned her back on you and chose her father."

"No... I'm all right."

"No, you're not. I'm hearing you fret over the past, and I don't know what to say... Haiti, and all that part of you, is such a distant world from mine. It all seems so complicated and disturbed. I'm just a London boy."

"Oh, but Thomas, my life's happy now, being with you. The small size of Cambridge relates to the Port-au-Prince I knew. That's comforting. And I too am really far from these things of the past. It's not just you. What can I say? Memories swarm over me all of a sudden. How do I control them?"

"Put them on a leash! That's how!"

"Oh, come now, funny boy! But watch out! I still roam at night. You'd think I'm a wild animal who misses stargazing, but it's window-gazing I do."

Thomas laughed. "I think I read about a werewolf alert in the papers."

"You aren't that far off!" I exclaimed, laughing with him. "My childhood was filled with mysteries of Vodou. We had werewolves, monsters at the crossroads as tall as houses, and she-devils lurking on rooftops wanting to catch children to eat them... I heard all sorts of tales in the dim light of the small bedrooms our housemaids had... And I loved the scents in these rooms... They smelled of black skin that bathed with Rosita soap. They smelled of palmakristi oil, strong and pungent. But it's the best for conditioning hair... Cotton mattresses, too, had a distinctive sweet scent... a mixture of the cotton itself and the particular body smell of the person who slept there. Anyway, my senses and my imagination were in a constant uproar."

"Darling, you do know that the English love ghost and horror stories, don't you? They're favorite bedtime stories for children. We go to sleep trembling, and then ask for more the next day."

"Not me. I don't like horror stories. I've had all the fright I can take."

"Ah... you're no fun!"

"*No fun*, you say. How can a child not be frightened by zombies? And a Catholic child at that? As if daily political murders weren't enough! Where's the fun when no one explains the difference between Christian miracles, black magic and murder? I grew up hearing of Jesus raising Lazarus from the dead and of zombies as walking corpses. How was I to know that Lazarus wasn't a zombie? In the end, what a child registers is that the dead aren't necessarily dead. The dead walk around with a grim look, and you don't know what's on their mind… probably revenge… or if they even have a mind… And they don't need to sleep. They're dead. And yet they're not. Try and have a good night's sleep after hearing that when you're seven years old."

"Why *revenge*?"

"Why not? How would you feel if someone had turned you into a zombie?"

"Hard to imagine, Io. I'll grant you that."

"Well, watch some Hollywood movies, and you'll get it. They do a good job recreating the infantile imagination in those films, besides showing how racist they are… And ask around, nobody in Haiti dies a natural death, and accidents don't happen by accident either. Accidents are curses that worked…. This cultural milieu's the perfect environment for a child's brain. Children suspend judgment naturally. From a child's viewpoint, Christian and Vodou wonders are the same. It takes years to sort that stuff out."

"Oh my… it's all too much for me to absorb in one sitting, darling!" Thomas stirred and stretched his arms. He looked at the sky through the window to his right and said, "My only revenge against life is to be happy with you."

I smiled. "You're my dream as well… And fortunately, a sustainable one."

Thomas groaned. He picked up my hands, brought them to his lips and kissed them. "I led a self-reliant life rewarded by music and meaningful friendships," he said. "But when I met you, I felt that you were a sign I couldn't ignore. I had to allow you in."

From the couch where we sat, Thomas and I were reflected in the large Venetian mirror handed down to me from my childhood. There were times when I would look at myself in it, and it seemed a window to the past. I felt as if I were bending over an enchanted pool that brought up images released from a universal akashic record. The mirror was the crystal ball of an invisible, inaudible medium who relished her power at unleashing visions drawn from my very soul. The mirror hung opposite us above the console. The white walls of our apartment were also hung with several of my oil paintings about Haiti. Each presented a unique tableau, an organized structure of a landscape existing outside of time, an orderly composition offering a different interpretation of nature's chaos.

Leo suddenly jumped off the window ledge and went to join his sister, Lucy, who slept on the Afghan rug in front of the fireplace. He licked the top of her golden head before laying himself down next to her.

I observed the cats dreamily awhile and then spoke again. "Thomas, you must know that saints helped me even when I was a child. They showed that human willpower can help us accomplish things beyond what is thought possible. We can withstand death through torture. Defy it even. Something far larger than us exists. There's a watchful force that's immensely delicate yet indestructible… Have you ever felt that?"

Thomas ruffled my hair. "Oh, lighten up, darling! That brain of yours needs vast amounts of dusting! Too much stuff in there!"

I was undaunted. "And yet, what great relief," I said, "to find that my own life's an ordinary one, not challenged by God's terrible favor, a life filled only with the ordinary martyrdom of family, social and professional banalities."

Thomas scoffed. "What do you mean, *ordinary*? There's nothing ordinary about you! You're larger than life, my darling!"

"Yeah, yeah… Eveline must've thought the same thing… She once asked me if I was as tall as the house. And mind you, we lived in a three-story house at the time. She must've been inspired by the same stories I grew up with… you see, she was already three years old when I brought her to this country."

"But, darling, I am being serious. As far as your impact on my life, you're truly larger than life."

"All right… But let me tell you about Walden Pond."

Thomas put on a mock-serious face. "Well now... what's this about? What about Walden Pond?"

"When I was there the last time, I swear I sensed that Thoreau himself was there with me... And when I came across other people also walking there, I imagined how they might see me, and it occurred to me how odd it is that one's life and whole person might look so banal from the outside and yet be so complex, even tortured, from the inside. Before I married you, I was more alone than monks are."

"What do you mean? You had more suitors than I've fingers and toes."

"Why this teasing? You and I both know how we met. You've always been interested in mystical stuff. If it hadn't been for the invitation from that group of self-appointed philosophers who were busy emulating some School of Philosophy that existed in Concord, you and I wouldn't've met... And what did you speak about if not music and spirituality? So, don't act like I'm the only heavy-minded one with inclinations to mumbo-jumbo and whose head needs *dusting*."

"Okay. You win. But admit that you loved that Chopin nocturne I was playing as you walked into your friends' living room."

"I'm not denying it. What was not to like anyway? And it was lucky that they were friends of mine who invited me to meet you. But what's gotten into you now?"

"I feel giddy. But remind me, my darling, of what it is you felt that first evening we sat together in the old Alcott House meeting hall?"

"What do you want to know?"

"I want you to tell me again what you felt when you looked into my hands?"

"Why?"

"Just humor me... Remember we were attending the first lecture of the conference? And the speaker prompted everyone in the audience to look into the palm of their hands."

"Of course, I remember. And I'll tell you again what I told you before. I saw hands that made me want to curl inside them."

Thomas laughed out loud. "And don't you ever, ever forget that you loved me right away either."

"I won't. But now it's your turn to humor me. Did you not fall in love with me under that very crucifix we've hanging right here? This very blood and gore and ultra-realistic eighteenth-century Mexican Crucifix I brought back from San Miguel Allende?"

"What are you getting at?"

"Remember how that first time you came to visit me, and I showed it to you? How I explained that real bone pieces were inserted in the wounds? I even took a magnifying mirror, I slipped it behind Christ's torso to let you see the lacerations on his back. I wanted you to see how they were carved and painted with great precision. Do you remember all that?"

"Yes, and so what?"

"Remember how I said, 'notice the painstaking care given to what isn't outwardly visible, and how the greatest violence done to us is often well hidden'?"

"What are you getting at, Io?"

"Never mind… And, Thomas, you also once told me that it was at that moment that you realized you'd fallen in love with me."

"And your point is?"

"My point, dear husband, is that you actually love the serious girl in me. So, don't you try and tease me while I'm sharing memories of things that've impacted my sensibility. Don't tell me that my brain needs *vast* amounts of dusting. That's cruel… even if it's funny."

"I daresay, it's terribly funny."

"Okay. It is. You win."

* * *

"ARE YOU DONE with the fax, Ma'am?"

"Yes. All done," I replied, aware of being rushed by people waiting to use the copy machine and feeling the pressure of being late while Thomas was waiting for me at home.

I had torn into small bits the photocopy of my father's old passport photo before throwing it away. Both my father's eyes had somehow remained on the same bit of paper. It felt as if he was looking at me from the bottom of the trash. I noticed it only when I picked up my bag from the countertop and threw a last glance down at the can before leaving. The photo of my father, once so familiar, suddenly seen in misarranged pieces, had felt strange. That last look I caught of his eyes had seemed like my first.

I left my father's face in the trash, I then thought as I left the photocopy store. Once outside, I felt invisible—just one more foreigner.

It has been many years now since my father died. I remember how I feared I would forever miss his gaze on my life. His gray-green eyes had a special glow when I entered a room. I thought that no one would ever care about me the way he did. But then, I had not foreseen the coming of Thomas.

Father was a man of few words. I learnt to read his eyes instead. It helped me maneuver around him. In times of depression later in life, these eyes would cloud over, turn grey, and quiver like a fish caught in a net.

Yet he was the father who had seemed like a monument, the pillar on which the family house rested, the ship's mast, the totem pole on which our faces were carved and through which our story was told. He was the thunder that warned and kept outsiders at a distance, the great bird with a hooked nose whom my sister Europa and I wanted to resemble. He flew high to survey the land before returning at night to nourish and restore us. When we looked at him, we knew who we were and where we stood in the world. When he laughed, we laughed. When, in later years, he trembled, we too trembled, and the house shook. And so, I ran. I ran before the house would shatter from the great quake of the only earth I knew.

I ran all the way to America to avoid being crushed, unaware that I would only get crushed further.

As a child, my father was an altar boy. "So, your name is Victor," the priest said to him the first day he met him. "That's good. A name sets destiny. You will do well." All my father kept from that experience was a love for the Latin Mass and organ music. Outside of the Mass, all music was noise. Once he became a man, he no longer went to Mass. He saw religion and Mass as good for women and children only. Thus, it was our mother who took us to church on Sundays. "Margueritte!" Father would call every Sunday from the garden where he planted trees on weekends, "Don't be late for church! Hurry the girls!"

At twelve years old, Europa was sent to a boarding school in Switzerland while I was sent to another in France. I dislike remembering that school in Saint-Germain-en-Laye, and how I stood in the schoolyard's alley of chestnut trees my first day there, lugging a leather bag filled with books. At the far end of the alley, there was a German blockhouse covered with moss and ivy, leftover from WWII. The school buildings themselves had been used for German headquarters. I soon learnt to climb up the blockhouse and sit alone on its rooftop, missing my family. In Haiti, Mother stopped going to church altogether.

I had been bored during Mass, like my mother was. However, I loved statues and paintings of bloodied saints, the quiet Virgin Mary, the drama of the Stations of the Cross, the storytelling of stained glass windows, the leftover smell of incense, lace-covered altars and the towering crucifix. Like it or not, the week had a crown, and Sunday was that crown. I felt its blinding luminosity within personal solitude. Whether at church or at home, I felt alone, surrounded by strangers, each one of us imprisoned and in pain.

* * *

SISTER BARBARA looked middle-aged when Father and I met with her. She was slight of body and had eyes of a crystal blue. My father had already become an old man when I took him to visit her on a Sunday. It had been difficult to get a private interview with the Canadian nun, then star of the Charismatic movement in Haiti because of her reputed healing powers. She lived at the Bourdon nunnery located in the hilly neighborhood above Port-au-Prince. By that time, my parents had been divorced for more than a decade.

I had known the Bourdon nunnery all of my life but had never been inside. People generally referred to it as the nuns' school rather than a nunnery since it also served as a primary school, and the nuns were teachers. As a group, they were known as the *Soeurs de Bourdon*—Sisters of Bourdon. I had always been mostly conscious of them in terms of traffic jams happening all around the school early morning and mid-afternoon when school ended for the day. It was an area to be avoided at those times. Even my father left earlier in the morning to go to the office just to avoid the traffic.

This was not a school attended by wealthy people's children. Boys and girls from slums and poor neighborhoods often came from great distances on foot or by public transport. Children walked along crowded sidewalks that were as potholed as the streets, wearing checkered green uniforms, holding hands with each other or with a grown-up accompanying them. Girls had vivid color bows tied at the end of stiff braids. Everyone was hurrying and perspiring and bumping into each other while careful not to stumble and fall, yet too often careless about crossing streets on a sudden whim. Public transport vehicles stopped whenever and wherever they pleased, cutting through traffic, swerving without notice, causing weekly accidents.

Our house, my grandparents' house, my uncle's house, my aunt's house, all were neighbors to each other on that same Bourdon hill and overlooked the nun's school. My grandmother's property was the closest to it, and they shared common boundary lines. When all of us cousins were small children and played in her swimming pool, we would hear the goings-on at the nunnery. From the second-floor balcony, we could look into the schoolyard if we were curious, before our gaze eventually chose to rest over the Port-au-Prince bay in the distance.

It was unsettling for me to enter these walls with my father standing on shaky legs, and on the verge of tears. He looked nothing like the father I knew, a man used to lording it over people. As it was, we had come as beggars. We were the poor in spirit come to receive alms. Cars were not allowed through the gates, so we had entered the yard on foot just as children from the slums customarily did. Sister

Barbara's office was on the second floor of the main building, closest
to the gates. The entrance hall was vast and dark and bare. It was
startling because, from the outside, the overall constructions at the
nunnery were handsome buildings of the colonial style and painted
a luminous cream color. High ceilings kept the rooms cooler, but the
high doors and windows were often kept shut to keep the sun, mosquitoes, and noise out. I held my father's hand as we walked up the
stairs, led by a nun who said that Sister Barbara would not be keeping
us waiting long. We were led into a small room with bare, white walls,
a desk in the middle, and three chairs. My father and I sat in the two
chairs that faced the desk.

As I would soon find out, Sister Barbara's fight was with Satan.
She viewed emotions as individual spirits who each have a will of
their own. Negative or painful emotions were the devil's avatars. She
spoke to them as she would to living entities. Her purpose was undi-
vided—she was driven to force evil away. In this struggle, she would
never bend or break. She led a life of prayer, frugality, abstinence and
service.

When Sister Barbara entered the room where we waited, she
looked at me in a fierce manner that seemed to say, "Make no mistake,
God is here." She then turned to my father. Her civilities were brief
before starting the interview with him.

"What is your name?"

"Victor."

"What is your pain?"

"Depression."

"Anything else?"

"Yes."

"What else?"

"Anxiety."

"Describe that for me."

My father became quiet and looked down at his hands. They
were balled into fists in his lap. "It's a paralyzing fear," he finally
murmured. "It's manageable at first until it escalates into sheer panic."

"Describe the panic for me."

"Panic's like electricity going up and down my spine, causing great trembling all over," he said after some hesitation. "It quickly reverberates and spreads to my extremities in unending waves that seem to burn my skin." He then went quiet again, his eyes focusing ahead into empty space.

"And then what?" Sister Barbara asked, taking his hands gently.

"What...?" my father—Victor—the old man—repeated pensively. Yet he slowly began to speak again, the flow of words increasing progressively as if thoughts were fighting to come out, stumbling over each other. "Then, my brain gets trapped in a dense cloud," he said. "And my eyes are blinded, and my body loses breath. It's something without texture, like fog. I can't touch it. There's nothing to touch. Yet it overwhelms and suffocates. I feel dizzy, although I'm able to walk straight. But I sit instead and slump into myself. There's pressure and throbbing at my temples... my head's ready to explode. Yet you, or anyone watching me, will see nothing... it's all happening inside me. I'm locked up, alone with it, and in it. Even then, I can't look in the mirror... it stares at me through my own eyes and shames me." Having said this, my father then stopped talking and cast his eyes down low. He even seemed to be smiling.

"Do you know the Lord's Prayer and the Ave Maria?" Sister Barbara asked.

"Yes."

She appeared to be tightening her hold on Victor's hands and said, "Pray with me." Her hands were large and had a fine bluish skin where thick ligaments seemed raised, creating deep, ridged hollows, each like a viaduct leading to long, bony, ruthless fingers. She prayed with eyes closed. Once she was finished, Sister Barbara opened her eyes wide and commanded harshly, "Spirit of Depression! Leave this man!

"Spirit of Anxiety! Leave this body!

"In the name of God-the-Almighty!

"God-the-Compassionate!

"God-the-All-Forgiving!

"God our Lord, Giver-of-all!

"In the name of Christ our Savior!

"Christ the son of God and God himself!

"Christ who died for us!

"In the name of the Holy Cross, I order you to leave this man!"

All during the prayer, I looked at my father. Next to Sister Barbara, I saw a small being in place of the force I knew. He was a child reciting the Ave Maria, as small again as the newborn baby loved by his mother as he once was when she first held him in her arms.

All of my father's praying, however, started and ended in that room. He never obeyed Sister Barbara's instructions to pray always. Some months prior to his death, he said to me with uncharacteristic tenderness, "My child, learn not to take things so much to heart."

* * *

SKIPPING ROPE during recess, I said to Europa one day, "The only thing wrong with you is your name. It's too big. A girl can't be named after a continent."

Europa took it badly. I should have known better. I had observed her every day of our common childhood while she swallowed two white sugar-coated pills stored in a blue tin pillbox with a screw top. I knew something was wrong with Europa but not what. I, too, was only a child.

What does a child understand about the nature of pain endured by another and carried as if a disgrace? What does a child understand about destiny and its differing selection between siblings who both crave equal apportioning? How was I to comprehend the broken emotions of a sister forever counting slights, thereafter unable to erase the scars they left inside? How could I know then what it felt like for her to face each day with a continually humiliated sense of self; to grow up amidst a large extended family in which she was the only member having to survive the ongoing shame of being found wanting in comparison to me; to be weighed down by the daily absence of praise from the very man whom Life had put in charge of raising her up?

"In the summer when I was seventeen," Europa said to me some thirty years after the fact, "I knocked on your door one morning. You didn't open. You didn't say 'come in.' All you said was, 'I don't want to talk. I'm not in the mood.' And that's my sister for you."

"Thirty years ago!" I exclaimed. "You're reproaching me for the mood I was in as an adolescent *thirty* years ago?"

"Yes… So?"

"And you're still angry with me? Heavens! You even look angry."

The corners of Europa's mouth took a disdainful, downward curve, and she said, "Your problem, Io, is that you don't like people."

"*People*? The problem's that I don't like *people*? Is this all you can see about me?" I realized and regretted at that moment that I had not learnt to read Europa's eyes the way I had my father's. There had been neither time nor necessity for that. As bereft as Europa might have been, she was not central to my survival. Father was.

Victor was an essential god to the survival of everyone in the family. He could not be ignored or trusted to be even-handed. Europa and I were swimmers in adjacent lanes, children struggling to stay afloat so they could reach a shore. I was not aware that there had been a competition until I realized that I was perceived as the winner. Both my mother and Europa resented me for it. Europa was jealous for herself while my mother was jealous for herself and for Europa. We were women competing for a man.

Europa had visions. Faces she saw were not human. A small, skinny child, she curled up under her sheets at night, hoping not to be seen. Monsters nevertheless came in the dark, stirring angrily in the corners of her bedroom, teeth gleaming, hungry; vultures flew out from under the bed while venomous snakes curled up the bedposts. Doctors said that Europa's brain was abnormally large and pressured by a skull too small to contain it. They wanted to operate.

"Operate what?" my grandfather screamed, himself a surgeon. "They don't know the first thing about the brain. My grandchild's not a guinea pig. She'll improve with time." It is then that Mother became over-indulgent with Europa, and Father became frightened and cruel.

* * *

WALDEN POND is the place where I go to collect myself. Henri Thoreau wrote that diamonds on the water made by glimmers from the sun would surpass any jewel on any crown, were it possible to assemble them.

One day, I sat on a tree trunk and daydreamed for a while until I noticed cigarette butts on the ground all around me. I leaned down and gathered more than a dozen of them, remembering my mother who always dropped her cigarette butts in the toilet bowl, apparently indifferent to the rage into which it would inevitably throw my father each time he walked in the bathroom. The white paper would have slowly come undone and the loosened tobacco shreds excreted a sickening yellow-brown color that stained the water. Wild disputes and threats of divorce invariably ensued. It seemed that Victor took it as a personal affront that Margueritte could neither stop discarding her cigarette butts in the toilet nor remember to flush them right after.

Scientific discoveries about the nature of memory reveal that every time we recall an event, we remember it differently. The more we recollect some circumstance, the more our account of it becomes a construct, develops into a lie, yet a lie in which we firmly believe. In this way, I have come to doubt my own memories and interpretation of how I have come to be so far from home, missing home, yet unable to return.

A different angle, a different view of the lake is what I opted for that Saturday when I arrived at Walden Pond and veered left. It was a glorious day, and many people were roaming about. I saw the pond itself as a ship, one surrounded by land rather than water. The dirt path that circles the lake is like a ship's promenade deck.

Coming out of nowhere, a child ran up to the edge of the lake and crouched low. He extended one little finger and dipped it in the water; he was excited, he laughed. That in itself was magical, this moment when two foreign bodies merged. Through the tip of one index finger and the ripples that extended from his touch, the boy apprehended a whole world. This knowledge and memory will forever exist in him and inform choices and experiences he will make in the future.

Looking for a quiet spot in the woods away from the shore where most people gather like seals, I crossed paths with a man, a woman and two girls both with long blond hair. The girls could have been twins, were it not for their different heights. They seemed about five and seven years old. Each girl carried a doll, the same bald baby. I reflected that the girls could have been company for each other yet had chosen their own separate friend in a doll. The younger of the girls walked ahead of the family. I observed roses and butterflies on her doll's dress. When the older girl noticed me looking at her sister, she ran to catch up with her and pulled sharply at her hair. It made me think of Europa.

I finally chose a tree stump to sit on and eat oatcakes. Chipmunks busied themselves all around me. One came close. I saw him pick up a breadcrumb and stuff it into his mouth. Then he came closer to me still, made quick little runs to the right, then to the left, taking brief pauses in between to look at me through shiny bead-like eyes. I threw him some bits of the oatcake. The chipmunk speedily came to grab the pieces and shoved them in his mouth. The rough edges of the broken bits of cake made jagged bumps in his neck. I noticed that he was stuffing them in a pouch somewhere beneath his mouth and not in his mouth. Then, the chipmunk ran off as suddenly as he came, but not far away. He quickly came back, neck pouch empty. I gave him additional morsels of cake. He stuffed them down quickly, ran off, and came back. The creature was hoarding.

* * *

WHEN IT RAINS, and the weather gets cold, I can't go swimming at Walden Pond where there is only sand at the bottom of the water; nothing threatening, only carp and trout swim past, colorless and discreet. I then sit at home, sensing the body of loss.

It rained most of August and some of July. It is as if my mother can tell when it is raining where I live. When it rains, she calls.

"I've written to my family in France," she said to me at the beginning of the summer, "I want Europa to go live in my country."

"Have you lost your mind, Mother?"

"Europa will be close to my family. No one in your father's family cares what happens to her."

"It's one thing to host someone for a few days, another to take responsibility for them long term. Europa cannot take care of herself. People have their own lives, their own burdens. Would you want their child if they sent her to you?"

"What would I do with it?"

"Exactly! Same for them. Besides, Europa isn't a child, and caring for an adult who's like a child is even more taxing."

"She's changed. She prays all the time. She stays home. She's nice now."

"Last time we spoke, you were at each other's throats."

"I'm telling you that she's changed. In fact, we're both making an effort."

"Staying at home in familiar surroundings and living in a town you know since childhood's not the same as finding yourself alone in a narrow apartment, in a foreign country, where no one knows you, and you know no one."

"She'll have my family."

"She won't. People spend their days at work. They come home late, too exhausted to enjoy each other. There's still dinner to prepare, children to help with homework and get to bed."

"It's their own fault. If they don't want children, they should stop having sex."

"Like you should've?"

"How dare you!"

"Besides, Europa will be making friends with street people because no one else will find her of interest, or profitable. She'll attract problems again."

"My family will not let me down."

"What choice do they have? Your expectations of them are unrealistic. Besides, what've you done for them all these years you've been away in Haiti? Where were you when they were in any kind of crisis?"

"You take her for a while then! She's your sister."

"I just got remarried, Mother. I need to devote myself to the man who has entrusted me with his own life."

"One does not prevent the other."

"Thomas and I've just started living together. Our place is small. We've no room to spare, and Europa inevitably eats all the space there is in any home."

"Take her on a trip then. Take her on a cruise. You'll have lots of space. You'll have the entire ocean!"

"Mother, I can't think about that right now."

"Why not?"

"I need time. Meanwhile, spare yourself your family's rebuke. Don't ask them for anything regarding Europa. You've lost touch with what life's like in the modern world."

"And you don't know what's going on in Haiti. You got away, while we're stuck here. They kidnap people every day. And then, it's one hurricane after another. People lose all they have. People have no place to live or sleep. People get killed for a piece of bread. People are hungry."

"Mother, you're not these people."

"And you, Io, you've lost touch with Haitian reality! I'm telling you that I'm sick, that Europa's sick, that we're perishing in this miserable, suffocating country where nothing works, where we're surrounded by thieves and rapists. Can't you see that I'm suffering?"

"Why tell me about the hungry people of Haiti I've lost touch with then?"

"Because I'm the hungry people of Haiti! Europa and I are going to be sick if you don't do something about it. I'm at the end of my rope."

"Sounds to me that you'd like to choke me with that little bit of rope you've got left."

"Why must you be nasty? I'm old now. Don't you understand? I'm an old woman! You think it's easy to be old? And my adult child's still on my back? You don't know my life. You don't ask, I don't tell. You're in your American dream world."

"You don't know my life, either."

"Because you don't tell me anything about your life. So, I don't discuss my problems with you, either."

"You're doing it right now. Plus, you want me to solve them."

"Stop it! You're just like your father. You always have to humiliate people. You need to crush."

"You called me, Mother. I didn't call you. I can hang up if you want."

"I'm telling you that I'm ill and you want to hang up? Nobody can talk to you. You start yelling, just like your father did."

"You're the one yelling. I raise my voice so you can hear me. I can stop talking altogether."

"Oh, God! There's nobody to help you in this world! Even your own daughter enjoys destroying you. All right then! I'll solve my own problems alone, and you can go back to the love of your new husband."

"Come on, Mother, all I'm saying is that whatever your problems, they're not those of the poor of Haiti. Don't use their misery to make me feel bad for you. Don't use your old age to make me feel guilty that I've some youth and happiness left. God knows it has come late in my life. I'm not old, but I'm not young. My old age will come too. You can be sure of that."

"My old age will come, my old age will come... what are you rambling about? I'm telling you that Europa needs to get out of Haiti! Do you hear me? She's suffocating! I'm not going to live forever. I do what I can while I'm here but, right now, she needs out. It's killing me! She's killing me. She's taking away the last years of my life."

"Can I talk to her?"

"Talk to her? Why? Well, yes...but she's on the roof now. She's not come down yet today."

"On the roof?"

"She sleeps there. You know your sister... can't sleep indoors... it's too hot, it's too this, it's too that. Always complaining that girl!"

"You said she's changed."

"Oh, stop that! Me too, I'm too hot! Haiti's never been so hot. Global warming. This country's going to explode. And we can't even use fans. There's no electricity, except for a little bit at night when it's already cooler, and we don't need it."

"Can you try calling her anyway?"

"Okay… just a second…"

Mother put the phone down. I heard her calling Europa at the top of her lungs. The dogs started to bark in unison. By the renewed intensity of the barking, I knew when Mother was coming back to the phone. She picked up the phone and said, "She's coming… one moment… here she is."

"Hello, sister!" Europa said cheerfully, "I've a surprise for you."

"A surprise… What surprise?"

"I'll tell you when I see you."

"When will that be?"

"Only God knows the details of our lives."

* * *

WHEELCHAIR ASSISTANCE for Europa was the first thing I requested from the airline so she would be accompanied and helped through US Customs. Getting Europa out of Haitian Customs was also a challenge. New laws in Haiti demanded proof of birth and ancestry. From Kinko's in Harvard Square, I faxed a copy of my sister's birth certificate to the Haitian travel agency taking care of Europa's travel documents, our father's birth and death certificates, and a copy of the first page of his last passport with his photo.

"I'm not upset with the wheelchair idea. Mother's wrong about that. I think it's funny," Europa said over the phone early on the morning she was leaving for the airport with the chauffeured car sent by the travel agency.

Mother grabbed the phone from Europa's hands and said in a strangled voice, "Thank you, Io! Thank you! Thank you! You're saving my life! I'm going to sleep for a week straight!"

Europa was offended. She refused to speak to me again but snatched the phone back from our mother and hung up.

Europa arrived in the US with the hunger of an escaped convict. The plane landed late, past dinnertime, at JFK in New York. When I saw black people exiting with tightly held bottles of Barbancourt Rum, I knew that the Port-au-Prince flight had finally started deplaning. Having had to wait for the wheelchair to be brought to her, Europa would be the last to exit.

I stood with Thomas in the waiting area. There was a fifteen-foot, silver metal railing that started right from an exit door apparently made of glass. The door itself opened at one end of a long, transparent partition wall. That very transparency of wall and door allowed people in the waiting area to see a section of that hallway coming down from the customs area. In this way, we could spot our loved ones a little ahead of time before they actually reached the door. The railing created a kind of passageway starting on the exit side of the door. It allowed room for keeping the crowd from overwhelming and blocking passengers coming through. There was competition for getting as close to the railing as possible. Having come early, Thomas and I had secured a spot at the end of the railing and right next to it. I held the railing firmly with one hand so no one would be able to push me off. Thomas did too. There was a great advantage to that position. We had an unimpeded view of the other side of the transparent wall as well as of the door and the clear passageway created by the railing. Once Europa exited, we would not have to maneuver through an effusive jumble of bodies to get to her. Haitians are a demonstrative people.

Judging from the black skin color and Creole-speaking of the great majority of people with whom Thomas and I were waiting, it was evident that we were surrounded by Haitian Americans living in New York, people greatly envied in Haiti for having made it to freedom and comfort in bountiful America. I observed them from the kind of privacy and isolation that Thomas's and my own pale skin color created around us. None of them would ever imagine that I am one of them, and like them, a survivor from a history of colonialism and dictatorships. None would believe that every generation of my family continued to fight for these revolutionary dreams of freedom and right to happiness, whilst all of us present at JFK that evening, instead of living in the birth country we loved, were a testimony to its failure. I wondered what survival story from the shipwreck they left untold. A harsh, cold, fluorescent light flooded the room. Being amongst Haitians, it made me remember the prison of Fort Dimanche and its torture chambers. Just hearing that name still makes Haitians tremble. It was no exaggeration when a *New York Times* article of October 1994 called Fort Dimanche The Auschwitz of Haiti. Built in the 1920s near the Port-au-Prince slums of La Saline, it was used during the three decades of the Duvalier dictatorships, both by father Francois and then his son Jean-Claude, all through the 1960s, 1970s and 1980s. I wondered what prisons, what hunger, what injustices Haitians around me, as well as those coming through customs, had escaped. All of us here in the airport were there because of direct or indirect influence on our lives by the Duvalier regimes. But it was highly unlikely that any one of them would have been survivors of Fort Dimanche. It was a place of death. I can't fathom the courage it takes for people under torture to keep silent or endure starvation with no sanitation in rooms where forty people were shut in a space no bigger than 12x13x12 feet. And here in the US, we were all escapees in one form or another. Haitians can speak their minds, unafraid of betrayal or death. And they made ample use of that privilege that night. It is, unfortunately, still a privilege in this world. They wore bright summer clothes and overflowed with an abundance of words, effulgent in their greetings and chatting, bodies buoyant with joyful expectancy.

I felt some apprehension but mostly great excitement at the prospect of seeing my sister again and giving her a good time. Europa loved to travel and always longed to go away somewhere, anywhere. The island was her prison, and her bitter complaints about it were constant. Everything about the world excited her. But she also loved rocks and collected those she picked up on her way, held them carefully while taking them home where she would examine each one silently for hours on end. She claimed that rocks had spirits that spoke to her. I deeply regretted that my sister never saw the house of fossils on Spencer's Island. Europa was easy to please and charmingly free of prejudices about people and places and delighted in every new encounter.

She felt the wonder and magic of every human being. Europa standing in the world and looking at it made me think of a destitute child
suddenly presented with a glittery toy. My daughter Eveline showed
that capacity for awe during the first year after her adoption. I'll never
know if she kept it all through adulthood, as Europa did. Europa's tenderness towards the smallest of creatures was heartbreaking. If a bird
she had heard every morning suddenly died, her grief was for the loss
of a seemingly irreplaceable friend. She cupped her hands to rescue
bugs whose wings were dangerously weighed down with water on the
swimming pool's surface, fretting desperately to take flight.

I was looking forward to seeing my sister's beautiful and easy
smile. It was shaped like a moon crescent, and she had perfect teeth.
When she was young, Europa had full, fine lips with corners turned
up as if forever ready to smile. I felt great tenderness just remembering her almond-shaped, chestnut eyes, and the gentleness they exhibited. Yet her eyes were easily frightened, like her smile also was, eyes
trembling and shifting away like those of a doe that suddenly faces
the stare of a man out hunting. My sister brushed her long brown hair
a hundred times each night to ensure it would grow healthy, and that
is how she explained its brilliance in sunlight. She loved lifting the
perfect oval of her face to the sun, closing her eyes like a bride ready
to be loved. Europa was tall, slender and walked with natural grace,
but she could not dance. She loved music, but her lack of self-confi-
dence showed in the way she moved to it—the awkwardness in her
steps and a strange hopping and tense shoulder lift when she should
be swaying.

Had it not been for the wheelchair in which she sat, I might not
have recognized my sister. Europa was dressed like a man. *Is this the
surprise?* I wondered. Her hair was cut short almost to the scalp, and
it was now gray. She looked aged as well, but her smile was the same
luminous one that took off years from her features when it flashed
across her dark-tanned face. Her eyes appeared to be smaller, but they
were still shiny and russet like a wild animal's. She wore cream-col-
ored pants and a blue, checkered man's shirt with long sleeves. Her
clothes were baggy and made her look skinny. Europa was coming

towards us, engaged in conversation with the man who pushed her wheelchair, but she opened her arms wide, still talking when she caught sight of me standing at the end of the railing.

With all manner of people waving hands at loved ones on either side of the long passageway created by the railing, and letting out shouts of joy, Europa appeared like a king on a palanquin entering a conquered town under the cheers of the populace.

The man pushing Europa's wheelchair turned out to be Haitian, and Europa was speaking Creole to him. The talking and liveliness were, however, all hers, and the man's resentful face stood in sharp contrast with her gleeful one. He never smiled, never returned greetings. He stopped the wheelchair, waiting in complete silence for Europa to get up while she appeared in no rush to do so and entirely unaware of the man's unpleasantness. She started telling him about the long trip, the uncomfortable plane, the bad food, the lengthy wait for the wheelchair whilst everybody had exited the plane, the endless lines at Customs, the officer who treated her like a criminal and took her fingerprints. All the discomforts about which she was complaining in great detail had nevertheless no visible effect on Europa's excitement and glee.

"Well, aren't you going to get up?" I finally asked her, speaking English to honor her language skills and acknowledge the fact that she had traveled. Europa spoke fluent English, and we would continue to speak it with each other during the trip because of Thomas. She learnt English while living in California with our father's sister for a couple of years, finishing high school. She also spoke Spanish, having studied it alone with books and practiced it during a couple of trips she made to the neighboring Dominican Republic, traveling on a whim and on her own. Each time, we, her family, had to rescue her because she had been robbed, ran out of money or fell in with a bad crowd, but generally, it was all three. She was, however, deservedly proud of her language skills, although no one except our mother ever praised her for it. She had a fascination for languages and a gift for learning them, aided by a fantastic memory for words. She loved to meet foreign journalists assigned to Haiti and pick up from them any amount of words or sentences they were willing to teach her. I once marveled at her glee in telling me *I love you* in Japanese. Europa has also loved me in Chinese, German, Korean, Italian, Turkish, Swedish, as well as in several African languages. But she never has loved me in French.

"Okay, Sister, I will," Europa said gently, while she got up from the airport wheelchair. The Haitian man turned the chair around and left. Europa approached Thomas with a seductive, childlike smile, saying in English, "Hello, Sir. How nice to meet you at last."

Thomas was won over on the spot. Europa smelled of vanilla, like a fairy who might have been living under the breadfruit trees of our childhood, by the brook where Father planted vanilla beans for their scent.

Thomas and I had flown from Boston the day before. We went to our hotel near the airport to drop Europa's luggage in her room before heading to dinner. We had reserved two expensive rooms at the Radisson, wanting Europa to be delighted by all aspects of her trip. It had been several years since she had had the chance to travel. Once we had all freshened up in our rooms, I went down to the hotel restaurant ahead of Thomas to find a table while he went to get Europa.

Thomas looked strangely amused when they finally joined me in the restaurant. While sitting down at the table, he leaned over and discreetly whispered, "You'll never believe what happened!"

It was not until Europa went to the bathroom that he explained why he had been laughing to himself. "Europa and I were alone in the elevator, going down," he recounted. "We get to the lobby. The elevator doors open, I step out. Sensing that Europa isn't following me, I turn around just in time to catch sight of her incredulous, indignant eyes as the elevator doors close back in on her. She went all the way up to the fourteenth floor and came right back down. Alone. The doors open again, and I see her still standing in the same spot, eyes glowing from outrage. 'Come on out,' I said, 'now!' She hops out without a word, walks past me with a sneer on her face, heading for the opposite direction from the restaurant. 'It's the other way!' I called. She turns around and comes back towards me with the same sneer. 'I don't see why they have to make elevators so aggressive,' she complained. 'Americans are so aggressive all the time, and with everything. I suppose that's why Io loves it here.'"

The restaurant's buffet section was the only place still open for serving food by the time we got there. Still, Europa was ecstatic over the variety of food on offer. She chose everything I did and then went for second and third helpings. She took a slice of every cake, relishing especially chocolate flavored ones, finishing up even those she thought tasted bad. I delighted in Europa's pleasure, marveling at how my sister could sit at a dinner table for hours, chew her food interminably, groan and grunt all the while appraising it all in comparison to Haitian dishes.

* * *

"A SURPRISE FOR YOU," Europa had said to me. Coming from her, "surprise" means trouble, not a gift. Europa takes it as her due that I never forget her on birthdays or Christmas, yet she never makes a gift or sends a card to anyone and remains bitter about feeling forgotten. She is resentful about the neglect of cousins who were her childhood playmates but argue about being now too busy with adult responsibilities to spend time with her. "If I had money and fast cars, they'd remember I exist," Europa says.

Our cousins had nevertheless loved Europa's company when we were children. They had found her fun to be with because she was whimsical, always in the mood to join in their games. I thought that she was usually handed the fool's part in those games, but she never noticed and was only grateful to be asked. I would sometimes object in her name, but she would protest. They did not enjoy me in the same way. I refused to play the goalie at their soccer games, arguing that I was the youngest and smallest and could not bear to have the ball kicked in my belly. I was found to be disagreeable. No one objected if I left to go play on my own.

Mother was not maternal. Conversation with children bored her. When she did talk to her children, it was to complain about human betrayal, the boorishness of Father's family, the sexual greed of men, the burden of marriage, the inadequacies of our father as a lover, and the enslavement of motherhood. When I protested about her telling me such things, she called me a bourgeois prude. My happiest moments were those I spent lying down on the grass to look at clouds or walking the neighboring hills with my dog. In later years, our mother discovered some meaning to motherhood, and her conclusion was, "You're my flesh and blood. I gave you life. You owe me."

While I chose exile, Europa could not. Her efforts to obtain from life what others did all ended badly. She just wanted to be loved but followed the wrong men—whoever smiled at her long enough. She never understood that a poor, uneducated black man in Haiti would only see her through the luster of her social status and milieu. She could not perceive that it was not their hearts that smiled at her but their need, not their protectiveness that yearned to hold her, but their greed. When they did eventually see her for who she was, namely a woman outside her family and class, marginalized, depreciated, they stopped smiling altogether. When they no longer smiled at her, it was because they no longer needed to. She had become a prisoner, dependent on her jailer. She followed her man outside her family, outside her childhood mansion. She joined his poverty, cooked his food, washed his underwear and accepted his contempt.

Mother went with me to visit Europa in the slums once. We took the goat path down the side of a ravine and at the bottom of which we crossed a rivulet that provided running water to this community of destitute people. We caught sight of Europa, alone outside a mud and thatched roof shack, squatting in front of a large tin pot, cooking over red coals. I noticed the contents of the pot at the same time that I recognized the earthy smell of red beans. Europa got up when she saw us. Her dress was soiled, her brow sweaty, her lips trembling.

When Europa eventually turned to God and converted to a Protestant faith, she still found untrustworthy ministers and people who use God to manipulate others for material gain. She held the world responsible for her failures, crawled back to her mother, again and again, blaming her most.

* * *

"I DREAMT OF NINE ANGELS," Europa said. "They came to instruct me on how to save the earth."

Thomas, Europa and I were sitting on the plane going from New York to Anchorage, Alaska, where we were scheduled to board a cruise ship going down the Alaskan coast all the way to Vancouver. The flight had left at 6:00 am. We had only slept a few hours, having woken early after having stayed up late watching Europa eat.

"Does the earth need saving?" I asked.

"Don't you read the news?" Thomas questioned.

"You know I don't," I said curtly. "It gives me nightmares." I was vexed. Thomas should have remembered that this was a sore point for me. "News is always bad news," I explained, but for Europa's sake only. "It always sounds like we are on the verge of the end of the world. Only the bad seems worth mentioning... It's the same with palm reading... Mother's a palm reader... She was always after us to give us news about our future. 'You'll know what to expect,' she'd argue. 'You can prepare for it.' No way. Not me... But Europa liked it. So, Mother taught her. She'll tell you."

"That's right! I learnt palm reading. It's a fascinating science. I do it all the time. People ask me. I'm good at it."

"I don't doubt it, Europa. But I survived this far without news about the world or my future, so I'll continue without. I'll find it all out soon enough anyway."

"Surviving's not living," Thomas said.

"Besides," I continued, "important news always lingers long enough to reach people like me. I'm kept painfully aware of the distress in the world, and how powerless I'm to change the course of events, even if I'd learnt about them the very day they happened."

"Mother loves the news!" Europa exclaimed.

"Well, that's news..." I said derisively. "Father used to get on her case for not following the news." Then I addressed Thomas with a smirk, "See, my love, there's hope for me yet."

"You've no idea how much Mother loves the news now!" Europa said. "She gets excited. She feels alive, especially if it's bad news."

Europa smiled, and added, "But it has to be on TV for her to be interested… If people come to her with news of what's going on in the
neighborhood, she doesn't want to know. She wants great, bad news
items… ones like the hernia epidemic going on in Haiti right now…"

"Oh! How terrible!" Thomas looked dismayed.

"It's from hunger. People don't eat enough, and they have too
much gas from having their stomachs empty for long periods of time.
That has gotten Mother all wound up. She stuck her nose in her father's
old medical books all over again. She gets completely absorbed with
illnesses. However, births and marriages completely irritate her."

"Her life's ending," I offered in explanation. "She doesn't want
to think of beginnings and of the world going on without her. Diseases, deaths and disasters make her feel better by reminding her that
she's alive and well in a home that still stands."

"Aren't you being hard on her, Io?" Thomas asked.

I shifted in my seat. "Before there was any television, radio or
even newspapers," I said in a curt tone, "news took a long time to
reach people. Some news never crossed the ocean. Lives weren't any
less significant then, and history no less in the making. Now that we
get huge, daily rations of negative information, would it really be
helpful for me to crowd my mind with countless, insignificant, repet-
itive news items?"

"I was asking about your reaction to your mother, not the
socio-historical significance of news."

I looked at Thomas furtively and mumbled, "You're right… I'm
hard on my mother."

Europa leaned forward on her seat so she could look at both
Thomas and me and asked, "Do you now see the importance of my
dream and how the earth needs angels?"

The dynamics between the three of us during the trip evolved rap-
idly: Thomas rarely entered a conversation between Europa and me but
answered when questioned. Europa never appeared to be addressing
Thomas when she spoke but was quick to notice if he was paying attention or not. I allowed Thomas his own space but let him know when I
wanted to be rescued from Europa. Thomas then talked about music.

While Europa waited to see the effect of her announcement about angels, I was thinking, *Europa looks like a fawn. She belongs in the woods where she can sing with birds and imitate the movements of lizards.* Then, I asked out loud, "Is one of the nine angels sent to save us from daily news?"

"You're making fun of me?" Europa said, turning her face towards the window, away from me.

"Not at all," I replied quickly. "If I were making fun of anyone, it'd be of myself."

Europa cast me a glance, then quickly went back to staring out the window, lips slightly quivering, saying nothing.

"What do angels look like?" Thomas asked. "Did they give you their names?"

"They do have names," Europa answered with surprising eagerness, and turning back around, "and their clothes are of different colors. One angel was named Faith, another Charity. One was called Wisdom."

"Virtues!" I said with enthusiasm.

"Yes…in a way…" Europa murmured, hesitant about how she should respond to my interpretation of her dream.

"What color does Faith wear?" I quickly asked to distract her from becoming insecure and sullen.

"Yellow."

"How did the angels speak to you in the dream?" Thomas asked.

"Telepathically."

"Is it similar to what happens when you read hands?" I asked.

"Yes."

"How do you know what to say when you look into the hands of a perfect stranger?" Thomas asked.

Europa paused a moment, then slowly explained. "I know what I must say. I hear it inside my head. It's like a dream, and a spirit speaks to me."

"Spirits speak to you?" Thomas asked.

"Yes."

"How?"

"I hear their voices in my head. They also tell me where to put my hands when I do healing."

Thomas was even more puzzled. "You do *healing*?"

"Don't you know this about me?"

"Thomas does," I said quickly. "I told him all the great things you do."

"I see…" Europa said, inhaling deeply.

"Do you want to read Thomas's hands?" I asked.

"If he wants…"

"Yes! He does!" I exclaimed, ignoring Thomas's beginning attempt to decline. I immediately insisted on changing seats with him so he could be closer to Europa.

I observed Thomas's large, immaculate hands while they were held in Europa's long, sun-tanned fingers. Her nails were short, uneven, and dirty. She scrutinized Thomas's palms for a moment and then shyly pulled out a pair of glasses from her pants' front pocket. They were kept in a black case that had indentations. Her embarrassment surprised me because my sister's new manner of dress gave the impression that she had shed all feminine vanities. Yet, she visibly disliked the glasses and handled them with a kind of disdain.

With the glasses now set on her nose, Europa bent her face down low over Thomas's hands the way a microbiologist might look into a microscope. She examined the fine web of lines in them like a lab technician would his DNA. After a long silence, Europa slowly raised herself back up, inhaled, and murmured, "Ah, yes…" She then took her glasses off, fumbling, looked far into the distance, seemed to be adjusting her eyes like one would binoculars, and spoke again. "You were certainly born under a high star," she said in a gentle tone, "but, like many of us, you were brought down. Still, you must remember to use fully the short time you have available."

* * *

EUROPA WORE NO RINGS on her slender fingers when she read Thomas's future in his palm. It made me sad to notice that and to recollect her many attempts at finding the lasting love of a man. My mind then wandered into loose associations around the remembrance of rings.

My first thought was of a young couple for whose wedding Thomas played a few months prior to the trip to Alaska: The Church of Unity in Boston was built in 1861 by a wealthy landowner with ideas unheard of at the time. It was to be an interdenominational chapel, the ultimate synchronistic place of gathering. It is a beautiful structure with elaborate stained glass windows. The pews are high paneled and accessed through a door like pews in old English churches. The Ten Commandments are the single evocation of religion to be noticed in the church, written in gold inscriptions on either side of the rose window in the apse. "Thou shall not commit adultery," I read, "…not bear false witness…not covet…"

The commandments left me pensive. I thought of my parents' marriage, of Europa's marriages and of my own. I reflected on how little or too late we come to understand what simple truths these guidelines represent.

At the Church of Unity wedding, the bride was from a family of sailors. She exhibited tattoos on her breasts in the low-cut décolleté of a sleeveless, strapless dress. The groom was a schizophrenic belonging to a distinguished, old Mayflower family. He looked very agitated. Had he been from Haiti, he would have been called a mulatto, an epithet that indicates class more than color.

With Europa sitting by me on the plane, I could not help but think of her losses and wish this kind of larger Boston society would have surrounded her in her life. A broader, more open, diversified social context that could have accepted the marriage of two disparate beings like that of Europa and any of her lovers; families unlike ours that could transcend class and cultural differences to celebrate their children's brave claim to a singular future of their own choosing, and help them achieve that. "Pray for them," the minister was saying to the bride and groom holding hands. I thought, *Such as I see them today, they will indeed need prayers.*

There was a 1965 black and white photo of my parents exchanging rings in the family album that has now been lost. Margueritte looked vulnerable and trusting. She was uncommonly beautiful. Victor smiled like a man who has won a prize. He had traveled to Paris for a vacation and surprisingly came home to Haiti three months later with a French bride. They had met through a family friend. Newlywed Margueritte left on a transatlantic ship for her new life in the Caribbean with an assortment of hats in her suitcases, wearing the emerald green one that day as she watched her father on the docks. He stood in a gray suit next to her mother, who elbowed him, mocking his tears while she waved a pink handkerchief.

At my own father's funeral, sitting across from him laid in his coffin and beside Europa in tears holding hands with our mother wearing black, I remembered the day a telegram came from France to inform us of our grandfather's sudden death. Our father had called us girls as we played in the garden by the cherry tree and told us to go comfort our mother upstairs in her bedroom. She seemed inconsolable.

Margueritte flew to Paris some months later to visit her father's grave. At the cemetery, she fell to the ground in her gray coat, whose color matched the marble gravestone. Wearing an ankle-length mink coat, her mother derided her grief and tears, "What drama! It's Victor Hugo's Hernani all over again!"

On her own deathbed, Margueritte's mother expressed her relief that her daughter had not been able to travel to see her. "One less unpleasantness to suffer!" she scoffed, "it's enough that I'm dying." She had been a statuesque, silken woman with blue eyes who made men sigh from desire. To me, she was the grandmother who poked fun at Haitians and tried to teach me how to play the piano.

My father never took off the gold signet ring he wore on his left-hand finger along with his wedding ring. It was removed only after he died of a stroke in his car and before the ambulance took him away. That ring had been an integral part of the figure our father cut in both Europa's and my memory of him. All aspects of the ring recalled the man and were connected to our childhood memories of him and early attachment—its size, weight, bulky look and initials standing out. The ring was enough to recall the man and his dominion over us. The ring was totemic. The ring ruled. Whoever wore it was the chosen one, and his successor.

My uncle gave me the signet ring when I flew to Haiti to attend my father's funeral. My heart beat fast when I tried it on. It was far too large. Had Europa been different, the ring would have gone to her by right, being the eldest child. Hoping that I could right the wrong done to my sister throughout her life, I gave the ring to Europa.

One day, I found myself looking for Moons of Jupiter on the Internet and read that "Jupiter's rings and moons exist within an intense radiation, trapped in the planet's magnetic field... Io and Europa are the names of two of Jupiter's moons."

It was thus accidentally that I learnt about the origins of my sister's and my name and gained new perspective on parental relationships in our family. While I found myself wildly elaborating on the negative pull and satellite existence within a cosmic spell under which she and I had lived in relation to our father, Europa had fallen prey to yet another spell.

The man with whom Europa had fallen in love was a sorcerer, a bòkò. In the countryside where doctors are not trusted, not in sufficient number and proximity, or even affordable, these sorcerers are a necessity, albeit a threat. Yes, they are believed to be able to ensnare or sell your soul to the devil, cast or reverse spells, destroy your health at a distance or chase evil spirits away. But they also have great knowledge of medicinal herbs, can reset bones, massage nerves, muscles, ligaments and internal organs back together in a wholesome balance. A bòkò will take any form of payment, whether money, valuables, market goods or your sister's soul.

As handsome as he was devious, Europa's new love had her eating out of the palm of his hand. In that hand, Europa dropped our father's signet ring. My heart then dropped into a hell of my own.

I tried to buy the ring back. Suppressing my pride and apprehensions, I went to the slums. I walked down a dirt path used daily by people and animals alike, accompanied by a frightened, reluctant but obedient Europa who pointed the way to the bòkò's house, cursing me all the while.

I sat in the dark room of this man's shack. While he flashed a large smile of gleaming white teeth interspersed with gold, he flaunted my father's signet ring on his right hand. It quickly became clear to me that, short of trading my own life, the value of the ring for the bòkò was beyond any price I could afford to pay. The man had agreed to the meeting so he could gloat and taunt me, exhibit his hatred for the privileged social class he saw in me. And so, for what past and present political misdeeds and civil neglect that social class inflicted on the country, this man would extract emotional payment through Europa with his cruel manipulation of her naïve and generous heart.

When Europa said to me over the phone that she had a surprise for me, I bit my tongue. *Have you gotten Father's ring back?* I thought instantly and wanted to ask. But saying it would have caused a row.

* * *

ON THE CRUISE, I had a dream. I saw an open-armed Christ rising above the Seguin Mountains of Haiti, where the red earth once seemed to me the body of all births and beginnings. When I woke up, I thought about our garden at home in Haiti, the earth that now holds the remains of Europa's babies, two sons, yet the same earth that left me barren.

The next morning, I woke up late. Thomas was already out, and so was Europa. I went on deck to find them and stumbled on Europa having a conversation with a passenger. "I've given birth to three children," Europa was telling the woman, "but all of them are now dead from illness in their first days of life."

Three? I wondered. *I know of only two.*

In another conversation with yet another stranger that day, Thomas and I standing near, Europa gave another version of her children's story. The second woman with whom Europa chatted appeared middle-aged and past her time of bearing children. Her husband seemed significantly younger, but he visibly doted on her. She looked radiant from a variety of overflow—fat, bright colors and glee. She loved being on a cruise and spared no words to express it, holding on to an expensive camera with a long and wide telephoto lens. Her husband stayed close, discreet yet attentive, carrying a tripod along with the rest of his wife's photographic equipment.

This happened on the day scheduled to explore Glacier Bay. The ship had stopped in front of a gigantic glacier and remained there until the end of the afternoon. Yet it was whales that the woman was raving about. She was not there to photograph glaciers but killer whales and orcas. She spent most of the afternoon on deck waiting to see them.

"They're gorgeous animals that thrive where I'd die," she said with great animation. "Whales are surrounded by all this ice. It's pure death if you ask me. But they live and multiply fine... You know, it's wrong to call them whales. They belong to the dolphin family. They're extremely versatile. They survive wherever they find it necessary to emigrate... You find them in all the world's oceans and in warm tropical seas too."

"Tropical seas!" Europa exclaimed. "That's where we're from, my sister and me. We're tropical fish!"

"Immigrant killer whales?" I asked, cutting in.

"Sisters?" the woman asked, turning to take a look at me, and then said, "You know, some type of orcas are composed of matrilineal family groups and are the most stable of any animal species."

"I had five children, alone, by myself," Europa said. "I'm an orca."

"How fortunate you are to have children!" the woman exclaimed with apparent genuine pleasure. "I didn't have that chance."

"Yep, five," Europa said again. "But they're all dead."

Christ, in my dream, bleeding as he was, soared like a great forgiving bird. He ascended towards a large sky whose sweep and embrace matched the wide, open movement of his arms. I felt compassion and not annoyance at Europa's insensitive lie to the orca-loving woman. I wondered about what profound unease might have been stirring in her that day, causing her to exaggerate the truth all afternoon on the ship and introduce herself to every new stranger as an astrophysicist-musician-writer-visionary-healer.

I could not help but think to myself each time, *Hildegard von Bingen wannabe.*

"And I can read palms!" Europa never failed to add.

One evening, Thomas, Europa and I were having drinks in one of the many lounges of the ship. A violinist and a guitarist were playing classical music. The violinist fascinated Europa. She repeatedly got up to go stand for long periods at a time right in front of him while he played, and stared. At one point, she came back to her seat looking perplexed, and said to me, "Do you know what Mother reproached me with the other day?"

"No… What did Mother reproach you with?"

"She said, 'I'm sick of hearing you complain that your life's gone all wrong because of bad karma! You're my bad karma. You've ruined my life.'" Having said this, Europa got sullen.

Thomas came to her rescue. "What's the bad karma you think you're paying for, Europa?" He was smiling encouragingly, trying to make light of the topic.

But before Europa could answer Thomas, I asked, "Ever heard of Hildegard von Bingen?"

"No. Who's she? Someone interesting?"

"Absolutely! She was a twelfth-century abbess, a mystic, visionary, scientist, composer and philosopher."

"Oh… She sounds just like me!" Europa exclaimed, delighted.

* * *

"FAITH BEGINS WITH AWE," I read in a book of mantras to be used for daily meditations inspired by Hildegard von Bingen's visions. I felt this kind of awe the day I stood on the ship at Glacier Bay, beholding something incomprehensibly vast, luminous and pure. God, I believed at the time, exists independently of us but is not hidden. I felt compelled to kneel as if through the humble folding of limbs and the abandonment of all arrogance in posture, I might express the magnitude of the impact the immense presence made in me—this glacier slicing through the mountain, unstoppable and relentless, grinding and spewing weak earth into exacting waters where only orcas reach the inscrutable depths wherefrom cries of the earth resonate in God's ear.

I stood mesmerized in the silence of this incalculable majesty. Even as the ship began to move away and the distance progressively increased between the glacier and me, even as the fog and the cold increased enough to have discouraged anyone from staying outside, and indeed people were hurrying in, I could not tear myself away. The enormous ship glided noiselessly through the iced waters. It left a triangular trail that rippled to a point, a trail no different in shape than that left by a duck on Walden Pond.

The sun was setting behind the glacier, and with its remaining gold, sent rays that gleamed and lingered over water as dark as liquid steel, water filled with life apparently foreign to our own, yet somehow connected. The multitude of small icebergs floating all around speckled the water's surface and looked like confetti left over from a parade.

"Something else, these glaciers, hey?" Europa whispered in my ear, startling me, standing so close that she almost touched my ear. "Your husband's looking for you."

"I cannot leave this..." I said dreamily.

"Me too... Did you see all the animals?"

"Animals?"

"Yes, the shapes all over the glacier." Europa's eyes shone like mirrors reflecting the dancing remnants of golden light.

"No, I didn't notice animals," I said absentmindedly, reluctant to lose my focus on the last images of the glacier and turn to my sister. I wished for something kind worth saying. Europa had such hunger to be acknowledged and respected. I acutely sensed my sister's needs, yet this time, I could not abandon my own self and be deprived of this lingering encounter with the divine. "Each time I heard the ice cracking and resounding like a great thunder god," I finally said slowly, "each time I heard the ice fall off, and then watched it sink, I felt it was a piece of me."

Europa looked uncomfortable. She listened politely, as one does with a stranger, and then said in a formal tone, "My sister's very deep these days."

"It was like a part of my own life was cut off and going under," I went on saying, ignoring Europa's audible unease. "But it seemed a necessary shedding of what bears no more significance." I was responding at that moment to an intuitive urge to show Europa that she too was other, and more, than the way she was perceived since childhood. She too could be freed and shed all this unfortunate excess she carries. "I don't know if it's like a kind of death or a rebirth instead," I told her, taking hold of her hand, "but either way, it feels necessary and good. This place has taught me something profound. I'm sad to leave it. I hope never to lose sight of it in my mind's eye."

"I know what you mean," Europa said, surprising me by letting go of my hand and putting her arm around my shoulders instead. "Let's go. Thomas is waiting."

* * *

WHEN WE WERE GIRLS, Europa and I, we once took a walk together in the hills across from our house in Port-au-Prince and came upon a mud-thatched, one-room shack. The hovel was the gray-brown color and cracked texture of the land all around it. The air was heavy, the hills barren except for a *bayawon* tree to which a donkey was tied, head and tail bent low.

In front of the shanty sat a very old black man, his white hair having the appearance of cotton. He was looking in the palm of his hands when Europa and I suddenly appeared in front of his house. To the child I was, the hands appeared larger than life.

When the old man looked up at us, the whites of his eyes were as yellow as ancient parchment. The man's chest was smooth but for a few scraggly gray hairs and two contracted nipples blacker still than the rest of his body. He held a drum between his knees and wore a ragged pair of brown pants, tied at the waist with a sisal string. His feet were dusty, so large and hoof-like, it seemed that no shoe could ever be fitted onto them. Next to the man was a small, three-legged table on which sat a human skull. In the skull rested a pipe. The pipe was gently smoking. A thin, gray filament was rising out of it. The door to the house was open, and I could see a bare banana husk mattress laid on the earthen floor.

Having observed our presence in silence, the old man started beating at the drum with both hands, playing a well-defined rhythmic pattern interrupted by a hard snap that he made at regular intervals on the wooden edge of the drum's stretched goatskin. He struck the instrument with such impetus that I shivered fearfully at the thought of what it might be like if he were ever to touch me.

The old man suddenly stopped the drumming and smiled. It was a wide, generous, engulfing smile. Teeth were missing, and the gaps in between were not regular like his drumbeats had been.

Europa was mesmerized. She stood stiff and attentive, the way she would later in life night after night on the Alaska cruise ship when the violinist played in the evenings at six. When the old man motioned with both hands for us to come near, I ran off while Europa went closer.

I stood at a distance, calling Europa, asking her to join me, but keeping watch of the old man while he talked to my sister. When Europa finally walked back to where I waited, she seemed dizzy. I took her hand and pulled her away. She did not speak until we were at a good enough distance from the old man, his shack, his drum, his skull, his dirt, his large feet. "What did he tell you?" I asked.

"I can't say," Europa mumbled, walking straight ahead, yet looking down, mouth hanging open.

"You mean he told you not to say what he said, or you don't know what he said, or you just don't want to tell me?"

"I can't say."

Many years later, after Europa had finally broken up her relationship with the bòkò, who kept our father's signet ring, she fell into yet another destructive relationship. This time, she was terrorized both by her new lover and his vodou priest of a father. The two men were in cahoots with each other to profit from her.

It is then that my old nursemaid came to visit. "Europa's soul's been sold by the bòkò," she said. "Her mind's weak now. You have to rescue your sister."

"How do I do that?"

"I can take you to people who can help."

"Help? If you want me to use the same measures to save Europa that were used against her to sell her soul the way you say it's been, I'm out."

"You're her sister. You're the only one here who can do it."

"I'll not fight evil with even more evil."

"You're leaving her in the hands of the devil then. All the bad choices you see Europa do and nothing ever working out for her, it's because she lost her soul."

"If the bòkò's the one who sold Europa's soul, how come she chose and followed him way before he got to selling her soul and they lived together?"

"Maybe she chose him because he'd already accessed her soul?"

"Ah, yes? Still, if bad choices are due to her soul having been sold to the devil, then Europa was sold since she was a child, and it's not this bòkò's doing."

"You talk like that about your own sister? Shame on you."

"The way you're talking, it's as if nobody in Haiti lives a natural life or dies a natural death. Anything goes wrong, and it's the devil that's gotten your soul... Besides, if all that vodou stuff worked, I'd be a goner too. Since my father died, plenty of people wish me dead. They see me as the wall between them and Europa's money. If something has gotten hold of Europa's soul, it'll eventually have to contend with God. And God will free her. I can't, and especially not by tying myself at the stake next to her... I have to wait until God steps in."

"Suit yourself then. But your sister's life is on your conscience, not mine."

Europa's new lover was no less frightful than the bòkò had been, with his father always whispering things into his son's ear, or mumbling to himself, crouched nearby. Furthermore, the whole family moved in with Europa— lover, father, mother, sister and brother-in-law—in the small apartment rented with money from her new trust fund. Soon after, he practically sequestered her, holding her hostage under constant surveillance by his family members. They took turns watching my sister. Europa once escaped through the bedroom window with a paper bag full of her few belongings while the family member guarding her at the time was using the bathroom. She went back, however, after spending two days at our mother's. The lover then barred and nailed all the windows of their apartment. The bathroom was the only place where she could go in alone because it had no windows.

Europa's inheritance money, left in a trust fund, was administered and paid out in a strict, monthly allowance. In spite of these limitations, she was seen by the family as a walking coffer of riches. These people who had only lived in crowded shacks, relieved themselves in bushes and outhouses, fetched water in distant streams or neighborhoods' communal faucets, were now walking on marble floors and flushing indoor toilets. They nevertheless did damage to the kitchen floor where they set down the hot coal used under the cooking pots, as they would not use the electric stove that frightened them.

Europa was also sexually assaulted every day. The man wanted her pregnant with a child who would be an irrefutable legal bond to her and her money. While they refused to let her cook anything for fear that she would poison them, the man and his family nevertheless fed her so little and made her live with such distress that Europa increasingly lost weight and repeatedly miscarried.

Mother was hysterical over Europa's situation and called me in Massachusetts every day. She and I worked out a plan for Europa's rescue. It took a lawyer, a justice of the peace and four policemen to get Europa out. It was a noisy but quick affair. Seeing the law and its hired guns knocking at the door, lover et al fled out the bedroom window.

Mother and Europa continued to live in terror. The vodou priest and his son were at their gate every night for a month. They made deafening noises with rocks they banged violently against the metal gate, yelling vile curses all the while, threatening to dispatch their army of bloodthirsty spirits, vouching that the two women would suffer unendurable, slow agony until they finally begged for death.

Mother's neighbors sent notes of complaints about the noise, blaming her for the vulgarity of the situation. She took up praying and started a diary, which she eventually mailed to me.

* * *

EUROPA'S FAVORITE FOODS are shrimp, smoked salmon, strawberry yogurt, oatmeal with stewed prunes, fresh pineapple, grapes, apples and bananas. All of these were heaped high on the oversized plate she chose for eating breakfast. Salmon went into her mouth with oatmeal and prunes; shrimp went in with banana. Europa's eyes glowed. She chewed without hurry. She drank milk.

Thomas, Europa and I were having an early breakfast in the twenty-four-hour dining room on the seventh floor of the cruise ship. We had docked in Skagway that morning, and the three of us had signed up to take the small scenic train, the old Yukon route railway, going up the Klondike trail, the original trail of the first gold rush, climbing up and over White Pass Mountain.

When my sister got up to go for a second helping of breakfast, I thought she went for a little extra or for something that she had not yet tasted. But Europa returned with a large plate heaped high with the very same selection of foods that she had on her first plate. Seeing my surprise, Europa smiled like a Cheshire cat and sat down with a deeply contented look.

"I hope you can eat all that in five minutes," I said, "because we've to be at the meet for the Klondike Trail excursion."

Thunder.

"Why didn't you tell me that? I wouldn't have gotten all this food!" Europa snapped, and a scowl quickly replaced her previous smile.

"How could I guess you'd get all that food again?" I said. "You were told the time of the meet, and you have a watch. Can't you time yourself? But, eat what you can, and leave the rest."

"I can't eat all that in five minutes!"

I felt alarm. "Leave it," I ordered. "The waiters will pick it up. Look around you. People leave what they don't want."

"I can't waste food!" Mounting anxiety showed in Europa's eyes. "I don't believe in wasting food. I'm going to put it in my room. I'll find you at the meet."

"You'll get lost in the interminable halls of this ship!" I cried. "And you're not allowed to take food to your room. Besides, with shrimp, salmon and banana, your room's going to stink!"

"What do you mean I'm 'not allowed'? It's my room!" Europa got up from the table and picked her plate up with a resolute gesture. She grabbed her jacket and scarf and started to leave.

"Yes, it's *your* room, but the cruise ship has rules, and passengers are under agreement to follow them!" I was trying not to shout, yet I was feeling deeply at a loss.

Europa seemed suddenly hesitant.

"Food's served in the dining rooms!" I cried again. "You imagine the mess if everybody brought platefuls of food in their rooms? That's the whole point of a dining area! And besides, you're not going to be at the meet on time."

"I will."

"You won't. You get lost all the time. And we can't accompany you to your room either because there's no time for that now."

"I'll get to the meet on my own."

"I don't want to miss the tour because you don't show up, and we don't have the heart to leave you behind. The cost of the tour won't be refunded either, and that too would be a waste."

"I'm not going to waste food! And that's that!" Europa walked away in a huff, holding her plate firmly.

Thomas remained calm. His involvement would have increased the tension. Yet, his pallor indicated his upset. My jaws were clenched yet trembling. I picked up my jacket without a word, and Thomas got his. Weeks of planning seemed to be crashing down. I saw a fiasco. I imagined a disappointing day in town going from shop to shop, three idle tourists with not enough money to buy joy back.

Thomas and I went directly to the meet. Two minutes later, Europa showed up, on time.

"Gold in the Klondike!"

Beginning in 1897, when most of the good Klondike claims were already staked, an army of hopeful gold seekers boarded ships in Pacific port cities and headed north towards a vision of riches to be had. The Canadian government required those going to the goldfields to bring with them a year's worth of food supplies so they would not starve to death during the long Yukon winter. Recommended supplies included 400 pounds of flour, 200 pounds of bacon and 100 pounds of beans. People poured into the newly created tents and shacks in the town of Skagway.

The White Pass Trail out of Skagway presented men with the greatest hardships. During the first year, twenty to thirty thousand gold seekers spent an average of three months packing their outfits up the trails, needing to cover a distance of about thirty-five miles, yet also having to trudge hundreds of miles back and forth along the trails, moving gear from cache to cache. There were murders and suicides on the way, disease and malnutrition, and death from hypothermia. The White Pass Trail was the animal killer. Prospectors overloaded and beat their animals, trying to force them up the rocky slopes. More than 3,000 animals died on this trail. Many bones can still be found at the bottom of Dead Horse Gulch.

* * *

THE KLONDIKE TRAIL was no longer experienced as a death trap, but conflicts, disappointments and sadness between Europa and me often left me with the feeling that a death had occurred. It was a great strain for me throughout the trip to try and avoid hurting Europa's feelings while she seemed to see me always as an intentional master of insensitivity. Being with her was like walking through a lovely garden hiding a minefield. There was a constant risk of explosion. The fact that Europa and I spoke French to each other when Thomas was not with us made matters more difficult. French was the language of our childhood and past intimacy. We could not pretend to be strangers and polite company to each other. Words in French impacted us more profoundly than anything said in English. This was so especially for

Europa for whom English was essentially a foreign language she had mastered. Speaking it must have felt to her like a kind of playing with an intricate toy, rather than using an essential tool, or weapon, as the case might be.

After the ride through White Pass Mountain, tourists were scheduled to have lunch in Jewel Garden, west of the Skagway River Bridge in the Skagway Valley.

Seeing the gardens, Europa first stood spellbound. She then walked around nonchalantly, ecstatic over the flowers, their colors, their textures, insisting on being photographed in the middle of every flowerbed, ignoring signs meant to keep people on pathways. While I accompanied my sister, yielding to her disorderly whims, Thomas was taking the guided tour around the garden. Europa smiled for the camera, bowed, opened her arms wide, and finally voiced her great regret that she was not wearing a wide skirt that could spread open like a corolla. I was startled by this first and only mention from my sister of her change in appearance and dress, but only said sweetly, "It doesn't matter if you're wearing pants, you look like a Madonna anyway, and these flowers seem like God's offerings to you."

"Don't compare me to an image of superstition!" Europa snapped. "I've converted. I'm a Protestant now, a Seventh Day Adventist. The Virgin Mary and the cohort of Saints, that's idol worship."

"Is that the surprise you had for me?" I asked in a low voice.

"What surprise?"

"Never mind 'what surprise...' Just tell me, how did you become a Protestant?"

"I met a Pastor..." Europa said slowly, observing me before continuing. "I felt welcomed by him. In the Catholic Church, nobody ever spoke to me. Mulattos are a bunch of snobs. Even their children look at me like I am dirt. In the Protestant Church, the pastor's different, and children fight to hold my hand. They may be poor, but they respect me and let me play the piano during the service."

"Since when do you play the piano? And how come they have a piano. Isn't it a poor people's church?"

"It's an electric piano someone brings on Sundays."

"It's a big church, then?"

"No. There's just one room, twenty by thirty feet maybe. Cement blocks, and a corrugated iron rooftop."

"How did you convert? Was there a ceremony?"

"I was baptized in the sea one morning, near Montrouis, with eleven other people."

"Who're they?"

"My brothers and sisters now. We were dressed in white. New clothes. We entered the sea…"

"All dressed?"

"Yes…we entered the sea, and the pastor baptized us, one by one."

"Did you get there by public transportation?"

"Yes."

"Did you get back to town with the same public bus?"

"Yes."

"Thirteen soaking-wet people? I hope you changed to dry clothes before getting in the bus!"

"You're so arrogant, Io. You always have to make fun of people."

"Don't lose your sense of humor over your faith. You must be able to laugh at yourself, or you'll die before your time. Jesus knows that. He was here on earth too."

"How do you know what Jesus knows?"

"How do you know Jesus is okay with a faith that doesn't venerate His mother?"

"What?"

"Europa, tell me? Are you the only white person in your church?"

"What?"

"Has the pastor started asking you for money yet?"

"He knows I don't have any."

"So, if he *knows*, that means the two of you've talked about money then?"

"What?"

"Listen… do you really suppose that a black pastor from the slums of our Bourdon neighborhood believes that a mulatto woman

from the hill mansions has no money? Have you ever met an impov-
erished black Haitian who doesn't think that all mulattos or white
people are rich? Do you think the pastor welcomes you because he
sees that you're one of them, that you belong, that you're a sister?"

"And why not?"

"Oh, come on Europa... Of course, the children want to touch
you and hold your hand! You're the closest thing to a Mount Olym-
pus divinity they'll ever approach in this Haitian caste system of ours
where paler skin makes you a kind of divinity... and I bet they com-
pete to touch your silky hair."

"You're so cynical, Io... I feel sorry for you."

"I know my people."

"You don't speak like they're your people... and they certainly
wouldn't see you as one of them."

"Wow... I never would've expected my own sister to question
my Haitian identity and belonging. I'd leave that to people who lack
knowledge about the historical complexity of nations of the world,
the shifting of borders and the never-ending migratory movement of
its populations... Nobody questions the Americanness of children
born of Mexican, Japanese, Chinese, Indian or African immigrants.
Americans don't have to be white to be Americans, and I don't have
to be black to be a true Haitian."

"There goes Io being testy again."

"Yes, I'm testy about these issues, and I make no apology. I've
had to suffer this all my life, and I've lost patience with those attitudes
by now. Caribbean cultures are cultures of contact between two or
more nations. Caribbean people are, therefore, a complex mix. No one
in the Caribbean's just one thing. We owe that to the slave trade. We've
Spanish, French, and English blood circulating wildly in our genes,
not just African. And not to forget Germans and Lebanese and Chinese
and whoever else came after the 1804 slave revolution. We deal with
that skin color variety with a wealth of vocabulary about the many
shades of white or black... you probably know more of them than I
do, seeing how you love language... it's like the Eskimos and words
for snow... And it wasn't so long ago that anyone with a bit of black

blood was considered black. Napoleon's Code Noir was explicit. You know all that very well, Europa… I may not be outwardly fully black, but I'm fully Caribbean and fully Haitian… just like you… and people at the top of the social ladder, if fewer in numbers, are still part of the whole… You're the best illustration of that, Europa."

"What do you mean?"

"You were born at the top of that ladder. And yet you're so Haitian that you've managed to insert yourself in other levels of Haitian social reality."

"Didn't you just mock me and question whether I belong there?"

"Understanding the many layers of society and knowing how to insert yourself in either layer doesn't mean that you belong in one instead of the other. It means that you are part of the whole enough to maneuver within the particulars… Even if part of you feels at ease in the new niche, all of your being doesn't, and you never fully belong anywhere."

"How would you know what I feel?" Europa said resentfully.

"Because I too am a mix."

"Io, you're nuts, that's what you are."

"Maybe. At least I don't use my mental fragilities to avoid responsibility for my actions, the stupidity of my choices and the distress I cause my family."

"Yeah, right… here comes Io, above and better than anyone."

"Describe me as you wish, but if you were the real Haitian you claim to be, you'd be fleeing from Protestantism and run to Vodou ceremonies instead."

"I'm fed up and done with Vodou."

"Your former lovers were good for something, after all."

"Io, you're clever enough to ridicule or justify anything, especially when it comes to belittling me. However, admit that I'm not welcomed by my family, and they look down on me because I don't have money. They're the ones who love others for their money, not my pastor and his church members."

"These are the ways of the world, Europa. The rich mulatto class isn't unique that way. People struggle to get ahead and then to keep what they acquired."

"But poor people love me even if my hands are empty."

"The children maybe…"

"Do you see my family inviting me over? You go to their dinners. I never do. They invite you to their birthday and Christmas parties. You share their cakes and fancy foods. I don't ever. They drive past me in the streets in their big air-conditioned cars and don't stop to give me a ride."

"They don't see you."

"Me? The single white person walking down the street where everyone else's black. You really believe they don't see me? Me, the Europa they grew up with?"

"Maybe you threaten them?"

"How? I've nothing. I've no power. I never hurt a fly."

"You create havoc. And when you don't, we've to anticipate when you might."

"What havoc? You say that to hurt my feelings."

"*What havoc?* For instance, and this is what I've been told happened… You pay our cousins a surprise visit. You bring along some mendicant or a bòkò friend of yours. The watchman at the gate lets you in because he knows you're family. Your cousins come to the door to welcome you and find you with some poverty-stricken company to whom you're busy showing off everything they have, trying to impress a poor bugger who has more cunning than you can ever imagine existing in one person… You might as well take a thief in and point to him valuables he shouldn't miss. And you really think you don't threaten them?"

"Well, maybe I do… They've too much anyway… They hoard all the country's wealth. They're the thieves."

"Could be. But they don't want to lose it any more than your bòkò lover wanted to give our father's ring back, or the other family who locked you up in the apartment wanted to lose access to your bank account."

Europa was about to answer when Thomas suddenly turned up. "Just as well…" she mumbled between her teeth. "This is a dead-end conversation anyway."

Thomas put his arms around me, smiling, filled with delight.
"You should've taken the tour! The guide was very instructive... And,
had I been allowed to pick some, I would've brought you, ladies, a
flower each."

"Europa doesn't want flower offerings," I said, switching to
English.

"And why not?" Thomas was cheerful.

"She says that's idol worship."

"You can never let go, Io, can you?" Europa snapped, also in
English. "You must dig your knife in any chance you get."

Thomas looked puzzled. "Seems I've missed something?"

I gave Thomas a caress on the cheek, saying, "Better let flowers
live than behead them."

"Ah...a touch of drama!" Thomas said good-humoredly. "I recognize my wife here."

"If drama's what you like, there's more where that came from!"
Europa said curtly with a disgruntled look.

"Thomas, what did you learn on the guided tour?" I asked,
ignoring Europa.

"All sorts of things!" Thomas said, his joyousness unabated.
"The guide explained the reasons behind the making of the garden,
besides attracting tourists, and the choices for the flowerbeds, the
organic way in which the flowers are grown and the magical design the
garden makes when seen up from a plane... Their having planned for
that effect of being visible from the air makes sense if we remember
that private planes are a common form of transportation in Alaska."

"I see a life lesson there," I said.

"What do you mean?" Europa asked.

"I mean that the farther and higher we stand from flowers, people and life itself, the more their mystery and meaning's revealed."

"So, Io, my love," Thomas asked, a twinkle in his eyes, "if I want
to remain charmed by the mystery you are to me, and all the while
wishing that the meaning of it be revealed, I better stay at a distance?"

"No, Thomas. Molière also wrote that 'women's greatest ambi-
tion is to inspire love.' I'm a woman. I don't want you to be charmed

by mystery and seek to pierce it. I want you close, blinded and hope-lessly under my spell." Saying that, I laughed, kissing Thomas lightly on the forehead.

Europa looked irritated. "Can't you speak about flowers as flow-ers and enjoy them simply for what you see?"

"Come now, Flowers," Thomas said. "Let's have lunch. I'm starved. Breakfast's long past."

* * *

BACK FROM THE TOUR that evening, the three of us went straight to our rooms. I was glad to find myself alone again with Thomas in our room, albeit a short while. I then called for the head steward of our floor, the fifth floor.

She was a young, pretty woman from the Philippines whose hus-band also worked for the same cruise line yet was assigned to a differ-ent ship. Her manner was calm, and her long black hair neatly gathered into a bun at the top of her head. At the time I met her, she had just returned from a three-months' stay in the Philippines. She told me how much joy it gave her to be with her daughter for a long stretch of time but now missed her more than ever. She had gotten used to cooking for her little girl, putting her to bed, watching her sleep. She showed me a picture of a proud, chubby, nine-year-old girl dressed like a cowboy, standing next to the grandmother who takes care of her with money sent by the parents working on the cruise ship. She explained how lucky they feel, having enviable jobs. Back in the Philippines, they were hungry. Listening to her, I remembered being a child and how my mother would discourage my show of affection, *Don't kiss me, you'll ruin my make-up. And I don't want to get attached when we are separated someday. I'll suffer more.* I kept these thoughts to myself and only spoke to the head steward about Europa's plate. "She has problems throwing food away," I explained. "Please take it out of the room for her. It will spoil, but she still won't be able to trash it."

The woman smiled. "I've prepped the room already for the night. I saw the food. But I'll go back after you leave for dinner. I'll remove it."

"Thank you," I said in a soft tone, embarrassed, and feeling like a traitor. I rushed back inside my cabin just as Europa was opening her cabin door to peer out, probably wondering about the people talking outside her door.

At dinner, Thomas wore black tie. I wore a blue gown with a matching jacket. Europa wore black slacks and a pink polka-dot silk blouse—a present from me. The femininity of Europa's blouse made an unexpected contrast with her short gray hair. Her winning smile and dazzled eyes matched the dizzying dots. Any irritation from earlier in the afternoon had vanished from her face. But I was still uneasy. Thomas started the conversation, but Europa was quick to take over and began recounting at length, and with infinite delight, her memories of the day. Jewel Gardens, she said, she would like to take home with her, but at the top of White Pass Mountain, she had felt cold and spoke of it as if it had been a personal aggression similar to that done by the New York Customs officer who took her fingerprints. However, a photograph of Europa standing next to a stuffed bear, taller than her, and wearing a new bald eagle sweatshirt bought at a White Pass Mountain tourist shop, would make anyone doubt any unpleasantness she complained about.

We had gotten a window table, and I was able to focus on the Alaskan shoreline going by—its high cliffs and green pine slopes edging the sea. The soft, rippled pattern the ship made on the water seemed to be flowing out of my very being. I closed my eyes to recreate the enveloping comfort of a life experienced long ago. I searched for the buried memory of an amniotic bliss in a space where I once, albeit briefly, found sustenance and a different sense of breath. But that imagined womb life turned sour almost the instant I evoked it. I was not alone in it. A twin challenged my right to life. A double punched at the amniotic sack and pulled at my umbilical cord. The double in the womb, my shadow side, albeit imagined, did not complete me, but depleted me instead. Fleeing that fictitious, amniotic harbor, fleeing also what little of the conversation reached me, my thoughts drifted to a letter I had received from a dear, old friend the day before we left for the Alaska cruise.

I was carrying the letter with me like a talisman, a protective reminder that somewhere else, in a place other than at this dinner table, away from my sister, not belonging to collective family memory, on a stage of my own, there I also exist. In other people's minds, in other hearts, in other circumstances of life, in other world views, I exist. Outside of myself, even, I exist still. Separate from limitations other people impose on my views and expectations of myself, I exist. I live in a friend's heart, a heart that singled me out for the kind of devotion friendship exemplifies.

I took the letter out. I rested my foot lightly on Thomas's under the table while I read and filled my mind with its recall of another world: "Viergela came over, and we cooked a huge pot of guavas. We made guava jam. It's really more like stewed guavas, you know, like the old-fashioned style the cooks at home made when we were children. We rarely see guavas anymore on the shelves in the Petionville markets or on the sidewalks' stalls. A woman came to my gate with a big basket and offered them for a fair price. I could not resist."

"What're you reading, Io?" Europa asked, visibly annoyed, a smirk on her lips. "Isn't it rude of you? We're having dinner together."

"I'm sorry, Europa. You're right. It's rude. But I need to read this now."

Thomas intervened quickly, "Let's ignore Io. You and I've got a lot to talk about, and we don't need her, do we?"

Europa was startled. "What?" Then she said with a smile, "No, we don't indeed." I, too, smiled, recognizing my sister, forever eager to play a game. "We don't need Io. We'll ignore her," she said again, her eyes taking on the glow of children's sharing secrets, whispering in the darkness behind stairwells.

I winked at Thomas and resumed my reading: "Viergela peeled the yellow-ripe guavas and left them whole with all their little round seeds inside, their coral-red flesh and slightly acid fragrance. Viergela agreed to follow my wishes about putting very little sugar because of my diabetes. But who will want to eat them with me this way? They will not keep very long since the refrigerator is never cool enough with the shortage of electricity—two hours here, two hours there, you can't keep anything cool enough anymore. As for freezing meat, forget that.

"Haitian people around me live their simple lives, which means being in constant need, out of work, with hunger as your bedside companion, the usual illnesses hardly identifiable, visits to the doctor and prescriptions impossible for lack of money. And there is the general nightmare at the beginning of the school year, such as buying books, uniforms, copy books and paying high tuition fees. There is also the end of the house lease and no money to renew it. Sometimes a baby dies, or her mother, a father in jail, another gone to try his luck in Santo Domingo. And yet still, a lot of laughter, commentaries full of life on all and nothing, along with faces that reappear after long eclipses, familiar names, forgotten, coming back.

"You asked about our Esau in your last letter. He is permanently worried and anxious because he has not found work in two years. There is no longer anyone able to afford his wood cabinets or tables. His wife suffers of an eternal ill in her lower belly; her sister has lost her mind and errs in the streets of Port-au-Prince while her husband is in the hospital to die; their three small children have taken refuge with Esau, their aunt Lonise, and the little boy Quéqué, in their one-room hut that leaks everywhere when it rains, and they huddle together on an inundated beaten-earth floor.

"Esau takes care of the three little ones as if they were his own, wakes up in the night when they are ill, ill himself from the grief of not being able to take them to the doctor and afford medicine. He says to them, 'my little children, you can't stay, there is no room.' They say, 'yes…we'll go back to our father's place.' In the morning, they go back downtown Port-au-Prince on foot, but in the same evening, they are back. Esau tells them again, 'my little ones, there is no food here, you will go hungry.' They say, 'it does not matter, we'd rather be hungry with you than at our father's.' Esau tells me, 'what else can I do but face the fact that we have four children?'

"These days it is Sava, the eight-year-old who cries every night—fever, stomachache. Finally, Esau manages to get him to the doctor and, after another delay, manages to buy him medicine. Diagnosis: beginning of hernia because of hunger and gas. There is the danger, however, that if he continues to go hungry, the hernia will reappear in spite of the medicine, and then what will he do?

"Two, three, four times a week, Esau meets with Auguste, or Jean-Marc, or another carpenter and wood-working colleague. They go for some very long search on foot all the way to Tabare, or even further, in the plains of Fontamara or Carrefour-Feuille, where they were told there might be some work. They come back exhausted in the evening, famished, having found nothing, and ready to leave again in the morning in another direction.

"So, my dear Io, it is the prime condition of our belonging to the world to find ourselves caught in and weighed under incontrollable conditions, to have to live with it all and to even die from them. Life is a strange package deal. Banal considerations these are, I admit, but in fact, there are no others to make. As for your own family, have you ever thought how so many people, our dear ones in particular, have the mania of not wanting to conform to conventional canons of behavior, and yet if they had the sudden idea to conform, how disappointed we would somehow be?

"It is now late afternoon, nearly dusk, and my house is slowly filling with the familiar sounds of the hour—workers that shovel sand piles at the other end of the street, the last exclamations of mechanics at the close of their day, the distant rumbling of a generator. The air is cool. There is a gray autumnal luminosity already. My dog, Mickie, is watching it all at the gate, wagging her tail in her everlasting hope that someone will come in. It will soon be the hour when small lizards and tiny frogs start their melodious whistling throughout the countryside."

* * *

DOLLY HAD BEEN KETCHIKAN'S main evening attraction. Creek Street, where her house stood, was the red-light district and is now only a rather short row of quaint tourist shops. The street briefly follows the creek from which it gets its name. Tourist guides now joke that in those early days of settlers and the gold rush, both men and salmon went up the stream to lay eggs. At the end of August, Thomas, Europa and I were still able to watch hundreds of salmon spawning in the shallow waters below us while we stood on Creek Street across from Dolly's old house.

One can now visit Dolly's house just as one would the Moulin Rouge in France. Dolly looks straight into the eyes of tourists from photographs that show her as plump and lively, with large, intelligent eyes.

In the Tlingit Indians' language, Ketchikan means "Thundering Wings of an Eagle." Thomas, Europa and I went to visit the community of Tlingit Indians who live in Saxman Village, a couple of miles from Ketchikan. After taking an initial bus ride, we crossed on foot a small section of the Tongass National Forest. Tlingit Indians keep a traditional tribal house. They are known as sculptors. They carve totems.

The island on which Ketchikan is built holds an annual record for rainfall that, in 1949, was 202.55 inches. As a result, the forest floor is continuously covered with a brilliant, thick, green moss that carpets even the deep, rounded hollows that abound there. "I wish I could curl up and live in that green moss," I said out loud to myself. "Even *I* would eventually be able to lay an egg…" I remembered my cat, Lucy, back home in Cambridge, the afternoon I surprised her and watched her silently, stretched as she was in the middle of the queen-size bed, belly up over the brocade bedspread, purring loudly, alone; her paws were curled in, eyes wide open, circling around, taking in her surroundings.

Thomas, Europa and I were part of a small group of visitors to Saxman Village from the cruise ship. The tribal house and the totems were the main attractions. Europa was excited, intimidated, inspired and spellbound. She stood upright and proud at the foot of the clan's totem pole for me to take a photo of her. This was the Thunderbird Clan, evidenced by the bird at the top of the totem. "Totems have four different uses," the guide explained. "They serve to identify the clan, tell clan stories, commemorate an event, or stand as a memorial."

Europa was the first to get up from her seat in the tribal house when the chief of the Tlingit Indians invited anyone to join in the traditional dance they were soon starting. A little girl in red handed Europa the embroidered, glittering ceremonial dress she should wear. That day, Europa discovered how it feels to be honored.

"Io, you might want to lay an egg in the forest," Europa said after the dance, "but it's here that I'd stretch my mattress and lay my egg."

I was startled. I did not think anyone had overheard me. Europa and I were lingering together inside the tribal house, even as Thomas and the other visitors were exiting quietly. Europa had returned the ceremonial dress right away, albeit reluctantly, thanking the chief, with a bow.

"Lay your egg, and then what?" I asked.

"And stay forever."

"Stay forever? To live with Indians, and become Indian?"

"Absolutely."

I was amused. "Is it then 'Goodbye shrimp, bananas, cottage cheese and papayas'?"

"Yes."

I smiled at my sister, thinking about the ranger who came aboard ship earlier in the day to talk about life in the wilderness. I said, "You mean that you're ready to eat whale, walrus, caribou, bear and muskoxen for the rest of your life?"

"Yes."

"Are you ready to forget about your pastor, being a good Protestant, and a true Haitian? You want to be Tlingit now?"

"Yes."

"I guess that's the closest you'll ever get to a Taino Indian and the true, indigenous Haitian." I couldn't help sniggering.

Disdainfully, Europa said, "There's an Inuit saying that the great peril of our existence lies in the fact that our diet consists entirely of souls."

I was amused. "A whale, walrus and caribou diet doesn't sound vegetarian or without much soul-eating to me. But where did you learn that? A voice in a dream?"

"I read about it."

"Where? And how do you even remember such quotes?" I asked, wonder and delight arching my eyebrows.

Europa lifted her chin haughtily. "Does it surprise you that I read and might remember quotes? You think I'm an idiot? The fact is, I've an amazing memory."

"Sorry for you," I said, chuckling. "I know how painful it is to remember everything."

"You're wrong. Memory is useful and good because people can't trick you a second time if you remember what first happened," Europa said, pursing her mouth in a smirk while casting a glance around to check if anyone was waiting for us to leave.

"Never mind tricks," I said, as undeterred in my good humor as Europa was in her seriousness. "The problem is that we don't get to choose what we remember, and it's not always what's useful for survival that memory chooses to hold on to. And then it takes years of meditation exercises to forget painful memories unless we resort to hypnotherapy… Either way, with too much memory, we're doomed!" I laughed, exhilarated by the wildly imaginative presence and strong primary colors of totems and carvings all around us inside the tribal house.

Europa was annoyed. "No. It's without memory that we're doomed," she said.

I did not respond. Something was slowly taking shape in my consciousness, an impression arising from the dignity, humility and otherworldly detachment in the way that Europa was standing in the dim light of the wooden tribal house. "Europa?" I asked softly, almost in a murmur, "Is there a *soul* in your belly?"

"What?"

I got closer to Europa and placed one hand on my sister's belly. "What I mean is, are you pregnant?"

Europa backed up from me. "Strange question all of a sudden, wouldn't you say?"

"Well… you still could answer."

"Do I have to?"

So, that's the surprise! I found myself thinking. *Ah, my sister… my sister…* I hid my face with my hands, shaking my head from side to side as if abandoning it to the back and forth of an ocean tide.

Europa bent down, trying to peer through my fingers and see my face, asking, "What're you mumbling?"

"...my sister... my shaman..." I was saying slowly with deep tenderness.

Europa straightened her back, uncomprehending. "Io, are you making fun of me?"

I uncovered my face, a faint smile on my lips. "No. I'm not... I'm traveling... You're sending my mind on a flight in the company of mythical beings... Thunderbirds! Eagles, bears, snakes, frogs, whales, turtles and sea-woman!" I said with mounting excitement. "They're looking down on us from their totemic heights! It's a fertile world we find ourselves in... Dear God, how one is humbled!"

Europa was alarmed, flapping her arms. "Io! What're you saying?"

I looked up to the ceiling as if it were an actual, vast, open sky at dawn. "I'm saying that the world opens anew, and anything seems possible again."

"Stop it, Io! I don't understand you."

"Understand? No need for understanding. The time has come for kneeling, for obedience, for reverie...trance...oracles...drumming... amulets...feathers..."

Europa stomped her foot impatiently. "Io, stop it, I tell you!"

But I did not stop. I could not. I kept speaking as if I were stringing words making an invisible necklace to honor Europa. "Shaman my sister... Soul of the forever-hunted now hunting within you... Healer of the dead that walk still... Mediator of an inarticulate world grateful for any word uttered in their stead..."

"Io! You don't make sense!" Europa put her hands on my shoulders, ready to shake me but not daring to.

"*Sense*? Europa? You, of all people, want *sense*?" I said with greater calm still. "Have I ever told you how I see you, deep inside of me, what I perceive at those rare moments when I see us beyond this flesh that entraps and diminishes us?"

Europa crossed her arms. "What do you see?"

I looked in a far, dim corner of the tribal house, focusing inwardly, opening my hands and fingers like a container, lifting them slightly. "I see you upright with totemic solemnity. Europa speaking to birds, bird herself, bird with a nest still to be found... but a nest, like all nests, that cannot, will not, resist the winds, these incomprehensible winds of life that devastate, then rebuild... Europa touched and chosen by God, carrying a strange vocation... the vocation to challenge our sense of normality and social superiority, defy established perceptions about the worth of a self and an identity to which we cling at all costs... and even when it means that we must destroy one another for it. God gave you a terrible burden, Europa, my sister, myself. He gave you the vocation to disturb..."

Europa was trembling. "I can't stand this! Io! Stop it, I beg you."

I stopped, but asked again, very gently, "Are you pregnant, Europa?"

Europa made an irritated gesture of the hand. "What's this?" she asked with annoyance and turned her back to me.

I stood still and asked again. "I ask you, are you pregnant?"

Europa turned around sharply and looked me in the eyes. "Yes!"

I backed up, jerkily, as if I had received a blow. "Ah... how I bow to you, Europa! I'm struck indeed... God the Incomprehensible! A piece of the glacier chips away from my heart again... Pregnant Europa-bird, disowned Europa-child, Fate's child, accepting what comes because this is what she's made for... incomprehension, disbelief, abandonment... she holds the flag of the hardship country, my Europa... Europa-shaman, woman-shaman, Paleolithic woman-shaman, Greek pagan, Elysian priestess, my sister, impossible believer in the intrinsic harmony of the universe and the goodness of man. I ask for your forgiveness, Europa. I thank you for bearing life for us all... for me... regardless... I'm innocent of your fate and its ills, but I'm at fault, nonetheless. I've not loved you as myself.

"I'm ashamed and desolate... so close to you, and yet so far. Could we remake ourselves within a new virtual reality where we retrace steps ill taken? Can we stop the fiction of our lives? Close it shut and lay it down the way we do a book we don't like? Could we dance at the margin of the imaginary, and find an easy love for each other? Can we live again a single, innocent day of childhood, staring at the Caribbean ocean? Walk on the red earth mountains of Furcy, where the breeze carried to us the invisible, scented music of pines? Could we gaze once more at the blue, unfolding undulations of the mountain range that ripples all the way down to the sea?

"No. We can't. We don't. Instead of the wonderfulness we could have again, we've got what irritates instead... noises... noises particularly... and the idiocies of people, people in public transportation, people at the office, people in church. Oh God! What boredom, what a great mass of boredom we must endure! We run from boredom only to find trouble."

Europa paced uncomfortably, looking intermittently at the door and checking to see if anyone was listening. "Io! What's happening to you? Are you drunk? Stop!"

"*Stop*, Europa? Obviously, life can't be stopped." I shook my head sadly. "Your new child attests to this." I fixed my gaze on her, but I looked beyond. I asked softly, "Is there a father for your child, Europa?"

Europa's mouth twisted. She lowered her head and looked in the palm of her empty hands. "There isn't. There's never a father. You know that. And when there is, it might've been best if there hadn't."

"Listen to me, Europa, even if it's the last time you ever do... All I can ever be is a mother of dreams, a mother of nothing I can really hold in my arms—unlike you. I live in an imaginary world... You, on the other hand, have tasted the earth itself. You've been the earth. It has given itself to you again and again, however bitter, to be tasted and felt and to be known by you intimately. It hasn't chosen me... All these years, Europa, you've wasted envy on me."

"I? What do you mean?" Europa let her hands fall to her sides, inhaling deeply.

I then took Europa's hands in mine. "I ask you, Europa. What's the meaning of my disposable life on earth? Alas, such ridicule we live, and with such force! Ah, but hear this, World... a new life's coming again! A child is to be delivered to us! A promise has been kept."

IV. Cacao

Io in the Year 2010...

CHARLOTTE WAS A PIG that crossed the water after the January 2010 earthquake destroyed Port-au-Prince's slums and wealthy neighborhoods alike. Charlotte thus lost her home in the slums along with the people who lived there. These were people who had fed her scraps they threw to the ground where she was tied at the back of their bare cement-block shack, a foot away from its wall—Charlotte ate banana and sweet potato peels, burnt clumps of cornmeal or rice scraped from the bottom of cheap, blackened cooking pots, and, on rare, relished occasions, she would find cacao pod husks suddenly put in a pile near her.

The waters of the brook had always served as a boundary between Charlotte's world and my mother's. The water that streamed down a pebble-and-sand flat bed, insignificant most of the year, grew into a deluge during the rainy season, eating at the slums, snatching and drowning people and livestock in its torrent. Unlike Charlotte's, my mother's world was protected—it stretched expansively behind a long, sturdy wall built on the opposite side of the stream to keep Charlotte and her kind away. The destructive, muddy current left the boundary wall unmoved.

I was a child when I watched the wall being built. To me, it seemed as indestructible as the Great Wall of China, as exclusionary as the Berlin Wall, and as defensive as the new Israeli West Bank

Barrier appears to me now. After the wall burst open, like bread being broken in pieces to be shared, Charlotte's eyes were tempted by what she saw.

Such a funny name my mother gave her when she found this pig in her garden. A grungy, gray mother pig with floppy tits, bleeding in places where her tough hide had been torn by bramble and barbed wire which had fallen from the top of the wall that no longer hid the slums that continuously crept up arid hills. Walls no longer hid the ugliness. Charlotte did what the poor from all the Port-au-Prince slums did, and even those who came from the countryside where they too starved—she ran for it!

It was not hard for pigs or people to abandon all they had since they had nothing. The slum-gypsies came in gray masses, down from the barren hills ridden with detritus. They dragged their wounds along, invading the manicured lawns of public gardens, even the pristine slopes of the Pétionville Club's golf course, planting their sticks and make-shift tents, sitting under imported cloth showing prints of fruits and flowers not indigenous to the Caribbean—installing their squalor in full view. They lined up daily to see what food the United Nations, or their luck, would bring.

It seemed, after the earthquake, that boundaries had fallen for good, that Haitians had become one people under grief, that rebuilding and restructuring Haiti would never again mean separating Haitians by color or class.

My mother assumed that Charlotte had survived the earthquake, but that her people had not—those who had owned and fed her while planning to feed on her someday. If her owners had perhaps survived the crashing down of their meager shack upon their own underfed bodies, they would still have been dumbstruck for a long while, unconcerned enough about the fate of a damn pig as to not realize that the pig was food, the very stuff for which they would soon be desperate. Had they been alive but not in shock, Charlotte's owners would've slashed her throat right then and cooked the beast on the spot. But they might also have looked for human survivors first and forgot about the pig that had just been given a freedom whose boundaries she would immediately explore. Still, even after a week had passed, no one had come to claim Charlotte, so it was fair to assume that the creature was orphaned.

My mother took to Charlotte, but her dogs didn't. They repeatedly defied rules around separate feeding schedules and assigned sleeping areas that she immediately established in order to protect Charlotte. After all, being born a pig is a kind of life condition that involves being held hostage by one's own form and other creatures' responses to it, even if outrageously pampered canines. So, it was a matter of hours until Charlotte's Eden in my mother's garden was turned into a penitentiary in which she was outnumbered by what might have seemed an army of dogs—ordinary pets turned predatory camp guards with their territorial, vengeful, teeth-bared attacks.

The alarmed shrieks of a pig—grating, screeching, discordant—are the most wrenching sounds on our nervous system. Why was Charlotte screaming? It couldn't be that the dogs were hungry and were trying to snatch away Charlotte's ration of rice, cornmeal and pig's meat since they had their own, and my mother doted on them. It couldn't be that they resented my mother's occasional sharing with Charlotte some bits of dried chocolate cake a friend of hers would bring back from trips to Jacmel since they themselves wouldn't touch it. And it couldn't be that the dogs were trying to protect my mother's garden and flowerbeds from the destruction caused by the weight of Charlotte spreading herself indolently over the most fragrant ones—they themselves were creating their own devastation through all their furious digging of useless holes—searching for parcels and bones they might have dreamt of—and shitting under bushes of imported, delicate plant specimens. No, the dogs just enjoyed terrorizing the pig.

Two weeks passed, and Charlotte was finally claimed. A man showed up one day, saying Charlotte was his. Pigs can't speak for themselves, so Charlotte couldn't tell my mother whether this man had just heard of a vagrant pig being fed by a crazy white crone and saw an opportunity. So Charlotte left, forced out with a short, sisal rope around her grisly neck, tail down between her muddy hind thighs, like a dog's—mortified, hurt and frightened. It was clear then, that from whichever side of the wall she found herself living, Charlotte's life experience as a pig was dominated by the constant menace of those she relied upon to protect her life, but also by Death itself.

One afternoon in Cambridge, Massachusetts, I found myself remembering Charlotte while sipping hot chocolate on Brattle Street, a street I love for its elegant mansions and trimmed gardens that evoke for me an idyllic childhood in pink taffeta, and children chasing after birthday balloons.

My childhood had unfolded in such a different world. In the 1970s, Haiti was not just another place in time, but another place in the mind—the air, the sounds, the flesh, all coalescing to create a flavor of the heart, a way of feeling, a singular definition of what being alive meant. Those were the challenging years of Jean-Claude Duvalier's dictatorship that followed the previous two decades during which Papa Doc, his father, appointed himself president for life, made Haitians call him Papa, while his way of disciplining the nation's children was to create a torture prison, a death-dungeon called Fort Dimanche. Papa Doc was a dictator known to have sat on the toilet in front of his government advisors, naked but for a soldier's green, round-top helmet, grinning to the radio reporter who held a live broadcast microphone in front of him while he uttered in a low, nasal voice, "I'm an immaterial being..."

Sitting in the chocolate house in Cambridge with cacao pod husks displayed on shelves, sold for decorative use, or reproduced in old botanical pen and ink prints hung on the walls, I could not have expressed how far I felt I had come from my former world in Haiti while I held a book about *Sanapia, Comanche Medicine Woman*, a case study in cultural anthropology. And yet, strangely enough, the book unwittingly also took me from Cambridge's New England elegance and culture all the way back to my memories of Haiti's vodou religion and politics and the ways they had affected my sister's and my life, all of which did not seem so different from the Comanche experience and concerns.

I had found the book in Ann Arbor, Michigan, where I had gone to help raise funds for a medical group that did charitable work in my ruined island. This book, too, in a way, was all about violence and death. How to protect oneself from magical curses? How to heal from the illnesses they caused? How to escape the snare of death, or even how to return from it? These issues being all the things human beings inflict on one another, moved by greed, revenge, or jealousy. The motives are immemorial and the same all over—people acting as if hell does not lie in wait. Death is however unique when it is your own to face, while each death is identical to the other in the way that it makes you cry out when you see it, if only because it is uglier than you had imagined—death not from God, but come from experts in articulating savagery.

The slim book about Sanapia that I found in Ann Arbor came from a used bookstore. Dusty, narrow aisles of floor to ceiling shelves and stacks were filled with haphazardly piled volumes, sorted vaguely by subject, that threatened at any moment to topple over. Antique chairs and climbing stools cluttered the passages. Wooden, life-sized sculptures of African deities stood at the cross-sections of the aisles. They seemed meant as makeshift street signs left to help identify one's location in this singular maze, where I eventually sat on a low stool next to an overwhelmingly severe fertility goddess. Her elongated breasts that ended in the point of a large nipple were like Charlotte's many teats, and perhaps the unconscious reason for which I might have plunked myself there. I noticed on a book across from me the photograph of a strong, wrinkled woman's face, printed in red. I picked up the book. The title of one chapter caught my interest—"The Resurgence of the Ghost complex."

The atmosphere, space and decoration of that bookstore were so unusual that I remained there for a long time, too distracted visually to really look into the book I kept in one hand all the while I roamed around. Flipping through the book now in the Brattle Street chocolate house was a different experience than it might have been at the bookstore. The only excitement at the chocolate house was the chocolate itself, as well as the few French pasties—chocolate eclairs, millefeuilles and madeleines—that they sold to enhance and expand the hot chocolate experience. But, looking into the book about the medicine woman as I did that afternoon, I discovered the complexity and depth of its subject matter and appreciated what a singular and bold anthropologist it must have been who got interested in doing field study in Comanche healing rituals and magic. I also came to realize that much of what was called "medicine" in it was only imaginative ways of using spirits to eliminate people. Witch doctors behaved no differently than warriors. No wonder that my mind, while reading about Sanapia, had wandered to Charlotte's world of African breasts and colonialism, its ghosts and corpses. Yet my mind soon ran away from the memory of Charlotte's world and that of Sanapia's exterminated people. Perhaps it was too intense and too familiar. My mind wanted escape. So, I hurried back to the simpler world of the chocolate house where I had come to relax. I wore earplugs against the noise from other customers, while Sanapia's story felt noisier from the clamor of human grievances.

* * *

I ABANDONED MYSELF to the scrutiny of wear marks on the chocolate house's wood floor for a long, dreamy while. We had similar floors where I grew up. I spent listless childhood hours looking at the termite-hollowed, dark wood planks on which my family walked.

A servant waxed the wood floors of our house each week. He spread the wax with a worn cloth, working a small area at a time. When the wax had dried over the whole surface of a room, he began the monotonous buffing of the wood with the hard-bristled shell of a dried half-coconut. He did this until floors in every room shone with a warm glow under our feet. We nevertheless remained constantly attentive at every step we took for possible splinters piercing from indented areas caused by the never-ending hunger of termites.

A red rug runs through the middle of the Cambridge chocolate house, starting at the door. Red carpets recall princely times and abundance. People feel comforted by them. I started looking at customers' feet, feeling distracted by the many kinds of shoes proceeding toward the cash register—sneakers, boots, clogs, a sudden pair of espadrilles even—enclosed as I was in the muffled cocoon of my plugged ears. I felt entertained by what human beings express of themselves in their choice of shoes and the way they stand in them—solidly anchored, pacing or prancing like young horses. I tried to imagine what bodies matched the feet and invented faces for them. I noticed how feet, even though they come in pairs, still seem lonely and exist independently from each other.

Then, I saw the blue-suede shoes.

They were the same early-night-sky hue of suede shoes that my father had bought when we traveled to Paris as a family in my early teens. I never saw my father wear them. I thought it a very feminine thing to do, buying shoes because they are irresistibly lovely, and even though not practical, comfortable or even needed. I would sometimes open my father's closet to look at them in their intimate repose. They seemed the kind of shoes that would disappear once their fairy-work was done.

I looked up to see the face of the man who now wore the blue-suede shoes decades later. He was olive-skinned, middle-aged, dark-haired and balding. He was slim, wore blue jeans, a black shirt and a gray tweed jacket. Our eyes met, and he winked.

I was startled—such an un-middle-aged, un-white-American thing to do! That playfulness, that sudden familiarity in being noticed, singled out from the crowd, that childlike invitation and boldness— how odd, how rare, how delightful! I smiled out of embarrassment but realized immediately how my smile could be misinterpreted, so I looked right back down at my book.

I let a little time pass, then looked up furtively. The olive-skinned man was just taking a seat opposite mine at the table on my right while a man with whom he was chatting edged his way between our two tables before he finally seated himself next to me on the red, leather-padded bench that ran the length of the wall. This other man had a square jaw, thick, short gray hair, full lips and warm blue eyes. I sensed a body full of energy by my side, someone physically fit.

While I could surreptitiously look at the olive-skinned man across from me, I could only observe the blue-eyed face from the mirror stretching all along the wall opposite us. I felt curious about the men, so I removed my earplugs slowly but saw in a flash that the dark eyes of the man opposite me had noticed it. I smiled and quickly picked up my book again. I leaned back against the wall to read and learn more from Sanapia about how to break a deadly spell.

* * *

"...CUBA..." The word caught my ear. The man who had winked at me was speaking. I leaned forward. "...my family was able to go when it was still possible to leave Cuba. It was at the beginning of the changes with Castro. My uncle in Miami sponsored us... Some years earlier, his wife had said to him, 'I'm leaving for America with the children. Come with us or stay in Cuba...' He didn't want to leave, and he didn't care for his domineering wife, but he went anyway... It's a good thing he did. He later made it possible for us to join him. It cost him a thousand dollars for each one of us. It was a lot of money then."

"How old were you?" The blue-eyed man spoke casually.

"An adolescent."

"Your English is amazing. Is it because you came here very young?"

The Cuban looked amused. "Actually, I was sent to school in Spain first. My accent changed, and my Spanish no longer sounded Cuban... Afterward, I went to university in Paris. I speak three languages, but I sound foreign in all three."

"I don't hear an accent when you speak English."

"I fool a lot of people." The Cuban shrugged his shoulders. "For years, I put Cuba out of my mind," he said. "I've been in investment banking all of my adult life... For the last fifteen years, I was a top executive in a large Boston investment company. I played tennis with the president of the company for twelve years. I played golf with the other executives as well. No one, I mean, no one, knew that I was Cuban... I'm retired now."

Each time I tried to catch a glimpse of the Cuban's face, he detected any slight movement of my head or eyes, even if he was in the middle of a sentence. Each time, he smiled only impercepti-

bly, yet his blue-eyed interlocutor discerned it and briefly turned to
check what I was doing. I pretended not to notice any of it while the
Cuban never stopped talking either. "...Ah... Cuba... at some point,
I started dreaming of the place. But I kept it my secret. I probably
had an unconscious fear of being shut out by people once they knew
I was Cuban... The business world has a club mentality. It wasn't
until it became possible for Americans to go to Cuba that I had my
secretary prepare my travel documents, and my full identity was
revealed. Everybody was shocked. People kept making remarks. 'All
this time... you've been Cuban all along... and none of us knew?' I
worried they felt misled or betrayed."

I knew what the Cuban meant. These are familiar issues. Ironi-
cally, I was also keeping my Caribbean identity a secret while he was
divulging his. Yet, being near a fellow Caribbean made me happy.
Perhaps the Cuban sensed my excitement, and it puzzled him, causing
a singular interplay to start between us.

* * *

"TAP! TAP!" The sudden sound on my table gave me a jolt, and I
turned around. The little girl had tapped twice, and her eyes caught
mine before she rushed back to her mother onto whose lap she quickly
climbed. She was sitting opposite me, like the Cuban was, but to the
left, with her red velour pants, laced-up shoes and gray socks, and no
shirt in spite of the winter. She appeared a happy, rosy-skinned, well-
fed child.

I had been spotted, and the girl wanted me to see and play with
her, too, without pretense to the contrary, the game she noticed me
playing with the man to my right.

But then, sitting on her mother's lap, red pants hanging haphazardly beneath her belly button and also low enough to expose on
her backside an inch of the crack in her bottom, the child turned to
her mother for a kiss. Then the girl grew quiet and self-conscious.
She stopped balancing her feet, puckered her lips and slowly tasted
the chocolate from her spoon. She siphoned the liquid noisily while
scratching her belly. Seeing this made me thoughtful. *My mother*

wasn't one on whose lap a child could sit, I reflected. *A nursemaid fed me, bathed me, soaped me with a cloth, rinsed and dried me, wrapping me in a towel, her skin avoiding mine.*

While I still wanted to eavesdrop on the men's stories to my right, I could not tear myself away from the child. She lightly fingered a soiled, crumpled napkin and kept glancing furtively at me.

"Tess!" The child turned around to look at her mother, who held her cell phone like a camera and wanted her attention. *She's jealous,* I thought.

* * *

THE STORY OF CHOCOLATE is connected to thousands of little girls, mothers, friends, lovers, old men and lonely old ladies. But chocolate also has its own story.

Delight in drinking cocoa had also been the Mayan's in 600 AD as it was now in that child sitting next to me. Then, the Aztecs took it from the Mayans in the fourteenth century. The Spanish explorer, Hernando Cortez, recorded the use of cacao in the Aztec court of Emperor Montezuma. Cacao beans were even used as currency. Four cacao beans could buy an Aztec a rabbit.

Irony had it that a Haitian and a Cuban were sitting side by side in a chocolate shop in Massachusetts. We were West Indian immigrants, both of us descendants from populations once enslaved and exploited by Spanish and French colonizers driven by their greed for cacao, and the wealth they could amass from it. Cacao was gold.

Many Africans see it now as an icon of the torture inflicted for centuries on people enslaved for its cultivation. Cacao in the Caribbean was then for Western colonizers what oil in the Middle East now represents for the modern Western world. Cacao drove the politics of nations the way oil now does. Some history books state that chocolate was discovered in Haiti.

I was charmed by the child's oblivion of the history behind this cup of hot chocolate that she sipped delicately and for which so much blood had been shed. I smiled further as I suddenly remembered reading that chocolate was introduced to the United States in 1765 by an Irishman who imported it from the Caribbean into Dorchester, an area of Boston only a few miles from where I was sitting—a Haitian eavesdropping on a Cuban, both of us drinking hot cocoa.

My sister has loved chocolate more than anyone I know. I couldn't help thinking of her with a sharp pang. I imagined Europa sitting here with me and how delight would fill her face with a child-like glee, eyes strangely aglow with disbelief that such exquisite plea-sure could exist, and she be allowed to have a share in it. Yet choco-late was the cause of the last conflict between us.

Our Alaskan cruise was over, and Europa was supposed to be packing her suitcase to return to Haiti. I entered her room to help. "I don't need help. Leave me be." Yet the suitcase was on the floor, open and empty. Clothes were strewn all around, along with bags within bags, holding nothing. "And don't touch anything. I know how to pack." We had bought new clothes for Europa during the trip to replace all the worn and faded ones with which she had traveled. Yet things were spread around in undifferentiated piles. Evidently, every-thing was precious. Yet the suitcase would never contain it all. Europa needed to sort things out. Still, she obviously could not bring herself to throw anything away, or leave anything behind, even her collection of empty plastic bags, those that had contained things we bought for her along the way. Some of them were visibly stuffed in corners of her suitcase. It was sadly evident that Europa did not want to go home. Remembering this moment now makes me think of Charlotte being reclaimed, dragged out of my mother's garden, returned to the life of a Haitian pig in the slums, abused and preyed over, if not killed for her meat right away.

I left the room, returning an hour later. The suitcase was com-pletely full, yet half the things remained on the floor. Several half-eaten bars of different flavors of chocolate laid on top of the clothes, one of which was her favorite since childhood, a large size Toblerone we had put by the bed in her hotel room before she arrived from Haiti. She ate it with parsimony all during the trip, never offering any of it, and still, lo and behold, a little was left. All the chocolate wrappings were torn and loose. I could not help but warn her, "Europa, all this chocolate's going to ruin your clothes. The heat in the Haiti airport will melt it in no time. You'll have a mess in your suitcase. Even if you wrap it all in one of those plastic bags, it'll be chocolate soup that you'll find when you unpack at home." "Get out," Europa said between her teeth. "You always have to make me feel I'm an idiot. Just like when we were kids. You haven't changed a bit."

I was slumped on my bed afterward, looking at the floor, when I unexpectedly noticed Europa's toes facing mine. Europa's unmistakable, lovely long toes with overgrown toenails, chipped and dirty. One never heard my sister enter or leave a room. She was either suddenly there or suddenly gone. I looked up. She had tears in her eyes. "I've been meaning to tell you," she said, "that I saw my new child in a vision the other night. I wasn't asleep. It's a girl this time. The two of us were in a landscape with soft outlines. Everything was blue, even the trees. She was waving to me in the distance. She stood near a river. Then she motioned for me to come to her... then it all vanished... but now I know... I see it all clearly... I want you to be her godmother and even though you already are her aunt. And I want her to have your name... that way, you'll have a chance at being a mother too... she can succeed you... she'll have two mothers. Alone, I'll never be enough."

* * *

"...GUANTANAMO..." The name jolted my consciousness back to Cuba and to the men on my right. This time, the blue-eyed man was talking. Reflected in the mirror, I saw how his face lit up with a smile while he reminisced. "I was a young man in the army, stationed in Guantanamo," he was saying. "I was excited. For a Polish immigrant kid who grew up in Brooklyn, Cuba was exotic. Just imagine what it meant. I'd read a lot about Guantanamo. I learned how it was the oldest overseas US naval base. It was leased from the Cuban government in 1903 to be used as a fueling station."

While the blue-eyed Brooklyn man talked, my own mind went back to the time of my adolescence in Haiti when I had befriended a boy whose father was a US embassy consul. His mother made regular trips to the Guantanamo base to shop at the PX, and she described the base as a semi-arid desert with terribly hot temperatures. But the PX was air-conditioned, and so were the Subway, Pizza Hut, Taco Bell, McDonald's and Breyers Ice Cream establishments. Guantanamo has since then always been part of my consciousness. With the influx of Haitian refugees to the US in 1990, the word "Guantanamo" was constantly heard out of the lips of Haitians.

All the while, my thoughts roamed inside my head. The Cuban was listening attentively to his friend and shaking his head in disbelief. "Guantanamo... a fueling station?" he mumbled. "How strange. I spent so many years trying to forget that I was Cuban, and now it seems that I've everything to learn and feel about it."

"Oh, but the Cuban government's been opposing the presence of the US in Guantanamo," the Brooklyn man said. "They claim it's invalid under international law. But, of course, the US keeps saying that it's valid."

The Cuban squirmed on his stool. "But more than a fueling station, wasn't it the detention camp for Haitian boat people?"

"For a while... But the camp was eventually declared unconstitutional in 1995. Haitians picked up on illegal boats were no longer detained there... it was also a detention camp for Cuban refugees."

"I heard that," the Cuban said, his voice cracking. "It's a prison now, right?"

The Brooklyn man was quick to reply, "Of course. Its use as a prison since 2002 is more for Afghan and Iraqi prisoners tagged as 'unlawful combatants.' The present-day Guantanamo Bay Detention Camp isn't the Guantanamo I knew. I was there much earlier. They call it Camp X-ray now."

It was my turn to squirm on my bench and remember. I thought, Cuba's Camp X-ray and Haiti's Fort Dimanche! Horror dungeons... both American soldiers and Haitian Tontons Macoutes behaved like Nazis, Peronists, conquistadors, crusaders... But the Cuban interrupted my thoughts. "What did the Guantanamo base look like?" he asked.

The Brooklyn man's answer was precise. "What the US originally leased was forty-five square miles of land and water at Guantanamo Bay on the southeastern end of Cuba."

"Wow! That much land..." The Cuban became silent for a few seconds, and then asked, "Did you know that Guantanamo's a Taino Indian name?"

Yes, I do! I thought to myself. *Taino Indians were Haiti's indigenous population as well.* My mind was racing, and I wanted to tell them *Haïti's a Taino word. It means Mountainous Land. Christopher Columbus discovered Haiti in 1492 and renamed it Hispaniola... The Spaniards enslaved the Tainos of Haiti and decimated the whole population through their cruelty and the diseases they brought... When Haiti was taken from the Spaniards by the French in 1697, African slaves took the place of the former Taino population.*

The Cuban's friend seemed not to have heard his question about Cuba's Taino name and was looking in a vague distance. "I was in Guantanamo at the time of the 'Cactus Curtain,'" he finally said, in a confiding tone.

The Cuban shifted uncomfortably on his seat, took his cup, held it briefly and then put it back down without drinking from it. "What can you tell me about that?" he asked.

"The Cactus Curtain was the name given for the line that separated the US naval base from the Cuban-controlled territory... Cuban troops planted an eight-mile-long barrier of Opuntia cactus along the northeastern section of the seventeen-mile fence surrounding the base. They wanted to stop Cubans defecting from Cuba to the US."

The Cuban frowned, eyes narrowing. "What year was that?"

"1961. Man... I was so young."

The Cuban laughed nervously.

"But that wasn't all," the Brooklyn man went on saying. "Afterwards, both US and Cuban troops placed some fifty-five thousand land mines across the perimeter of the no-man's-land and around the perimeter of the naval base. This was the largest minefield in the Western hemisphere."

The Cuban inhaled deeply.

"But I assure you, they're no longer there. President Clinton ordered the removal of mines in 1996."

"It still lasted thirty-five years!" The Cuban exclaimed.

The Brooklyn man relaxed. "You must understand that Cubans didn't want their own people to vacate Cuba any more than the Americans wanted them to enter the US"

The Cuban looked uncomfortable. "Was the minefield effective?"

"Yes and no. After the Cuban revolution, some Cubans were desperate enough to try anything so they could take refuge on the US naval base, because, once they got there, if they got there, they could claim political asylum. Once they reached the naval base, they were welcomed and protected. So, regardless of the mines, people by the dozens took the risk... Some made it, some got blown up."

"*Cabron!*" the Cuban cried out, banging his fist on the table. He then apologized for his outburst. "Sorry... It's not you I am calling a 'bastard'... it's just an expression."

His friend nodded. "It was indeed hard to witness... even at a distance... but we were ordered by our superior officers not to watch the minefield anyway. You see, both the US and the Cuban sides had guard towers. The Cuban guards were watching the US guards with binoculars more than they were watching their own side of the minefield. They could guess from the angle or movement of a US guard's face and eyes if he'd detected someone crossing. Cubans shot many of their own escapees this way... So the US guards were asked to look in the other direction if they perceived or even sensed a body in the dark, and wait until that person got to the base... It was very emotional when people made it."

The Cuban made a sad smile. "But what a way to be separated from your family. Your mother or brother blown to bits right next to you!"

The Brooklyn man relaxed his shoulders and sat back. "That's why Clinton had them removed... The mines were replaced by motion-and-sound sensors."

"That's wonderful to hear."

"Yes. But the Cuban government hasn't removed its corresponding minefield outside the perimeter."

The Cuban scratched the back of his neck and then fidgeted with his shirt collar. "Was Cuba your only experience in the military?" he asked.

"No," the Brooklyn man said, suddenly looking pensive.

"Where else did you go then?"

"I was at Abu Ghraib."

"Iraq?"

"Yes."

"Wow. That must've been hard."

The Brooklyn man bent forward so he could speak softly and avoid being overheard. "The public only heard about the worst actions... If those photographs hadn't leaked, we would've thought of Abu Ghraib only as a US effort to protect America from terrorism, whether Iraqi, Al Qaeda, Taliban and the rest. We didn't create Abu Ghraib. We took it over once we occupied Iraq."

"In 2003, yes?"

"Yes. The army was given ninety days to reopen the prison. They requested assistance. What they got were a bunch of young MPs who'd had no training for being prison guards... Sadam Hussein's face was painted on walls all over the prison. Thirty-thousand people are presumed to have been tortured there by Sadam's army... killed and buried right there."

The Cuban put his hands under his haunches and said somberly, "A haunted place for sure..."

"Yes... 'The Ghosts of Abu Ghraib' is a documentary made about it, but it details the period after the US army took over... The title's appropriate, but these young, unqualified, untrained MPs-turned-prison-guards were given power they weren't emotionally equipped to handle."

The Cuban smirked. "What do you mean *not equipped?*"

The Brooklyn man looked around him uncomfortably and contracted his large shoulders. "I mean they'd been ordered to put their weapons away and yet they had to guard people tagged as dangerous and unlawful combatants… people they were sure would gladly have killed them the first chance they got… understand they were unsophisticated young Americans with no sense of political and cultural subtleties who were suddenly given power over people they mistrusted, despised and feared… There were only 300 personnel to watch over thousands of prisoners. The initial space Sadam Hussein created was for a thousand prisoners, and it quickly grew to have three thousand and more. So, of course, cells were cramped, and makeshift cells were created haphazardly… The security of America was on the army's mind, and certainly not the comfort of prisoners."

The Cuban appeared more at ease to talk about Abu Ghraib than he did about Guantanamo and seemed eager to know more. "Didn't *60 Minutes* do a show about Abu Ghraib around 2004?" he asked, digging a hand in his left pocket and jiggling things in it. "I saw that show. It seemed they didn't talk so much about the ignorance and lack of sophistication of the guards to explain the torture of prisoners… I think they argued the blame rests on the politically sophisticated army and the upper echelons of government, those being the very people who later tried to do a cover-up of their own actions and place responsibility on the MPs of the night shift… It's the guards who were prosecuted for taking pictures illegally and exposing the whole mess. The interrogators themselves weren't prosecuted for killing prisoners under torture."

"I agree it's all impossible to justify," the Brooklyn man said, sitting back and resting his head on the wall. "One can only try to understand… America was in a panic after 9-11. The State Department was in a panic. The military intelligence was in a panic. The young MPs were in a panic… The whole issue was how to fight an enemy you don't know and can't even see… The answer at the time was to interrogate enough people so that you eventually end up with some intelligence."

The Cuban scoffed, leaning forward, "You mean by a kind of law of averages?"

"Well, yes… You must understand that Abu Ghraib was mortared and attacked every day. The road in front of Abu Ghraib was the most dangerous in the world at the time. Skeletons of exploded tanks and burnt corpses lay along the street... The devil had gotten control of the stage."

The Cuban brushed his hair back with both hands and blurted out, "Was it also the devil that got control of Guantanamo and wouldn't leave Cuban territory to Cubans?"

The Brooklyn man scratched his throat and shuffled his feet nervously. "I know what you're getting at," he said, "but I'm not talking about international politics here. I'm not trying to justify the big players in the world economy. I'm only talking about the psychology of the people at the mercy of those big players... all the young MPs who grew up in the safety of American suburbia for the most part and had to harden themselves to the daily horror they witnessed... People became aggressive, even sadistic, as a reaction to the fear in their gut all day long and their anger against terrorists. Unconscious tendencies normally kept under check by upbringing or by society had gotten loose and out of hand."

"You mean the savage in us was let loose?" the Cuban said, straightening his back. He stretched his arms and inhaled deeply before responding, looking doubtful. "But it seems it wasn't just the distorted emotions of fragile young MPs that were at play here, was it? Weren't MPs given specific orders on how to prepare prisoners for interrogation? It seems they outdid themselves at the task... so-called preparations involved solitary confinement, no bed, no blanket, no sleep, no rest, no food, repeated showers while blindfolded and sustained sensory deprivation with hoods over their heads for hours or days on end... Americans became the kind of enemies they themselves hated... a foreign people one couldn't see and whose identity one knew nothing about."

The Brooklyn man nodded, looking down. "That's also true," he said.

The Cuban shifted on his seat. "I can't even imagine how vulnerable, humiliated and frightened these prisoners must've felt. I mean, they were forced out of their homes and arrested indiscriminately. And while in prison, they were insulted and tortured by people they couldn't see and in a variety of ignoble ways... electrocuted, raped, forced to masturbate, themselves or others, piled on top of each other in a pyramid, not knowing who was on top, who was under... all the while hearing dogs growling near their faces or their genitals... Come on, the world has seen the photographs. And, tell me, how did poorly trained guards, if they were truly left to their own devices and their fears as you say, how'd they come up with methods of torture known to have first been implemented in Guantanamo and also used by the Brazilian military? Tell me that." The Cuban at that point leaned forward and put a hand on his friend's wrist. "Tell me... How can one claim the young MPs invented methods of torture that were already known and used?"

The Cuban's friend did not move his arm away but closed his eyes, smiling sadly. "It's a good question... But, do you know that tests have shown that even mature, middle-aged men will inflict unbearable pain on others if they feel the orders come from a so-called legitimate authority?... Soldiers admitted they went numb..."

"Did you witness people being tortured when you were at Abu Ghraib?" The Cuban interrupted. "Did you?"

The friend opened his blue eyes and said calmly, "I witnessed interrogations, not tortures... But I did know about them."

The Cuban looked his friend in the eyes while pointing an index finger on the table. "Didn't America sign the Geneva Convention that prohibits torture in 1949?"

The Brooklyn man held the Cuban's gaze. He seemed at peace. "Yes. But Al Qaeda didn't. They followed no rules, they took no prisoners, they kidnapped people and executed them... In 2002, President Bush said that Geneva Convention rules no longer applied to the war against terrorism in the Middle East. Rules of interrogation changed. Torture was re-defined... What's suffering? What's physical injury? Under the new definitions, what Sadam himself had done in Abu Ghraib wouldn't have qualified as torture."

The Cuban looked at his friend quietly for a short while as if trying to find words, finally saying, "In Abu Ghraib, a man died under torture behind a white sheet that interrogators had hung in front of his cell so that inmates on the other side couldn't watch. But he could be heard… One of his friends later said in an interview that they listened as his soul cracked."

Aimé Césaire should've heard this, I thought, both horrified and mesmerized by the conversation I eavesdropped on. *Césaire may have died still a Frenchman,* I thought again, *his beloved Martinique still a colony in spite of the Negritude movement, but his analysis of colonialism and the hegemony of the white world all over the planet after WWII still holds… torture prisons and all… Césaire is still as relevant today as he was then… he'd say it was deep racism going on in Guantanamo and Abu Ghraib, and even in Fort Dimanche, even if it wasn't Americans doing it…But Duvalier learnt his methods of population control from them… the American occupation of Haiti lasted nineteen years… he was a child when they arrived and a grown man when they left… that little country doctor was filled with renewed black self-hatred started from colonial times… It's all there again in Guantanamo, Abu Ghraib and Fort Dimanche… greed for power and wealth… capitalist societies justifying imperialist aims and hiding behind notions of national security… who knows what new forms and targets imperialism will take in the future and what masks it will use?… colonialism hid behind Christian ideals as well… let's blame God for what we do to each other in his name… the Christian crusades, it's all imperialism… Césaire wasn't wrong when he blamed Europe for Hitler… it created its own demon… Hitler learnt from European colonialism what Duvalier learnt from Americans… the first concentration camp was created in Namibia by German colonists… Nazism was nothing but a new form of colonialist wars… it was okay as long as it was done to Africans, Arabs or Indians… savages… Hitler stepped out of bounds by doing it to white people… the humiliation of the white man, that wasn't okay… Césaire was right, Hitler's our own demon… MPs in Abu Ghraib behaved like Nazis… Ah…* I was about to leave in sadness and disgust when I heard the Brooklyn man say something that made me curious all over again.

* * *

"I SAVED ONE MAN'S LIFE," the Brooklyn man said in reply to the Cuban. "Yusef's voice in Abu Ghraib is what I hear at night when I'm alone under a white sheet."

"Yusef?" The Cuban asked, smiling. "Who's he?"

"He'd been a chemistry teacher. With the war going on, and after, he more or less sustained his family by selling cigarettes in the streets. One day, he tried to sell me some. He was friendly. I didn't feel hatred from him, not even fear. I liked him. We struck up a conversation. He told me his name and asked for mine.

"And then, later on, I was walking with MPs in a hallway at Abu Ghraib. I heard my name, Steven! Steven! There was joy and urgency in that sound and hope too. I stopped walking and turned towards the voice.

"Yusef was gripping the iron bars of his cell with both hands. He cried, 'It is me. Yusef. I sold you cigarettes. We spoke. You told me your name. Remember? We are friends… we are friends. You liberated my country. We are friends!' And then, one MP hit Yusef's hands with his stick and ordered him to retreat to the back of the cell. Yusef persisted, taking the pain. He was repeating the same things over and over with extreme anxiety. 'It is me, Yusef. We talked on the street! We are friends!' I hadn't recognized him at first, but slowly I did. I told the MP to stop hitting him. Finally, I said, 'I remember you Yusef. How did you get here?' He said that men came in the middle of the night. Neighbors lied about him. They said he was a Sadam supporter, like his brother-in-law. They said he was hiding him. Yusef admitted it was true what they said about his brother-in-law. But he kept insisting, 'I am not like him. I do not know where he is. My brother-in-law would not hide himself in my house. His wife is my sister, my daughter is his niece. He would not put them in danger to protect himself. Please, Steven. I am innocent.'

"I told Yusef I'd look into it. And I did. Then I went to talk to him. He wasn't in his cell. One MP admitted that Yusef had been under interrogation since I spoke with him. They thought that he made friends with Americans so he could spy. They reported him. I asked them where they'd taken him.

"I found Yusef standing on a box wide enough for only two feet to rest, naked but for the black hood over his head, his hands tied behind his back. I ordered the men to help him down from there, untie him and get him his clothes."

"Wow!" The Cuban exclaimed. "You must've been some kind of high-ranking officer to be able to give orders in that place."

"Yes. I was. Anyway, Yusef heard me speak to the men, and he cried out, 'Steven! I know your voice! Inshallah! You are here!'

"It's only when Yusef had been able to dress himself that I told the men to remove his hood. I didn't want him to be naked when we faced each other. With his clothes on, Yusef stood straighter. Tears ran down his eyes. He said thank you repeatedly. 'Thank you, Steven. Inshallah! God bless you!' His eyes were red, his cheeks pale and sallow.

"I asked him if he was hungry. And yes, he was. 'Bless you', he said again. He'd had no food since I'd seen him in the cell.

"I last saw Yusef the very next morning. I'd arranged for a helicopter to take him back to the city and to his family. Yusef stood in the yard of Abu Ghraib, dressed in clothes that had become too big for him. His hands were tied behind his back. His eyes were bandaged with a black cloth. He could hear the helicopter, but he didn't know where he was and why he was there.

"I must also tell you about the stench at Abu Ghraib, from feces, urine, detritus, who knows, perhaps gas from corpses still decomposing. Human misery leaves a stench. Someone described Abu Ghraib as a desert bowl of misery. Yusef was standing in the middle of it all, bent, shrunken.

"I told the men to remove Yusef's bandage briefly, and I saw that tears were streaming silently through eyes he still kept shut tight. I told him, 'Yusef, have no fear. No harm will come to you any longer. This helicopter, these men, they will take you home. I'll come along, but you can't leave here without your eyes being bandaged. It's a security measure. You mustn't see Abu Ghraib from above and be able to describe it. They'll take the bandage away before we come down in the city.'

"Yusef then opened his eyes but said nothing at first. Tears began to flow more heavily when he spoke. And he exclaimed, 'Steven! Allah sent you to save me! I knew it when I saw you. I recognized you right away. I knew that you would take me out of here. It's happening as I thought, and still, I cannot believe it. Thank you! May Allah bless you always!'

"The image of Yusef that I've forever in my mind is the one of him sitting inside the helicopter with his legs close together, shoulders relaxed, eyes bandaged, smiling, praying, thanking God, his voice mixed with the noise of the chopper's helices. I can't tell you how many times I heard Yusef praise Allah during that short ride to take him home."

* * *

I DECIDED TO LEAVE. I'd had enough. Human suffering and acts of courage felt overwhelming. Images of violence and misery I witnessed in Haiti were flooding my mind. I put the book about Sanapia in my backpack and zipped it shut. On an impulse, before getting up, I leaned forward towards the men. "I want to thank you for your courtesy in letting me eavesdrop on your conversation," I said with a smile. "I heard the name Cuba. I couldn't resist. I'm also a Caribbean."

The men smiled. "Where in the Caribbean?" they asked simultaneously.

"Haiti."

"I would never have guessed!" the Cuban exclaimed with a grin.

I shook my head, "No one does. I stopped telling people I'm from Haiti, so I don't have to argue my identity or prove it." The Cuban chuckled but said nothing. "When I speak Creole with Haitian taxi drivers in Cambridge, they assume that I'm a missionary who went to Haiti. I don't tell them otherwise because the minute I tell them I lose my humanity."

The Brooklyn man looked puzzled. "What do you mean?"

"Because of my skin color, I'm immediately associated with the resented mulatto class of Haiti, and people's demeanor towards me switches instantly."

"That's sad…" the Cuban said.

"No. It's just a reality. It's like you not telling the bankers that you're Cuban."

He smiled.

The Brooklyn man cleared his throat. "How did you come to this country? Were you one of the boat people?"

"No."

"I didn't think so."

"I'm not the prototypical Haitian you used to meet in Guantanamo. I came here to study anthropology at university."

"Nice. What do you do now?"

"I'm a writer. I'm also a painter."

"What do you write about?" The Cuban asked.

"What we're talking about. What it's like to be a Caribbean inside and outside of the Caribbean. How to stand with one foot here and the other somewhere else. How to belong while my identity is defined by a series of negations. My accent, the way I move, dress, react. Everything I am reveals what I'm not."

The Cuban laughed softly and sat straighter. "I'm also trying to write. I don't want to be a banker anymore. People where I worked knew me as John. Now I'm Juan again, the name my parents gave me. I started a novel. When I went to Cuba, people refused to take me for Cuban. Yet I've this dark complexion you can see, hair on the chest and arms. I think I look Cuban, but they don't see it. And when I speak Spanish, forget it. I lost my Cuban accent in Spain years ago. Even if I don't say anything, they still don't recognize me. It must be what you say. I've been gone a long time. I must've picked up other ways of moving, other gestures. And when they see my daughter next to me with her white skin, straight blond hair, green eyes, then I'm done for."

"Cuban men must go wild over her!" I blurted out. And out of embarrassment, I quickly mumbled, "I mean… opposites attract, don't they?"

"My wife's a very pale-skinned American blond," he started to explain, and then caught himself, "but, let me introduce myself. I'm Juan."

"And I'm Steven," the Brooklyn man said, offering his hand, "What's your name?"

"Io."

"An unusual name," Juan said with a charming smile.

I was slightly embarrassed by the sudden attention to me and so tried to shift their focus back to Juan's family. "Is your daughter your only child?" I asked.

"I've a son too. Actually, it's the four of us who went to Cuba. Me, my wife, my son and my daughter. Before that trip, all my son knew is that he's this white kid from Concord, Massachusetts, and we go to Martha's Vineyard every summer. I tell him, You're not white. Wait until we go to Cuba, and I take you to our hometown where my grandfather was mayor. And so, we get there, to my hometown, a little, bitty, lost, nobody of a town, and I feel at home like I'd forgotten what it's like. Houses are run down. Termites, poverty and neglect have been eating at them for decades. Streets are dusty, deserted, pot-holed. The asphalt is on the verge of fossilization. The town square's vacant. Shadows on the ground from a couple of coconut trees stretch themselves across the yellow grass and street. They made me think of chalk marks from a prisoner counting days in his cell."

"How did your son react?"

"In Havana, I wasn't Cuban, and my son wasn't Cuban either. But, once I stood in my hometown, all was different. The first old guy I bump into asks me who am I? What do you want? I felt so happy that someone actually saw me and talked to me. I told him my name and why I was there. He was stunned. He asked, Arenas? Your name is *Arenas*? You must be the grandson of... and right there and then, in front of my son whose jaw had dropped, this old man tells us my family's entire genealogy and history. He wraps his arms around my shoulders and leads me inside a bar, with my son, my daughter and my wife following. I felt like my childhood and ancestry had come to reclaim me. I was beaming like an idiot. That joy I felt had started even on the plane. I wasn't the only Cuban going home. Once we saw the island, we were one weepy mass of people crying. Cuba! Cuba! Ah... I tell you... that was something else."

"You should read the *Oxford Book of Caribbean Short Stories*," I said to Juan. "You'll discover how much you actually belong. You'll see how much your issues are issues of Caribbean identity. You speak of your delight at being *seen* in your hometown and recognized too. I know these feelings well. I walk in the streets of America every day. I'm not seen. But I've learnt how to feel that I exist because *I* see, not because I'm seen. And still, I'll never forget being back in Haiti and dining at a familiar tennis club. My family were all members of that club. I recognized an elderly gentleman who'd been a friend of my father's. I went to pay my respects. He was ecstatic. He said, You're Io? Victor's daughter? How well I remember your father! What a good friend he was! And then he leaned over and asked me what happened to Rose, my father's sister. He said she was a beautiful Rose. He danced with her at the Choucoune's dance floor on many occasions. He knew my grandparents and even my great-grandmother. He thought she was a delightful woman, remembered her as a passionate bridge player gracious enough to let her guests win. Oh, but do sit down with us, he said. Child, meeting you takes me back to the days of my youth! But tell me, where's Rose now? He kept bringing up my aunt Rose. This old man pulled me the way you, Juan, were pulled into the town bar. I was pulled to the heart of my family's past. I was suddenly cocooned with such genuine interest in my being that I wondered why on earth I'd ever left and was there any meaning to the pain of separation while it might've been so much easier to stay. Read those stories, Juan, and you'll see how not belonging's also a way of being Caribbean. Migration's at the root of Caribbean life and identity as is its blue-suede sea."

"Blue suede?" Steven was startled.

I laughed. "Oh, never mind that. But tell us, Steven, where'd you grow up? I fantasize about how it must feel to live in one's birth country, having physical and human connections that go way back."

"It may sound strange," Steven said, "but I don't have any greater sense of belonging than the two of you have. I grew up in Brooklyn in the 1950s. It was like a war zone. We were immigrant kids from various ethnic backgrounds fighting each other, mocking each other, different gangs stabbing at each other for one more yard of sidewalk space. My mother was Polish, my father, a Swede. But my mother never let her kids be racists. She never forgot how it was when her parents came to this country, and only black people were kind to her family and showed them how to survive in America. I went to the army as a very young man. Everywhere I was stationed pretty much felt like the war zone I'd known in Brooklyn. But I'm no longer in the army. I'm a psychology professor. Really glad to be out of the army. In fact, Juan and I just met at a conference."

Juan then said, "This may also sound strange now, but while I just told you about feelings of belonging in Cuba that were roused in me, Cuba again now feels far. It's here that I feel I belong. And I don't feel foreign in any way with the three of us together. Every part of me is understood, recognized, at ease. I don't have to explain myself."

Steven suddenly stood up, "I think we have to leave."

I then also noticed how two members of the staff were rolling up the red rug, bringing out mops and buckets of water. How late it had gotten while we chatted.

The cold outside stunned my face.

Steven was blowing warm breath on his gloveless hands. "Juan, you've to invite Io to your party on Saturday."

Juan smiled but said nothing.

I noticed Juan's silence and tried to cover it up. "Don't they make here the best cup of hot chocolate you've ever had?" I said, changing the subject.

"Oh, yes!" Juan quickly said, grabbing at the chance to evade Steven's question.

I thought, *he's probably worried about his wife's reaction at some Caribbean Chiquita showing up at her house. The way this man winked at me and kept looking at me, he's probably a typical Caribbean man who's been a handful for his wife.* But all I said was, "It'd make an interesting story if I were to tell how the three of us met here tonight."

"What do you mean?" Juan was looking at me now.

"Haiti, Cuba, Brooklyn. Three war zones. Camp X-ray, Fort Dimanche, Abu Ghraib. Three torture prisons. All of that history held between the three of us. Such heavy material revealed over small cups of delicate, pungent, hot chocolate!"

Juan said, "Did you know that present-day production of Cacao in Cuba is in the Guantanamo region?"

Steven snickered. "What irony! Cacao and Camp X-ray, all in the same region."

Juan was talking and shifting his weight from one leg to the other, tapping his hands together to keep warm. "You'll be surprised to hear that cacao plantations in Guantanamo date back to the seventeenth century," he said. "It was this part of Cuba that became the center of cacao production because it was the landing place of the French when they traveled from Haiti."

Steven laughed. "So, it was the French's fueling place before it became America's?"

Juan gave Steven an odd look and said, "But it's Cortez the Spaniard who started to cultivate cacao in Haiti and all over the Caribbean."

"Absolutely!" I exclaimed. "But Haiti's production dwarfed all of them... even Venezuela's whose economy was dominated by cacao production for nearly 300 years."

Juan frowned. "How strange it is we meet in New England, talking and knowing so much about Cacao?"

Steven's face sobered as well. "If you ever write that story, I would love to read it. Let me give you my card. We can keep in touch."

"I have a card too!" I gave a card to Steven and another to Juan, who did not offer me one back. "About Saturday..." he started saying. But I interrupted him. I put my hand gently on his, "I wouldn't be able to come, Juan. I'm so sorry, my husband and I already have an engagement."

"You're married? What's your husband's name?"

"Thomas."

"Haitian?"

"English."

"Do you have children?" Steven asked.

"I don't."

"Any relatives from Haiti who live in America?"

"Yes. Some in Virginia. Others in Florida."
"Siblings?"

"I've had a sister who lived in Haiti."

"Had?"

"Yes. She died in childbirth, in a way. Not so long ago, actually. A little over a year ago."

"What happened?"

"Her child was stillborn. A little girl. My sister died the next day."

"Something went wrong with the birth?"

"No, besides the fact that the baby was not alive. We don't know why my sister died. My mother wouldn't allow an autopsy. She said she didn't want her child butchered, and an autopsy wouldn't bring her back. I agreed. I believe my sister died of a heartbreak. Her *soul cracked* like you said earlier about the man in Abu Ghraib who was tortured behind a white sheet."

"Oh, Io, I'm so sorry. What's her name?"

"Europa."

"Were you in Haiti at the time?"

"Come on, man," Juan interrupted. "Stop the questioning. Can't you see she's about to cry?"

"It's all right," I said. "Steven means well. And speaking helps. Pain shouldn't be kept secret. Isn't it pain that we just talked about? And wasn't it beneficial that these torture prisons were exposed to the world? It's good to examine pain going on in and around oneself... see what hand we had in it."

"I've got to go," Juan said. He looked uncomfortable. "We must say goodbye."

I sensed his unease and thought, *he's embarrassed to have confided in a total stranger. Now he feels exposed. He wants his image and safety mask back. Saul was right that day on Spencer's Island when he said to me that it's funny how where we come from is often where we wanna be rescued from... But can we ever be rescued?*

Yet all I said was, "It's been a pleasure to meet you both." We then shook hands with each other as only old friends do and parted forever.

V. The Love of Mothers

Io in the Year 2012...

IMAGINE A CHILD, an extra being in the plenitude of the world, a contented creature who slips out to the garden holding a gift from her mother. She walks in yellow flip-flops, the tip of her toes overhanging slightly, gathering dust. A white sheet from the hallway closet is tucked under her arm. She intends to spread it open over the freshly mowed grass where she will lie on her willowy back to watch the slow procession of white cumulus in the sky. Her body takes in the feel of the Caribbean light, the sea breeze coming from the Port-au-Prince bay, and sounds rushing in from nearby tropical birds.

She also carries memories in the mind that already define her sense of self and images that shape her idea of the world. These memories include the high ceilings of her parents' house, the garden areas where grass won't grow, the stairs that take you everywhere and nowhere, and where she imagines herself being an American Indian shooting arrows and running with imaginary friends.

She is still at that age when one does not question one's place in nature and in the world even while she overhears increasingly each day from her family numerous comments that articulate fears about a changing society. She listens to conversations about murders in the night, coups-d'états, dictators, hurricanes and ensuing floods, and the menace of earthquakes.

Yet the girl is filled with wonder. Her name is Io. I am Io.

Forty-odd years later, you find me tossed into the great American melting pot of nations. I have joined the hundreds of thousands of displaced people confounded daily by the whirling of disparate lives and dissimilar cultures, yet all of them living under one flag.

I have not escaped Haitian history. I have only joined another. Many of us who were dispersed have died, yet my family is enlarged. I have remarried. My husband's mother calls me Daughter.

Kin and kinsmen are nevertheless not the same. At the root of colonizing schemes, political or familial, there is a deep confusion, a claim that God's creatures need to be saved from their ignorance of an established order and higher good. We violate each other in God's name. We savage the savage.

* * *

THE FUSS OVER QUEEN IDIA is that the British stole her mask from the king of Benin and won't return it. And now that same mask has become a symbol of Pan-Africanism. I learnt about this sixteenth-century mask from a Nigerian I met at the Harvard Co-op Bookstore. Queen Idia's son had ordered the mask from an artist in honor of his mother's successful reign. These were glorious days of power, wealth and immense national pride about the history of Nigeria. Nowadays, however, the great-great-great-grandson of the Oba of Benin, the very king deposed by the British, is a taxi driver in Massachusetts who lives in Lynn. The British carted 3,000 artifacts from the Benin kingdom during their colonizing rule of Nigeria in the late nineteenth century and way into the twentieth.

I told Thomas this story and about my meeting a Nigerian called Freddy, how regal he looked when he walked on the mezzanine aisle of the bookstore with his cup of English Breakfast tea. Thomas was in a playful mood that day and said, "What kind of a Nigerian name is Freddy? A Nigerian name ought to be exotic, therefore rhythmic, multi-syllabic, impossible to pronounce or remember. Like a good old-fashioned Indian name used to be. Give me a name with allure, a phonetic thrill, a challenge to spell, defiant, extravagant, and impossibly over-the-top!"

"Thomas! Where do you get such notions?" I said, laughing in spite of myself.

"Silly me," Thomas replied with an exaggerated sigh. "What do you expect? I'm English. A Brit! I dress up with Verve! Verve is my own show of human lunacy, my grass skirt, my ankle bells."

"But Thomas, you should look up Queen Idia's mask on the Internet. It's a gorgeous work of art outside of the fact that Africans have turned it into a symbol of the African world struggle against colonialism. It's funny that I should have heard about it at a university bookstore where people of all nations move up and down the stairs. I see Native Americans, Mexicans, Chinese and Japanese, Irish and English and Israelis, not forgetting Haitians, and Pakistanis, and Indians, Nigerian survivors of the Biafran war as well as Ghanaians, Iraqis and Palestinians. All of us people who suffered some form of colonialism or imperialism at one point or another."

"Or still do," Thomas said. "But you know, I feel the same way you do at the bookstore when I'm conducting an orchestra, and I look at the faces of the musicians in front of me. Each one is unique in shape, color, features, and each one alludes to one race or another. It's like the entire world is gathered in front of me."

"The older I get," I remarked, "the more reverence I feel in front of every human being I meet. Each one of us is a separate, whole universe. And yet we are deeply interconnected. We're more intimately bound to each other than we can ever comprehend. We meet each other for a reason. It's not a coincidence. There's an invisible maestro watching. I'm sure of that."

Thomas embraced me, "You mean I'm not the only maestro in your life?"

"Oh, silly Thomas! But about us being all interconnected in a wild orchestra of color and shape, did you know that 500 Haitian free men of color helped Americans in the Revolutionary War? That time when they were trying to drive the British from Savannah?"

"Haitians were in on it against us too?" Thomas said, feigning upset. "How did that happen?"

"The siege happened in 1779. And a very bloody one. These Haitians were called the *Chasseurs-Volontaires de Saint-Domingue,* meaning the Volunteering-Huntsmen of Santo-Domingo. They were the largest unit of soldiers of African descent to fight in that war."

"Why *Saint-Domingue?*"

"Haiti was called Saint-Domingue at that time. It was still a French colony. The island was renamed only after the 1804 slave revolution."

"I've never heard of this!" Thomas showed real surprise.

"Well, you should've. It's not well known in the US I grant you that. Haiti's role in the American Revolution and its independence was a point of national pride for Haitians. There's now a monument dedicated to these *Chasseurs Volontaires* in Savannah."

"Who were these men?"

"Free men who volunteered, as their name tells you. They served as a reserve unit to American and French forces fighting the British. As battered American and French soldiers fell back, the Haitian troops moved in to provide a retreat. And what's more, after returning home from the war, Haitian veterans soon led their own rebellion that ended in 1804. That's how Haiti gained its independence from France."

"This is an amazing story!"

"Indeed. And remember I was telling you how the world's nations all come to the Harvard Co-op Bookstore? Well, the siege of Savannah itself showed the Revolutionary War to have been a world conflict more than any other engagement of the Revolution."

"How's that?"

"Number one, significant foreign resources of money and material contributed to the eventual success of the cause of American independence... Number two, there was the crucial importance of human resources... The quantity of foreigners who fought in the war was amazing. There were French, Poles, Native Americans, African slaves and free men of African descent, Germans and Hessians and Austrians, and then Scots, Welsh, Irish and English... and Swedes... and American and West Indian colonials. This battle was known to be the most culturally diverse of the whole war."

"What a wonderful thing, Io! And very moving too."

"Absolutely! This force made of men from many nations was assembled in three armies... They fought for six weeks for the possession of Savannah."

"Six weeks? That's quite a long battle!"

"Yes. And it left the largest number of casualties the allies suffered in a single engagement."

"Io, how come you know so much about this?"

"I looked it up on the Internet. Someone had sent me a group email about the Savannah monument."

"Ah... the great brain of the Internet..."

"And you know what else I found on the Internet?"

"What? Your father's lost signet ring?"

"Thomas! That's mean."

"Sorry... Sorry... I don't know how that came up... but tell me, what did you find?"

"While I was searching for information on Queen Idia, I stumbled upon an Ashanti queen."

"Who?" Thomas asked, showing a curious smile.

"An old queen mother whom the British imprisoned. This was in Ghana. The queen refused to wear clothes as a protest and to shame both the Ashanti men and the British. I saw a black and white photograph of the skinny, dignified crone, exposing her hanging old breasts... And she still looked regal."

"*Regal?*" Thomas frowned. "How's that possible?"

"And yet she was. Nudity was her weapon and shame its bullet. The Ashanti queen was a warrior queen. A woman accustomed to the use of weapons. She shamed the British by showing the world their abuse on an old woman and queen. They didn't look so civilized after this. Imagine how the British would feel if Queen Elizabeth was thrown in a Nigerian prison, and she protested by showing herself naked for the whole world to see."

"Yes, that's painful to imagine," Thomas said.

"I think the Ashanti queen wanted Ashanti men to feel shame as well. This was her way of making them realize their cowardice. How they allowed a mother, a grandmother, and their queen at that, to be imprisoned, dispossessed and demeaned."

"Indeed," Thomas murmured, bending his face. "That would be a great shame for me to see my mother like that and to have failed to defend her."

"And Thomas, also remember that the Ashanti were proud warriors. This must have been devastating. But you know…"

"What?"

"Queen Idia and the Ashanti queen were two different women and two different queens, even if they were both involved with colonialism."

"What do you mean?"

"The way I see it, one queen suffered from colonialism while the other inflicted it."

"Which did which?"

"I would say that the Ashanti queen suffered, and Queen Idia inflicted."

"That's debatable, Io. The Ashanti were involved in the slave trade at some point."

"Well, yes… But anyway, for the sake of my argument, let me say that Queen Idia's mask had been commissioned by her son, the king of Benin. He wished to honor her contribution to the power and enrichment of his reign. I read on the Internet that Queen Idia's wars of conquest had extended the ancient empire of Benin to unbelievable heights and wide geographical reach."

"Impressive woman!"

"For sure. But Queen Idia was a colonizer nonetheless… African people in the sixteenth century whose land and rivers she annexed couldn't have been any happier about that than were twentieth-century Nigerians about the British taking over their country… And look at the Taino Indians in Haiti. They mustn't have been happy either when Christopher Columbus came ashore from his three ships. *La Pinta*, *La Nina*, and *La Santa Maria*… And after Columbus received a warm welcome from the Indians, he killed some, imprisoned the rest, enslaved them, stole their land, and put them to work on it, until disease and hunger decimated the whole lot of them... And that's when they went looking for Africans to replace the Indians."

"Ah yes, it's all terribly awful," Thomas exclaimed, "but the table has turned now, hasn't it? Idia is now glorified for her colonialist wars. Her mask has become a symbol of pan-Africanism, and we rotten old Brits are recognized as thieves."

"Which they were," I said.

"Ah... the world is mad!"

"But Thomas, in all fairness, just because history recorded Idia's own colonizing acts, doesn't mean that the Ashanti queen mother never inflicted some form of abuse on her kin and kinsmen."

"I thought you said that the Ashanti *suffered*, and Idia *inflicted*?"

"Well, yes. But the Ashanti Queen's nudity was a powerful aggression besides also expressing her distress. It seems she would've had her sons die rather than dishonor her by staying alive under British rule. Where was the mother there?"

"Perhaps honor took precedence over all other considerations?" Thomas argued.

"So it seems. And perhaps queens and mothers, it's all the same? Mothers being, at times, a form of colonizing queens. If they are not able to colonize surrounding tribes and seize their land like Idia did, they colonize their children and appropriate their lives... All of us American children or foreigners strolling in the Harvard Co-op Bookstore, we're all runaways. It's not just me. Some form of violence lingers in our core. Colonization is all we knew."

* * *

I FOUND PEACE in reading the letter Thomas sent from England, and in knowing that he was home, walking again in the civilized world of his childhood. It was a world of arboretums planted with species saved from the slash and burn and havoc reaped in all their places of origin; species newly brought to a world of undeviating, tree-lined avenues and bridges adorned with streetlamps. Thomas is back in the place where he first developed dreams for his life, sipping tea with the mother who sat his old teddy bear on her living room's flowered couch.

"Dearest Love, I have not neglected you," he wrote to me. "Communication is difficult on the Blackberry, and Webmail is awkward to maneuver. Also, I am on a whirlwind tour. I want to make the most of my brief time here. I am keenly reminded how every moment is indeed precious. Last night, I stayed up until one o'clock talking with my uncle Eddy. He is also my godfather. He makes me feel that I matter. I got up at 8:30 this morning, tired, but feeling there was still much more to talk about. Later today, I will meet with my aunt Margot and her husband Peter for lunch. She wants me to follow them home afterwards. She wants to share family memorabilia and stories before she loses or forgets them. You know that she has no children. I seem to be designated as the family historian of my generation. Later, I will drive back to my mother's place, maybe a three-hour drive, and spend the night there. More family conversation awaits me. Already, on Thursday, my mother and I spent a jam-packed day of talking and catching up, all the while driving to familiar places that feed my soul in ways that only specific places can because of all they represent and contain. My long email to you on Friday (accidentally erased and lost) was my attempt to keep you involved. I did relay and describe to you my remarkable meeting with David W. earlier that day. I walked into his study and found two fortepianos and a library that is almost identical to mine. The two of us had a grand time together. He made lunch. We have ideas and history in common. We had a lovely conversation, and I shared with him my thoughts and vision of what I can do of significance in the world. Being in England reminds me of how large and hopeful I once felt. Everyone receives me with understanding and encouragement. You like to say how we need friends, should have as many as we can, and that some of our tasks are very demanding and we, therefore, require much support. It is unreasonable to expect it all from any one person. I am enjoying a renewed connection with England, especially with people of like mind and interests. I also want to keep track of what's going on with you. Thank you for copying me your various emails of interest, and for writing, and for loving."

* * *

"WE HAD THE EXPERIENCE but missed the meaning," I read in T. S. Eliot, "the past experience revived in the meaning is not the experience of one life only but of many generations." I mulled a long time over this sentence. Thomas was still away, and I was sitting alone at Burdick's, my favorite chocolate shop in Cambridge. I always felt that a writer must think in those same lines as T. S. Eliot describes, and analyze our existence with this constant level of sensitivity and awareness. We all should evaluate the meaning of our life experiences in relation to those of our parents and the generations before them, to see what behaviors we perpetuated to our benefit and that of others, or not, and examine what we learnt, or failed to learn.

I returned home mid-afternoon to find an email from Pierre, a childhood friend, now a psychoanalyst living in New York. Pierre's father committed suicide when he was a boy. Pierre's mother said that his father was on an extended trip to Europe in order to explain to him this sudden and lasting absence. In those days when he was a little boy, Pierre wore a lime green suit on Sundays. He grew attached to a tall, handsome black man he followed around the house, watching him do housework. Antoine was a faithful servant whom a spinster aunt of Pierre's tried to teach to read. His daytime domestic work done, Antoine would sit on a wooden bench every afternoon in the back courtyard, wearing his best clothes, smelling of Palmolive soap, ready for the lesson. He changed back to his old work clothes afterward to resume his early evening duties. Unable to learn, Antoine eventually became depressed and killed himself one Sunday in the windowless room he occupied. Returning from Mass with his family, the child in a lime green suit found his tall friend hanging from a rafter.

Pierre's emails are usually brief, cryptic, telegram-style. The new one had an atypical length that surprised me: "There is no excuse for my long silence," Pierre wrote, "but we are in a stupor. After all these trials, the latest is now a personal earthquake. Here is a family story: my brother and his wife were planning to visit. Her sister suddenly went mad. Seriously mad. She feels she is inhabited by huge snakes. This is happening right now in a suburb of Miami. A servant is blamed for the curse. One could laugh but only up to a point. Maybe there is a Haitian syndrome where every childhood, golden or not, is poisoned by a servant or some other person, all in a world of witches."

I responded to Pierre's letter right away, writing that, "on Sunday, August 22nd, 2010, at community gatherings around the United States, the Bahamas and Haiti, kites will be flown at 4:53 pm in commemoration of the January 12th earthquake to tell the world that Haiti is a country that will rise stronger than ever from the rubble and from its personal history of political, economic and social turmoil."

Pierre usually answers emails right away. Three hours after replying to him, I still had no response, so I became concerned. I called him on the telephone, taking the risk of disturbing the dinnertime with his family.

"A Vodou priestess with Alzheimer's," I heard Pierre say at the other end with no other form of hello. "Have you ever seen one?"

"Well, no, Pierre... why?"

"Manbo Zila's mind is gone. I found that out from the Haitian grapevine. Could it be that spirits took back their gifts?"

"I don't know. But why are you concerned about her?"

"I met her once. A powerful woman. Sharp as hell. Hard as a nail. But what I am really wondering about are the ways in which a person may lose her mind and go mad. Alzheimer's is a form of that."

"I agree."

"Perhaps that's the real death. The death of the body is no more than a perfunctory affair, like funerary arrangements that drag on because of some incompetence somewhere. What do you think of that?"

I laughed. "Your question takes me by surprise. My thoughts are not formed on the subject."

"I understand. My own thoughts are not formed yet either," Pierre said in a voice that seemed surprisingly far and distracted. But then his tone picked up fast, and he said in an almost cheerful way as if it were one run-on sentence, "In the meantime, her descendants have taken her place here in New York. They're all Americans now, fat and delighted at finding themselves hugely successful in the spiritual professions. And my advice to you, Io, is to check both sides of the streets before crossing over. And eat salt."

"Salt?"

"Yes, salt. Just think how *zonbi pa manje sèl.* Right? Remember how we grew up hearing this, and learnt that zombies don't eat salt? Well, evidently, salt is the antidote!"

"Would salt restore Manbo Zila?" I asked.

"Only if the Alzheimer's diagnosis is wrong. Do you think the diagnosis is wrong?" Pierre was giggling. "Could it be that it's not Alzheimer's Manbo Zila suffers from, but zombification instead?"

"That'd be quite a *coup-de-theatre!*" I exclaimed.

"I bet the family wouldn't like that one bit," Pierre said, laughing again. "I can see the headlines. The Revenge of the Zombies on the Vodou Priestess. Or, something like Zombifying the Old Zombifyer! Or, better yet, The Zombified Zombifyer."

"I like all three. But less is more, so maybe the third one's best?" I said, grinning. "It doesn't matter if the family likes it or not. Zila was a public figure. The world is involved in her affairs just as she involved herself in the affairs of others. Besides, it'll give them something to mull over before they mindlessly and greedily embark in her career. Either way, they won't escape her influence on their lives. There's no escaping family. Families are essential to who we are. Like it or not, we have to deal with that."

"You think so?"

"Thomas is in England for a family funeral right now. When he comes back, we'll be going to a family reunion of mine."

"Well, all I can say is good luck."

* * *

I MET THOMAS AT LOGAN AIRPORT. "How was London?" I asked. He showed me a photo of a London storefront sign on his cell phone as a form of answer. It read English, African, Asian and Indian

Groceries. "You see," Thomas said with a sigh, "London is not the city I knew. Home is no longer home. What was I hoping for anyway? Serves me right."

I took his hand, and we walked to the parking lot to get the car. As soon as we got to our apartment, I made him drop his luggage and led him to bed. We held each other while chatting. Our two cats were stretched belly up on the bed with us. This was their way of letting Thomas know how relieved they were that he was back. White and golden furs were blending with the colors of the quilt. Thomas remarked how time had dissolved for him at home in England. It was as if he had never left his city, in spite of the great changes he found there. He described the funeral. His already widowed cousin had asked him to walk with her behind her mother's coffin. At the funeral parlor, Sanskrit texts were read while the coffin rolled into the incinerator. Thomas kept sighing in between sentences as he talked. He recounted the lunch he had with his cousin before going to the airport. They looked at the river running below the restaurant's balcony. His cousin said with tears running silently down her cheeks, "When my husband died, all I wanted was to jump in the river... be gone with him..."

"Thomas, why does this make me think of my adolescence? It must be the mention of water and being immersed. I used to snorkel in the sea at Montrouis. It's a stretch of beach near Port-au-Prince. I spent entire afternoons of my adolescence teasing sea anemones."

"Sea anemones? What kind?"

"I don't know their name. They display a circular fan at the top end of a hollow tubular stem. The anemone pulls its fan into the stem the second you come near. The fan goes inside the stem so fast that you don't even have a chance to touch it ever so slightly. I tried again and again. The fan remains hidden until the anemone relaxes and lets it out and spreads it open. There was a long strip of them that ran along the shore of my uncle's beach house."

Thomas laughed. "You were not *teasing* them. You were torturing them," he said. "And speaking of torture, I heard a BBC World Service interview of a liberal English Imam and the vice-president of the Muslim Student Federation of the UK. A young woman student had come out publicly to admit she'd been brainwashed into violent Muslim extremism at an English university. She'd seen videos and other propaganda that showed the West committing terrible acts against Muslims, including acts of torture. She confessed that she was so angry that she wanted to be the first woman suicide-bomber in England. The Imam then criticized the student organization during the BBC interview. He called them Right-Wing Fundamentalist Muslims who espouse Wahabi theology."

I snuggled closer to Thomas. "What's *Wahabi?*"

"Apparently, Wahabi is a theology that regards women as distinctly second-class. The Imam argued that some of the Muslim treatment of women, including the wearing of the veil, all stem from tribal customs that are not Koranic. He claimed that women were highly regarded in the early days of Islam. They were integrated as leaders and teachers. But now, various splinter groups, such as the Wahabi, are more tribal in their customs."

* * *

"A PARTING SHOT," Thomas burst out, "a bomb! A pernicious, poisoned, many-layered explosive! That's what your aunt Rose dropped in your lap!"

"Serves me right, too, in a way…" I said with sadness.

Thomas and I were sitting on a plane flying back to Boston from Florida, where we had gone immediately after Thomas's return from England. My Aunt Rose, my father's sister, had turned ninety. The family reunion was at her daughter's Sara.

Even eighty-nine-year-old Aunt Cécile traveled with her daughter Thea to come celebrate her sister-in-law's milestone birthday in Florida. She too would soon be ninety. It had been easier for her to come since she was staying in Thea's home in North Carolina since the earthquake devastated Port-au-Prince where she lived. She sat in a wheelchair pushed by Thea. The morning of the trip, she had gotten a fresh haircut and her weekly bath. Still, the trip was a challenge. Aunt Cécile asked to urinate every half hour while she also suffered from chronic diarrhea since the earthquake. Thea was unfailingly loving and only grateful that her mother agreed to the trip. She thanked God daily for this renewed closeness to her mother, the chance to return some of the nurturing she once received and strengthen ties that death would soon sever.

Of Aunt Rose's six children, two natural sons and two adopted sons were missing. Of the two natural sons who could not come, Jacques had died long ago, and Alex had a change in mind. The party had been his sister's idea, and she took the lead on all the planning. Alex did not want the gathering to be at his sister's house, although it was a large and comfortable one. He wanted the party at Destin Beach, a half-hour drive away. He refused to hear concerns about the intense heat at the beach, the humidity, the bugs, the inconvenience of transporting food and chairs for twenty or more people, or of the early closing time of the beach.

Alex had strong emotions and handled them as best he could. He began to lose his hair and gain weight right after his brother died. He now keeps his head clean-shaven. A heart attack in his fifties and the ensuing triple bi-pass surgery had motivated Alex to sign up for a weight loss program and register at a gym. He progressively became slimmer, slim, slender, skinny, and then "dried-up," as his mother called it. She argued that her son now looked more like her father than her son. "I don't recognize you," Aunt Rose cried out. "Your whole face droops and looks like a mask!"

Alex came up with arguments regarding his absence. "How respectful towards my mother would it be," he asked, "for me to join in the gorging over exotic meals reminiscent of former times and family pride while, after the earthquake, thousands of Haitians are still without homes and food? What does it mean that my mother is honored for having survived ninety years of plenty at a time when thousands of children in Haiti would never live to see their first decade? And let us not forget that for people huddling in the makeshift tent-slums sprouted all over Port-au-Prince, this is life as usual, meaning no food, no roof, no medicine, no job, no education, no future, and watching your children die in infancy."

Alex had been a lonely-looking little boy. He had known times of hunger and homelessness after his mother fled Haiti with her three children during the Francois Duvalier dictatorship, and she feared for their lives.

* * *

AT SARA'S, the men were eating Haitian hors d'oeuvres, and the women were creating floral arrangements when we heard that Alex was actually in the south of Haiti, working in construction, helping rebuild an orphanage destroyed by the earthquake. I immediately thought, *At least he's consistent. He puts his beliefs into action.*

It was Thea's brother, Lucien, who broke the news to everyone except for Aunt Rose and Aunt Cécile. He had just arrived from Haiti with his wife, Julia. He hadn't yet left Haiti when he received a call from his cousin Alex who had just landed in Port-au-Prince and was about to board a small plane to Jeremy. *He's paying tribute to mother and family, after all,* I thought, *Jeremy is his family's ghost town, the place where his father's family came from and where they're all buried.*

Aunt Rose and Uncle Bob had adopted three Mexican-American boys from an orphanage in California after Jacques died. The oldest of the three was Jacques's spitting image. The boys were half-brothers, sons by different fathers, given up to Social Welfare by their mother, who could not cope. Bob was Rose's second husband, a handsome French adventurer who came to Haiti looking for good fortune and found Rose. Bob was not the father of Rose's children, and this Frenchman was gratified to finally be called Father by his Mexican adoptees.

As soon as he reached eighteen, the eldest boy disappeared without a trace for years, and this until Thea decided he was family, put a search on him, found him, and met with him. The boy was now a diplomat, a gay man living with another. He said that he had no interest in seeing his adoptive parents, especially after enduring years of adolescence listening to Bob's endless store of anti-homosexual jokes. The middle son spread terror in town during his own adolescence, drinking, thieving and raping. Aunt Rose slept with a machete under her pillow like she once did during the Duvalier dictatorship. The boy was eventually caught, lived in and out of jail, in and out of marriages throughout adulthood, until he suddenly came back, middle-aged and fat, claiming repentance just so he could stick around and watch, and one day claim his share of inheritance. He called his mother on the day of the party, pretexting car problems. Aunt Rose refused to come to the phone. The third boy was a grateful and loyal family man who found God. He was baptized in the Southern Baptist Church, went to church early morning and late afternoon every Sunday, had a string of lovely, polite blond children who called him Sir, and his daughters were only allowed in a swimming pool if they wore knee-length shorts and T-shirts.

Everyone else in the family was there, or almost. "Had he been alive," I said to Aunt Rose, "my father would've been the first among us to arrive here, loaded with gifts." She smiled. I missed Europa. I felt my mother's absence, too, and suffered great pangs thinking of her, a brave, lone outcast from the family and the Haitian bourgeois society since divorcing my father. In truth, she never really belonged anyway and seemed marginal even whilst married. Everyone expressed regret for the (unexplained) absence of Thea's husband's, but no one mentioned Europa. My sister would not have been at the party even if she had been alive. She was an undesirable; this was tacitly understood and accepted, although not openly an outcast like my mother. I always suffered from my mother's and my sister's absences at family gatherings. Mentioning Europa would have been heard as a reproach. I cowered, content to have a family that made room for me and did not devour me like Europa and my mother did. I admired Alex's courage to stand alone and express his outrage. But he is a man. Gender differences are real. All my cousins created and lived within stable, loving family units. I needed family support, albeit distant. Being my father's favorite child was my *laissez-passer*, and I preferred to have it than not.

* * *

MY FATHER HAD BEEN DEAD fourteen years when Aunt Rose asked me, "Tell me, Io, do you think your father died of a natural death?" This happened half an hour before Sara would be driving us to the airport. Thomas and I were the only relatives left from the reunion.

Mulling over that question on the plane next to Thomas and wondering what might have been going on in Aunt Rose's mind when she asked that, it seemed that her voice entered me and spoke without reserve in my head, *Oh no... You don't leave that easily and abandon me only to more decrepitude, enjoying an easy conscience about having been a good niece. No... You don't depart unaffected, unharmed, beautiful still, rejuvenated even. Your father handsome all his life, and now you? No... You don't run back to the airport and to the rest of your life on stable legs, my old husband's lust following after you. Everyone thinks I'm oblivious to what's going on while you treat him like he's some petty thief trying to steal any feel of your bare skin. No! You're the actual thief here, and I won't let you leave the house with all that I possessed of memories now yours. My brothers got all the education while my mother imposed a marriage on me at sixteen, only to see me end up divorced ten years later with small children and no money. My brothers never offered help. They sided with my husband. My body may now be a joke, but it's still a body. I'll cling to it even if it humiliates and aches me to hell. No way, Little Niece... you don't go in that plane and sit with a sense that you've had enough of me, my children, my grandchildren, my great-grand-children and all that's mine. I'm not going to let you feel smug in that plane. You may see them bicker, sense the strain of raising a family, observe the wear on their faces, hear the regrets, but you're the loser, not them, not us, not me, no. You'll never know the joy of recognizing yourself in another. You'll never look at a handsome man and be able to think, This is my son! How proud my father would be to see how his grandson takes after him! No. Those joys are never going to be yours as sure as I'm not going to be the old aunt who now may die. Your own story is worthless. You understood nothing and gave me no joy. You made no difference. You did nothing to lighten my old heart of a mother. And I want you to know that my brother, that son of a bitch of a father of yours who got to live an entire long life and never worried about me, well, I'm not interested in your honoring him or his honoring me. Life wouldn't be so unjust as to reward scoundrels like him with a painless death!*

In that last hour together, Aunt Rose had sat by me in that body no longer born by its own legs, a diminished measure of its original height. She looked at me with defiance when she asked my views on the circumstances of my father's death. Sara's and my husband were English speakers. Everyone was usually careful to speak in English rather than French whenever either man was present. They were both present at that moment, and yet Aunt Rose addressed me in French. Fortunately, Thomas understands some French. Throughout the world, language and accent differentiation are used to create intimacy, signify acceptance, belonging or exclusion. With the socio-linguistic situation of Creole and French in Haiti, determining class and level of education, and therefore setting the stage for cruel marginalization and separatism, Haitians are particularly sensitive to the use and manipulating power of language. Aunt Rose was always a careful person in her appearance, her words and gestures. She dresses each day with strong colors, matching pants and blouses, matching earrings and necklaces and a splash of *eau de toilette* on her gullied throat. She sustains herself each day with a creative killing instinct, appetite for drama, and lust for control. Her black mane is now a prickly halo of cropped white stubble that serves to signify the place of the face, and frame it. She looked at me with green eyes, once large, once mysterious, but now round, narrowing, mimicking a bird of prey.

My father used to reproach me, "You're stubborn like Rose's mule." And my mother reinforced his statement with, "You're like a viper from Rose's garden!"

After three days of celebration, feasting on family memories, enjoying group commiseration, boasting about surviving life's punishments, discussing the passed-down maladies, neurosis and attributes that nevertheless make us unique and uniquely bonded, the parting shot hurt.

It was delivered after three days of having my ears buzzing with the deeply accented English of upper-class Haitians come to America, and after I had felt compelled to defend my mother only once. "She was ahead of her time," I argued over cornbread and grits. "She was an early feminist. She didn't do anything that Caribbean husbands don't commonly do when they're busy betraying their perfectly lovely wives and bragging about it to their buddies."

Yet the best story from the Florida reunion was of a dog.

The dog's name was Jet. This happened before Francois Duvalier became Haiti's president and dictator. His predecessor was President Magloire, who had been loved by the Haitian bourgeoisie and mulatto class. Jet had been President Magloire's brother's dog. The president's brother moved out of his house after having been my grandmother's neighbor for many years, leaving his dog behind. Did he move because Grandmother cropped the hedge-trees that served to separate the two properties? "They block my view of the bay!" she argued. Did he change residence because she poisoned his pet guinea hens? "They disturb my siesta! I asked him to get rid of them," she explained. Or did he abandon the neighborhood because at church she publicly embarrassed the actual president, his brother? "He was sitting in our family pew and on my seat." So, she asked the president for her seat back. He had gotten up, bowed, lifted his hat with utmost courtesy and left the church. Grandmother sat down contentedly. She was always devout.

The dog that was left behind crossed over to Grandmother's garden. She hated dogs. Cousin Alex found the dog. Jet adopted Alex, who named him Jet. The two bonded. Alex was Grandmother's favorite because he looked like her late brother. She refused him nothing. She allowed his new Christmas train set to take over the living room's Persian rug. Jet sat on the rug with Alex to watch the train go by, eyes rolling round to follow the train, jaws drooling as if the toy were a rat he craved. "Sweetheart…" Grandmother finally moaned, "the dog's behind sits on the rug. Can't you have him sit on the mosaics instead?"

"No." Alex pursed his lips, got up without a word, moved the train piece-by-piece to his tiny bedroom at his mother's house next door.

The next day, Grandmother sent him a note of apology with the maid. Still, Alex did not come back. The following morning, Grandmother personally brought cake to the house for Alex and cheese cubes for Jet. She knocked at Alex's bedroom door. Alex opened the door and stood there with Jet by his side, both looking glum. Grandmother offered cake to Alex and set the cheese cubes on the floor for Jet. Alex refused the cake; Jet did not touch the cheese cubes either. Grandmother pleaded. The next morning, a sullen Alex brought his toy train back to his grandmother's, followed by Jet. Waiting for Alex to finish setting the train tracks back on the living room rug, Jet went out and jumped in the swimming pool. Each time Jet was seen taking a dip in the pool, Grandmother had the entire pool emptied out. With a single garden hose pouring water into the pool, it would take three or four days to fill it.

* * *

"JET WAS AN INTELLIGENT DOG," Aunt Rose was saying. "I concede that." All the cousins were gathered around her at Sara's house like children around a storyteller. "He was a dog living in times of curfew. He knew to be silent and watchful. The night that soldiers with loaded rifles parked their truck in front of our gate and came knocking at the door looking for my ex-husband, Jet stayed quiet. He didn't make a sound, he who loved to bark. He was hidden with us, the children, the maid and me, huddling in the darkness of the gardener's room that was sectioned at the back of the house. But the imbecile the soldiers were looking for was not at my house. He was not even in hiding!"

Sara then interrupted her mother. "All of you, just so you know," she said, "the *imbecile* my mother is talking about is my father."

"Sara, be quiet," Aunt Rose said. "The reason I call him that is that I saw him the next day walking leisurely on the Champs de Mars! I warned him, 'They're looking for you!' And the idiot replied, 'who is *they*?'"

"Mother, that's enough of calling my father names! He's dead."

"I know he's dead!" Aunt Rose snapped. "I know better than anyone that Duvalier disappeared him. We'd all be dead too if it weren't for me doing everything to get us out of there before they got your father! He should've taken my lead and left instead of doing all he could to keep me in Haiti. Can you all imagine that in those days, wives couldn't take a plane without the written consent of their husbands, Ex or not?"

"Why were the soldiers looking for him?" I asked.

Aunt Rose acted surprised. "You ask me *why*? I'll tell you *why*! He was a colonel in the army, and he was suspected of being part of a military junta that was plotting to overthrow the government. The night we were hiding in the servants' quarters is the night when I decided the time had come to leave the country."

"No, Mother," Sara interrupted with impatience, "it's after The Night of the Mulattos that you decided to leave Haiti."

Aunt Rose turned towards Sara with a look of indignation and a puzzled frown, then suddenly brightened. "Well… yes! You're right! What an affair that was!"

"What was it?" I asked.

Sara smiled. "I'll never forget the terror we felt," she said. "Rumors had gone around all day that on that particular night all mulattos would be killed and that anyone who killed a mulatto wouldn't be prosecuted. Mother spent the day filling and sewing four little so-called safe packages. She used one handkerchief for each one of us. She put one-quarter of all the cash she had in the bank in each one. She divided all her jewelry too, so we'd each have something to sell in exchange for cash or food if we got separated. We couldn't be loaded with food or anything heavy. It was no use trying to run that day or that night. Everybody in the neighborhood knew us, and whoever didn't would spot our light skin easily. We felt watched, so we stayed in the dark. I cried the whole time that Mother was sewing the pouches. I cried even when our maid Dieudonne tried to reassure me that *Nobody's gonna kill you, Miss Sara*. She wanted to take me and hide me in her own house. She and all her family could've been killed for protecting a mulatto. Mother wouldn't let her. I cried the whole night as well. But nothing happened. Dawn came. Nobody had been killed. Not us, not anyone."

Aunt Rose suddenly stood up with her cane and legs working surprisingly well in unison at that moment, an imperious look on her face, ordering silence for a speech. "That morning," she started, "I said—No more! I'm not going to live like this anymore!" Aunt Rose became silent and studied our faces and composures to judge the effect of her dramatization and, apparently satisfied, she continued. "Every generation in my family, every generation in the history of us mulattos have been compelled to leave Haiti because of political unrest and the fear of slaughter. Each time it's the 1804 slave insurgency against the French all over again. Except this time, it wasn't the French, it was us. And now my turn had come to be slaughtered? I said, No way. I am out. And I am not coming back when things calm down either. I also warned my brothers. If you're smart, you'll do the same. It's never going to be calm for us here. This isn't our country. At every turn, every generation, we're shown that this isn't our country. We don't have a country. I've had enough of that. I'm going to leave and find my own country. Whichever it is, I'm going to find it, I'm going to adopt it, and I'm going to be loyal to it. My brothers looked at me like I was an idiot. Men think women are idiots."

All worked up and looking like she felt all over again the fright of those days when she was planning her exile, Aunt Rose turned to Sara and said, "I told your *imbecile* of a father that same day that he may not be allowing me to leave the country with my children, that he may refuse to sign my visa, but I was going to show him. Wait and see. Piss in your pants is all you'll be able to do about it!" Aunt Rose then burst into laughter, and Sara quietly left the room.

"Sara! Where are you going?" Aunt Rose shouted.

"To the kitchen, Mother. I have lots of people to feed."

"Ah, yes…" Aunt Rose breathed with regret.

I came to Sara's rescue, asking Aunt Rose, "How did you manage it? How did you circumvent the law?"

"Your great-grandfather!" Aunt Rose's voice boomed, turning her whole body towards me. "That's who did it!" With the mere thought of her grandfather, Aunt Rose's withered face lit up. "My grandfather loved me! My mother may not have loved me, but her father adored me. Ever since I was a baby, he took me all over with him, even took me where children weren't allowed, and a girl at that."

"Why didn't your mother love you?"

"She had more interesting things to do," Aunt Rose said curtly, and then paused. She looked right and left, checking faces again, and argued, "You ought to know the history of your family."

"Tell us then…" Thea's brother, Lucien, said with his habitual calm. His wife, Julia, was sitting on the left side of Aunt Rose propped in the middle of the olive-green couch while Thea sat on her right. I was crouched on the floor next to the rock base of the tall fireplace, my toes playing with the thick pile of the carpeting. Ensconced in the peach armchair that matched the color of the walls, Thomas seemed most eager to hear the stories. Yet, these were only stories for him and not the structural events of his life. He was entertained, but not stirred as we were.

"You see," Aunt Rose said, raising her chin up and straightening her back, "The grandfather who adored me was a prominent man of law and a great orator. When he was due to debate in court, all of Port-au-Prince shut business down to go listen to him. It was great theatre, the only theatre at the time. My father had met him through some business they were doing, and he was invited to the daughter's, my mother's, twentieth birthday party. They were married shortly after. My father took her to Paris. Your uncle Edouard was born there. Then, the Great War was declared, and my father was mobilized. He proved to be a courageous man on the battlefield and was decorated. I wear his medal around my neck. See?"

The cousins then all wanted to see the medal, each one pushing the other to get closer to Aunt Rose until she got annoyed. "Enough! All of you. Listen to me! You don't know how long I'll live, and you may never hear this again!"

Having moved her audience back to attention, Aunt Rose smiled. "So, when the war was declared, and my father was mobilized," she said pompously, "my grandfather, the prominent man of law, demanded that my father send his daughter back to Haiti with her child so they could be safe from the war. My mother was quite happy to be back. She cared nothing for motherhood or loyalty to a husband fighting in the war. She was always at some tea party or at a club card game. When it was time to breastfeed your Uncle Edouard, a servant who kept watch at home came to inform her. She would ride back to our house in her carriage while the servant walked back. Port-au-Prince was a small place, and we all lived close to each other in the same neighborhood. Breastfeeding over, she would return to her card game. She never played with any of her children. The war over, my father returned to Haiti to his now-estranged wife and son. My mother eventually had a second child. That was Victor, Io's father."

I laughed. "I guess they weren't estranged very long!"

"Unfortunately, if you ask me!" Aunt Rose snapped. "This new child somehow became, and remained, the only child she loved. No one could touch Victor, including our father. She spoiled him and fussed over him. He behaved like a spoiled child for the rest of his life. All your father ever thought of, my dear Io, was himself. By the time I was born, a valueless girl at that, my mother had no love left for me. My father tried to compensate. He did love me, but it's my grandfather who adored me. He took me to his club, where I stayed quietly near him the whole time while he played cards with men involved in politics. When the men questioned the presence of a child, he'd shrug his shoulders—Don't pay her any mind, she's a good girl. That's also how I came to know one of Grandfather's students at the law school. This young man came to the house all the time. It turns out he eventually became president."

"Which president was that?" Lucien asked.

"Vincent. After he became president, he still remembered me from when I was a child, and he'd send a limousine from time to time for me to come visit him at the National Palace."

"You should see it now!" Lucien said, raising his eyebrows and shaking his head. "It's a pile of rubble since the earthquake."

"Yes... I saw images on the news... very sad..." Aunt Rose murmured, lowering her face. "It was a uniquely beautiful building. George Baussan was the architect who designed it in 1912. Of course, we knew the Baussan family."

"I saw these images of the destroyed palace too," Sara said, surprising us, coming back from the kitchen and settling on a chair a little behind me as if to be ready to get up at any moment.

"What about the limousine?" Lucien asked.

Aunt Rose seemed revived by the question and quickly answered. "Anyway, in those days when the president would send the limousine for me, Grandfather was long dead. I guess we met out of nostalgia for this great man we both loved. I still remember Grandfather when he was at the height of his fame and men came hush-hush one night to see him. It was very late. The men behaved with great mystery, and fear too. Even then, my grandfather let me stay in his office. They'd come to offer him the presidency. In those days, men of power decided on everything. No vote or anything. My grandfather pulled at his mustache gently, cleared his throat, and refused. He told them how honored he was but was more interested in staying alive to care for his family."

"Did he ever regret refusing the presidency?" Lucien asked, breaking his usual reserve about personal matters and emotions. "He could've done a lot with the power."

"I don't know if he regretted it. He wouldn't have lived long enough to use the power. Look at the history of Haitian presidents. You'll see... Anyway, this was a long way around to answer the question of how I got out of Haiti. It must be obvious now that it's thanks to my grandfather's political connections that, years later, I got a visa to leave the country, despite my ex-husband's efforts to the contrary."

"What happened?" I asked. "Was it President Vincent?"

"Yes. I remember very well my last visit to the palace," Aunt Rose recounted with a smile. "But I didn't see him that last time. I had sent word that I needed help, and why. It was all hush-hush again one night. Limousine, black men with dark glasses leading me into a windowless office, piles of papers stacked everywhere, but one paper is miraculously pulled out, it concerns me, and an exit visa is stamped on it. Leave the country quickly! That's all I remember hearing while my heart was pounding wildly. I asked no questions. I went home, I picked up my children, I closed the door, I left home. At the airport, two officials looked at the documents, they looked at me, they looked at each other, something was evidently odd, but they stamped the document and let me go."

"Where did you go?" Thomas asked, surprising everyone.

Aunt Rose smiled, visibly pleased. "First to Jamaica, then Martinique, then France, and then, like most of us here, America. I'm now an American. I take my new nationality seriously. I am grateful. We're safe. Io, I wouldn't let that English husband of your waste time any longer. Thomas, you're new to the family, but take my advice from an old aunt. Get your American nationality." Aunt Rose fell silent and smiled sadly. "Jacques would be here today too if he'd not gone back to Haiti and its politics. It must've been a family disease he inherited. I warned him." At that, Aunt Rose shrugged her shoulders.

"My brother was an idiot like his father!" Sara blurted out with tears in her eyes.

"Sara, my girl, shut up!"

"Why should I?" Sara protested. "That's how you speak of my father! I've nothing good to say about my father, but I keep my mouth shut. Respect your elders and the dead. That's what you taught us, Mother. My father's dead. My brother's dead. I loved my brother dearly, but I don't thank him for getting involved in politics and putting our family name in the macabre Haitian list. Even for what's happened to you, Mother, I don't thank him."

Aunt Rose was shocked. "What about me?"

Sara looked exasperated. "You're forever paranoid you're being followed, spied upon, or your phone tapped! But let's be real. Who are we for anyone to bother spying on us? We are nobody, damn it! We are invisible! Just a bunch of Haiti's throwaways who've managed to make good in America. That's who we are now. Anyway, dinner is ready. The table is set."

* * *

HAITIANS PACKED in a small space, touring Florida. There were seven of us in Sara's van heading for Destin Beach. Caribbean people go to the ocean as if to a shrine. English and French words were bouncing inside the car with everyone talking what was easiest for whoever sat closest.

In Sara's kitchen, I had said, "I don't want to leave here without having seen the ocean once."

Everybody thought this a great idea except for Aunt Cécile sitting in her wheelchair next to me. Almost in a whisper, she asked me, "Is this so you can continue walking barefoot?" I flinched. I know how going barefoot in Haiti is perceived to be a low-class or a poverty issue, so I held my tongue. I was leery of Aunt Cécile's soft-spoken comments since my last visit to her in Haiti at the time when my daughter, Eveline, was refusing to see me, and I felt broken. I liked her gentle presence during adolescence. I visited her often and sat quietly under the almond tree on the outdoor terrace while she spoke to me about God. During that last visit, however, she spent an hour telling me with an impassive face about several divorce situations she knew where the women lost their children, and that these women deserved what they got if they were foolish enough to divorce a man. I remember thinking at the time that Aunt Rose hadn't lost her children. But she hadn't been living alone in America then, as I was. She had social status and family support.

Having gotten no answer from me, Aunt Cécile asked again, "Are you in the habit of going barefoot in the house?"

"Yes, Aunt Cécile," I said, "when it makes sense or feels good." But I was actually thinking *No more servants for us in America, Aunt Cécile! With twenty-five people coming in and out of the house all day and children knocking about, Sara surely appreciates having one less pair of dirty shoes on her rugs.*

Aunt Cécile rested one hand lightly on mine and then tightened her grip, asking, "My eyes aren't good these days. Can you tell me, Io, if you see other people here going barefoot?"

"Aunt Cécile, I don't pay attention to other people's feet. Their feet are their business. But if you can't see theirs, how come you see mine?"

My old aunt recoiled. "Cold air is blowing on me," she moaned. "Io, do you know where it's coming from?'

"No, Aunt Cécile, but probably from the air conditioner."

"Find Thea for me. Right now."

"Thea went out to the garden."

"Go tell her to come back. I don't want to go to the beach. I have seen enough beaches. I want to lie down in my room. I'm going to be ninety years old in December. I don't feel well."

Thea walked excitedly into the kitchen at that very moment, having just been told about the beach proposition. "Mother, I'm back!" she announced with a large smile, her eyes brilliant with gaiety.

"Good, Thea. I'm glad you're here because I don't want to go to the beach."

Thea's shoulders and smile dropped. She then pulled a kitchen chair next to her mother, sat and tried to cajole her. "I think you'll enjoy the beach. It'll make you feel better. And I would really like to go too, Mother."

"No. You have to stay with me."

"Aunt Cécile!" Sara called from the other end of the crowded kitchen, "Thea will put you to bed, but she can go to the beach. I'll stay with you. I live here. I can see the beach anytime."

Aunt Cécile darted her eyes severely in Sara's direction, but then only mumbled softly, "If you say so, my dear."

Thomas was driving Sara's van, and the air-conditioner was going strong. Lucien and Julia, who had come from Haiti and were therefore used to tropical temperatures, instantly felt cold and asked if it could be turned down.

"No," Aunt Rose said right away. "It'll be too hot. If you're cold, put your jackets on." She was sitting next to me in the back and suddenly poked my arm with her elbow, whispering in French as if she and I had been plotting, "At the house, I sat next to Cécile for a reason."

"What reason, Aunt Rose?"

"I wanted to see for myself."

"See what?"

"Cécile doesn't miss a thing. She watches Thea like a hawk. As soon as Thea leaves the room, she starts moaning. My back hurts. I can't breathe. Come and scratch my head. I want to lie down. And Thea is there as fast as a slave. Did you notice? And did you know that Thea gets into the shower with her mother to wash her? If Thea doesn't watch out, her mother is going to ruin her life. Her husband's going to leave the house. That Cécile, I know her well. All meekness and religion, but she has an iron will and is as selfish as they come."

I whispered back, "I see no love for me in her eyes."

Aunt Rose straightened up with a mock-puzzled look and then elbowed me again in the ribs. "But Cécile doesn't have love for anyone, Io. Never had. Except for Lucien maybe? See how she obeys her son like a child. He can do no wrong." Aunt Rose paused for a few seconds and elbowed me again. "Yet, she's a clever dog. She makes Lucien feel that he never does enough. But she reserves the bitter reproaches for Thea. That girl's a saint. Cécile will win. Mark my words."

Having flown in earlier than the others, Thomas and I had benefitted from two separate tours of the area already but had not yet made it to Destin Beach. We were on that road for the third time, however, and for the third time, Uncle Bob pointed to the boat hangar. "Look at that! Isn't that wonderful? An airbrush artist was commissioned to paint it!"

I, therefore, looked for the third time at the metal boat hangar on whose gray wall three gray whales with open mouths swam in the wavy stripes of a gray ocean. Aunt Rose cheerfully agreed with Uncle Bob out loud, poking me in the ribs with gusto once more, saying, "That's an artist who is paid a lot for his work. He must be good!" I noticed Thomas looking at me in the rearview mirror at that moment. I smiled back at him. *That's a poke at me,* I thought, *and not in the ribs this time. Good job, Aunt Rose and Uncle Bob... They both know how I struggle as an artist. And I have to look at that ridiculous and ugly whale and hear how successful the painter is. If you call that a painter.*

Aunt Rose and Uncle Bob then insisted on showing us every single landmark of theirs. We saw a Walmart and a discount store where Aunt Rose buys artificial flowers and metallic-gold frames for landscape paintings she picks up at fairs and garage sales. With great excitement, she demanded that we *Stop the car right now*, and come out to see the front of yet another discount store. It was a brick hangar whose façade was an immense mosaic collage made of pottery shards and miniature plastic toys. We had an array of dinosaurs, supermen and mermaids. I thought *Maybe post-earthquake Haiti should export shards and rubble to decorate Florida's storefronts.*

Once at the beach, we found that no one had brought a bathing suit. Everyone had either felt too old, too rushed, too hot, too thirsty, or too worried about getting sand in Sara's van. We all looked at the ocean with longing and soon left.

On the way back, we stopped at a sandwich place where busgirls wore red miniskirts and ruffled aprons made from pink gingham cloth. They moved shapely, bare legs like hurried automatons, speeding unawares past large murals of undulant palm trees fanning above ocean waves crashing on white sand from which pink flamingos were taking flight. As we entered the place, Lucien exclaimed, "It's really pleasant to be in Florida!"

Seated alone at a table with me where we waited for the others to join us with the orders of sandwiches, Aunt Rose carefully hung her cane on the back of her chair and turned to face me. "I'm very well impressed with your husband," she said. "He isn't at all what I imagined."

* * *

"MY LIFE IS UNEVENTFUL," Sara said to me, "and that's the way I want it."

Sara married at eighteen. Her husband, Chris, was twenty-six. He came from America's Deep South while Sara came from Post-Colonial Haiti. Both grew up without a father. They said their vows in a small Puerto Rican church with two hired witnesses.

Chris was a toddler when his father disappeared without a word, abandoning his wife and eight children. Many years later, his eldest sister hired a private detective and found their father on his hospital deathbed. Another wife and set of children were gathered around him.

"He had no time for me when I needed him, and I've no need for him now," Chris told his sister. "I'm not coming."

Sara's own parents were divorced by the time she was six. On visitation days, her father sent his chauffeur to pick up the three children at their mother's house and drive them to the downtown Port-au-Prince restaurant where he waited. They ate the same meal of steak and fries each time, at the same table, under the distracted eyes of their father, who drank and discussed politics with friends at the bar.

The Rond-Point was a landmark restaurant, one of four business establishments built around the perimeter of a circular plaza in the middle of which stood a permanently dry fountain. Early in his dictatorship, Papa Doc Duvalier had the fountain destroyed and replaced by a cement sculpture taller than the Rond-Point, showing two hands in a handshake, one black, one white, presumably as symbols of the harmony between opposites hoped for since the 1804 slave independence.

Papa Doc spent the years of his presidency fighting the mulatto elite that feared his black populist ideas and lobbied against him from the start. Mulattos, who opposed the government, were hunted down by the dictator's militia, imprisoned, tortured and killed. In the end, Papa Doc became so paranoid about keeping power that he killed all Haitians up and down the color scale with no distinction between friends or foes, and the Rond-Point's pacifist sculpture was proved an enduring lie, besides being singularly ugly.

When lunch was over, Sara, Jacques and Alex were invariably driven by the chauffeur to see a French movie at the Rex Theatre. The chauffeur sat with them, delighted with the entertainment, albeit watching a film spoken in a language wholly foreign to his Creole-speaking ears. When much later in life, Sara heard of her father having been murdered for conspiring against Duvalier, she asked, "What happened to the chauffeur?"

Obsessed with Haiti, Aunt Rose and her daughter have recreated the Haitian gardens and lush environment they knew. The Florida climate makes it easy for them. Sara's long curving driveway is lined with pink azalea bushes that start at the gate. The garden is organized around the goldfish pond whose attraction for the children is neither its beauty nor the fish, but the frogs. Store-bought, luxury frogs. Sara's grandchildren stand at the pond in hundred-degree temperatures all afternoon armed with fishing nets, attempting to catch frogs they are sworn to return to the pond alive, but don't. The kids peer patiently at the water through lotuses, water lilies, hyacinths and elephant ears, searching for the round, glassy eyes of frogs hiding below, or for those that lie motionless in the bush amid cinnamon ferns interspersed with stag horns, Calla lilies, purple hydrangeas, white impatiens and pink caladium. Live oaks towering above the pond and disseminated all about the vast lawn dangle Spanish moss along their branches all the while the whole garden resounds with the continuous chirping of birds.

Sara's youngest grandson is the garden's fawn. He is a four-year-old freckled redhead who takes his coloring from his grandfather Chris, but not his quiet involvement with growing things. The child would rather catch frogs than grow corn. His punishment for killing frogs instead of throwing them back in the water is "time out" when he must stand and face a corner of the kitchen while his brothers and cousins appear indifferent to his predicament. They drink sodas with their afternoon snack of crackers and cheese, ending it with vanilla ice cream Sundaes topped with chocolate fudge oozing down in unctuous rivulets beneath a layer of loosely sprinkled crushed peanuts. Sara towers over the bunch of them obediently seated at the kitchen table, and her eyes glow.

Chris's vegetable garden would have earned him the respect of his wife's family servants in Haiti. It did not appear to bother the help that their windowless rooms were built in the least attractive end of the garden near the dumpster or shared a wall with the cemented garage affixed with a startlingly loud buzzer used to summon them. They did, however, stand disapprovingly each afternoon, lips pinched in a downward curve, while hosing interminable rows of flowering plants that produced no fruit. For them, beauty was not in the form but in the purpose of things.

Servants yet suffered, cramped in small spaces, missing their own.

In their rooms, the women kept a large photo frame in which they assembled their relatives' black and white passport photos for trips they never took, except the one to the cheapest photo shop downtown Port-au-Prince in a back alley behind the cathedral that has now crumbled from the earthquake.

The men kept fighting cocks, some scruffy, plucked-pink, underfed, virulent creatures that stared all day at the gray cement floor. The animals were kept safe and out of sight in the damp corner of a windowless room, tied to a forked nail hammered into a whitewashed wall.

Both men and women persistently plugged the widening cracks in the walls of their rooms with black hair collected from combs and brushes permanently sticky from hair-combing oils. This practice meant to incur protection from evils that infiltrate the night and simper in the dark.

To us, however, children of the elite, what servant quarters unwittingly taught us is that servants were people who thrive in close proximity, living in noxious clusters like farm animals, inviting tenderness. They slept their deep, tired sleep of servants, laid over cotton mattresses worn thinner each year, stretched over noisy, rusty springs that sank in the middle.

Servants nevertheless saved money which they exhumed ceremoniously during Sunday afternoon visits to relatives, fishing shriveled wads wrapped in odd cloth out of cotton brassieres or pant pockets, handing them over to pay for the care of a child they might hug once a week, not staying a minute longer than was possible so they could return by nightfall to their narrow space of servitude.

* * *

IN FLORIDA, AUNT ROSE had been seated in a large armchair. That day was her ninetieth birthday. Her eyes darted fiercely at everyone while Sara was lining family members up, giving them each a flower to offer her mother. Aunt Rose's children held a red rose each. Grandchildren held a pink rose each. Spouses, nieces and nephews held a daisy each. In addition to a daisy, Thea, Lucien and I held a white rose each to offer in the name of our fathers—Aunt Rose's two deceased brothers—Edouard and Victor.

Above the fireplace in front of which Aunt Rose sat, there was a large painting of two peacocks that had been done by her mother. Julia was ecstatic over it while she waited in line with Lucien. I tapped her on the shoulder. "My grandmother took up painting in her old age," I whispered. "She mostly painted flowers. But did anyone tell you the story of how she poisoned her neighbor's peacocks? And that was President Magloire's brother."

When my turn came and I stood in front of Aunt Rose seated low, I went down on my knees to speak to her at eye level and give her the white rose. "This is for my father," I said. "He would've loved to be here." I then burst into tears and rested my head on my aunt's bony thighs dressed in black polyester pants. Aunt Rose caressed my hair, saying, "I know…" I finally got up, and Aunt Rose stuck my father's white rose and my daisy in the large vase at her feet, turning her attention to the next person.

Once the vase was filled with all the flower offerings, it was placed at the center of the dining table. Lucien led Aunt Rose to her chair in the dining room. She sat under multicolored balloons, and banderoles hung from the ceiling. Their garish party colors contrasted with her black, long-sleeved blouse, though laden with embroideries of white roses swirling around the neckline. Aunt Rose wordlessly surveyed the lavish food displayed on the dining table covered with a white linen embroidered tablecloth. She seemed unmoved until she suddenly frowned, her gaze having stopped at the emerald-green cake that her adopted son Maurice's wife—a petite, blonde native of Flor- ida—had made especially for her.

* * *

I COME FROM a culture of violence. We continue to reflect it in the ways we behave, consciously or not. My Aunt Rose's parting shot reflects that. My cousin Alex sent me a Jewish meditation from the Baal Shem Tov—Facing Yourself. It is argued that God sets us up to have a confrontation with a person who exhibits the very flaws that exist in us but which we do not see in ourselves. God keeps setting up these confrontations until it dawns on us that we, too, exhibit the behavior that we so dislike in another. What Alex is trying to tell me is obvious enough, and his protectiveness of his mother's behavior is understandable.

I nevertheless question, "Doesn't evil exist in and of itself?"

Violence takes many guises.

I remember the children who helped us get ready for school in the morning. Adolescents working with an empty stomach while helping others their age, us, the children driven to school like princes and princesses in fairy tales they would never read. They remained behind, clad in rags, to help the maids—clean dishes, make beds, scrub toilets. It is only after the early morning chores were done that they were given a half-cup of black coffee and a three-inch square of *biswit*, that cheap Haitian bread made with lard.

What has become of them? What can become of a country filled with adults who were these children? I also wonder about what happened to Aunt Rose, to the young woman full of hopeful vitality for whom men once competed on the dance floor, and whose lips are now just a tight, red slash.

I now understand ghostliness. I once had filters like a photographer does. I used them to color the world around me, filter and cloak and soothe all forms. I am now my own interpreter of absolute change.

It used to be easier to stand in front of people and feel whole. I did not know before how much I needed these old walls. Walls my father built, walls that smothered me yet confirmed my existence and identity. "This is who you are. Here you breathe. Here's where you exist." These walls of my childhood home were my inner land, the living grave of ancestral spirits, *my house of fossils*, the land from which to draw strength and continuance yet visit in sacrifice. In Haitian Vodou culture, such a place is called a *démanbré*. A literal translation could be the "dismembered." It implies severed pieces, a whole sectioned into many parts, yet remaining a determinate place where one goes to recover one's being, claiming those disjointed, cut up, pulled apart limbs in order to recompose as one needs or sees fit. These walls of my house may have already been cracked, rough, discolored, pealing, saltpeter foaming and disfiguring them, but they contained and pacified me, reflecting me in infinitely subtle measures. They seemed strong enough to deny my modern invisibility and disconnectedness in a foreign land, and yet they were not strong enough to have resisted the earthquake.

* * *

OLD FAMILY PHOTOGRAPHS at Sara's house were hung in the hallway to the bedroom where Thomas and I slept. Two of them, in particular, held my attention one night, enough so that I pointed them out to him. Two large-size, yellowed photographs of family gatherings, taken at some long-ago Christmas. In one photo, the family stands in rows by generation and gender.

The men in the photo are stiff. Grandfather, Jacques, Uncle Edouard, and my father wear formal dinner jackets in the hot Caribbean night. My grandfather is first on the left of the row composed of these four men standing at the back of the couch. Each of their wives sits on the couch in front of her husband standing behind it. Jacques, however, stands among the men in place of his father behind his mother, my Aunt Rose, already many years divorced. He was sixteen, as tall as my father, Grandmother's favorite child, strikingly handsome. Seated at the far right of the couch and in front of her husband, my mother is enjoying being able to spread her naked shoulders and arms that emerge out of a sleeveless, low-cut décolleté. The long and large skirt of her emerald green taffeta evening dress stretches over and covers half of Aunt Cécile's legs, seated next to her, looking timid. It took years for Cécile to reveal her devouring jealousy towards women her husband lusted after, my mother especially. In the photo, my mother, Margueritte, is either oblivious to the pain she causes or she is taking a subtle revenge for the many slights, snips and slaps inflicted on her by her two sisters-in-law since she arrived in Haiti, a gorgeous new bride in full glory, innocence and foreignness.

We the grandchildren, although sitting on the Persian rug at the feet of each of our mothers, seem more unanimously hanging at our grandmother's feet, squeezed as she was while sitting to the left end of the couch, a plump queen bee plopped beneath her husband. To us, and even if Aunt Rose, as a daughter, remembers her differently, our grandmother was an uncontested goddess of love and plenty. Her constant good humor was a relief from the colonial rule under which mothers in the photograph held us (except for mine), even if their piercing claws were hidden under an abundance of ornate rings that glittered like the buttons on the butler's jacket.

In the second photograph, the family is seated at a long mahogany table covered with an embroidered, white linen tablecloth. The food is not yet on the table, but glasses are full. Grandmother's butler, Louis, appears in the upper left corner of the image, his face closed. The black and white photograph does not deny him the actual colors of his world—his white cotton uniform, the white of his eye around the black of the iris, his dark face. He is holding a silver tray, standing straight as a column, a fixture to wealthy people's lives, a convict of need.

"Christmas dinner was brilliant!" I recalled for Thomas's benefit once we were in bed. "We started with crispy fried tidbits… malanga *acras*, pork and beef *griots*, brain marinades, fried plantain… All laid out on silver trays. Louis first passed them out to parents having rum cocktails before dinner. Children were served after the grown-ups… Uncle Edouard's favorite cocktail drink was a Martini. I kept hoping he'd offer me the olive at the bottom of his glass, but he never noticed me staring. He never saw me, period… We drank cola sodas. And sometimes we chanced snatching morsels directly from the tray as it came out of the kitchen. Louis pretended not to see.

"My grandmother's kitchen smelled like fresh dough. But at Christmas, the smell of turkey took over. I was apprehensive about seeing the turkey dead on a tray. I'd watched it being fattened for a whole month. When I tried caressing the unseemly beast or just talking to it, it got agitated and ran in circles. It couldn't do much else in terms of movement. It was attached with a short string around a stick in the ground... The turkey was served with *gratinés*... Of course, there was always creole rice and red beans. There's no Haitian meal without rice and beans. Beans in a separate sauce or cooked with the rice. That's my favorite... My father loved palm-cabbage *gratiné*... Aunt Rose preferred breadfruit *gratiné*. I love that too... My mother never took to Haitian food."

"Haitian food's great!" Thomas protested. "What a loss... poor woman."

"Yeah, well... after the meal, I scrutinized the turkey's carcass in the kitchen. It bore no resemblance to the oddly proportioned creature I'd come to love. Not even an abstraction of it. It was more of a sunken ship, rotted on an ocean floor like I'd seen in books. Nothing like the anxious, gawky and oddly coiffed gray bird I'd known... I imagine the brigantine *Marie-Celeste* looked like a turkey carcass too when they found it at the bottom of the Port-au-Prince bay... You remember that story, right?"

"Yes, Io. You told me all about it. And I loved it."

"Okay, Thomas... okay... but all this remembering makes me sad... and I'm suddenly thinking of my friend Pierre. Something he told me the other day while you were still in England. Quite upsetting. Not only because I love him, but probably because his truth is also mine. "

"What truth?"

"He said he was his own mythology. And that we're, meaning him and me, in this post-Darwinian, post-colonial world. Not fish, not fowl, not eagle, not lion, not crocodile or lizard, but here we are anyway... He didn't mean *post-colonial* literally, of course, but it feels like it. Our servants are still nearly slaves in the way we've let them live... Pierre wondered if, looking back, we'd know where we'd fit in our original milieu. Meaning Haiti. He said he doesn't count his possessions like his relatives in Haiti do. You know, like owning two of this, three of that, or how many trips made to wherever. At the end of the count, if there's enough, his relatives will come to the conclusion that they're successful westerners and that him, or me, or even you, Thomas, being married to me, are aberrant dummies to be staying in America when we could live like kings back home. They ask Pierre what he's doing here. They think he's betrayed them. Betrayed his origins and his ancestors who left him money he should be proud of. What's to be proud of? Pierre asked them. We're just lucky, but for a short time only, because soon we'll find that we're the difficult generation positioned at the edge of post-colonial history. He said to think of him as a demilitarized zone. We are tightrope dancers, wrong move or compromise, and we'll fall into the void... That's what Pierre said."

"Your friend is a tormented fellow," Thomas murmured.

"He isn't the only one, I'm afraid... Even when I was a child... I saw how plants bleed sap. Just break a leaf or snap a stem... red poinsettias bleed a white sap... I would touch that sap lightly, dab some on the back of my hand. I examined its texture, its scent... You know, I wonder what kind of a child Aunt Rose was?"

"Hard to imagine!" Thomas said with a small laugh.

"I disagree. I can see her... a child who observes everything... intelligent and sensitive...   but rebellious as all get out! Ah... Thomas... at any given time, we're all that remains of the world we knew."

* * *

THE SKY LOOKED CLEAR, and the temperature was in the low seventies when Thomas and I landed in Boston. The air was cool enough to sober spirits but not to make one shiver. I could not wait to call Pierre and tell him about my family reunion. We had to follow-up on our last conversation about the impact families have on our lives. I nevertheless waited a week to filter things on my own first. When I finally called him, Pierre sounded happy to hear from me. He asked, laughing, "So, how did it go?"

"Why are you laughing before I've said anything?"

"Was there no funny business you can tell me about?"

"All I can say is that my aunt gave me a parting shot."

"Aha! I was right! What happened? Tell me everything."

"How much time do you have?"

"All afternoon. Today is Saturday. I'm off. No patients. You're my patient now. Go on, I'm listening. What comes to mind?"

"Everything comes to mind!"

"Aha!"

"Yeah, aha… everything had gone beautifully until the last day. We'd been at my cousin Sara's house the whole time. Thomas and I were the last of the company to leave. We still had an hour before going to the airport. We were relaxing and chatting with my aunt Rose who had turned ninety, my uncle Bob, Sara and her husband Chris. The *parting shot* came soon after we'd come out of Sara's computer room. Thomas had wanted to show my website to my aunt Rose, uncle Bob and Sara. Chris didn't look. He never gets involved outside of his wife and children. He observes, however. He's not indifferent. Anyway, Thomas had found it strange that my family knew nothing of my website and next to nothing about my life's work. In the computer room, he read out loud some of the praise written on my website. Sara was impressed. My aunt said how proud my father would be. My uncle tried to crack a joke, as usual, and my aunt snapped at him."

Pierre sniggered, asking, "What did she say?"

"Something like, Bob that's enough!"

"Brief but a good shot." Pierre seemed delighted at the prospect of my story. Family behaviors and complexities fascinated him. He was a psychoanalyst, after all.

"My aunt's a good shot, for sure," I said. "My uncle visibly recoiled, poor fellow. He can't stand not being the center of attention, so he's endlessly telling jokes as a way of getting it. As for my aunt, she said that my father would be proud, but she expressed nothing of her own feelings. Only Sara looked genuinely pleased for me."

"Do you think your uncle and aunt were jealous?"

"Wait till you hear the rest… Back in the living room, the conversation somehow started on Haitian men's marital infidelities. I told my story about a cousin-by-marriage of my father's—and of my aunt,

of course—who'd groped me in the sea when I was fifteen. He'd nick-
named me his fiancée ever since I was a kid. Maybe he'd come to
believe it. Nobody could see what he was doing under the water. He
was my aunt Rose's childhood friend, and the husband of her favorite cousin. Aunt Rose and her cousin spoke on the phone every day.
I've thought a lot about this conversation since the parting shot was
fired… My own husband had just wanted to honor me by reading the
praise on the website. I wonder if the contrast was too strong to bear,
and if my aunt suddenly felt both protective and angry for her cousin.
Also angry at me for not keeping the family dishonor secret. Perhaps
she'd felt an inner pinch of shame and dishonor in the computer room
already, seeing my husband's pride in me, while hers was trying to
crack a joke, as always, and being somewhat of a joke himself… She
did tell me at the beach that he was better than she expected…"

"What? She said *that*?"

"Yes… a caress and a slap at the same time… I told you she's a
good shot."

"But what was she expecting? I mean, why was she expecting
something bad, to begin with?"

"Maybe because of my sister's choices of men when she lived?…
Or she felt the urge to let me know she didn't think much of my previous
husband?… Ah, who knows!… Maybe it's her old rivalry with my father,
and she resents him getting post-mortem satisfaction from me?… Or old
jealousy towards my mother that she transferred onto me?… Anyway,
my uncle Bob is famously unfaithful. That's a given. And you know how
people in Haiti will make jokes about a cuckolded woman, but never at
a cuckolded man? My aunt and her cousin are very close, and perhaps
their self-images are enmeshed?… It could be that my story might have
stirred personal wounds about the dishonor and ridicule women get from
unfaithful husbands. Even now, Uncle Bob pretends senility to try and
kiss on the lips every woman he meets, family included. Even me. My
father was different… Yet Aunt Rose decided to remember him as a
womanizer. She started telling about his lust for women and secret mis-
tresses. She claimed he was about to remarry at the time he died… She
even suggested I knew this woman well."

"Did you?"

"How would I know? My aunt refused to tell me her name."

"An old ruse. She's clever, Io!"

"Maybe. But I told my aunt that being a womanizer's the one thing that can't be said about my father. She scowled at me, claiming there are things I don't know. And that's when the parting shot was fired. She looked at me coldly and asked, 'Do you really believe that your father died of an accident?' I was stunned. I could only mumble that everybody knows he had a stroke in his car."

"Oh my… Io, I'm sorry…"

"Then she screamed, saying, 'That's not what happened! I went to the morgue! I saw his forehead! You didn't!' I was crushed, Pierre, and yet felt compelled to explain what really happened, instead of laughing off her madness."

"How could you laugh it off anyway? Come on…"

"I suppose you're right. Anyway, I argued that he hit his head on the windshield. The impact made a gash. But Aunt Rose didn't let me continue. She looked at me menacingly and screamed that my father killed himself with his car. He was suffering from depression. He committed suicide. And then, worst of all, my cousin Sara chose that time to interrupt and say softly, Oh, I thought you knew… Knew what? I asked her. Then I started telling her and everybody there how I have never heard such a ridiculous version of my father's death. It didn't even match events every eyewitness described, or the official records and death certificate. I recounted how my cousin Lucien was called right away at the scene. He took my father's gold signet ring off even before the ambulance showed up. Then I turned to Sara specifically and reminded her how she hadn't even been to Haiti for my father's funeral. All she knew of my father's death came from her mother. I felt bitter. I reproached Sara that she hadn't even called me after my father died."

"Wow! How did she take that?"

"She twisted in her chair, looking at her husband. Chris was puffing on his pipe. Uncle Bob gaped at his wife. Aunt Rose was observing everyone, eyes rolling from face to face. Thomas kept quiet, his eyes fixed on me. He never knew my father. Then I looked at Aunt Rose in the eyes and asked her why she was telling me this fourteen years after the fact… can you imagine, fourteen years! Dead as he is, my father certainly wasn't the one who was going to suffer from this."

"Fourteen years, Io? Really? Talk about Haitians digging up corpses!"

"Ah… Pierre, you're going to make me laugh. I don't want to laugh yet. Let me focus… yes… well, my aunt slapped my arm and then got up with remarkable swiftness. She stared at me and said with virulence that there are things I don't know. So, I asked her why she wasn't telling me the things I don't know since they made such a difference. But then she slowly walked to the center of the room, turned around, came back and stood right in front of me, looking down at me. And without batting an eye, she said it was my mother's fault… My father killed himself because of my mother."

"Unbelievable, Io! If it weren't you telling me this, I wouldn't believe it."

"Yeah, but I'm not done… So then, I argued that my parents had been divorced twenty years already when my father died and that she even claimed he was about to remarry, and that her argument, therefore, made no sense. You'd think that would deter her? But no. She said he killed himself because he found out she'd had lovers all through their marriage. She'd made a fool of him all over town. He killed himself for shame, and to punish her, and make her suffer a public blame. He killed himself out of revenge."

"Twenty years after the divorce? It's you she was killing out of revenge, Io."

"That's just what I told her, Pierre. I almost laughed at first. I'm sure I had at least a smirk on my face when I argued back. I asked her who else in the house but me could be hurt by her absurd version of my father's death. I even said I was glad Europa was dead too and would never have to hear this. Had Thomas not been there, Pierre, I would've left the house right then. But I also felt that Sara didn't deserve this kind of parting scene. Plus, she needed to know the truth. This was a family story, after all. We'd spent three days together sharing family stories. So, I started explaining things out loud for whomever in that room might listen, ignoring my aunt, looking ahead, past her, and strangely, she let me do it. This whole conversation had been in English for Thomas and Chris's benefit, and I continued in English. I said that what actually happened was that my father had been diagnosed with arteriosclerosis of the brain. He increasingly suffered dizzy spells. Two days before he died, he'd fallen in the shower. His doctor ordered that he not drive anymore. So, my father hired a chauffeur. That fatal day, right at the point where the road forks into his driveway, 200 yards from home, my father ordered the chauffeur out of the car and give back the keys. He took the driver's seat, turned the key, and started down his driveway. He had a heart attack just seconds later and hit a post a few feet from his gate. My cousins Lucien and Julia were called right away. They live practically next door anyway. They came immediately and took him to the hospital where he was pronounced dead. Uncle Edouard was still alive at the time, and he, as well as everybody, corroborated the story of his death, including Europa. Nothing and no one came to challenge it… and that was it. When I was done, I looked at my aunt in the eyes."

"How did she respond?"

"Same. Unmoved. She said I needed to know the truth. I'm not even sure Sara heard the whole thing because when my aunt got up shakily and walked towards the kitchen, she asked Sara if she was still driving us to the airport. So, she knew Sara had left, but I don't know when. My uncle Bob had also wandered to another room. Thomas seemed really upset but said nothing. Probably too polite to speak up. It was his first time with my family. He got up saying he was going to get our luggage. Chris was the only one who stayed. He kept puffing on his pipe, sitting calmly in his usual chair by the fireplace. He spoke very gently to me, saying that Aunt Rose was wrong to have done that. The way his voice sounded at that moment, his southern accent was so strong and unintelligible that it seemed he was the foreigner, and not me."

* * *

"LET ME TELL YOU THIS," Pierre said. "Dizzy spells are a common telltale about a major stroke coming up. Victims of strokes while driving all have some gash on the face from hitting their head. Your father died of a stroke, that's certain. But I haven't heard anything as nasty as what your aunt did to you in many years. It should bother you. It bothers me."

I shivered. "Explain to me why you see it as *nasty*."

Pierre groaned. "Hearing a different version of your father's death feels like you're losing him all over again," he explained, "and especially such a terrible death as suicide. If you were to believe it, it could destroy you. We must mourn by making peace with the loss. What you know of your father's death is part of what you used in order to mourn him and to accept that loss. This process becomes part of your identity. If that structure is shattered, you fall with it too. How we mourn a loss as significant as that of a parent is a huge part of who we are and how we face life afterward. By attacking the story around your father's death, your aunt threatens the basis of your mourning process. She exposes to danger the very fabric of the new being who emerged."

"Sara said that I'll never get an apology from her mother and that she feels completely self-justified."

"That's right! But she knows what she did, and she did it intentionally, I've no doubt. She may be regretting it, though."

"Sara admits that her mother can be nasty with her too. She lets it go out of family loyalty. I told her I know about family loyalty all too well, but I'll no longer participate in covering up abuse. I kept silent too much already about what I witnessed. Particularly about my sister... Sara then said I must follow my beliefs. It was obvious she was annoyed and defensive, especially when I explained that my reaction isn't just about me. Thousands of children all over the world get abused and keep quiet out of family loyalty. Enough of that."

"What did she say?"

"Nothing. But right after I spoke to her, I wrote a long letter to my aunt and emailed it to all my cousins, including Sara."

"Did they respond?"

"Julia called me from Haiti and said that Aunt Rose is ninety years old, so we'll have to forgive her. My cousin Alex wrote that he gives his mother the benefit of the doubt as to her intentions. He's learning that respecting others includes giving them the space and time to come to terms with their lives and reality. He accepts more and more that he can only change himself and, in so doing, also change the world. People let go of their paradigms when they're ready to. Facts have little or no bearing on how we see the world. Feelings are neither right nor wrong, and facts don't necessarily change our feelings."

"What nonsense! Feelings can be wrong! Your cousin Alex is full of it!"

"He wasn't happy with my views about suicide either. And he obviously had been fed the same suicide version of my father's death. He tried to reconcile me with it. He wrote that the way my father's life ended is a parenthetical statement at the end of an otherwise full life. He argued that suicide is an honorable letting go. He did, however, grant me the right to believe that suicide is from pain one is no longer capable of handling and that suicide sometimes involves aggression towards others."

"Damn right there's aggression in suicide!" Pierre snapped. "We're not part of the Japanese culture, and suicide in the West isn't Hara Kari. But my dear Io, you're like a shrink alone in her own mind, and your instincts are right. A great violence has been done to you. I told you why. You've mourned your father's death with one particular image of what it was. By challenging your story and the kind of peace you've made with the story, your aunt is attacking your ability to survive loss, and continue living. It was indeed a parting shot from your aunt. Her intent was to harm, and possibly even kill."

"But what have I ever done to her?"

"Nothing. It's what and whom you represent. I have listened to eighty-year-old people still eaten up inside with jealousy of some sibling, and actively wanting revenge."

"You think that's what's happening with my aunt?"

"I don't know. One thing I know, however, is that *she* knows."

VI. Haïti Homecoming

Io in the Year 2014...

I FELT NO FEAR sitting in an aircraft caught in large air pockets that shook it repeatedly. These clusters of emptiness in the atmosphere are the familiar signs of approaching Haiti from the air. But the man sitting next to me was a worse irritant.

He had the window seat and stuck a film camera held by suction cups on the small window, thus blocking the little view I could have of the mountains I was eager to see. I nevertheless frequently stretched my neck to catch a glimpse of the earth I loved. He saw nothing of my discomfort even though he looked at me furtively now and then and seemed busy eavesdropping on the rare exchanges in English I had with the air hostess, even though only about my snack or beverage preferences. He must have eventually been satisfied because he finally turned and introduced himself in French. "*Je m'appèle Jean-René. Je viens de Paris,* " he said, extending his hand. I understood that he must have detected my French accent when I spoke and assumed we had common ground enough to start a conversation.

After a few banal exchanges about where we each were traveling from, he finally noticed my renewed attempt to look out the window but misunderstood my reasons for it. "*La terre ici est muette. Ne vous fatiguez pas à regarder et comprendre,*" Jean-René declared, telling me that the land below is mute, don't bother trying to see and understand. "It is Haitians who are the problem," he explained further. "The chaos they create in their country is unbelievable."

"*Non. La terre n'est pas muette*—the land is not mute," I said calmly. "It communicates by showing. And this is my land. I am Haitian. And, following what you just said, I too am part of the problem."

"*Oh... je suis désolé...*" he mumbled, adding embarrassedly that he meant no offense. My skin color is so light, he hadn't realized I was Haitian.

"No offense taken," I said. "I just wanted to be clear about who I am." I then fell silent again and slid back into that impressionable stream of thoughts that he had interrupted when he introduced himself, and I started imagining what more I might say to this presumptuous Frenchman from Paris, keeping my thoughts to myself because I was not interested in engaging him. *Read its red-earth fissures,* I thought sadly. *Cracks, ravines and gullies, land blistered and raw like a brain... Listen to the story its eroded hills tell... 298 years of slavery... 32 coups d'états since the slave revolution... brutal American occupation started in 1915 and lasting nineteen years... adding to yearly climate upheavals... four hurricanes in 2009 alone... the 2010 earthquake left 300,000 dead in thirty-five seconds... so no, this earth isn't mute... it's you who's unable to see and hear the murmur of waves moving to a wounded shore... This earth holds countless words inside its breast... From the slave trade, to colonialism, to imperialism, and to the present lucrative industry of international aid, men have plotted to rape this land and the people who own it.*

Had Jean-René known my thoughts, he might have stopped trying to make conversation. "Millions of seedling trees have been planted all over Haiti," he said. "Haitians are only now understanding that the drought is caused by the deforestation of the mountains."

'Only now' are they understanding, he says... we're back to dumb Haitians being the problem... and he thinks he found a topic of interest to me... Well, at least he noticed that I care about the land...

"What kind of trees are they planting?" I asked absentmindedly, all the while recalling the mass reforestation of Haiti with Nymes some decades ago, and the contempt poor farmers and fishermen living in eroded coastal regions felt towards this foreign intervention. It was a time when these trees that produce nothing edible were brought in abundance to areas where people had no food—country people largely dependent on fruits of the earth for their daily sustenance. Haitians living in these rural areas greeted these reforestation efforts with derision and indifference. They were then judged to be slow-minded, uncooperative and illiterate natives by foreigners who thought at the time that they knew better than Haitians what Haitians needed.

The ills of illiteracy are often blamed on its victims. Its perpetrators belong to the colonialist or imperialist systems whose interests they defend. In general, extended and expanded illiteracy in Haiti created a constantly renewed and vast pool of cheap manual labor—defenseless and disadvantaged people in the midst of socio-cultural and scientific progress. It is no wonder they became a largely fatalistic people who feel at the mercy of gods they never seem to successfully placate.

"I do not know what kind of trees they are planting," Jean-René said, shrugging his shoulders. "My area of expertise is solar energy. I work for a company that installs solar disks."

Oh, dear... what a bore... He's going to feed me some technology, numbers and data... "Solar disks have been long overdue!" I nevertheless gasped as air pockets suddenly shook the plane again, sending my stomach up into my throat, thinking *Why am I always compelled to be polite even when I'm feeling imposed upon? Men don't seem to have that compulsion.*

"Oh, yes!" Jean-René exclaimed in a self-assured tone. "But it has been long overdue for 75 percent of the earth. We have got to stop cutting trees down for charcoal."

"Yes..." I said, "but bear in mind that no Haitian in the countryside would ever cut down any kind of fruit-bearing tree." Jean-René did not reply. I grew quiet again, detached, and murmured sadly, almost inaudibly, *But yes, we do have to stop cutting trees down so that each prayed-for rainfall stops washing the land away...* Yet I smiled inwardly, my mind filling with images having to do with charcoal. I saw anew these many moments in childhood spent crouched near a pot cooking on hot coals in the servants' quarters. I felt again my skirt bunched between my legs, pink skin showing around the edges of scabs drying up on my knees. I was waiting for our food to be ready. The point at which the cook came to check the cooking time and bent over the cast-iron pot to lift its lid was a thrilling moment. Sweet-scented, vaporous steam rose from the rice and beans, enveloping my face and squinting eyelids, the inside of my nostrils briefly stung by its sharp heat. Intimacy around hot coals included many hours in the penumbra of the laundry maid's room, sitting over the edge of her cotton mattress that was loosely covered with a single faded sheet. I loved to observe and feel the repeated magic in her careful gestures while she transferred hot coals into the black iron used to press the family clothes, careful to keep gray ash from spilling out of its side holes.

Jean-René interrupted my thoughts. "I do not like living in Haiti," he said, somehow thinking that this too would be of interest, "but I like my work there. What I do is extremely needed."

Oh, thanks for your sacrifice, I thought. *Such a big man...* I ignored him while other thoughts and images flooded me again. I saw two contrasting visions of my country. One image was of a fertile land sprouting anew with a multitude of green seedlings growing upwards towards the sun whose energy both plants and people would grasp and revere. The other image was of the wounded earth left in the aftermath of the 1804 slave revolt against the French colonialists, and which earned Haiti the title of being the First Black Republic. In violence, slaves had stolen the land of Haiti from the people who had, in violence, stolen them from their African land, bringing them to an island they had, in violence, stolen from the Indians. Being called the First Black Republic was an epithet full of glory for which Haitians have been paying an overwhelming economic, political and psychological price ever since. This price is not hard to comprehend judging only from hardships suffered just from the first Franco-American embargo of 1806, to having to pay in 1825 a 92 million gold francs indemnity to France for its losses in the slave trade and exploitation of Haiti's land resources, this sum being ten times Frances's own yearly budget in those days; and then there were the nineteen years of American occupation started in 1915 until finally, the last US embargo inflicted in 1993.

From these images, other thoughts came flooding. I reflected on the dichotomy constantly manifested in Haitian culture. I wondered if it is inevitable in post-colonial Caribbean cultures, anthropologically described as cultures of contact, alluding to a human event in a place where two or more different nations or races come to meet. And so, there seems to be an eternally constant polarity between two things in Haiti's socio-economic reality that impedes progress and the development of a communal identity. Division started during the slave revolution of 1804 and continued ever since, regardless of common goals of freedom and autonomy. We still display two different modes of occupying the land. The Creoles and the Bossales population of the nineteenth century still live on the same island where they perforce interact but remain foreign to each other, one resentful of the other's presence while wholly dependent on it. We still suffer intolerable contrasts and polarity between the whiter Creoles born from the sexual rapport of slave mothers with white colonialist masters, versus black Africans then called Bossales; the powerful versus the powerless; Catholicism versus Vodou; French speakers versus Creole speakers; mansions in sparse, exclusive neighborhoods versus shacks in vast slums.

Yet, during Francois Duvalier's dictatorship, an attempt was made to create a black elite and middle class. It was effective to a degree. Division lines started blurring, and a greater socio-cultural complexity has occurred, one profoundly influenced by other political and socio-economic factors as well. The proximity, wealth and power of the US to Haiti is the greatest one. A progressive and definite weakening of French culture, language influence and status in the country is occurring. Since Duvalier, people of the economic elite have been sending their children to US universities rather than to France, either because they already lived in the US in exile or would more easily be able to flee there if the sudden need arose.

Canada has been very welcoming and respectful of immigrants from the beginning, and there is a rich community of Haitian exiles there. I remember how my parents' generation, grandparents and great-grandparents were all sent to France for higher education. This is no longer the case. The use of the French language by the mulatto elite class in Haiti is thereby becoming less comfortable and fluent. In the meantime, Haitian Creole is changing both in Haiti and in Miami's Little Haiti. Language in Haiti is increasingly influenced by the great majority of Creole speakers living in the country due to the mass exodus of the educated, French-speaking population started during the Francois Duvalier dictatorship. At the same time, English is brought in through television, as well as by the necessity to take advantage of technological advances and tools used in all areas of commerce and health care. One television set in the slums will serve many families. People crowd into a small room and outside the door to watch, whether they understand or not. Children pick up English words and incorporate them into their exchanges in Creole. Street people now beg in a kind of English that sounds like Creole but isn't, asking, "*Giv mi won dala…*"

My thoughts were again suddenly interrupted, but thankfully not by Jean-René this time. It was the announcement that we were about to land. Tray-tables had to be put up, and seat belts fastened. As if meant to illustrate the thoughts I just had, the announcements were made in English, French and Creole.

Regardless of these issues I had just been mulling over, I knew that the home situation for me in Haiti would be unchanged and modeled after what they were in the days of my childhood. I would be speaking French at home with my cousins and their friends, Creole to the help in the house, the chauffeurs and other workers, and English to my husband at night. In those late-night conversations with Thomas after a long day of juggling back and forth through many variations of socio-linguistic situations, I would feel disconnected from everyone and foreign even to myself. I would go to bed with a lonely sense of self, a sensation that began during my adolescence and first political flight to France.

At the second announcement made by the air hostess, I made a greater effort to gather my thoughts and focus on what was going on around me. I opened my purse to check on my passport and the customs documents to be filled out that were distributed earlier to all passengers. It was at that time that Jean Baptiste tapped me on the shoulder. "*Ce serait bon qu'on se revoie*—It would be fun to see each other again," he said. "I am staying at the Hotel Montana in Bourdon. Here is my card in case you forget my name. I give it to you now because once we exit the plane and start going through customs, we might lose sight of each other. Not to mention the free-for-all struggle to identify luggage and keep it close at hand so a thief does not rip it out of your hands."

"*Je n'oublierai pas votre nom*—I will not forget your name," I said with an embarrassed smile. "I do not have my cards with me. But I know the Montana Hotel. The owners and their families have been family friends for generations."

"How about that! *Magnifique!*"

"*Oui*. It is great… But, do you know that the hotel was pretty much all destroyed by the earthquake?... I do not think it is back to its former glory yet. Yet, the owners started rebuilding right away… And do not worry, it is probably now constructed according to earthquake safety regulations. Many people from the UN died in that hotel… One of the two sisters who own the hotel almost did. I am told it was her son who persisted in looking for her among the wreckage, insisting that she was alive. He crawled under the rubble, calling out for his mother until he did find her… He risked his life."

Jean-René's mouth hung open. "*Incroyable*—Incredible! How brave!"

"Yes…" I smiled. "That is Haitians for you."

* * *

IT HAD ALREADY BEEN TEN YEARS since I last walked on this land. I had escaped on the last seat of the last plane out of Haiti after the Port-au-Prince airport had been shut down. Massive popular riots against President Aristide in 2004 had made the country unsafe, once again. It had been fortunate that my mother, my sister and I had already sold the family property of which I had charge as executor of my father's estate. Albeit in dramatic and rushed circumstances, I said goodbye at the time to the two women closest to me with a lighter heart than I should have, relieved to be returning to my life in America, even if that meant being perceived only as a divorced woman with an estranged adopted daughter.

Now, for my return to the place I once called home, Lucien and Julia would be waiting for me at the airport. Fearing for my husband's safety, I had traveled without him. My mother was no longer strong enough to suffer standing in the heat, the pervasive dust and the crowd at the airport, and I was apprehensive to see how affected by age she had become. I was also both sad and relieved that Europa would not be waiting at the airport either. It had always been painful to reconnect with my sister during these visits home. She saw me as the fortunate one who had escaped the family tragedies while she remained imprisoned in them. Her loss, abandonment and resentment were all-pervasive, and I felt choked by both the desire and the inability to save her. Because of my deep Christian faith and belief in an afterlife, I felt certain that Europa was now ministered to by angels in another realm—certainly, she deserved angels—and losing life on earth was no loss at all.

As for my own survival, I had developed the art of deadening myself before landing in Haiti. Perhaps these internal workings were what Jean-René kept interrupting, and why he irritated me. It was a partly unconscious process I had unwittingly learnt since I was a girl, at the time when I was first torn away from family and sent abroad to be shielded from political violence. I learnt to shift into a kind of emotional passivity and take the position of what is called by anthropologists a participant-observer.

My cousins were already in the habit of sheltering me. Their hosting me on this new trip home was not the first time. My father had been a compulsive builder. Our family house had gone up and up, one floor at a time. When he was left alone in his four-level mansion—children grown, wife having deserted him—he turned every

floor into an apartment for rent. When he died, I inherited a life of
tenant farming. I inherited trouble. Biblical prophecy foretells that
sins of forefathers will be brought upon their descendants. While on
the plane bringing me home, I had thought of Jean-René as a soul
coming back to repay his French forefather's sins in helping clean up
the human, economic and political mess they created.

I have wondered what sins I, too, was paying for during my life of
taking care of rental apartments. I was in charge of trouble during the
day while Michel, the watchman, took care of trouble at night. Great
trouble once came from one of these long-ago tenants. She was a Haitian woman educated abroad who held a high-ranking job in government finance. She soon turned into a werewolf, refusing to pay rent.

The house that my father had initially built stood on the upper
part of our land. There were two gates used to access the house. The
main gate stood on the upper part of the property while the second
one was way down at the bottom. During that time that I took care
of tenants living there, and before I eventually sold the property, land
and building, I always used the upper gate to return home at night.
Everyone living or working there knew my habits. I lived in a base-
ment-floor studio apartment underneath a stack of tenants who filled
my days with complaints about toilet malfunctions, water shortages,
dead inverters or the new spread of black spawn from frogs that
spoiled the turquoise-blue water of the pool.

But one evening, coming home around eleven o'clock, I felt a
sudden urge to change my route. Right before the point in the road
when I would be turning into the top entrance driveway leading to the
gate near which my father died, a whim inspired me to drive past the
entrance, go around, use the long loop the road made before entering
the narrow driveway that led to the bottom gate which, unlike the
other one, was always kept locked.

I stepped out of the car into the silence of the night and walked
the few steps to the locked gate. I inserted the key in the padlock and
pulled the chain off. I opened the gate wide, went back to the car,
drove it quietly through, parked it, switched off the motor and head-
lights.

I came out of the car to be instantly startled by the dark shape of a man moving speedily towards me, low to the ground, crab-like, until he stopped right at my feet, crouching still, and lifted his face towards mine. It was Michel, the night watchman.

"*Shush... pa fè bri, kache kò w*—Hush... make no noise, hide!" he whispered in Creole. "I've been watching out for you to come home. There's a car full of military with machine guns. They're parked right around the top gate. They're waiting for you. They want to arrest you. They mean to kill you. It's the lady on the third floor doing this. She has friends in the government. This afternoon, she ripped your telephone wires. She did it herself. You can't make calls anymore. She cut the electrical wires too."

"*Ki jan w fè konnen se li*—How do you know it's her doing?" I asked calmly, trying to resist the contagion of Michel's panic.

Michel stood up, staring me in the eyes, breathing very close. "*Mwen wè li ak de grenn je m! Epi, m te la nan bariè a lè yo parèt. Machinn nan plen zam ak nèg*—I saw her with my own two eyes! And I was there at the gate when they showed up. A car full of weapons and men."

"So?" I asked, still trying to deny the danger in what was happening.

"*So?*" he repeated after me, slightly mocking. "*So,* the car stopped at the gate right in front of me. It was eight o'clock maybe. One soldier came out. He asked if you were home. He knew your name. I said No. He said Okay and went back in the car. Then they backed the car and parked around the corner of the small parking area, opposite the gate. The way they parked, you wouldn't've seen them when you came down the alley, and with all of them packed in there. They're still in there now. Not one of them has come out of it since. You can't stay here! They'll arrest you! You'll disappear! We'll never see you again."

It was late, but the night was still hot and without the usual breeze from the bay. Only dogs barking in the hills could be heard. A thin film of sweat shone under the moonlight on Michel's skin. Bushes made dense, body-like forms in the dark. Michel was pacing, shaking his arms as if to rid them of insects clinging at the elbows. My thoughts were racing for what may have seemed an eternity to this man, unnerved with fear as he was.

"*Mwen va al kay kouzen m pou aswè a*—I'll go to my cousins for the night," I finally said. "But I first have to get my nightgown, some clothes for the morning and my toothbrush."

Michel moaned and flagged his arms. "*Ou pa ka al la! Ya wè w*—You can't go there! They'll see you!"

His concern for me made me smile despite my increasing alarm. "I won't use my flashlight," I reassured him. "The full moon's bright enough. Besides, the gate is on the other side of the building. My apartment faces this side… Go back to the top-level gate as if you're making your rounds and you're still expecting me."

I ended up spending eight days at my cousins' house, waiting until my lawyers and their own friends in the government had cleared the way for me to go home again and had forced the lady-werewolf to leave the premises, rent unpaid.

At first glance, the apparent hatred towards me by my tenant on the third floor was not justified, but it is explainable if one considers the social and political context of the island. My tenant was a black woman with a French university education and who, at that time, had a well-paid government job. My father had taught me to be careful about choosing my tenants. Nothing in this woman's appearance or outward circumstances foretold her subsequent behavior. She eventually became three months late in her rent and gave no reason for it. She just didn't feel like paying it any longer and hoped to get away with it by using her political clout. This problem was not uncommon for anyone owning property in Haiti at that time. Ownership was at your own risk, and the real law was that of the thug. People appropriated anything they coveted, and if you didn't like it, they paid to have you zombified or shot, or did it themselves. Someone owning land on which they did not actually live was busy fencing it with solid walls. These walls guaranteed nothing in terms of someone not building or forever squatting on your land, but it helped. Perhaps only long enough for you to find a buyer. I was more at risk being an unmarried woman manager in a machismo culture, and one perceived as having lost her footing in Haitian society by living abroad for many years.

Another aspect of the problem might have been the old historical color and class resentment. As far as I could see, my tenant lacked nothing in education and refinement compared to me, but there is no accounting for the way she perceived me or for old hatred towards the mulatto class from which I was obviously issued. I owned property while she didn't. The balance still looked in my favor. She had power to ruin my good time on earth, reverse the unequal balance she perceived, and she went for it. It is highly unlikely that she knew my family history and realized how invested we had been in this island since its beginning as a republic. Every generation of men in my family have been involved with overthrowing governments to right some perceived wrong while women struggled to keep the children safe. There are only a handful of us left in Haiti. The Duvalier dictatorship took care of that. Considering the woman's age, it is most probable that she grew up under that dictatorship and still harbored its poison in her breast.

In retrospect, however, the stay at my cousin's house had been fun. It was like those summer nights of childhood when cousins were always there to chat with. But also, the tension was familiar. Impending violence was the kind of excitement I knew. I did not have to go to the movies for it. For all Haitians then, the stuff of fiction or cowboy movies was the stuff of real life.

* * *

OLD AUGUSTIN WAS A NEW SERVANT. He was the first person I saw at my cousins' house when we got back from the airport, a man looking taller, thinner and more brittle than the blue broom he held. Lucien and Julia had picked me up at the airport and drove me straight to their house. Augustin was working in the entrance hallway when Lucien opened the front door. The old man immediately offered to take my heavy luggage from Lucien's hands to carry them in the room he knew the maid had prepared for me. During the following days of my stay, Augustin would still be the first person I bumped into every morning. Each time I would be struck by his eyes. They swayed about like black and white flags atop a rigid pole while he swept the white marble floor, appearing to be dizzied by the vast orderly house which he was newly hired to clean early every morning, and dazed by the daily effort it took for him to define himself in it.

The ride from the airport had been the usual strain I knew. Each traffic light stop is a new opportunity of awareness at being a player in a human tragedy. Beggars swarm around the car, knocking wildly at all windows. They see light-skinned passengers inside and assume it is soft-hearted foreigners who just landed, unused to the shocking sight of poverty, unaware of the ropes of street charity, all of it making them easy targets. The people's distress outside the car is such that one cannot risk opening any window to any degree to give anything. Beggars would instantly start slapping and fighting off each other to get the first grab of whatever morsel is handed out, then pummel the one who got it, snatch it from him and run. You'll lose your arm and anything on it if you try giving alms. There is not enough time at a traffic light to help each beggar, and even if there was time enough, the number of hands reaching out and competing is endless. The brutality is such that one rarely sees women begging at streetlights. The distress inside the car is also suffocating, but our discomfort only a moral one, if any. One must pretend not to notice the beggars because any eye contact causes a greater avalanche of pounding at windows and windshields. Each second of time passing is crucial for passengers' safety, and also for a beggar's chance to move or intimidate us into giving. But one cannot afford to feel anything at those times. Going from the airport to the house is an exercise at hardening the heart, killing compassion and disregarding good conscience. Without that, one could not stand to visit Haiti. In between traffic lights, the dirt and misery are overwhelming. Inside the car, people chitchat as a way to put blinders on.

"*Et comment était ton vol*—How was your flight?" Julia asked. Speaking French somehow cocooned us in an illusion of refinement and safe distance from the Creole mad desperation going on in the streets outside the car. Language established an "us" and a "them." And being part of the "us" was always a better affair.

"*Bien*—Good," I mumbled, unable yet to abstract away from the beggars and the poverty all around us. "The usual air pockets when we get close to Haiti... I made friends with the man sitting next to me. A Frenchman. His name is Jean-René."

"Ah? What is he doing in Haiti?"

"Seems he installs solar disks for some international aid company... he is staying at the Montana."

"The Montana? Ha! A luxury hotel like that? Same old story. International aid never reaches the poor, or very little of it... did you know that eighty percent of foreign aid goes to sustain staff's salary and lifestyle? It's well-known by now. There are all sorts of scandals. These people supposedly come to help the poor, and they live like kings! They rent villas with swimming pools, they enjoy a battery of servants or they stay at luxury hotels like your Jean-René, scouting for sexy black girls they can use for quick fun and then drop when they go home... Slave owners did the same thing... And to top it all, they judge us and look down on us. In their hearts of hearts, they are all racists."

"Ah... Julia... there is no real freedom when you are too poor to say no... But how are things for you nowadays?"

"Not good. Nothing has changed. People are hungry. The government does not care. Nobody feels safe. Kidnappings have increased. The ransoms have increased. People of our color are a target. They see mulatto, they think Money... And there are street gangs in Haiti now too. Drive-by shootings."

"Why is that? What happened?"

"Yes, my dear, gangs... Even tourists are not safe. People say it is the police doing it. They have not been paid in months... something we have never seen in Haiti! I mean gangs, not government employees not being paid... But that is ever since Americans emptied their prisons of illegal Haitian immigrants and sent them back home... Can you imagine? These people grew up in New York, they do not speak a word of Creole, they do not know anything about Haiti and do not care… they are just a bunch of murderers and rapists, and the Americans just sent them to us. Between hunger and crime all around, we do not know what to do and how to live anymore… and you cannot help everybody, so you just close your eyes and live among yourselves… And good help is really hard to find in Haiti nowadays too. It is not like it used to be. Nothing is like it used to be. This is not the Haiti you knew. You cannot trust anyone any longer… If you have cash or jewelry beyond what you can keep on yourself, we will put it in the safe for you… I told my sister-in-law the same thing. Thea arrived yesterday with the little girls, her two granddaughters. I am worried about everybody's safety. All of you here at the same time, it is worrisome, I cannot deny that, even if I am happy to see you… But Thea is staying with her mother and not with us. You will be staying with us in Thea's old room, downstairs."

I felt a surge of pleasure to learn that Thea was home again too, and that she would be separated from me only by the few steps leading from one house to the other. They were built a few years ago as a replacement of the serpentine path we used as children to visit each other. The old childhood passageway is now a steep, narrow flight of stairs that leads up to what is now Aunt Cécile's house. Her new house stands above her old house, and this old house had now been Lucien's and Julia's home for a long while. Lucien and Thea's childhood house has undergone several renovations and aggrandizements since we played there as children and celebrated my cousins' birthdays with orange-flavored cakes and canned asparagus sandwiches.

Thea and I used to play with dolls in her old room. She was gentle with me as if I too were a doll. It was calming. There was no downstairs then. It was a one-level house. The current second floor is where the family den, large bedrooms and bathrooms are now spreading at the top of a white marble flight of stairs, accessed through thick, white wrought-iron doors kept double locked at night. These renovations were done a couple of decades ago prior to Lucien moving his wife and children back to his childhood house. Thea had already made her life in America many years ago at that time. In the old days, she wore soft bangs over her kind, brown eyes, and her long blond hair was parted in two equal braids that the maid re-braided each day. There were silk ribbons tied in a soft, ample bow at the end of each braid. My own hair was long then too, but dark, and left to do what it pleased throughout the day after the hasty, brushing I performed myself each morning.

Aunt Cécile was deathly ill. Thea felt sure that her old mother would be cheered by the presence of her great-granddaughters, two blond angels with soft curls, seemingly flown out of an Italian Renaissance painting.

Julia seemed very preoccupied and unnerved by the recent dismissal of the young servant replaced by Augustin to be enjoying anyone's visit. A new servant to be trained in the house demanded extra vigilance, and she could not relax as much with company as she might otherwise have. The dismissed servant had been with them for a decade but had been caught stealing from a wallet full of money. "Hundreds of dollars were disappearing," Julia explained, "and we could not understand how it was happening. And all of it in US dollars, I tell you. We finally came to suspect him, although it did not make sense. He had been with us for so long, you see. But he knew the schedule of our lives like the back of his hand as if he had a clock in there with which he timed us by the second... Anyway, the day we caught him, he had been watching for Lucien to enter the bathroom for his morning shower. Once Lucien was inside, he had two minutes to rush upstairs and slip into the bedroom. Your cousin never spends much time under the shower. He goes in and out. But that day, he turned the shower on but did not go under. Instead, he silently went back to the room... Ah... it was terrible... the boy cried, and cried, and denied, even with the dollar bills in his hands. He pleaded...but he is lucky we did not hand him over to the police. God knows what they would have done to him in there. Nowadays, they do not waste time or jail space for the likes of him... you know what I mean."

* * *

BEES. BEES SWARMED with renewed agitation. They moved under the red-flowered Tiffany lamp that hangs from the ceiling right above the bar, at the level of a brightly colored painting of turbaned children wearing Turkish ruffled pants and skirts. They are having a feast of fruits at a round table, cutting golden papayas open, slicing watermelons, laughing wholeheartedly in a turquoise-colored room under an abundance of vivid banderoles and confetti. Bees buzzed as if they were joining the party in the painting under the Tiffany lamp, whose light was always switched on at night as a precaution. Bees had at first only been tolerated at the house when they established their hive above the front door before they were truly welcomed there. Bees are believed to be a good omen in Haiti. They bring wealth and good fortune to the household. So, my cousins decided that discomfort from bees flying around was worth tolerating. Even though it is a popular belief held mostly by the servant class, Julia paid heed to it and kept the bees she detests. The largest hive was eventually moved up and above the terrace on the top floor of the house where their honey is now harvested periodically by the servants, served as a delicacy for Lucien's breakfast of toast, scrambled eggs and a cup of Selecto coffee.

Augustin had not started the early dawn watering of the garden when I heard the first shot.

The ceiling fan was softening all sounds in my room, and I had at that moment just gone to pee in the bathroom adjacent to my bedroom and to the bar area where bees swarmed. Dogs and roosters in the nearby hills had not sounded their alarms yet. The sky was still a dark shade of blue, seen through the latticework of the bedroom window behind which grew hibiscus and birds of paradise whose leaves responded like soft drums to Augustin's morning water hose.

The second and third shots got my heart racing. They came as confirmation that the first had indeed been a gunshot.

I knew I should stay in bed and lie low. My father had lectured us children often enough that one does not move, or stand, after the sound of a gunshot. You should get down instantly. In my mind, I could still hear him speak, *If you're standing, you'd be giving yourself*

up as a target. You must determine what's going on first, and where.
Yet, I felt in me a child's growing agitation and excitement—fear and
fun were old companions.

Flashlights swerved past my window, over the bushes. And
disappeared. Then returned, in the silence. I heard my cousin's and
Augustin's hushed voices.

"Augustin! *Kote w wè l pase*—Did you see where she went?"

"*M panse li fè bò baryè a*—I think she went near the gate."

Hearing this, I got up and went out to join the bees.

I found Julia near the mahogany front door left ajar, standing by the bar
and the bees. She had no make-up on and wore a snug turquoise-blue
housedress. She kept looking out to the garden, biting her lower lip.

"Ah…you are up?" she said, not looking at me, eyes focusing
on the darkness.

"Happy birthday, Julia…" I said softly.

She smiled but did not turn to face me. At that moment, Lucien came through the darkness from the left of the front doors and
stopped to talk to his wife, holding a gun in one hand, barrel down. He
wore striped pajamas. *Like a convict*, I thought. Then, his thirty-year-
old son came to the door as well, coming from the right, frowning.

"Did you catch her?" Julia asked her husband.

"No. She just disappeared. Augustin thinks he saw her by the
gate. But it does not make sense. That is the completely opposite area
from where I saw her when I was on the terrace upstairs. I had her
right in the aim of my gun. I saw her clearly. She was lying belly
down in the grass. But after she heard me ask Augustin for a rope, she
realized that I was not going to shoot at her but wanted to catch and
tie her up… By the time I came down, she had split."

My cousins' son was pacing on the stone entrance floor, swing-
ing his gun in his left hand. "I would have fired two shots if I had not
been afraid to wake the little girls!" he said.

"It is a good thing you did not!" his mother snapped, and she
closed her arms onto her breast as if she were cold. Then, she turned
to her husband, "So, it is a woman?"

"Not even… a fifteen-year-old girl wearing rags."

"Rags?"

"Yes…. I think she must have jumped over the wall beyond the swimming pool and into our grandmother's garden."

"She would have killed herself!" Julia argued. "That is so high! Did she get wounded? Is there blood?"

"I do not know… I will look on the lawn later when it is daylight. She must have taken a chance and jumped… It is the only way I can explain her disappearance."

"What a thing to happen today!" Julia said. "On my birthday!" Then she turned to me, "You had better go back to bed, Io, and catch some sleep… I am going to get dressed for the six o'clock morning Mass at Saint Peter's… Today is the Feast of the Assumption. I want to get there early."

I went back to my room. I walked past the bees already swarming under the light of the Tiffany lamp, heading for my bed, still not knowing much of what had just happened and who had fired the shots.

I managed to go back to sleep, albeit a restless one, and had a nightmare. Its contained violence and sinister mood resembled much of those I have had since adolescence. These dream events felt painfully real and haunted me for several days after they occurred. It was as if they had not been made-up scenes by the unconscious, but were recovered memories of incidents I had witnessed during my youth under the Duvalier dictatorships, or emotions I had suffered and still held in. The dream I just had told a familiar story, the likes of which prisoners at Fort Dimanche might have once commonly experienced and not just dreamt, at a time of Haitian history when people would have chosen death over prison.

It was still dawn in the dream. A colorless dawn. Vendors had not yet come in great numbers. Rinds and faded odd lettuce leaves were lying about the hardened ground of the small open-air market. The night rain had carved ragged holes in the thatch roofs of the stalls. "*Makout yo te fenk la*—The *tontons macoutes* were just here," a young girl warned in a forceful Creole. "They came in a helicopter. They saw the place was empty, so they left."

A man appeared, cleanly dressed in freshly pressed khaki pants and shirt, asking the gathering vendors if they knew of his brother's whereabouts. Vendors at that moment made such noise in their greetings of each other and with the clatter of wares that the man was not heard and the arrival of two *tontons macoutes* in uniform was not immediately noticed.

When the man saw the *macoutes,* it was too late to hide. He straightened himself and stood stiffly, knowing that they were looking for political dissidents and that his presence and manner of dress in a peasant market at dawn would be suspect. He raised his chin up, looking in the distance towards the sea. The man seemed to have found strength there, because, anticipating the unavoidable *macoutes'* questioning and his probable arrest, he started taunting them. "How can I help you, gentlemen?"

One *macoute* slapped him. "Who do you think you are?"

The man stared the *macoute* in the eyes. He then suddenly grabbed the mother of pearl handle of the heavy gun that hung on the *macoute*'s right hip. His index finger was already on the trigger when the *macoute* quickly snatched the gun back with both hands, turned it around, pointing the barrel at the man's face.

The man looked again in the distance as if he were noticing something he had not before and as if he had a friend beckoning him from there, calming him. He said to the *macoutes*, "Give me a cigarette. I can't go like this, naked like this."

One *macoute* laughed, saying, "Why not?" He pulled a pack of Splendid from his pants' pocket.

The man reached for the unlit cigarette presented to him, placed it hesitantly between his trembling lips, then fell onto his knees. Then he bent even lower down to the ground, reached ahead of him and grabbed two handfuls of muddied soil that he lifted imploringly in a gesture of offering to the sky. He dropped on top of his head all the mud in his hands, mumbling, "For you are dust and to dust you shall return."

He then dug for another two handfuls of mud closer to his knees and was wiping his face with it when the first bullet struck him in the ribs.

The man cried out.

He must have expected both the shot and the pain, and yet he was still stunned by it—this death he had to recognize, confront and accept, death having come to him with so little time for preparation.

The second bullet made him cry out again, and he fell face down into the mud. "Ah…this is terrible… terrible…" he moaned.

The *macoute* was shooting to wound, not to kill, not yet. The man would have to feel his death come slowly.

The man heaved himself heavily. His whole body jerked convulsively with each additional bullet. "Ah… this is terrible…this is terrible…" he groaned and sobbed.

By the time I had woken up and got dressed, feeling deeply unsettled by the dream, Julia was back from Pétionville. She announced to me first thing, "It is a good thing I went to mass early. I would not have found a place to park or a seat in church. It was absolutely packed!"

"I will go to church with you on Saturday afternoon," I said as a form of apology for not accompanying her earlier. "Also, my mother sent word that she wants to see me. No doubt, she will have heard of the night's excitement, being just down the hill, and she will be itching with all sorts of questions."

"That is for sure," Julia said. "The servants' grapevine must be buzzing strong. They have nothing else to do… Anyway, we'll be celebrating my birthday at the Pétionville Club tonight. You are welcome to join us. Be here at six sharp."

"The club is still active? I thought the golf course had been turned into a tent city. What is the American actor's name again? The one helping refugees there?"

Julia made a brusque movement of the hand as if she were shooing a fly. "Sean Penn. But the tents are way down at the bottom of the golf course. You do not see them. The club is fine. Every Wednesday, they have a special buffet and entertainment. Luckily, today's Wednesday."

"And your birthday!" I was pleased to trumpet.

She responded with a lovely smile. "But what we benefit from higher up on the golf course are the people from MINUSTAH, the UN peacekeeping force. It is like they are protecting the club for us. We feel safe."

"I wonder, Julia... what about news spreading that they are the cause of cholera outbreak? There's talk about rape too..."

"Well, Io, we do not have real contact with them. All I know is that the MINUSTAH people at the club are all Brazilians, and they are friendly... For them, it is like being on vacation. They have nothing to do. You see them sitting around all day, drinking sodas... And they get paid more because Haiti is supposed to be a dangerous assignment."

* * *

CHRIST'S WOUNDS still bleed on the cross that stands outside the pastel-colored ruins of the Port-au-Prince Cathedral.

From that cross, Christ overlooks the gray mass of the open-air market that spreads in the mud-and-rubble streets of the former Port-au-Prince. Under the toothless shade of crumbled walls, destitute Haitians continue to exhibit the survival skills of cacti and rodents. Cars honk their way through, carving themselves a slim passage inside the thick puzzle made of stalls and people. Dust-covered papayas, bananas, fly-covered meats, grimy balloons strangled together in bunches of garish colors, ruffles-and-frills baptismal dresses for infants of unfortunate births, mint-flavored toothpaste, rose-scented soap bars, and parts from computer carcasses apparently immune to rust and rot are incessantly bargained over by an unstoppable swarm of beings whose human forms blend, merge and collide in an infinite, anxious ocean of putrefying matter.

Most of Port-au-Prince's churches crumbled during the earthquake. The church of Saint Louis King of France, where my father's funeral was held, became an empty lot fenced with scraps of rusted metal roofing sheets, joined and nailed together on imported two-by-four wood posts. This had been a family church since the days my great-grandparents built it.

The Sacred Heart Church where I did my First Communion had also collapsed. In its place, weeds and gravel were all I saw.

The magnificent National Palace was turned into rubble. Its white innards and secret archives were left open to the winds, offered to thieves and foreign journalists alike. Palm trees were nevertheless still erect in the front, as they seem to have been in all eternity, eternity being, for me, my own lifetime.

The red and blue national flag was still high up on a pole, but it too had given up to winds and thieves and rot, as once, years ago, anti-Duvalier rebels' heads were, stuck on a pole through the red slash of severed necks—punishment for having tried to overthrow the dictator. These bi-color cloth symbols of Haitian national identity were left to the appraisal of passers-by, strolling on the sidewalk along the green iron fence bordering the lawn of the palace, or given to the gaze of odd people watching through narrow windows of public transport buses. These drove by at an incoherent kind of speed, faces of passengers framed within the written invocations in primary colors saying, "SAINT JUDE, PATRON OF DESPERATE CAUSES, HAVE MERCY."

"*Kote Ri dè Mirak*—Where's Miracle Street?" I asked my chauffeur.

I knew that I would be experiencing my country again through the safe cocoon of old, established, family privileges, but I did not yet know that I would be driven through the ruins of my childhood city in an air-conditioned, bullet-proof car, driven by a tall, skinny young man who had lost his mother in the earthquake along with the other thirteen members of his immediate family.

Jean-Marie was a quiet man who, since the catastrophe, had been living with his wife, infant son and daughter under a gray plastic sheet roof held up in the front by two broken-branch, makeshift pillars, and in the back, by the single remaining wall of his small house. This was a calm young man whose attentive smile as he opened the car door for me every day made me feel lost for words. He had to leave his tent at 6:00 am to get to the house by 8:00 am. It wasn't that the distance was great. Not at all. But he first had to walk carefully, climb over and stumble through the uncleared ruins of his own neighborhood until he reached the main street where he waited for public transport to drive by. This is not a culture of written bus schedules. In those early hours, the busses are filled with people trying to make it to work, and they do not always stop. The first bus would eventually take him downtown Port-au-Prince. Once there, he then had to wait for another public transport going towards Pétionville. These were the most crowded in the rush-hour mornings. It was deeply moving to me, and a cause for wonder, how Jean-Marie nevertheless smelled of fresh soap every morning and wore impeccably clean pants and T-shirt in spite of his living situation and transport conditions. And when I finally dared ask him how he managed that with no house and no running water, he just laughed. He never told me. Yet he could sense my admiration and compassion, and he was pleased to have been noticed.

The first time that my cousin sent him to pick me up at the house and drive me, Jean-Marie said, "Bonjou, Madame Io," with a large smile. Employees of any kind will always include Mr. or Mrs. before one's first name or family name when they address people of superior social status. Using the first name instead of the family name may be a discreet form of affection unless the employee just doesn't know the family name, and this would have been the case between Jean-Marie and me.

Having said hello, Jean-Marie then stood politely and courteously to open a side door for me to sit in the back, as is customary between chauffeur and passenger. But I said, "*Non. Mèsi Jean-Marie. M'ap chita devan avè w. M'a wè pi byen*—No. Thank you, Jean-Marie. I'll sit in the front with you. I'll see better." He seemed embarrassed at first that I had crossed boundaries. But he quickly got used to it, was always talkative and helpful.

"*M bezwen wè Ri dè Mirak*—I need to see Miracle Street, Jean-Marie," I said again. "I really need to see it." Miracle Street was where my father, my cousins' father, our grandfather, and a whole genealogy of men of my family had held their offices.

My father went downtown Port-au-Prince every morning for forty years and worked on Miracle Street next to the Nova Scotia

Bank, across from Mr. Stark's glass store, itself next to the sandwich and ice cream shop where he sometimes took us kids for rum-raisin ice cream on Saturday night. I thought of Miracle Street and the Nova Scotia Bank a lot when I traveled to Canada ten years ago and stayed in Spencer Island in the house full of fossils. The street and the bank had been landmarks of my childhood, emblems of my father and paternal ancestry. Now that I was in Haiti again after ten years of absence, I wished to see the old street's features, behold them once more as they were, and not as I feared to discover them—desolate, fractured, haunted. It was as if finding the old street would be like finding my father again, remembering my first pencil, the one he gave me—milky white with a single red ball that seemed magical, and the French words *Farine Boule Rouge* written in black, meaning Red Ball Flour.

My father and my cousins' father were importing a brand of flour called "Red Ball." I do not know which country they came from, but these imports at the time gave me a glimpse of the larger world beyond Haiti and one about which I fantasized. These pencils were promotional items. Yet it seemed to me then that the pencil my father gave me was the only one of its kind. It did not matter that there were boxes of them stacked deep in the back of the family butter factory which produced cooking butter for the Haitian population during all the years of my life, up to the very day of the earthquake that destroyed offices, factory, the childhood miracles of Miracle Street and all of Port-au-Prince.

"*Men... kote Ri dè Mirak,* Jean-Marie—But... where is Miracle Street?"

"*Nou te fenk la*—We were just there," Jean-Marie answered sweetly. "That's where you bought the two fans for your mother."

"That was Miracle Street?"

"*Wi. M te panse w te konnen*—Yes. I thought you knew..." His voice was as gentle as a sea breeze. "*Men sa pa fè anyen si ou pa te rekonèt li*—but, it's okay that you didn't recognize it."

I was close to tears. "No... it's not okay..."

Jean-Marie took a quick, furtive glance at me while driving, careful to watch the road and the people crisscrossing it. "I remember when the buildings were destroyed," he said. "You walk through town, and the whole time, you don't know where you are. That's how it was for me too." Jean-Marie spoke as if he was just remembering those times, but I knew his words were meant only to soothe me. I knew that. He was addressing the part of me who lives beyond the social boundaries that separated us and that partakes of our shared humanity. He was simply being kind. "I was home, and yet I was lost," he said again. "But I got used to it. It's like I learnt the face of my country all over again. Every building, every street has a before-and-after face."

I laughed, but only out of a sadness mixed with a dark sense of humor. "I know what you're saying. It's like ads you see for acne medicine or weight loss. Except that here, the change is a disfigurement rather than an improvement… And speaking of disfigurement, Jean-Marie, I forgot to ask you what was that big building downtown we passed on the way down? It's like a big, blue box."

"Oh, that's the electric company, Madame Io."

"Ugliness remains," I said, "easily identifiable while we struggle to recognize the ruins of everything else."

Jean-Marie was silent, taking my words in, and then said, "I learnt to identify the ruins and see the differences between each. To you, right now, the streets are like rotted mouths. They all look the same. But to the dentist, each one's different."

"Jean-Marie, please take me back to Miracle Street. I need to see it and know it. Please drive slowly when get there."

We were proceeding down Miracle Street, and it was painful for me to recognize some of it. My mind was piecing these broken slabs and chunks back together to recreate the buildings I knew and loved. These were my family ruins. We were driving down the street slowly, as if following an invisible funeral.

"*Gade on Blan devan bank Nova Skosya a*—Look at this white man in front of the Nova Scotia Bank!" Jean-Marie suddenly exclaimed. "*Genlè de vakabon ap bal pwoblèm*—Looks like two bums are hassling him."

I looked ahead of us in the direction Jean-Marie was looking and recognized Jean-René, the Frenchman who had sat next to me on the plane. "*Vanse machinn nan jis devan l pou n sa ranmase l. M konn msye*—Drive the car closer so we can pick him up. I know him."

Jean-Marie pressed on the accelerator and made a sudden stop in front of the group. Noises from both the charged-up engine and screeching tires startled all three men.

"Jean-René! *Montez*—Get in!" I called from the front-seat window while observing the two men instantly running away. Jean-René did not hesitate either. I am not even sure he recognized me before he opened the car's back door and rushed in, wearing a yellow and red Hawaiian shirt, white Bermuda shorts, flip flops, sunglasses and a flat-top boater hat. *What's that get-up about? Maurice Chevalier or Frank Sinatra on a holiday? Seriously? How does he not expect to be harassed? Doesn't he know that people around him are desperate?*

"Ah… *Merci*—Thank you!" he said to me, ignoring Jean-Marie. "*Vous tombez à pic. Je filais un mauvais coton*—You have perfect timing. I was in a jam."

"*C'est à Jean-Marie, mon chauffeur, qu'il faut dire merci. C'est lui qui vous a repéré*—You should thank Jean-Marie, my chauffeur. He's the one who spotted you."

"You thank him for me. I feel shaken and out of sorts right now, and I do not speak Creole."

"You do not speak Creole? *Merci* is the same word in French and in Creole… How do you work in this country if you cannot communicate with the workers?"

"I speak French to them… they manage."

"*They* manage, and you cannot? *They*, the illiterate people, while you cannot in spite of all the learning you have had since birth?"

"It is good for them to speak French… a real language… and certainly more useful to them in this world."

"What world is that? Where and when will they ever travel that French would be useful to them? I cannot believe that you come to this country and snub its people's language… Besides, any linguist can tell you that Creoles are *real languages*… It is racist social contexts that have prevented them from developing fully." I could not help myself. Without a preamble, I started right in on him. I wanted to slap him for being such a fool, and all my pent-up resentment burst forth. "Immigrant workers coming to France are expected to learn French, so why is it you cannot learn Creole in a Creole-speaking country?"

"I do not have time, and I do not know how much longer I will be coming here."

"You will never get out of here, to begin with, if you keep going out in the streets of Port-au-Prince dressed like that. Might as well carry a sign that says, 'I am a tourist. I have excess money to play with. Come and get it.' You are asking to be killed."

"*Vous êtes dure*—You are hard on me."

"*C'est pour votre bien*—It is for your own safety."

"*Ah... Merci donc.*"

"Yes. And I will be taking you back to your hotel right now before I go home. I am not letting you out alone in the streets of Port-au-Prince dressed like that."

"Streets? What streets? It is going on four years, and Haitians have not even begun to rebuild their city in spite of all the international aid."

"What international aid? In whose pockets did the money fall? This country has been raped by one foreign power or another ever since Columbus. And that was in 1492! And you are going to blame the victim for their scars? But I see that slavery has left you a scarred man too."

"What do you mean?"

"Your disdain for black people... your racism... you are emotionally stunted and insistently blind over centuries and centuries of ills against a targeted black population... those are your scars... you carry them in the mind and in your soul."

"Wow... I will ignore your insults... but tell me, how *targeted* are they now? We are helping black populations all over the world."

"Slavery, colonialism, apartheid, racial segregation with occidental powers gorging from slave work and territories they stole. That is *how targeted*... the damage is huge. Look at the division and occupation of all of Africa that was organized in 1885 at the Berlin conference... and twenty thousand workers killed by French colonists alone during the construction of the Congo-Ocean Railway, while the first concentration camp German colonists created in Namibia was for black people. Always black people."

"*Vous y allez fort, ma chère*—You are striking a bit hard, my dear. And all that was long ago. We are not in the nineteenth century anymore. You live in the past, my dear."

"What past? I am speaking of present issues. I am speaking of Africa's development thwarted because its people had no rights and no power for centuries. Africa emptied of its population and its riches... and I suppose that you are going to blame Africans for all that like you are blaming Haitians for their misery when you know nothing of the burdens of their history, and how history keeps repeating itself. You need to open your eyes to the gifts of colonialism that keep on giving while climate upheavals keep grinding them down deeper."

"*Oh... mais ne vous fachez donc pas*—But do not get angry."

"I am not angry... I am educating you... I am giving you things to think about for the rest of your life."

"Ah... a teacher. Very good. I want you to be my teacher. I love that."

"Good. Because you will keep going to countries with developmental problems. It will make you a better man to think of your role there and of the world history that ended up bringing you among these people. Learning to speak with them would be a first step."

Jean-René let out a short laugh. "You would make a great preacher. But I want you as a friend, not my preacher... And look! We have just reached my hotel. Let us have a drink and discuss how we will change the world. Shall we?"

"No. Thank you. I am glad I got you out of a tight spot downtown. But I must take these fans to my mother, and Jean-Marie needs to go home. His day's work is done."

"Dinner then? Name the day."

"Thank you. But again, no. I will be leaving soon. I am here for a short stay. And I am a married woman who respects her husband. In this country, a married woman does not have dinner alone with a stranger."

"Oh, but these are antiquated, traditional views. You are too smart to stick to them. It is only dinner."

"Why do you want me to let go of my *antiquated, traditional views* when you hold on fast to yours?"

"What antiquated views of mine are you talking about, my dear Io?

"Your racism, my dear Jean-René."

I thought that the fans would help my mother chase away the mosquitoes, the heat and the smells coming from her neighbors' private generators. But when she saw my gift, she was annoyed.

"Not just one, but *two* fans!" she jeered. "My poor child... we never have electricity when we need it. What do you want me to do with those things?"

I argued with her. "What is that high, enormous, ultramarine-blue box of a building of the electric company for, if there is no electricity?"

"A bright touch of ugliness," she said. "Every city has them."

"I refuse to laugh, Mother. That building devours the landscape like the Presidential Palace used to. It is in your face wherever you stand in Port-au-Prince. At least the Presidential Palace was beautiful... You mean that they have money to build a monster of an electric company but none to run it?"

"Yes."

"What kind of power is it that has no power?"

"Haitian power," my mother scoffed. She then turned her humped back to me, searching for the nearest chair. She waddled carefully to it, reaching out with a quivering left arm, sliding and scraping one black sandal at a time until she could finally clutch the chair's padded arm with fingers swollen with arthritis, then turn halfway in a brusque movement that showed no trace of her once legendary grace, and with a groan, she sat heavily down.

Oh... my dazzling mother... I thought. *Where have you gone? How painful to see you like this, a wreck deprived of its bold sails, chest harrowed by contrary winds, drained of all contents, deserted by family... you're my Marie-Celeste, my luminous brigantine who long ago visited from afar, and stayed, and brought hope, charm, ideas... Your vitality is nearly finished, your destiny played out, the bay of Port-au-Prince surely to be your final stop... But I'm not ready....*

"God is angry," my mother was saying. "He shows it with the heat. He shows it with the deluge. My poor Europa would be going out of her mind from it... it drives me mad too... I cannot get used to her being dead... I cry all the time... As you can see, her photos are all over the house... Poor child! The earthquake would have broken her heart and killed her stiff on the spot if she hadn't been dead already... Maybe there is a God, and he knows what he has spared her, but I miss her every day that I breathe... But God has not spared me at all... I suffer, but I do not want to die. I am afraid of ending up in a coffin like my child... I cannot make sense of the coffin... my beautiful Europa, just ashes in a box... And the other night, you were not here yet, there was a storm as if it was the end of the world. It sounded like bombing during the war. I was not afraid then, I was a child, I was excited, but I was afraid that night... I stood at the window, gripping the wrought iron bars, looking out. Rain so strong it would have lashed my back as hard as a whip. I swear... Anybody out that night got a whipping, for sure... I kept thinking, God is angry, God is angry, Oh by God, he is really angry... even the dogs were afraid... They hid under the bed. They took turns to come get me. They fretted around me and nibbled at my ankles. It was like they were saying, 'What are you doing there, Mommy? Come with us under the bed. We are afraid...' I was afraid too, but I was hypnotized by the sky, how thunder and lightning tore at the darkness... God's anger was splendid! You ought to have been there!"

* * *

THE SONG GOES like this: "*Yoyo, se on bon ti gason ki konn di, 'Mademoiselle, je vous aime'*—Yoyo is a nice young man who often says, 'Miss, I love you...'"

We had sung it in our youth, and now we were all middle-aged.

My cousins and their friends had gathered at the Pétionville Club to celebrate the birthday that had the good fortune to fall on a Wednesday-at-the-Club night. I had driven with Lucien, Julia and Thea in another bulletproof car than the one Lucien lent me for the duration of my stay.

I was eager to see the club again, even if it did not hold any really happy memories for me. I had been a mediocre tennis player who never could show off her game using the best tennis racket or wore the latest tennis outfit that others envied; I would never relax in a bikini around the pool because I could not ignore the probing look from prospective boyfriends while I felt insufficiently endowed with hips and breasts; I was anxious at club parties because the clash between the exacting sensuality young men expected from me and the romantic love I dreamed of instead, caused me to walk about with a hole in my stomach.

The club had gone through many changes since the earthquake sliced its main building through the middle. Repairs and improvements have, however, made use of and kept that disastrously opened middle section, an architectural trauma transformed into an open terrace that turned out to be quite pleasant when the sky is blue. It allows tables and chairs and colorful umbrellas to be carefully arranged for tennis players to settle, seeking refreshments after a game, men indifferent to the pungent scent of their sweat. The bar, restaurant, kitchen and bathrooms are now on one side of the open-air divide while elegant lounging areas with plush, bright sofas and white wicker armchairs stretch on the other side. The white walls of this relaxing salon are ornamented with paintings of oversized tropical flowers that create a comforting sense of the bountiful exuberance and reliability of life.

That Wednesday of Julia's birthday, however, waiters wearing red pants and Hawaiian shirts made the constant back and forth crossing between both areas under a torrential rain. They held silver trays in one hand and a black umbrella in the other. They brought us the mixed drinks we ordered, as well as a continuous flow of assorted appetizers that added up to a full meal at evening's end—paté on melba toasts, cheese and lobster puffs, shrimp cocktails, mini pizzas, meat pastries, fritters and marinades, and countless other Haitian specialties. Because of the weather, our family and friends who gathered to celebrate Julia's birthday were the only people present. We had the club and the artists of the show all to ourselves.

The singer, Roulo Courtin, held a guitar at the microphone. The aged singer had also been a performer at parties during our youth. He now had brought two of his sons and a daughter to sing with him and regale the audience, their voices nevertheless drowned out by the rain. When they started the Yoyo song, however, we didn't need to hear the words—we knew them by heart—the song and Yoyo had never left us.

The Yoyo in the song is a simple, young black man who has the singular grace of an even disposition. Everyone is fond of him. He sells peanuts. He enjoys his customers so much that he will use for them the only French he knows, saying, "*Mademoiselle, je vous aime,*" because he knows how it gives the ladies a brief illusion of being sophisticated, set apart, as true French speakers in Haiti are, and even if these customers are actually like Yoyo—native Creole speakers, historically, socially and forever eluded and marginalized by the French language.

Yoyo is poor, uneducated, unattached, a street vendor always giving more than what you ask for. The song tells how, "*lè w mande l pou dis li ba w pou kenz*—when you ask him for ten cents' worth, he gives you fifteen." And still, when you ask him for fifteen, he'll give you twenty's worth, "*ak tout degi la dann*—and with extra added on."

Yoyo measures the peanuts he sells in a shot glass. Despite his poverty, he is delighted with life as he knows it and with the social order in which he has a very low position. Yoyo, therefore, was the best kind of poor, black peon—you could rely on him for continuous good mood, honesty in the face of wealth, humility in the face of debasement, and pride in service brought to the point of giving you more than what you ask for. Yoyo represents the perfect, disappearing, old servant class, the poor who are content to remain poor, the very kind of servant Julia said you can't find in Haiti anymore.

My cousins' friends were friends of my own youth as well. I had not seen them in decades. I watched them enter the lighted halls of the club that night as if they were ghosts—people once alive, having dramatically changed form, unrecognizable from the wear of years. They seemed the deeply contaminated living dead, lepers whose disease distorts and eats away their features but who have dared this once to come out of the nearby hills where they hide. They had survived much, having immured themselves with a few trusted servants and all the objects of modern comfort they hauled from America. I felt a profound tenderness for them, and a malaise—I saw myself in them.

Yoyo's song came again as an encore, and we stood to sing along in a kind of salute to the death cortège of something once dear and venerable. We, the women, were singing, not the men. The men were waiting for the emotion over Yoyo to cease so they could continue with politics and economics, and the hot subject of the day. At song's end, boisterous Tony was the first to speak.

"You should have shot her dead!" he declared buoyantly, addressing my cousin. "You let her live. She'll come back. And with help."

Tony was still tall and wearing his disturbingly self-confident grin. He had been the handsome catch whom all upper-class girls of my generation had swooned over, even if he was Lebanese. A distant cousin of mine's marriage to a Lebanese man had created some uproar in the family at the time. Her father spoke of disowning her. It no longer is an issue now. Lebanese are respected for being hard-working, appreciated for their single-minded devotion to family, and assimilated through the status given by having accumulated lots of money.

In the old days, Tony flirted with all the girls, at times flaunting his catch-of-the-day, particularly on the carnival floats in February, where he stood with an open shirt, pouring Barbancourt rum down his throat or over his hairy chest. But Tony went and married a girl from Nicaragua to whom he is devoted. He is now balding so severely that he seems flat-headed, and the top portion of his head to have been lopped off. He squints through glasses so thick that his dark eyes are distorted to the size of duck eggs. His teeth are long and yellow, lengthening still. His face is fashionably unshaven, therefore prickly, showing salt-and-pepper stubble that intimidates mosquitoes, so they concentrate on his wife's legs instead. He sits in a slouch and crosses bare, bony legs that end on oversized feet shod in dirty sneakers with no socks. When Tony stands up, the slouch down his lower back transfers into a curve on his upper back.

"I wouldn't have hesitated," Tony argued again loudly. "Two bullets in the head. That is what she longed for!"

"Kill her, and I will have the police on my back?" Lucien questioned calmly, scratching his throat afterward.

"Give the police some money under the table," Tony advised with a grunt and a chuckle, "and they will go away, grateful you shot some thief for them." He kept rubbing his lower thighs near his knees as if he were trying to pull at his khaki shorts to cover them. Perhaps he was somehow self-conscious of his bare legs. I was surprised at how casually he was dressed at an evening club gathering, but nobody seemed to mind.

"Nowadays, the police look for any reason to put you in jail," Frantz said, joining in the discussion with his customary well-reasoned diplomacy. "You kill somebody on your land, and you will do two days of jail, no matter what, even if you were defending your life, and even if the thief is found with a gun in his hands… And you do not want to find yourself in jail. Not in Haiti. Not now, not before, not ever."

Frantz has worked hard all of his life to amass wealth and control his shyness. The frustrations brought by his lifelong efforts have made him an angry man. His blue eyes have a warm yet ruthless gaze. His son, Baptiste, his French daughter-in-law and their two children lived in a house they rented from Lucien, situated right below my cousin's house. It was from Baptiste's house that the gunshots had originated.

Baptiste is the love of Frantz's life, and Baptiste's youngest child is the spitting image of his grandfather Frantz when he was a boy. When we were children, Frantz's shyness was so painfully uncomfortable that it seemed contagious, and any attempt to talk to him made me blush.

"Okay then, it is simple," Tony was saying, "you kill her and throw the body out the gate. You wash your hands of it, and nobody can pin it on you." He leaned forward to look at my cousin closer as if to add weight to his argument. "The corpse is not in your home. You do not know a thing about it. Not your business. Wash your hands of it." He executed the gesture he had just mentioned, and sat back in his armchair, grinning.

Lucien smiled too, but with some irony, turning to Frantz. "Who shot who anyway?" he asked. "There were three shots fired."

"She shot the first shot," Frantz answered with confidence, picking up his drink. "She had a gun! At least, that is what Baptiste's security guard said... and that he fired the second one... But who knows what the truth is, right?"

"That girl in rags could not have owned a gun!" Julia interjected suddenly, holding a shrimp. "Where would she have had the money to buy one? That makes no sense... Besides, I am glad my husband did not kill her. All this upset... A woman killed in my yard and on the day of the Assumption at that? Ah, no... Baptiste, your security guard is lying to cover up the fact that he was sleeping... that girl must have made some noise that frightened him. He shot in the air, not knowing where to shoot." Julia then turned to Baptiste and asked, "And where was your wife in all that commotion?"

"She was alone in the house with the boys," Baptiste said, adjusting himself in his seat, then crossing his legs. "She locked herself up in a closet with the boys. She is French. She is not used to all this... I was out of town. I came back this afternoon."

"But tonight, she is coming to spend the night at my house in La Boule with the boys," Frantz declared, pointing an index finger in the air. "I do not want the kids exposed to more of this if the thieves come back."

"They are not going to come back to our house. We were not the ones being robbed. It was the small house next door," Baptiste argued, uncrossing his legs and leaning forward to pick up a mini pizza. "The owner is a woman. She is away in the Dominican Republic. Every time she leaves town, she gets robbed. I do not think she cares. Last time, they cleaned her furniture out. This time, the girl was not alone. The security guard says there were two men with her. They left a suitcase. They are coming back for it. No doubt about that."

"Why would they take this kind of risk to retrieve an empty suitcase?" Frantz's wife asked, holding her rum cocktail with her customary, upright elegance. She was Baptiste's stepmother, and usually careful not to interpose herself between her husband and his son. "And even if it was full, they know we will be waiting for them to come back."

"The suitcase was not empty," Baptiste remarked affably. "It was full of food. They emptied the fridge."

"They must be desperate to risk all that just to empty a fridge!" Frantz's wife pointed out. Tony was twisting in his seat. "That is what I was telling you!" he exclaimed. "You should have killed her! When these people are hungry, they are desperate and, therefore, dangerous. They act without thinking, and you cannot predict what they will do."

But Frantz was still following his own mind's track, stimulated by Lucien's previous question. "If the girl is supposed to have fired the first shot," he asked his son, "and your security guard the second, and supposing that he is not lying, who fired the third?"

"I did," Lucien said.

"And you missed her?" Tony cut in, laughing delightedly.

"I would not have missed," my cousin argued, clearing his throat. "I shot in the air to frighten her and told her to freeze. That is when she laid down in the grass, and I got a good look at her... But then she heard me tell Augustin to get the rope, and she realized that I was not going to shoot her. So, she made a mad dash, and going so fast that I do not know where she went... It was dark, lots of bushes. That helped her."

"Your Augustin probably helped her!" Tony interjected with amusement. "Did you check the servant's rooms?"

Lucien was startled. He paused, then seemed to dismiss Tony's suspicious idea and turned to Baptiste instead, "But if she had a gun, where is it? Did your night watchman find it?"

"No," Baptiste said, raising his eyebrows and rubbing the back of his neck with one hand. "Maybe she dropped it in your own yard when she laid in the grass?"

"If she had a gun when I fired in the air to frighten her, would she not have fired back?" Lucien replied while signaling to one of the waiters. "Maybe she dropped it when she jumped the wall between your house and mine? That wall is high too... I will have Augustin look for the gun around the wall in the morning. If she lost a gun, she will come for that before she comes for the food."

"Maybe," Baptiste said thoughtfully, looking down at the table and its display of hors d'oeuvres, "but the wall around my house is not that high. Every time thieves come in the neighborhood, they end up jumping into my garden. My garden is an escape route, I swear..."

"Sweetheart," Julia interposed. "Get barbed wire installed on their wall tomorrow, and on ours too. I insist on that."

"Yes. I will take care of it," Lucien assured his wife, casting her an affectionate glance.

"Barbed wire might be more effective than paying for a security guard," Frantz remarked, shifting position in his chair. "Guards are getting more and more expensive, and they are even more scared than you or me... Security companies just put a uniform over some country peon, a gun in their hands, pay them a pittance, and charge you a fortune for a kind of security you never have or feel... I have three of them at my Pétionville store, not to mention two at my house. I have yet to find any one of them awake when I make a surprise check... And you cannot trust them either, no matter what you pay. Sometimes they are the ones to bring the thieves in. They inform on us. They know when we are out of town. Have you not noticed?"

"I trust my security guard," Baptiste argued, putting his drink down on the table by the platter of juicy, crunchy meat marinades that the waiter had just brought. "But it is not because he is a good guy," he said, picking up a fresh, warm marinade, gobbling it whole. "I have got a technique. I reward him each time I make a surprise check and find him awake."

"How do you manage that? I would like to meet a security guard you find awake when you check!" Tony said.

Baptiste leaned forward, picked another marinade, taking his time, letting Tony wriggle in his seat, then explained slowly. "Once or twice a month, I set my alarm in the middle of the night, a different hour each time. I get up, get out, and I silently sneak up on the security guard. I do that for the store too. It is the only times I ever go out of the house at night without calling my security guard first and ask if all is okay out there. I usually do not move out of the house until he has made a round and tells me that I can come out. I just do not risk it. And even if it is seven o'clock, and we are just going out for dinner."

"If you were out of town," Julia remarked with an ironic smile, "your security guard knew that you could not be paying him a surprise visit, and we now know that he was lying to cover up the fact that he was sleeping... I was right. The girl never had a gun in the first place."

"How do you reward them?" Tony asked Baptiste with a frown before he could react to Julia's comment. "Money?"

"Yes. Money," Baptiste said with a smirk and sat up, inhaling deeply. "I double their pay for each time I find him awake when I do a surprise check. I do that for the security guards at the store too."

"What?" Frantz protested, smiling. "That is my money you are throwing away, Baptiste. You are working for me, remember!"

"Maybe so," Baptiste answered, confident in his father's support. "I have yet to find any of them asleep. Since I started doing that reward thing, I have never been disappointed by any of my security guards. What I pay them is worth the tranquility."

"What do you pay?" Tony asked, scratching an ear.

"Three hundred a month. The legal rate."

"What? That is too much!" Tony moaned, rubbing the top of his head. "And since when do you have to pay the legal rate? Nobody does that."

Baptiste raised his eyebrows and observed with a smirk, "It depends what peace-of-mind is worth to you and how much you want your family to sleep at night."

Frantz had been looking at the floor with drooped shoulders when he suddenly raised his blue eyes and beamed at his son.

* * *

I FOUND MY COUSIN'S MOTHER on her dying bed, my gentle, God-fearing Aunt Cécile, her whole being oddly returned to the beginning of time, going from butterfly to the helpless stasis of larvae. She seemed enfolded in the luminous, crystallized, slow-to-die, muffled-cotton cocoon of a blind, transcendent silence within which she lay with faint breathing. She kept enduring in her late determination to feel unconditional love for everyone. In that determination, she found inspiration to summarize all she could remember of me by saying with a slight yet easy smile, "Ah, Io... she is always so nice..." I had just returned home and came by her bedside, Thea having just told her that I was there to see her.

My father's sister, Aunt Rose, was also dying of cancer in Florida, my uneasy, passionate aunt. She was receiving daily injections of morphine to soften a death that she complained was too slow to come. "How long do I have?" she asked the doctor the day he told her his diagnosis. On her way back to the house, she said to her daughter, "Sara, if die is what I have to do now, let us get it over and done with!"

Round-shaped lumps swelled around Aunt Rose's neck and in odd places of her body. The doctor said that she had developed many more lumps that were invisible because they were internal. At first, Aunt Rose would touch different areas of her body delicately as if to make contact with that unknown in her, but soon afterward held silent her feelings and thoughts about her coming end. When her intestines got blocked, help came.

The nurse took a long look at my aunt's shrunken form and face, and whose olive-green eyes were scrutinizing her back. She reached a decision and started to turn my aunt on her side. She then lifted the wrinkled nightgown, pulled down the sallow panties and bared the old woman's bony rear. My aunt said nothing.

The nurse put rubber gloves on and made them snap at the wrists. Aunt Rose closed her eyes.

The nurse inserted her index finger into my aunt's rectum to create an opening, and then slipped in the longest finger, the one commonly gestured as an insult. She dug until her fingers felt the fecal ball blocking the passage. She pushed deeper in, past the ball, so she could curl her fingers around it. She then dragged the hardened excrement out with slow care. My aunt moaned.

Afterward, the nurse took an enema bottle, inserted the funnel into the old woman's hemorrhoid-lined rectum and filled her with solution. "Hold it ten minutes!" she ordered.

"I never would've accepted to come to my daughter's house to die if I'd known that dying would take so long," Aunt Rose grumbled, and then said no more. She had not eaten in several days.

After ten minutes, the nurse lifted my aunt like a bagful of leaves and sat her on the pot. The invalid pooped until she collapsed.

Sara was holding her tears when she told me, "Mother wants no funeral, no flowers, no sermon, no family reunion, nothing. 'Stick me in a box and burn it up,' is what she asked. We will respect her wish, regardless. That is all I can say."

In due time, my own mother will follow my aunts. Under the lavender cologne, red lipstick, black mascara, rouge, and pale face powder, there is only a shrunken crone. Even her dentures were missing some teeth. She stands on two arthritic knees that she describes as carnivorous piranha fish biting her raw flesh whenever she moves, and she holds herself up with two metal canes she keeps at arm's length and repeatedly insults. My mother's last act of the last scene of her life is pure bravado. She will accept help and take my arm for support only if no one is there to see it. When I tried telling her about my aunts, she protested with peremptory, dismissive gestures of both arms, "Stop it! That's the last thing I need to hear. It's too depressing. I'm sorry, but I intend to die only once. I don't need to die again and again through the deaths of others."

When I came to pick her up the morning of my last day in Port-au-Prince to go to the airport, I found her dressed in green, a red hibiscus in her hair, smelling like a field of flowers. When I offered her my arm, she refused, "*Absolument pas*—Absolutely not!" She pushed herself up stoically from her chair with great difficulty. "Go wait in the car. I'm coming. I don't want you to remember me looking like a wreck."

It seemed an eternity had passed when she finally emerged from her front door. I was sitting in the back of the car while Jean-Marie sat on the driver seat. We both watched in silence. My mother closed the door slowly and carefully, and then she turned around, squinting slightly, not wearing her glasses. She looked up as if to judge the distance remaining between her and the front seat of the car that would take me away. I was debating whether or not to go help her when I heard Jean-Marie exclaim, "*M tèlman renmen wè l! Li tèlman toujou ge*—How I love to see her! She's always so joyful!"

* * *

COMING BACK from downtown Port-au-Prince with Jean-Marie on the previous day, the last Saturday before my departure from Haiti, unable to process the vastness of the human misery existing so close, I arrived just in time to find Julia and Thea ready for church, walking to the car, wearing lipstick and French perfume. Their smiles warmed me. "Are you coming with us?" Julia asked. "We are going to be late. So, you come right now or not at all."

Remembering my birthday promise on Wednesday that I would go to church with her the next time she went, I ignored my fatigue, and said, "Yes, of course." I followed them to the air-conditioned, bulletproof car for a ride to Saint Peter's Church in Pétionville.

I had not been to Saint Peter's for many years. I had been married there once. My father's sadness had weighed on me. We walked down the aisle to the altar briefly together before he handed me over to a stranger.

My cousin's son had gotten married there a year ago as well. When we entered the church, Julia pointed out two man-sized wrought iron candelabras standing on either side of the altar. "They are from the wedding," she explained. "We gave them to the church. There were four. I kept one for our house here and one for the beach house."

Julia and Thea chose to sit in the second row, right by the center aisle, across from the altar. During Mass, I turned around a few times to observe people behind me. Even though my cousins were kneeling, praying, seemingly preoccupied only with the proper ritual responses, I felt as if they were frowning at my impious, unfocused behavior. I turned back to face Jesus's stern eyes staring at me from a portrait inspired by the Shroud of Turin, hanging on the pillar to my immediate right.

The church was completely filled with elegant members of the Haitian bourgeoisie wearing fineries over rounded, well-fed limbs. A few humbler people sat in the back of the church and on the far sides, sticking close to the walls whose whiteness made their black faces and bare arms stand out. Most of them huddled nearest to the entrance and side doors as if they wanted to slip out unnoticed once Mass was over.

The sermon was delivered from a microphone standing in front of the altar, dead center. The priest's voice was overly amplified through enormous speakers hung high. They crackled, hissed, and thumped. There were twelve novices divided in equal numbers who stood on either side of the priest. The red robes they wore did little to hide the bulge of over-indulged bellies and the full cheeks of young, untroubled faces.

The priest was speaking about the significance of communion. The volume was already painfully loud, and still, in his eagerness to admonish us, the priest began shouting, "You must become consumers of Jesus! It's of vital importance that you eat Jesus! You have to become daily consumers of Jesus! Eat Jesus, my brothers and sisters! You must eat Jesus! Amen."

I looked at my cousins. They seemed reverent. Unable to run, I looked up through the high windows, past the treetops and into the azure sky.

Acknowledgements

I owe a sense of wonder to Roderick Kettlewell, my husband before God and men, for his willingness to share love and life with me, and never doubting me.

I bow down to the memory of the late John Sampas, who unceasingly believed in my work and found so many ways to support and move it towards recognition. I greatly miss the poetry, generosity and complete gentility of his soul.

Susan E. Reed's patient, critical reading of an earlier version of the whole manuscript, was immensely helpful in getting me to rethink the whole in terms of its parts. These were the unforgettable gestures of a true friend.

Anne Davenport and I sat next to each other many years ago in her office at Harvard when she gave me precious editorial comments for the first chapter of the book, *The Ghost of the Mary Celeste*, in its earlier form. What I learnt from her then, and always, has enriched my skills as a writer and my person.

Stimulating editorial comments from Ian Graham Leask at Calumet Editions seemed, once again, issued from a magical realm of inspiration. He appears to know ahead of time the perfect form of a book.

I am deeply indebted to both Gary Lindberg and Ian Graham Leask, my publishers at Calumet Editions. It will take years to appropriately and fully comprehend the beneficial influence they will have had in my life.

Last but certainly not least, I want to express my gratitude to all those who are endorsing this book, old and new friends who restore me with their moral support, hold me up, push me further towards light, and help me live.

About the Author

MARILÈNE PHIPPS was born and grew up in Haiti. She is a member of the Academy of American Poets and a recipient of the NAACP's Award of Excellence for outstanding commitment in advancing the culture and causes for communities of color. Phipps held fellowships at the Guggenheim Foundation, Harvard's Bunting Institute, the W.E.B. Du Bois Institute for Afro-American Research, and the Center for the Study of World Religions. Her collection, *The Company of Heaven: Stories from Haiti,* won the 2010 Iowa Short Fiction Award. Her poetry won the 1993 Grolier prize, and her collection, *Crossroads and Unholy Water,* won the Crab Orchard Poetry Prize. Her memoir, *Unseen Worlds,* was released in 2018 by Calumet Editions. She has contributed to American anthologies and collections such as *The Best American Short Stories*; *Haiti Noir: The Classics*; *The Beacon Best*; *Ploughshares*; *River Styx*; *Callaloo*; and *Harvard Divinity Bulletin*, and she edited *Jack Kerouac Collected Poems* for The Library of America. Her website is at www.marilenephipps.com.